The Unofficial Harry Potter Companion

The Persons, Places and Things in the Harry Potter Series of J.K. Rowling

Compiled by

Duane M. Searle

ISBN-10:1470003481
ISBN-13:978-1470003487

DEDICATION

For Kaitlin, Charlotte & Melanie.

CONTENTS

ACKNOWLEDGMENTS

On behalf of Muggles everywhere, the compiler of this dictionary wishes to thank J.K. Rowling for presenting Harry Potter to the world in such an irresistible package and for providing a lasting means by which parents and their children can read in wonder together.

PREFACE

While riding on a train ride from Manchester, England to London during the summer of 1990, an obscure author named Joanne Kathleen ("J.K") Rowling had an epiphany of a little boy that she developed into the protagonist for a series of children's books about magic and wizards. Rowling named her character Harry Potter and he is now known around the world.

In a nutshell, Harry is an orphaned wizard boy who experiences trials and tribulations with good and evil forces while receiving formal magical education at the mythical Hogwarts School of Witchcraft and Wizardry in England. Harry's best friends are faithful Ron Weasley and brainy Hermione Granger. He is a frequent target of the school bully, Draco Malfoy, and is pursued by the evil, dark wizard Lord Voldemort. The reader learns early on that Lord Voldemort murdered Harry's parents and was gravely wounded by an unsuccessful attempt to take Harry's life as well. The incident left a lightning bolt-shaped scar on Harry's forehead that makes Harry instantly recognizable to many in the wizarding world as the boy who ended the reign of Lord Voldemort. However, Harry soon learns that Lord Voldemort intends to regain the power he lost and kill Harry in the process.

In July 1997, J.K. Rowling's first Harry Potter book was published in Great Britain by Bloomsbury Publishing under the title: *Harry Potter and the Philosopher's Stone.* Ten years later the Harry Potter series was completed with seven titles, the last of which was released at midnight, prevailing time, on

July 30, 2007. The action in each book takes place during a different year in Harry's life. With each book, Rowling reveals more persons, places and things and provides further insight into those persons, places and things already introduced. It is not an exaggeration to state that thousands of them are introduced through the books.

As the series progresses, the number of recurring characters, imaginary settings and magical objects continues to expand beyond the limits of some people's ability to remember them without outside assistance. While it may not be necessary to remember the vast majority of them for an understanding of the basic plot, an awareness of them enhances a reader's appreciation of the story's complexities and of Rowling's craftsmanship. At a more basic level, the ability to recall many of the details in the Harry Potter series simply makes the books more enjoyable to read.

There should be a resource for Rowling's readers to use that refreshes their recollections of what those items mean and when and where those items come from in the books. The following pages consist of a comprehensive dictionary of all the persons, places and things that are mentioned in the Harry Potter series.

An effort has been made to not only provide a basic definition for the items listed here, but also to help the reader trace them back to their original sources in the books. In some cases, an item's relevance to the overall plot is briefly discussed.

The references in this dictionary are abbreviated by book title, chapter number and page number from the hardback editions sold in the United States. For example, the reference for a name found on page 168 of chapter 10 of *Harry Potter and the Sorcerer's Stone* appears in this dictionary as "SS 10, p. 168." The books in the series are abbreviated as follows:

Harry Potter and the Sorcerer's Stone **"SS"**
Harry Potter and the Chamber of Secrets **"CS"**
Harry Potter and the Prisoner of Azkaban **"PA"**
Harry Potter and the Goblet of Fire **"GF"**
Harry Potter and the Order of the Phoenix **"OP"**
Harry Potter and the Half-Blood Prince **"HP"**
Harry Potter and the Deathly Hallows **"DH"**

Many of the items in this dictionary appear repeatedly in more than one of the books. For these types of items, the dictionary generally lists the *first* place where they are named or explained. Where important facts or information are added in the books about an item, more than one reference may appear in the dictionary entry for that item.

As a result, the reader should not assume that if a dictionary entry for an item lists only one reference, that the item appears only once in that book or across the Harry Potter series. The reader may discover the item elsewhere in that book or be surprised to find that it resurfaces in a later one. Discovering these parallels in the books makes the Harry Potter series fascinating to read.

However, there are exceptions to this general rule of construction for the dictionary. Given the complexity of the last book, *Harry Potter and the Deathly Hallows*, and the myriad of cross-references to other items from the remainder of the series, this resource includes every reference made in that book to the thousands of items in the series. In many of these cases there is no explanation for the dictionary entry, just a cross reference at the end of the entry to "DH" by chapter and page number. These references demonstrate that J.K. Rowling has truly outdone herself in pulling the persons, places and things together one last time in the final book of the series.

Within some of the dictionary entries brief information is provided regarding the origin of certain plants, actual place names in Great Britain and less familiar locations. This information is derived from outside resources and is usually placed at the end of the entries in parenthesis in order to set it off from the content that is found in the Harry Potter series.

On March 12, 2001, J.K. Rowling published two corollary books to the Harry Potter series. Printed under pseudonyms, the books are: *Fantastic Beasts and Where to Find Them* by Newt Scamander and *Quidditch Through the Ages* by Kennilworthy Whisp. Both books are mentioned in *Harry Potter and the Sorcerer's Stone.*

Fantastic Beasts and Where to Find Them is a special edition of the actual book that Harry used during his first year at Hogwarts. Harry's own handwritten notations appear on some of the book's pages. While *Fantastic Beasts* presents the longstanding debate over which creatures should be considered "beings" versus "beasts," it is primarily a dictionary of numerous magical creatures, including mammals, birds, fish and insects.

Quidditch Through the Ages is a reproduction of a popular book in the wizarding world that details the chronological development of the sport of quidditch. Inside the cover of this book is a plate that shows the names of several students who borrowed the book from the Hogwarts library. It lists eighteen students from O. Wood to H. Potter.

The dictionary entries for the corollary books in the series are abbreviated as follows:

***Fantastic Beasts and Where to Find Them* "FB"**
***Quidditch Through the Ages* "QA"**

It should be noted that the first of the corollary books includes several introductory pages, but is not organized into chapters. *Quidditch Through the Ages* contains both introductory pages and chapters. The introductory pages in each corollary book are referenced in this dictionary by the corresponding Roman numerals listed in, or deducible from, each book. For example, a reference to the sixth introductory page in *Fantastic Beasts and Where to Find Them* appears in this dictionary as "FB, p. vi."

Because *Fantastic Beasts and Where to Find Them* is itself a dictionary, the information on magical beasts found there is not provided in detail within this dictionary, except where it provides other information that leads to related dictionary entries. The same approach has been taken for some of the information from *Quidditch Through the Ages*.

Finally, there is an appendix to this dictionary. It contains quick reference lists of key information from the Harry Potter series. The lists are helpful for recalling at a glance the names of:

Beasts and Creatures; Books and Publications; Charms; Countries and Exotic Locations; Currency; Curses; Food and Candy; Great Britain Locations; Hogwarts School of Witchcraft and Wizardry Students, Professors, Staff and Subjects of Instruction; Joke and Gag Devices; Laws; Magical Devices and Objects; Ministry of Magic Divisions; Plants; Potions; Quidditch Broomsticks, Players, Teams and Terminology; and Shops and Stores.

It is hoped that this dictionary will enhance the reader's understanding and appreciation of the Harry Potter series. Long Live Harry Potter!

ABBOTT - AZKABAN

Abbott. The name on a gravestone at the churchyard in Godric's Hollow. DH 16, p. 325.

Abbot, Hannah. The first student sorted by the Sorting Hat during Harry Potter's first year at Hogwarts. Hannah was a member of the Hufflepuff house. SS 7, p. 119. She was one of the students who was frightened by Harry's parseltongue incident at the first meeting of the Dueling Club. CS 11, pp. 198-199. During the panic that ensued at Hogwarts over Sirius Black's entry into the school, Hannah expressed a wild theory to her Herbology classmates that Sirius could turn himself into a flowering shrub. PA 9, p. 166. In another Herbology class the following year, Hannah mentioned that Eloise Midgen tried to curse away the acne from her face and her nose fell off instead. GF 13, p. 195. During Harry's fifth year at Hogwarts, Hannah was a prefect, along with Ernie MacMillan, for the Hufflepuff house. OP 10, p. 188. The following school year, Hannah's mother was found dead and Hannah was quietly removed from the school. HP 11, p. 222. DH 16, p. 325; 31, p. 621.

Abercrombie, Euan. The first student sorted by the Sorting Hat at the beginning of Harry Potter's fifth year at Hogwarts. Euan was sorted into the Gryffindor house. OP 11, pp. 207-208.

Aberdeen. A location that the Knight Bus flew over when Harry Potter rode the bus. As the bus moved abruptly from Anglesea to Aberdeen, Stan Shunpike spilled hot chocolate on Harry. This event occurred after Harry ran away from the Dursley residence during the summer prior to his third year at Hogwarts. PA 3, p. 41. Aberdeen was the residence of Prudence, who was the sister of Madam Modesty

Rabnott of Kent. QA 4, p. 12. (Aberdeen is a historic county and seaport in Northeast Scotland.)

Abergavenny. The destination for Madam Marsh when she was a passenger on the Knight Bus. Harry Potter was also a passenger on the bus at the time. This event occurred after Harry ran away from the Dursley residence during the summer prior to his third year at Hogwarts. PA 3, p. 36.

Abominable Snowman. Another name for the Yeti. FB, p. 42.

Abraxan. A breed of Winged Horses that were powerful giant palominos. FB, p. 42. Rubeus Hagrid tried to make up a story about falling off of an Abraxan horse when Dolores Umbridge asked him about his facial injuries. This event occurred during Harry Potter's fifth year at Hogwarts. OP 20, p. 437.

Abyssinian Shrivelfig. A plant that Harry Potter pruned in a Herbology class during his second year at Hogwarts. During that particular class, Ernie Macmillan apologized to Harry for suspecting him of attacking Hermione Granger, who had actually been attacked by the monster from the Chamber of Secrets. CS 15, p. 268. (Abyssinia is the former name of Ethiopia.)

Acanthia Way. A street in Little Norton. Doris Porkiss lived at No. 18 Acanthia Way. OP 10, p. 191.

Accidental Magic Reversal Department. A department located in the Ministry of Magic. This department dispatched two of its workers to clean up the magic that Harry Potter inflicted on Marge Dursley prior to running away to begin his third year at Hogwarts. Harry was so angry at Marge for her insults that he accidentally caused her to inflate like a balloon. As a result, the workers from the Accidental Magic Reversal Department were summoned to puncture Marge and modify her memory of the incident. PA 3, p. 44.

Accidental Magic Reversal Squad. A squad located in the Ministry of Magic. The wizards who worked for the squad were known as Obliviators. GF 7, p. 86. According to Arthur Weasley, a couple of wizards were fined by the Department of Magical Transportation for apparating without a license and splinching themselves. They had to be sorted out by the Accidental Magic Reversal Squad. Arnold Peasegood was an Obliviator for the squad. Arthur pointed out Arnold to Harry Potter and Hermione Granger at the camp on the grounds of the Quidditch World Cup. These events occurred during the summer prior to Harry's fourth year at Hogwarts. GF 6, pp. 66-67; GF 7, p. 86. The squad was incorporated in the Department of Magical Accidents and Catastrophes and was located on level three of the Ministry of Magic. OP 7, p. 130.

Accio. The magic word for the Summoning Charm that propelled an object to the wizard who invoked the charm. Molly Weasley used the Summoning Charm to force Ton-Tongue Toffees from George Weasley's pockets before he left the Burrow for the Quidditch World Cup. GF 6, p. 68. Harry Potter also made use of the Summoning Charm for an important event during the Triwizard Tournament. GF 19, p. 353. Mad-Eye Moody used the charm to retrieve the Marauder's Map that fell out of Harry's hands that same year. GF 25, p. 472. Harry invoked the charm in a duel after the Triwizard Tournament. GF 33, p. 669. These events occurred during the summer prior to and during Harry's fourth year at Hogwarts. During year seven, Harry used the Summoning Charm to save Hagrid as he fell from Sirius Black's motorcycle. DH 4, p. 61. The charm was subject to interference from counter-enchantments. DH 10, p. 188.

Achievements in Charming. A book that Hermione Granger used to study for her Theory of Charms O.W.L. This event occurred during Harry Potter's fifth year at Hogwarts. OP 31, p. 709.

Acid Pops. Candies that were sold at Honeydukes in Hogsmeade. Ron Weasley pointed out Acid Pops to Harry Potter when they were in Honeydukes during Harry's third year at Hogwarts. According to Ron, Fred Weasley gave an Acid Pop to Ron when he was seven years old and the candy burned a hole through his tongue. PA 10, p. 200. During Harry's sixth year at Hogwarts, "Acid Pops" was the secret password to gain entry past the gargoyles to Albus Dumbledore's office. HP 9, p. 182.

Ackerley, Stewart. The first student sorted by the Sorting Hat during Harry Potter's fourth year at Hogwarts. Stewart was a member of the Ravenclaw house. GF 12, p. 178.

Aconite. Another name for the monkshood plant, also known as wolfsbane, that was used in potions. Severus Snape quizzed Harry Potter about the name of this plant during Harry's first Potions class at Hogwarts. SS 8, pp. 137-138. (Aconite is any plant that belongs to the genus *Aconitum* of the buttercup family.)

Acromantula. A magical beast that lived in the uncharted jungle of Borneo. The Acromantula was first sighted in 1794. FB, pp. xviii, 1 and fn. 1. Aragog was an acromantula. The venom of an acromantula was very valuable; Horace Slughorn estimated that a pint was worth about one hundred galleons. HP 22, p. 481.

Advanced Potion-Making. A book written by Libatius Borage that the Potions N.E.W.T. class used during Harry Potter's sixth year at Hogwarts. HP 9, p. 183. A new copy of the book that year cost nine galleons. HP 11, p. 220. One of the subjects covered in the book was Everlasting Elixirs. HP 15, p. 305.

Advanced Rune Translation. A book that Hermione Granger read during the summer prior to Harry Potter's sixth year at Hogwarts. HP 7, p. 129.

Adventures of Martin Miggs, Mad Muggle, The. The title of a series of comic books that existed in the wizarding world. A pile of these comic books was located in Ron Weasley's bedroom at the Burrow. Harry Potter observed these books on his first visit to the Burrow prior to his second year at Hogwarts. CS 3, p. 40.

Aethonan. A breed of Winged Horse that was chestnut in color and popular in both Britain and Ireland. FB, p. 42.

Africa. Hermione Granger suggested to Harry Potter that Sirius Black might be hiding in Africa and that it would take too long for Hedwig to take a message to him asking for advice about the painful scar on Harry's forehead. This event occurred during the summer prior to Harry's fourth year at Hogwarts. GF 10, p. 150. Africa was the native habitat of the Erumpent and the Fwooper. FB, pp. 16, 18. The Nundu was found in East Africa. FB, p. 31. Broomsticks were probably introduced to African wizards by European wizards. QA 8, p. 42. (Africa is a continent located south of Europe and between the Atlantic and Indian Oceans.)

Age Line. A golden, magical line that Albus Dumbledore placed around the Goblet of Fire so that students who were under seventeen years of age could not submit their names for the Triwizard Tournament. This event occurred during Harry Potter's fourth year at Hogwarts. GF 16, pp. 256, 259.

Aging Potion. A potion that Fred and George Weasley and Lee Jordan consumed in order to age themselves enough to qualify for the Triwizard Tournament. Fred and George were only sixteen years of age at the time that names were submitted for the selection of Hogwarts' champion and they needed to be seventeen years of age to enter. GF 12, p. 189. An Age Line around the Goblet of Fire prevented the potion from working as intended and Fred and George sprouted long, white beards instead. Two other students who tried the same potion for the Triwizard Tournament were Miss Fawcett of the Ravenclaw house and Mr. Summers of the Hufflepuff house. GF 16, p. 260.

Agrippa. A famous witch who was featured on collectors cards inside packs of Chocolate Frogs. Ron Weasley complained to Harry Potter that he was unable to obtain the Agrippa card. This event occurred on the

Hogwarts Express as Harry traveled to Hogwarts for his first year of school there. SS 6, p. 102.

Aguamenti Charm. A charm that Profesor Flitwick asked his students in Ron Weasley's class to study during Harry Potter's sixth year at Hogwarts. HP 11, p. 218. It had the effect of producing water. HP 26, p. 574. DH 11, p. 222.

Aingingein. An old game played in Ireland. Aingingein was an early version of Quidditch. Fingal the Fearless was a champion Ainingein player. QA 2, pp. 4-5.

Alas, I've Transfigured My Feet. The title of a play written by the French wizard Malecrit during the early 1400's. Dialog between two of the characters in the play, Grenouille and Crapaud, referenced the terms "quidditch keeper" and "quaffle." QA 8, p. 39.

Albania. The country in which Lord Voldemort was reportedly in hiding after his attempt to kill Harry Potter failed. This report surfaced during Harry's second year at Hogwarts. CS 18, p. 328. Albania was the country where Bertha Jorkins went on vacation and were never heard from again. This event occurred the summer prior to Harry's fourth year at Hogwarts. GF 5, p. 61. Lord Voldemort confirmed that he hid deep within the Albanian forest at a place that even rats avoided because small animals died there after coming into contact with a dark shadow. GF 33, p. 655. DH 15, p. 288. Helena Ravenclaw hid her mother's diadem in a tree stump in Albania. DH 31, p. 617. (Albania is a country in Southern Europe, in the Balkan Peninsula, that is west of Macedonia and northwest of Greece.)

Albus. The secret password to access the wizarding radio program, *Potterwatch*, during year seven. DH 22, p. 438.

Alchemy. A subject that African wizards were particularly skilled at performing. They were also adept at astronomy. QA 8, p. 42.

Alderton, Arkie. A well-known broomstick designer who was the father of a wizard on trial at the Ministry of Magic during year seven for being a half-blood. DH 13, p. 257.

Alecto. A witch who was a Death Eater during Harry Potter's sixth year at Hogwarts. Alecto had a brother named Amycus who was also a Death Eater. HP 27, p. 593.

Alihotsy. A magical plant, the leaves of which caused hysteria when eaten. The melancholy-inducing treacle of the Glumbumble was used as an antidote. FB, p. 19.

All-Africa Cup. The name of the quidditch cup awarded in Africa. The Gimbi Giant-Slayers from Ethiopia won the All-Africa Cup twice. QA 8, p. 43.

All-England Best-Kept Suburban Lawn Competition. An award that the Dursleys thought they had won from a muggle letter. However, the letter was actually sent to them by members of the Order of the Phoenix to get the Dursleys to leave their home. This event occurred the summer prior to Harry Potter's fifth year at Hogwarts. OP 3, p. 48.

Alohomora. The magic word for a charm that was used to open a lock on a door or window. The charm was first invoked by Hermione Granger to open a door on the Charms corridor so that she, Harry Potter and Ron Weasley could return quickly to the Gryffindor house and avoid getting caught out of bed. SS 9, p. 160. Hermione was unable to successfully invoke the charm against a certain locked door that could only be opened with a winged key. These events occurred during Harry's first year at Hogwarts. SS 16, p. 279. Hermione had better success using the charm to open a window in the West Tower of Hogwarts to help someone confined there escape. This event occurred during Harry's third year at Hogwarts. PA 21, p. 414. DH 10, p. 187.

America. The habitat for two magical beasts. Clabbert originated in the southern states of America. The Doxy preferred cold climates in America. FB, pp. 8, 10. See also, **United States of America**.

American Witches. A group of middle-aged, American witches stretched a spangled banner between their tents at the Quidditch World Cup. The banner read "The Salem Witches Institute." This event occurred the summer prior to Harry Potter's fourth year at Hogwarts. GF 7, p. 82.

Amortentia. The most powerful love potion in the world. It did not manufacture or imitate love, as that was impossible. Rather, the potion caused powerful infatuation or obsession. HP 9, pp. 185-86.

Amycus. A wizard who was a Death Eater during Harry Potter's sixth year at Hogwarts. Amycus had a sister named Alecto who was also a Death Eater. HP 27, p. 593.

Anapneo. The magical word for a charm that helped to clear the windpipe of a wizard. Horace Slughorn used the charm on Marcus Bilby aboard the Hogwarts Express on the way to Harry Potter's sixth year at Hogwarts. HP 7, p. 144.

Ancient Runes. A subject that was taught to students at Hogwarts beginning in their third year, if they elected to take the class. CS 14, p. 252. In deciding which classes to take for his third year at Hogwarts, Neville Longbottom asked other students whether Arithmancy was more difficult than the study of Ancient Runes. CS 14, p. 252. Hermione Granger took the Ancient Runes class during her third year at

Hogwarts. PA 4, p. 57. Ancient runes were read upside down. OP 10, p. 192. DH 16, p. 316.

Ancient Runes Made Easy. The title of a book that Hermione Granger read during Harry Potter's second year at Hogwarts. CS 14, p. 254. Hermione did not take the Ancient Runes class until the following year. PA 4, p. 57.

Andorran Minister of Magic. The Minister of Magic from the country of Andorra. When Barty Crouch was discovered by Harry Potter and Viktor Krum near the Forbidden Forest, Barty ranted and raved about a memo from the Andorran Minister of Magic. This episode of insanity occurred during Harry's fourth year at Hogwarts. GF 27, p. 556. (Andorra is a country in the East Pyrenees between France and Spain.)

Andromeda. A favorite cousin of Sirius Black who was also Nymphadora Tonks's mother. OP 6, p. 113.

Anglesea. A place that the Knight Bus flew over when Harry Potter rode the bus. As the bus moved abruptly from Anglesea to Aberdeen, Stan Shunpike spilled hot chocolate on Harry. This event occurred after Harry ran away from the Dursley residence the summer prior to his third year at Hogwarts. PA 3, p. 41. (Anglesey is an island and historic county in Gwynedd, which is located in Northwest Wales.)

Anglia. The make of Ford automobile that Arthur Weasley drove and modified with magic so that it could fly. The Anglia was capable of holding many pieces of luggage in its trunk. Seven members of the Weasley family and Harry Potter rode in the vehicle on the way to King's Cross to board the Hogwarts Express. CS 5, p. 66. Ron Weasley and Harry later flew the Anglia to Hogwarts and crashed it into the Whomping Willow. These events occurred during the summer prior to Harry's second year at Hogwarts. CS 5, p. 74.

Animagi. The plural form of animagus. See **Animagus.**

Animagus. The name given to a wizard who could transform himself at will into an animal. PA 6, p. 108. The following wizards and witches were Animagi: Minerva McGonagell, as an orange tabby cat, SS 1, p. 9; Sirius Black, as a dog, PA 17, pp. 338-339; Peter Pettigrew, as a rat, PA 17, p. 348; and James Potter, as a stag, PA 21, pp. 411-412; PA 22, p. 424. An Animagus was required to be registered with the Ministry of Magic and during the century in which Harry Potter lived, there were only seven registered Animagi, one of whom was Minerva McGonagell. PA 18, p. 351. Hermione Granger discovered that Rita Skeeter was an unregistered Animagus. For Rita's animal form, see GF 37, p. 727. This event occurred during Harry's fourth year at

Hogwarts. It was rare for Animagi to turn themselves into winged creatures that could fly. QA 1, p. 1.

Antioch. A wizard who may have been one of the legendary Three Brothers who owned the Deathly Hallows. DH 21, p. 412-13. See **Peverell.**

Anthology of Eighteenth-Century Charms, An. The title of a book that Harry Potter consulted in order to find a way to breathe underwater in the second task of the Triwizard Tournament. This event occurred during Harry's fourth year at Hogwarts. GF 26, p. 488.

Anti-Cheating Charm. A charm applied to the O.W.L. examination papers distributed during Harry Potter's fifth year at Hogwarts. OP 31, p. 708.

Anti-Dark Arts Spell. A magic spell used to repel the effects of the Dark Force. Hermione Granger suspected Professor Quirrell of casting an Anti-Dark Arts Spell in order to guard the Sorcerer's Stone. This event occurred during Harry Potter's first year at Hogwarts. SS 13, p. 227; SS 15, p. 246.

Anti-Dark Force Spell. See **Anti-Dark Arts Spell.**

Anti-Disapparation Jinx. A jinx that prevented a witch or wizard from disapparating. Albus Dumbledore placed the Anti-Daiapparation Jinx on several Death Eaters in the Death Chamber of the Department of Mysteries. This event occurred during Harry Potter's fifth year at Hogwarts. OP 36, p. 817.

Antipodean Opaleye. One of ten pure-bred dragons native to New Zealand and known to migrate to Australia. The Opaleye was arguably the most beautiful type of dragon. Muggles mistook the eggs of this dragon for fossils. FB, p. 11.

Anti-Umbridge League. A name suggested by Angelina Johnson, but rejected, for the group of Hogwarts students that referred to itself as Dumbledore's Army. This event occurred during Harry Potter's fifth year at Hogwarts. OP 18, p. 391.

Aparecium. The magic word for a charm used to reveal writing that might have been concealed in a document. Hermione Granger unsuccessfully invoked this charm during Harry Potter's second year at Hogwarts to read the apparent blank diary of T.M. Riddle. CS 13, p. 233.

Apothecary. A shop located on Diagon Alley. Harry Potter purchased ingredients for potions from this shop prior to his third year at Hogwarts. PA 4, p. 52.

Apparate. The ability of a wizard to vanish from one location and to reappear at another. CS 5, p. 69. Underage wizards were not permitted to apparate. CS 5, p. 69. Hogwarts was constructed with enchantments in order to prevent anyone from apparating into, within or out of it. PA 9, p. 164. The converse action of apparate was disapparate. PA 22, p. 419; GF 4, p. 45. According to Arthur Weasley, apparating was very difficult and a wizard needed to pass a test and have a license in order to engage in apparition. The licenses were issued by the Department of Magical Transportation. GF 6, p. 66. Charlie Weasley failed the test the first time he took it, but passed it on his second attempt. GF 6, p. 67. Apparition was unreliable over long distances, such as the Atlantic Ocean. Only highly skilled wizards were wise to cross continents by apparition. QA 9, p. 48; 2, p. 4. Fred and George Weasley passed their apparition tests during the summer prior to Harry Potter's fifth year at Hogwarts. OP 4, p. 68. The specific age for taking the test was 17 years of age. An underage wizard could apparate with an adult wizard by holding on to the adult wizard's arm. Wizard dwellings were magically protected from unwanted apparators. HP 4, pp. 58-59. At the beginning of the second semester of Harry's sixth year at Hogwarts, the Ministry of Magic offered apparition lessons for twelve weeks at a cost of 12 galleons. HP 17, p. 354. Side-Along Apparition occurred when one wizard accompanied another wizard during apparition. HP 17, p. 356. Wilkie Twycross was the Ministry wizard who conducted the apparition class. HP 18, p. 382. According to Wilkie, the three D's of apparition were: destination, determination and deliberation. HP 18, p. 384. During Harry's sixth year, the test was offered on April 21. HP 21, p. 448. During year seven, Pius Thicknesse made it an imprisonable offense to apparate to or from the Dursley residence. DH 4, p. 46.

Apparation Test Center. An office in the Department of Magical Transport located on level six of the Ministry of Magic. OP 7, p. 129.

Appleby Arrows. A quidditch team that played the Banchory Bangers in 1814. QA 5, p. 17. The team was formed in 1612 and its chief rival was the Wimbourne Wasps. QA 7, p. 32.

Appraisal of Magical Education in Europe, An. The title of a book that Hermione Granger mentioned to Harry Potter after the Quidditch World Cup. The book contained information about the Beauxbatons Academy of Magic and Durmstrang Institute. This event occurred during the summer prior to Harry's fourth year at Hogwarts. GF 9, p. 123; GF 11, p. 166. DH 6, p.100.

Aqua-Lung. An underwater breathing apparatus that Harry Potter considered using for the second task of the Triwizard Tournament. This event occurred during Harry's fourth year at Hogwarts. GF 26, p. 481.

Aquavirius maggot. An insect that Luna Lovegood believed the Ministry of Magic was breeding during Harry Potter's fifth year at Hogwarts. OP 34, p. 772.

Aragog. A giant, black and gray spider that was blind and the size of a small elephant. Aragog lived deep within the Forbidden Forest and was brought there by Rubeus Hagrid. Hagrid found Aragog a wife, Mosag, and they had many offspring. Aragog was wrongly suspected of killing Moaning Myrtle when the Chamber of Secrets was opened for the first time. CS 15, pp. 276-278, 282. These events were explained during Harry Potter's second year at Hogwarts. During the summer prior to Harry's sixth year at Hogwarts, Aragog appeared to be dying. Rubeus Hagrid collected giant slugs to feed to him. HP 11, p. 230. Aragog died during March of that year. He was an acromantula. HP 22, pp 470, 480. DH 28, p. 561.

Arbroath. The location from which Guthrie Lochrin rode a broomstick in 1107. Guthrie ended his short trip in Montrose and complained that the broomstick caused him to suffer a splintered buttocks and bulging piles. QA 1, p. 2.

Archie. An old wizard who refused to take off a long flowery nightgown and put on a pair of pinstriped trousers to look more like a muggle at the Quidditch World Cup. Archie's justification for not changing his clothes was that he liked to feel a healthy breeze around his privates. This event occurred during the summer prior to Harry Potter's fourth year at Hogwarts. GF 7, p. 84.

Arcus. One of the reputed owners of the Elder Wand. Either Arcus or Livius may have killed Loxias in order to obtain the Elder Wand. DH 21, p. 412.

Argentina. A county in which quidditch was played. The Argentinian quidditch team made it to the quarter-finals of the World Cup in the last century. QA 8, p. 45. (Argentina is a southern country in South America.)

Argyllshire. A location which served as the subject of a map that was located on the second floor of Hogwarts. The Fat Lady hid in the map after Sirius Black slashed the painting she usually occupied at the entrance to the Gryffindor house. PA 9, p. 165. (Argyll is a historic county in West Scotland.)

Arithmancy. A subject that was taught at Hogwarts. The Arithmancy class was offered to students after they had completed their first two years of classes. CS 14, p. 252. Professor Vector taught Artihmancy. PA 12, p. 244. In deciding which classes to take for his third year at Hogwarts, Neville Longbottom asked other students whether the Arithmancy class was more difficult than the Ancient Runes class. CS

14, p. 252. Hermione Granger elected to take the Arithmancy class during her third year at Hogwarts and it was her favorite subject that year. PA 4, p. 57; PA 12, p. 251. She also suggested to Harry Potter at the beginning of Harry's fourth year at Hogwarts that he drop his Divination class and take the Arithmancy class like her. GF 13, p. 194. Hermione studied arithmancy during Harry's fifth year at Hogwarts. The class met during the same time as Harry's Divination class. OP 15, p. 315.

Arjeplog. A location in Sweden where the finish line of an annual broom race, which started in the tenth century, was located. The fliers raced from Kopparberg to Arjelog. The course went through a dragon reservation. QA 2, p. 4.

Armadillo. The bile from an armadillo was one of the ingredients in Wit-Sharpening Potion. The other ingredients of the potion were powdered scarab beetles and ginger root. Harry Potter worked on the potion during his fourth year at Hogwarts. GF 27, pp. 513-14, 518.

Armando Dippet: Master or Moron? The title of a book that was written by Rita Skeeter and was a bestseller. Dolores Umbridge kept a copy of the book in her office at the Ministry of Magic during year seven. DH 13, p. 252.

Armenian Warlock. A wizard who reportedly saved a village from werewolves. During Harry Poter's second year at Hogwarts, Gilderoy Lockhart became aware of the report and passed the heroic feat off as his own. CS 16, p. 297. (Armenia is an ancient country in West Asia that is now divided between Armenia, Turkey and Iran.)

Ashwinder. A magical beast. When frozen, Ashwinder eggs were of great value for use in Love Potions and were eaten whole as a cure for ague. FB, p. 2.

Asia. The game of quidditch was never widely popular in Asia, due to the fact that Eastern witches and wizards used flying carpets instead of broomsticks. QA 8, p. 46.

Asiatic Anti-Venom. A subject in a book that Harry Potter pretended to read during his fifth year at Hogwarts. OP 16, p. 331.

Asphodel. A plant, the powered root of which when mixed with an infusion of wormwood made a sleeping potion so powerful that it was known as the Draught of Living Death. Severus Snape quizzed Harry Potter about the name of this plant during Harry's first Potions class at Hogwarts. SS 8, pp. 137-138. (Asphodel refers to any of the various Southern European plants of the genera *Asphodelus* and *Asphodeline*, of the lily family, commonly known as the daffodil.)

Astronomy. A subject taught by Professor Sinistra in a tower at Hogwarts. CS 1, p. 204; PA 9, p. 165. Although first-year students were not required to purchase a book for this class, they were required to have a telescope for it. SS 5, p. 67. The students studied the planets by looking through their telescopes every Wednesday at midnight. SS 8, p. 133. Harry Potter studied a map of Jupiter during his first year at Hogwarts. Hermione Granger tested Ron Weasley on the subject of Astronomy in the library that same year. SS 15, pp. 246-247. Prior to his third year at Hogwarts, Harry was tempted to purchase a model of the galaxy in a glass ball so that he would not have to take another Astronomy class. PA 4, p. 50. During his third year, Harry, Ron and Hermione worked on star charts for the class. PA 8, pp. 145-146. African wizards were particularly skilled at performing astronomy. They were also adept at the subject of alchemy. QA 8, p. 42.

Astronomy Tower. One of the named towers at Hogwarts. The Astronomy Tower was one of the favorite places where Albus Dumbledore liked to go and spend time at the school. HP 23, p. 493.

Atlantic Ocean. One of the natural habitats of the Sea Serpent and the sole habitat of the Shrake. FB, p. 38. The first witch to cross the Atlantic Ocean on broomstick was Jocunda Sykes in 1935. QA 9, p. 48.

Atmospheric Charm. A charm that Hermione Granger suggested might have been used to cause rain in a room at the Ministry of Magic during year seven. DH 12, p. 244.

Atrium. See **Ministry of Magic**.

Aubrey, Bretram. A student at Hogwarts on whom James Potter and Sirius Black, as students, placed an illegal hex. James and Sirius were given double detention from the incident. Harry Potter discovered this information while serving detention in Severus Snape's office during Harry's sixth year at the school. HP 24, p. 532.

Augurey (Irish Phoenix). A magical beast. Augurey feathers repelled ink. FB, pp. vii, 2-3.

Auntie Muriel. See **Weasley, Muriel**.

Auror. The title for a wizard who was employed by the Ministry of Magic to apprehend Dark wizards. Mad-Eye Moody was a famous Auror. According to Charlie Weasley, half of the cells in Azkaban were full because of the efforts of Mad-Eye Moody. GF 11, p. 161. Ron Weasley informed Harry Potter that Aurors killed all of the giants in Britain because the giants were too fond of killing. GF 23, p. 430. Mad-Eye Moody advised Harry and Hermione Granger to think about becoming Aurors. This event occurred during Harry's fourth year at Hogwarts. GF 25, p. 477; GF 29, p. 570. Nymphadora Tonks and Kingsley Shacklebolt were Aurors. Two courses of instruction for Auror training were Concealment and Disguise, and Stealth and Tracking. OP 3, p. 52. Ron Weasley expressed interest in becoming an Auror. OP 12, p. 228. A wizard named Dawlish was also an Auror. OP 27, p. 620. During career counseling at Hogwarts in his fifth year, Harry stated his desire to become an Auror. In order to be considered for the position of Auror, a wizard needed to have a minimum of five N.E.W.T.s, with no grade in them under "Exceeds Expectations" and to pass a series of character and aptitude tests at the Auror office. There was an additional three years of training beyond wizarding school. The Ministry of Magic did not accept any new Aurors during the three-year period prior to Harry Potter's fifth year at Hogwarts. OP 29, pp. 662, 665. The following Aurors were stationed at Hogwarts for extra security during the next school year: Nymphadora Tonks, Proudfoot, Savage and Dawlish. HP 8, p. 158. Gawain Robards was the Head of the Auror Office after Rufus Scrimgeour left the position to become Minister of Magic. HP 16, p. 345. DH 5, p. 66.

Auror Headquarters. An office, incorporated in the Department of Magical Law Enforcement, that was located on level two of the Ministry of Magic. OP 7, p. 130. DH 12, p. 245.

Auror Office. The office in the Ministry of Magic from which Aurors operated. DH 1, p. 4.

Australia. According to Percy Weasley, Ludo Bagman was amused by the disappearance of his employee, Bertha Jorkins, and suspected that she misread her map and instead of ending up in Albania, landed in Australia. GF 5, p. 62. The Antipodean Opaleye dragon was known to migrate to Australia. FB, p. 11. Quidditch was introduced in Australia in the eighteenth century. QA 8, pp. 40-41. DH 6, p. 96. (Australia is a continent located southeast of Asia and between the Indian and Pacific oceans.)

Auto-Answer Quill. A magical device banned from the O.W.L. examination hall during Harry Potter's fifth year at Hogwarts. OP 31, pp. 708-09.

Avada Kedavra. The magic words used to invoke the illegal Killing Charm. Hermione Granger mentioned this charm in response to a question from Mad-Eye Moody. There was no countercurse to the Killing Curse and Harry Potter was the only known person to have survived it. GF 14, p. 215. The curse was used on a student who was identified at GF 32, p. 638. This event occurred during Harry's fourth year at Hogwarts. Two years later Severus Snape invoked the curse against Albus Dumbledore on the ramparts of the Astronomy Tower of Hogwarts. HP 27, p. 596. During year seven, Lord Voldemort used the charm to kill Charity Burbage for an article she wrote for the *Daily Prophet* in defense of Mudbloods. DH 1, p. 12. This was one of the last three charms invoked at the end of year seven; the others were *Expelliarmus* and *Reparo*. DH 36, pp. 743, 749.

Avery. A Death Eater who, according to Sirius Black, was able to worm his way out of being sent to Azkaban by claiming that he acted under the effects of the Imperius Curse. Avery was then set free and was still at large during Harry Potter's fourth year at Hogwarts. GF 27, p. 531. Avery was present in the Department of Mysteries when Harry retrieved the prophecy relating to himself and Lord Voldemort. This event occurred during Harry's fifth year at Hogwarts. OP 35, p. 788. Avery was a student at Hogwarts and a friend of Severus Snape, when he was also a student there. DH 33, p. 673.

Avis. The magic word spoken by Mr. Ollivander to invoke a charm that caused birds to burst from the tip of Viktor Krum's wand. Mr. Ollivander used the charm to test the working order of Krum's wand during the Weighing of the Wands Ceremony as part of the Triwizard Tournament. This event occurred during Harry Potter's fourth year at Hogwarts. GF 18, pp. 309-10.

Award for Special Services to the School. An award given at Hogwarts to Tom Riddle. CS 13, p. 231; HP 20, p. 430.

Axminster. A type of flying carpet that Barty Crouch's grandfather owned. The rug accommodated twelve people at a time and was acquired by Barty's grandfather before flying carpets were banned by law in Britain. GF 7, p. 91.

Azkaban. A wizard prison located on a tiny island far out at sea. CS 12, p. 224; PA 10, p. 188. More specifically, the location was somewhere in the North Sea. HP 1, p. 8. The guards of Azkaban were known as Dementors. They drained happy thoughts out of the minds of the prisoners who consequently went insane within a few weeks. PA 10, p. 188. Rubeus Hagrid was forced into Azkaban when the Chamber of Secrets was reopened during Harry Potter's second year at Hogwarts. CS 14, p. 262. Sirius Black was the first person to ever escape from Azkaban. PA 3, p. 41. Sturgis Podmore was convicted and sentenced by the Wizengamot to six months imprisonment at Azkaban for attempting to break into a high-security area in the Ministry of Magic. OP 14, p. 287. The Dementors revolted from their duties at Azkaban and aligned themselves with Lord Voldemort during Harry's fifth year at Hogwarts. OP 38, p. 845. Lucius Malfoy was imprisoned there that summer. HP 7, p. 130. For his attack on Tom Riddle, Morfin Gaunt was imprisoned in Azkaban for three years. HP 10, p. 211. His father, Marvolo Gaunt, was sentenced to six months in Azkaban for injuring several Ministry of Magic employees, including Bob Ogden. HP 10, p. 212. Mundungus Fletcher was arrested and sent to Azkaban during Harry's sixth year at Hogwarts. HP 21, p. 457. Percival Dumbledore was a prisoner at Azkaban after he attacked three Muggles. Perzical later died there. DH 2, p. 16. Another wizard prison was Nurmengard. DH 18, p. 360.

BABBLING BEVERAGE - BUTTERBEER

Babbling Beverage. A magical beverage that caused the person who drank it to babble. OP 32, p. 746.

Babbling Curse. A curse that Gilderoy Lockhart claimed in one of his books to have removed from a Transylvanian villager. Lockhart used Harry Potter to reenact the incident during a Defense Against the Dark Arts class that occurred during Harry's second year at Hogwarts. CS 10, p. 161.

Baddick, Malcolm. A student who was sorted by the Sorting Hat during Harry Potter's fourth year at Hogwarts. Malcolm was a member of the Slytherin house. GF 12, p. 178.

Bagman, Ludo (Ludovic). The head of the Department of Magical Games and Sports during Harry Potter's lifetime. GF 5, p. 61; GF 30, p. 592. Ludo helped Arthur Weasley get tickets for the Quidditch World Cup during the summer prior to Harry's fourth year at Hogwarts. GF 5, p. 61. Ludo played quidditch for the England team and also was a beater for the Wimbourne Wasps, prior to becoming the head of the Department of Magical Games and Sports. GF 7, p. 78. Ludo announced the Quidditch World Cup and was one of the five judges on the panel for the Triwizard Tournament at Hogwarts during Harry's fourth year at the school. GF 7, p. 92; 8, p. 102; 16, p. 254. According to Winky, Ludo was a bad wizard. GF 21, p. 382. During that same school year, Harry learned that Ludo had been tried before the Council of Magical Law for being a Death Eater. GF 30, pp. 592-93. Ludo was quoted in *Quidditch Through the Ages* as giving praise to that book. QA, p. iv.

Bagman, Otto. The brother of Ludo Bagman. Otto got into trouble with a lawnmower that had unnatural powers and Arthur Weasley smoothed the whole incident over. The event helped Arthur to befriend Ludo and occurred during the summer prior to Harry Potter's fourth year at Hogwarts. GF 5, p. 61.

Bagnold, Millicent. A witch who was the predeceasor of Cornelius Fudge as the Minister of Magic. When Millicent retired, many wizards wanted Albus Dumbledore to take over as Minister. OP 5, p. 93.

Bagshot, Bathilda. The author of *A History of Magic.* First-year students at Hogwarts were required to purchase the book. SS 5, p. 66. Harry Potter also used the book in preparation for his third year at the school. PA 1, p. 1. The book included a full account of a famous wizard retreat into hiding from muggles during the Middle Ages. FB, p. xv, fn. 4. Bathilda was quoted in *Quidditch Through the Ages* as giving praise to *A History of Magic.* QA, p. iv. Albus Dumbledore and Bathilda shared regular correspondence. DH 2, p. 17. Auntie Muriel claimed that her mother had been a friend of Bathilda and that Bathilda lived in Godric's Hollow. DH 8, pp. 157-58; 17, pp. 334-35. Bathilda's great-nephew was Gellert Grindelwald. Rita Skeeter referred to Bathilda as "Batty." DH 18, pp. 355, 359.

Balderdash. A password used to gain access to the Gryffindor house during Harry Potter's fourth year at Hogwarts. GF 12, p. 191.

Ballycastle Bats. A quidditch team that played the Chudley Cannons. Harry Potter read about the Ballycastle Bats in *Flying with the Cannons* during his fourth year at Hogwarts. GF 22, p. 393. The Ballycastle Bats was the most celebrated quidditch team from Northern Ireland. The team's mascot was Barny the Fruitbat. QA 7, pp. 32-33.

Ban on Experimental Breeding. A law passed in 1965 that Newt Scamander helped write. The law prevented the breeding of new and untamable monsters in Great Britain. FB, p. vi. A bog-standard chicken that breathed fire was carried into the Ministry of Magic by Bob, who suspected that the chicken violated this law. This event occurred during the summer prior to Harry Potter's fifth year at Hogwarts. OP 7, p. 129.

Banchory Bangers. A quidditch team from Scotland renowned for the poor skills of its members and their post-match parties. In 1814, the Banchory Bangers was forced to disband after attempting to catch a Hebridean Black (dragon) to serve as its team mascot. QA 5, pp. 16-17.

Bandon Banshee. A creature that Gilderoy Lockhart claimed to have eliminated. Gilderoy informed his first Defense Against the Dark Arts class that the feat didn't just happen by his smiling at the banshee. CS 6, p. 99. This event occurred during Harry Potter's second year at Hogwarts.

Bane. A black-haired centaur who lived in the Forbidden Forest. Harry Potter encountered Bane during his first year at Hogwarts. SS 15, p. 253. DH 36, p. 728.

Bangladesh. The Ministry of Magic in Bangladesh regarded quidditch with some suspicion. QA 8, p. 46. (Bangladesh is a country in South Asia and north of the Bay of Bengal. It was formerly a province of Pakistan.)

Banishing Charm. A charm used to perform the opposite function of the Summoning Charm. The Banishing Charm had the effect of repelling objects. Harry Potter practiced the Banishing Charm during a Charms class in his fourth year at Hogwarts. GF 26, p. 479.

Barnabus Finkley Prize for Exceptional Spell-Casting. See **Finkley, Barnabus.**

Barnabas the Barmy. A wizard who was featured on a tapestry located on the eighth floor of Hogwarts, across from the Room of Requirement. Barnabas was depicted being clubbed by trolls because he had foolishly tried to train them for a ballet. OP 18, pp. 388-89.

Barney the Fruitbat. The mascot of the Ballycastle Bats who was well-known for his appearance in Butterbeer advertisements. QA 7, p. 33.

Barnsley. The location where Bungy the budgie lived, as reported in the muggle news by Mary Dorkins. Bungy lived at the Five Feathers in Barnsley. This event occurred during the summer prior to Harry Potter's fifth year at Hogwarts. OP 1, p. 4. (Barnsley is a city in South Yorkshire of Northern England.)

Barnton. The location in Britain that had a quidditch field with very tiny baskets as goal posts on the opponent's end of the field and large baskets on the home team's side. This inequity was pointed out by a representative of the Department of Magical Games and Sports in a *Daily Prophet* article printed on February 12, 1883. QA 6, p. 19.

Baruffio, Wizard. A wizard who said "s" instead" of "f" when he uttered a charm and, as a result, found himself on the floor with a buffalo on his chest. Professor Flitwick used the incident to illustrate to Harry Potter's Charms class the importance of speaking the magic words of a charm correctly. This event occurred on Halloween during Harry's first year at Hogwarts. SS 10, p. 171.

Baruffio's Brain Elixir. A magical liquid that Eddie Carmichael offered to Harry Potter and his classmates to help them study for O.W.L.s. Eddie offered to sell one pint of the elixir for twelve Galleons. This event occurred during Harry's fifth year at Hogwarts. OP 31, p. 708.

Bashir, Ali. A wizard who was upset with Arthur Weasley's embargo on flying carpets. Barty Crouch warned Arthur of Ali Bashir at the Quidditch World Cup during the summer prior to Harry Potter's fourth year at Hogwarts. Arthur's response was that he had informed

Bashir one hundred times that a flying carpet was defined as a "muggle artifact" under the Registry of Proscribed Charmable Objects. GF 7, p. 91. Percy Weasley mentioned to Ludo Bagman at the Yule Ball that Bashir was caught smuggling a consignment of flying carpets into Britain. These events occurred during Harry's fourth year at Hogwarts. GF 23, p. 425.

Basic Blaze. Some of the magical fireworks invented by Fred and George Weasley, collectively referred to as Weasleys' Wildfire Whiz-Bangs. They were sold for five galleons The other type of fireworks, Deflagration Deluxe, were sold for twenty galleons. This event occurred during Harry Potter's fifth year at Hogwarts. OP 28, p. 634.

Basil. A wizard who coordinated the portkey arrivals at the Quidditch World Cup. Basil attempted to dress like a muggle in a kilt and poncho. He knew Arthur Weasley on sight. This event occurred during the summer prior to Harry Potter's fourth year at Hogwarts. GF 7, p. 75.

Basilisk. A deadly monster, also known as the King of Serpents, that was a giant snake. The basilisk was hatched by a toad from a chicken's egg. It had deadly venomous fangs and if one looked directly into its eyes, one instantly died. CS 13, p. 247; 16, p. 290. Spiders were afraid of basilisks. CS 15, p. 278. The only weakness of a basilisk was a rooster's crow. CS 16, p. 290. The monster hidden within the Chamber of Secrets was a basilisk. CS 16, p. 290. The victims of the basilisk during Harry Potter's second year at Hogwarts were, in order of their petrification by the basilisk: Colin Creevy, Justin Flinch-Fletchley, Nearly Headless Nick, Hermione Granger and Penelope Clearwater. The basilisk was originally bred by Harpo the Foul and declared illegal during medieval times. FB, pp. 3-4. A tear of a Phoenix was the only known antidote for basilisk venom. DH 6, p. 104; 31, p. 622.

Bat-Bogey Hex. A hex that Ginny Weasley was reportedly good at invoking. OP 6, p. 100. She used the hex on the Hogwarts Express on the way to Harry Potter's sixth year at Hogwarts. HP 7, p. 146.

Bath. A city where a witch, according to Ron Weasley, owned a book that once you started to read it, you could not stop. The book forced you to walk around with your nose in it and you had to perform everything one-handed because you could not let go of it. CS 13, p. 231. (Bath is a city in Avon, in Southwest England.)

Bath Buns. Round sweet buns that Rubeus Hagrid baked and offered to Harry Potter and Ron Weasley during Harry's third year at Hogwarts. Harry and Ron knew better than to accept the buns because they were too familiar with Hagrid's bad cooking. PA 14, p. 273.

Bayliss, Hetty. A witch who lived in Norfolk and observed a flying car. Her account of the incident was reported in the *Evening Prophet.* The vehicle was in fact driven by Ron Weasley with Harry Potter as a passenger. Another eyewitness to the same incident was Angus Fleet. This event occurred during the summer prior to Harry's second year at Hogwarts. CS 5, p. 79.

Beast. A creature not deemed worthy of certain legal rights and that was refused a voice in governance of the magical world. A Beast was contrasted with a Being. FB, p. x.

Beast Division. A division in the Department for the Regulation and Control of Magical Creatures. The Beast Division was established by Grogan Stump. FB, p. xii, fn. 2. Newt Scamander worked in the Beast Division. FB, p. vi. The division included the Centaur Liaison Office and the Werewolf Capture Unit. FB, p. xiii, fn. 3. DH 12, p. 245.

Beater. A player on a quidditch team who used short baseball bats to prevent two jet black balls, slightly smaller than a quaffle and known as bludgers, from striking the other players of his team off of their brooms. There were two beaters per team. SS 9, p. 153; SS 10, p. 168. The function of the beater changed little over the centuries. The rules prohibited the beater from scoring a goal or handling the quaffle. QA 3, p. 10; QA 6, pp. 24-25.

Beaters' Bible, The. The title of a book written by Brutus Scrimgeour. Brutus was quoted as giving praise to *Quidditch Through the Ages*. QA, p. iv.

Beating the Bludgers--A Study of Defensive Strategies in Quidditch. The title of a book written by Kennilworthy Whisp. QA, p. v.

Beauxbatons Academy of Magic. A school for witches and wizards located in France. Hermione Granger mentioned to Harry Potter after the Quidditch World Cup that she read about Beauxbatons in *An Appraisal of Magical Education in Europe*. GF 9, p. 123. Fleur Delacour referred to the school as the "Palace of Beauxbatons" and boasted that it had a dining chamber with ice sculptures during Christmas. GF 23, p. 418. Beauxbatons' location was a mystery so that its secrets could not be stolen. GF 9, p. 123; 11, p. 166. The school transported its contestants to the Triwizard Tournament at Hogwarts in a flying powder-blue, horse-drawn carriage the size of a house. It was pulled by twelve, giant, palomino, winged horses. The horses drank only single-malt whiskey. The coat of arms of Beauxbatons consisted of two crossed, golden wands that each emitted three stars. The chief administrator of the school was Madam Maxine. GF 15, p. 243-45. These events occurred the summer prior to and during Harry's fourth year at Hogwarts. Students at Beauxbatons could not take the Ordinary Wizarding Level tests (O.W.L.s) until after six years of study. HP 5, p. 101.

Beedle. The author of children's stories in the wizarding world. His book was titled *The Tales of Beedle the Bard.* DH 7, p. 135.

Befuddlement Draught. A potion that Harry Potter studied during his fifth year at Hogwarts. The ingredients for the potion included scurvy-grass, lovage and sneezewort, which caused inflammation of the brain. The potion was similar to the Confusing Draught. OP 18, p. 383.

Beginners' Guide to Transfiguration, A. A book written by Emeric Switch. First-year students at Hogwarts were required to purchase the book. SS 5, p. 66.

Being. A creature deemed worthy of certain legal rights and given a voice in governance of the magical world. A Being was contrasted with a Beast. FB, p. x.

Being Division. A division in the Department for the Regulation and Control of Magical Creatures. The Being Division was established by Grogan Stump. FB, p. xii, fn. 2. The Being Division had a special office for Werewolf Support Services. FB, p. xiii. DH 12, p. 245.

Belby, Damocles. A student of Horace Slughorn who was the uncle of Marcus Belby. He received the Order or Merlin and was an outstanding wizard according to Horace. Damocles invented Wolfsbane Potion. HP 7, p. 144.

Belby, Flavius. A wizard attacked by a Lethifold in 1782 while he vacationed in Papua, New Guinea. Flavius recorded the event and it was the earliest known written account of a Lethifold attack. FB, pp. 25-27.

Belby, Marcus. Marcus was one of the privileged students to be invited into Compartment C of the Hogwarts Express to meet Professor Horace Slughorn on the way to Harry Potter's sixth year at Hogwarts. His uncle, Damocles, was a student of Horace Slughorn. HP 7, pp. 143-44. Marcus was a member of the Ravenclaw house. HP 7, p. 150.

Belch Powder. A joke powder sold at Zonko's Joke Shop in Hogsmeade. Argus Filch asked Harry Potter sarcastically why he was not buying Belch Powder in Hogsmeade like the rest of his little friends. This event occurred during Harry's third year at Hogwarts. PA 8, p. 153.

Belcher, Humphrey. A wizard who Albus Dumblefore used as an example of a wizard who had made mistakes. Humphrey incorrectly decided the time was ripe for a cheese cauldron. HP 10, p. 197.

Bell, Katie. A student who was one of the chasers on the Gryffindor quidditch team during Harry Potter's first through fourth years at Hogwarts. SS 11, p. 186; CS 7, pp. 107-08; PA 8, p. 144; GF 17, p. 285. The other two chasers on the team were Angelina Johnson and Alicia Spinnet. Katie's name appeared on the list of borrowers found inside the cover of *Quidditch Through the Ages.* QA, p. i. During Harry's sixth year at Hogwarts, Katie was the only remaining member of the team with whom he had started playing. HP 9, p. 175. One of her friends that year was a student named Leanne. HP 12, p; 248. During that same school year, Katie suffered a curse and was removed to St. Mungo's Hospital for Magical Maladies and Injuries. HP 13, p. 258. DH 30, p. 603.

Benedict, Brother. A Franciscan monk from Worcestershire who lived during the Middle Ages and wrote a manuscript about certain trouble he had with a talking "ferret" in his herb garden. FB, p. xiv.

Benson, Amy. A child who was an orphan at the same London orphanage where Tom Riddle lived during his childhood. The orphanage was operated by Mrs. Cole. Other orphans there were Billy Stubbs, Eric Whalley and Dennis Bishop. Amy ventured into a cave with Tom and Dennis during an annual outing and was never the same again in the head. HP 13, pp. 264, 268.

Bertie Bott's Every Flavor Beans. Special candy sold in the wizarding world and made in many unusual flavors. SS 6, p. 101. The flavors included: chocolate, peppermint and marmalade, SS 6, pp. 103-04; sprouts, spinach, liver, tripe, booger, toast, coconut, baked bean, strawberry, curry, grass, coffee, sardine, pepper, SS 6, p. 104; vomit, SS 17, p. 300; and ear wax, SS 17, p. 301. Harry Potter was introduced to this candy on the Hogwarts Express as he traveled to his first year at Hogwarts. SS 6, p. 101. Albus Dumbledore was unfortunate enough to eat an ear wax flavored bean at the end of Harry's first year at Hogwarts. SS 17, p. 301. The candy was advertised on the billboard at the Quidditch World Cup. The ad read: "A Risk With Every Mouthful." This event occurred during the summer prior to Harry's fourth year at the school. GF 8, p. 102. Rubeus Hagrid gave Harry a box of candy, including Bertie Bott's Every Flavor Beans, as a Christmas present that same year. GF 23, p. 410. DH 21, p. 406.

Bethnal Green. A location where a third regurgitating public toilet was reported in a memorandum sent to Arthur Weasley. This event occurred during the summer prior to Harry Potter's fifth year at Hogwarts. OP 7, p. 133. (Bethnal Green was a former borough of London, north of the Thames.)

Bezoar. A magic stone taken from the stomach of a goat and able to save a wizard from most poisons. Severus Snape quizzed Harry Potter about where to find a bezoar. This event occurred during the first Potions class that Harry attended at Hogwarts. SS 8, pp. 137-138. Harry forgot to list a bezoar as an ingredient in a Potions class test he took at the end of the Fall term of his fourth year at Hogwarts. GF 22, p. 396.

Bicorn. A creature whose horn, when ground into powder, was used as an ingredient for Polyjuice Potion. Hermione Granger read the ingredients of Polyjuice Potion from *Most Potent Potions* to Harry Potter and Ron Weasley during Harry's second year at Hogwarts. CS 10, p. 165.

Bigfoot. Another name for the Yeti. FB, p. 42. See **Yeti**.

Bigonville Bombers. A quidditch team from Luxembourg. QA 8, p. 41.

Billiwig. A magical beast from Australia. Dried billiwig stings were used in several potions and believed to be an ingredient in Fizzing Whizbees. FB, pp. xviii, 4. Xenophilius Lovegood used billiwig wings in his recreation of Rowena Ravenclaw's diadem. DH 25, p. 513.

Binky. A pet rabbit owned by Lavender Brown and that died around October 16 during Harry Potter's third year at Hogwarts. Sibyl Trelawney predicted Binky's death during a Divination class attended by Harry that year. PA 8, p. 148.

Binns, Professor. The professor of the History of Magic class at Hogwarts. Professor Binns was the only professor at the school who was a ghost. SS 8, p. 133. He routinely called students by incorrect names. CS 9, pp. 149-52. Professot Binns was a boring teacher and could make even goblin rebellions sound dull. GF 22, p. 392. DH 21, p. 415.

Birmingham. A location that the Knight Bus flew over after leaving Grimmauld Place on its way to Hogsmeade. This event occurred during the summer prior to Harry Potter's fifth year at Hogwarts. OP 24, p. 525. (Birmingham is a city in West Midlands, in Central England.)

Bishop, Dennis. A child who was an orphan at the same London orphanage where Tom Riddle lived during his childhood. The orphanage was operated by Mrs. Cole. Other orphans there were Billy Stubbs, Eric Whalley and Amy Benson. Dennis ventured into a cave with Tom and Amy during an annual outing and was never the same again in the head. HP 13, pp. 264, 268.

Biting Fairy. See **Doxy**.

Black. A wizard family. The family crest included the motto "Toujours Pur." DH 10, p. 187.

Black, Alphard. An uncle of Sirius Black who left Sirius a decent pot of gold that allowed Sirius to move out from his home when he was 17 years old. OP 6, p. 111.

Black, Bellatrix. The sister of Andromeda Black and Narcissa (Black) Malfoy. Bellatrix was one of Sirius Black's cousins and the wife of Rodolphus Lestrange. OP 6, pp. 113-14; HP 2, p. 21. She was a prisoner in Azkaban because of her connection to the Dark Lord, but she eventually escaped. HP 2, p. 26. During Harry Potter's sixth year at Hogwarts, Severus Snape believed that Bellatrix had taught her nephew, Draco Malfoy, Occlumency. HP 15, p. 322. DH 1, p. 9. Bellatrix' fate occurred at the end of year seven. DH 36, pp. 736-37.

Black, Elladora. An aunt of Sirius Black who started the family tradition of beheading their house-elves. OP 6, p. 113.

Black Forest. The place where Professor Quirrell reportedly met vampires and a hag. Rubeus Hagrid informed Harry Potter of the report when they observed Professor Quirrell in Diagon Alley. This event occurred during the summer prior to Harry's first year at Hogwarts. SS 5, p. 71. The Black Forest was also the location of a portkey that brought a large group of wizards to the Quidditch World Cup. This event occurred during the summer prior to Harry's fourth year at the school. GF 7, p. 75. Ellerby and Spudmore, a company located in the Black Forest, manufactured quidditch brooms such as the Tinderblast and the Swiftstick. QA 9, p. 50. (The Black Forest is a wooded mountainous region in Southwest Germany.)

Black, Mrs. The mother of Sirius Black. Mrs. Black was found in a life-size portrait behind curtains at Number Twelve, Grimmauld Place, London. OP 4, pp. 77-78. She died ten years prior to Harry Potter's fifth year at Hogwarts. OP 5, p. 82. DH 9, p. 170.

Black, Narcissa. The maiden name of Narcissa Malfoy. Her sisters were Andromeda and Bellatrix and she was one of Sirius Black's cousins. OP 6, p. 113. Narcissa was a Death Eater. DH 1, p. 8.

Black, Phineas Nigellus. The great-great-grandfather of Sirius Black who was, according to Sirius, the least popular headmaster Hogwarts ever had. OP 6, p. 113. A portrait of Phineas hung in Albus Dumbledore's office at Hogwarts and also at 16 Grimmauld Place and he was able to flit between the portraits. Phineas was a member of the Slytherin house when he was a student at the school. OP 22, p.472; 9, p. 178. DH 10, p. 178.

Black Pool. The location where Neville's great uncle pushed him off the end of a pier to test whether Neville was a muggle or wizard. Neville told this story to his fellow Gryffindor house classmates after the Sorting Ceremony was completed during Harry Potter's first year at Hogwarts. SS 7, p. 125. (Blackpool is a seaside resort in West Lancashire, in Northwest England.)

Black, Regulus Arcturus (R.A.B.). The younger brother of Sirius Black who was a Death Eater. OP 6, p. 112. Regulus attended Hogwarts and was a member of the Slytherin house at the time when Horace Slughorn was a professor there and the head of that house. HP 4, p. 70. A few days after deserting the Death Eaters, Regulus was killed by them. HP 6, p. 106. Regulus' middle name, Arcturus was not revealed until year seven. He had been a quidditch player at Hogwarts for the Slytherin team. DH 10, pp. 186-87. Regelus' fate was revealed during year seven. DH 10, p. 196; 36, p. 734.

Black Sea. A body of water from which a Ukranian Ironbelly dragon carried off a sailboat. This event occurred in 1799 and caused the Ukranian wizarding authorities to begin continuous surveillance of the Ironbellies. FB, p. 15. (The Black Sea is a body of water between Europe and Asia that is bordered by Turkey, Romania, Bulgaria, Ukraine, Georgia and the Russian Federation.)

Black, Sirius. The wizard who owned and allowed Rubeus Hagrid to borrow a flying motorcycle in order to take Harry Potter to safety after Lord Voldemort attempted to kill Harry. SS 1, p. 14. Sirius's escape from Azkaban was so important that it was announced on muggle television. PA 2, p. 17. Sirius was imprisoned in Azkaban for killing thirteen people with one curse in broad daylight. PA 3, pp. 37-38. Barty Crouch issued the order to imprison Sirius without a trial. GF 27, p. 526. In his youth, Sirius was a student at Hogwarts and his best friend there was James Potter. He was best man at James and Lily Potter's wedding and they made him Harry's godfather and guardian. PA 10, p. 204. Sirius was an unregistered animagus, in the form of a dog, and was known to his closest friends as Padfoot. PA 17, p. 348; 18, p. 355. The true account of the mass murders attributed to Sirius is discussed at PA 18, p. 351; 19, pp. 365, 369. Sirius was a member of the Order of the Phoenix and lived at his family's home: Number Twelve, Grimmauld Place, London. OP 4, p. 78. Narcissa (Black) Malfoy was one of Sirius' cousins. Arthur Weasley was Sirius' second cousin once removed. OP 6, p. 113. Harry used the code name Snuffles for Sirius during Harry's fifth year at Hogwarts. OP 14, p. 280. DH 2, p. 14. Sirius as a youth appeared in a story that Harry watched in the Pensieve during year seven. DH 33, p. 671.

Bladvak. The gobbledegook word for pickax. Ludo Bagman admitted to Harry Potter in the Three Broomsticks that bladvak was the only word of gobbledegook that he could speak. This event occurred during Harry's fourth year at Hogwarts. GF 24, p. 446.

Blagging. The name of one of the ten most common fouls committed in quidditch. QA 6, p. 29.

Blast-Ended Skrewt. A creature that looked like a deformed, shell-less lobster. It had no visible head and its legs stuck out in very odd places. It smelled like rotten fish and could burn, sting and bite simultaneously. GF 13, p. 196-197. A blast-ended skrewt was produced by crossing a manticore with a fire-crab. This information was conveyed in a *Daily Prophet* article written by Rita Skeeter. GF 24, p. 438. Harry Potter was introduced to the blast-ended skrewt in a Care of Magical Creatures class taught by Rubeus Hagrid. This event occurred during Harry's fourth year at Hogwarts. GF 13, pp. 196-197. After Halloween, when the skrewts had grown to over six feet in length, Harry considered them to be the most repulsive things he had ever seen. GF 21, p. 368. DH 2, p. 21.

Blasting Curse. A curse invoked by Hermione Granger with the magic word "*confringo*" to help Harry Potter and herself escape from Bathilda Bagshot's residence during year seven. The curse rebounded and accidentally broke Harry's wand into two. DH 17, p. 349.

Blatching. The name of one of the ten most common fouls committed in quidditch. QA 6, p. 29.

Bletchley. A wizard who worked in the Ministry of Magic and for whom the charm *Meteolojinx Recanto* worked to stop rain indoors, according to Arthur Weasley, during year seven. DH 13, p. 255.

Bletchley, Miles. A student at Hogwarts who was a member of the Slytherin house and keeper on its quidditch team during Harry Potter's fifth year at Hogwarts. OP 19, p. 400.

Blibbering Hundinger. A magical creature that Luna Lovegood believed to exist. Hermione Granger was skeptical about the existence of the blibbering hundinger. OP 13, p. 262.

Blood Blisterpod. A joke candy that Fred and George Weasley suspected they had mistakenly given to Katie Bell during a quidditch practice session. This event occurred during Harry Potter's fifth year at Hogwarts. OP 14, p. 293.

Blood Brothers: My Life Amongst the Vampires. The title of a book written by Eldred Worple, an old student of Horace Slughorn. HP 15, p. 315.

Blood Status. A status conferred by the Ministry of Magic on students seeking admittance to Hogwarts that they had wizard descent. This practice occurred during year seven. DH 11, p. 210.

Blooder. The old term for a bludger. QA 3, p. 9. Blooders were originally just flying rocks. QA 6, p. 21.

Blood-Replenishing Potion. A potion that Arthur Weasley took every hour after his snake-bite injury. This event occurred during Harry Potter's fifth year at Hogwarts. OP 22, p. 488.

Blood-Sucking Bugbear. A creature that Rubeus Hagrid incorrectly suspected of killing a rooster outside of his hut during Harry Potter's second year at Hogwarts. CS 11, p. 201.

Bloody Baron. The resident ghost of Hogwarts who was affiliated with the Slytherin house and the only ghost who could control Peeves. SS 7, pp. 124, 129. The Bloody Baron's name came from the fact that he was covered in silver bloodstains. At a ghost's council held during Harry Potter's fourth year at Hogwarts, the Fat Friar voted to allow Peeves the opportunity to join the rest of the school in the feast that followed the Sorting Ceremony. However, the Bloody Baron opposed the idea and his objection was final. In response, Peeves reeked havoc in the school's kitchen. GF 12, p. 181. The Bloody Baron had loved Helena Ravenclaw and when she refused his advances he stabbed her to death and then committed suicide. DH 31, p. 616.

Bludger. A jet black ball, slightly smaller than a quaffle, used in quidditch and that attempted to strike players off of their brooms. There were two bludgers in the game. SS 10, p. 168. Bludgers were sought after by beaters on each team, who could strike them with baseball bat-like clubs. A bludger was made of iron and measured ten inches in diameter. QA 3, p. 8; 4, pp. 21-23. DH 31, p. 625.

Bludger Backbeat. A widely-known quidditch move. QA 10, p. 52.

Bluebottle. A type of magic broom that was designed for the entire family and included a built-in, anti-burglar buzzer. The bluebottle was advertized on the flashing advertisement in the stadium at the Quidditch World Cup. GF 8, p. 96. This event occurred during the summer prior to Harry Potter's fourth year at Hogwarts.

Blurting. The name of one of the ten most common fouls committed in quidditch. QA 6, p. 29.

Boardman, Stubby. The lead singer of The Hobgoblins. *The Quibbler* reported that Doris Polkiss believed Sirius Black was actually Stubby Boardman. OP 10, p. 192.

Bob. A wizard who was employed by the Ministry of Magic. Arthur Weasley addressed Bob in an elevator at the Ministry during the summer prior to Harry Potter's fifth year at Hogwarts. OP 7, p. 129.

Bobbin, Melinda. A student at Hogwarts during Harry Potter's sixth year at the school whose family owned a large chain of apothecaries. Melinda was invited to a special party at Horace Slughorn's rooms in Hogwarts that school year. HP 11, p. 233.

Bode, Broderick. A wizard who worked as an Unspeakable for the Department of Mysteries. Arthur Weasley had no idea what Broderick did in that position but knew that it was top secret. GF 7, p. 86. Broderick was admitted to Ward 49 of St. Mungo's Hospital for Magical Maladies and Injuries because he believed himself to be a teapot. This event occurred during Harry Potter's fifth year at Hogwarts. OP 22, p. 486. Broderick was later found dead at St. Mungo's, after having been strangled by Devil's Snare. He was 49 years old at the time of his death. OP 25, pp. 546-47.

Bodmin Moor. A location in Cornwall where a Golden Snitch could not be captured for six months. This event occurred in 1884. QA 6, p. 23. (Bodmin Moor is a granite moorland in Northeast Cornwall, England.)

Bodrod the Bearded. A goblin rebel who Ron Weasley complained he had to study about for the History of Magic class final exam he took on the day of the third task of the Triwizard Tournament. Another goblin rebel's name was Urg the Unclean. This event occurred during Harry Potter's fourth year at Hogwarts. GF 31, p. 618.

Body-Bind Curse. A curse invoked with the magic words "*petrificus totalus.*" The Body-Bind caused a person's body to become as stiff as a board. Hermione Granger invoked the curse against Neville Longbottom during Harry Potter's first year at Hogwarts. SS 16, p. 273. The curse was broken if the wizard who invoked it died. HP 28, p. 608. DH 8, p. 138; 32, p. 645; 36, p. 733.

Bogart. A creature that liked dark, enclosed spaces (i.e. wardrobes, gaps between beds, cupboards beneath sinks and grandfather clocks) and was referred to as a shape-shifter. A bogart took the shape of whatever it thought would most frighten someone. PA 7, p. 133. It became confused if more than one person was in front of it. PA 7, p. 134. The best defense against a bogart was laughter and speaking the magic word "*riddikulus.*" PA 7, p. 134. Remus Lupin observed that Harry Potter's worst fear when confronted with a bogart was fear itself. Rather than being afraid of a bogart turning into an image of Lord Voldemort, Harry was most afraid of a bogart changing into a dementor. PA 8, p. 155. These events occurred during Harry's third year at Hogwarts. The following year, Harry encountered a bogart in the third task of the Triwizard Tournament. GF 31, p. 623.

Bogies, Curse of the. A curse that Professor Quirrell taught first-year students at Hogwarts. Ron Weasley threatened to use the curse on Hermione Granger or Neville Longbottom during Harry Potter's first year at the school. SS 9, p. 157.

Bogrod. A goblin who worked at the Gringotts Wizarding Bank during year seven. DH 26, p. 532.

Bole. A student of Hogwarts who was a member of the Slytherin house. Bole played the position of beater on that house's quidditch team during Harry Potter's third year at Hogwarts. PA 15, p. 308. The other beater on the team was Derrick. Bole graduated from Hogwarts during Harry's fourth year and was replaced on the team by either Crabbe or Goyle. OP 19, p. 405.

Bonaccord, Pierre. A wizard who was the first Supreme Mugwump of the International Confederation of Wizards. Pierre's appointment to that position was contested by the Liechtenstein wizarding community. OP 31, pp. 725-26.

Bones. A family of some of the best witches and wizards of the age, according to Rubeus Hagrid, who were killed by Lord Voldemort.

Other families that were similarly murdered were the McKinnons and the Prewetts. SS 4, p. 56.

Bones, Amelia Susan. A witch who was Head of the Department of Magical Law Enforcement in the Ministry of Magic. Amelia's office was on the same floor as Arthur Weasley's. OP 7, p. 123. She was an interrogator during Harry's Potter's disciplinary hearing held at the Wizengamot. This event occurred during the summer prior to Harry's fifth year at Hogwarts. OP 8, p. 138. Amelia was the sister of Edgar Bones. OP 9, p. 174. Although a gifted witch, she was murdered (along with Emmeline Vance) by Lord Voldemort. HP 1, p. 13.

Bones, Edgar. A wizard who was a member of the Order of the Phoenix and killed, along with his family, fighting for the Order. Edgar was the brother of Amelia Bones. OP 9, p. 174.

Bones, Susan. A student sorted by the Sorting Hat during Harry Potter's first year at Hogwarts. Susan was a member of the Hufflepuff house. SS 7, p. 119. She appeared at Hog's Head to discuss formation of a club to study Defense Against the Dark Arts. This event occurred during Harry's fifth year at Hogwarts. OP 16, p. 342. Susan had an aunt, uncle and some cousins who were killed by Death Eaters. OP 25, p. 550. She was the first student of the eligible sixth year students to be partially successful at learning to Apparate during Harry's sixth year at the school. However, she ended up splinching her left leg behind her starting point. HP 18, p. 385.

Boniface, Brother. A Franciscan monk who made Brother Boniface's Turnip Wine in Worcestershire during the Middle Ages. FB, p. xiv.

Boomslang. The shredded skin of a snake that was an ingredient for Polyjuice Potion. Hermione Granger read the ingredients of Polyjuice Potion from *Most Potent Potions* to Harry Potter and Ron Weasley during Harry's second year at Hogwarts. CS 10, p. 165. Hermione broke into Severus Snape's office to obtain boomslang that year. CS 11, p. 186. During his fourth year at the school, Severus Snape accused Harry of breaking into his office to remove boomslang skin and gillyweed. GF 27, p. 516.

Boot, Terry. A student sorted by the Sorting Hat during Harry Potter's first year at Hogwarts. Terry was a member of the Ravenclaw house. SS 7, p. 119. She participated in the first meeting of the Dueling Club during Harry's second year at Hogwarts. CS 1, p. 193. Terry's name appeared on the list of borrowers found inside the cover of *Quidditch Through the Ages*. QA, p. i. She appeared at Hog's Head, along with several other students, to discuss formation of a club to study Defense Against the Dark Arts. This event occurred during Harry Potter's fifth year at Hogwarts OP 16, p. 338. During year seven,

Terry was disciplined at Hogwarts for yelling in the Great Hall about one of Harry's feats that year. DH 29, p. 572.

Boothby, Gladys. A witch who crafted the Moontrimmer in 1901. Gladys' Moontrimmer was a leap forward in broom construction. QA 9, p. 48.

Borage, Libatius. The author of *Advanced Potion-Making*, a book that the Potions N.E.W.T. class used during Harry Potter's sixth year at Hogwarts. HP 9, p. 183.

Borgin, Mr. A wizard who owned a Dark Magic shop known as Borgin and Burkes in Knockturn Alley. CS 4, p. 50. Harry Potter landed in Mr. Borgin's shop by accident after using Floo Powder for the first time. This event occurred during the summer prior to Harry's second year at Hogwarts. CS 4, p. 49.

Borgin and Burkes. A Dark Magic shop in which objects were bought and sold and that was located in Knockturn Alley. Borgin and Burkes was the largest shop on that street. CS 4, pp. 50-53. Harry Potter landed in this shop by accident after using Floo Powder for the first time. This event occurred during the summer prior to Harry's second year at Hogwarts. The founder of the shop was Caractacus Burke. HP 13, p. 261. Tom Riddle worked at Borgin and Burkes, after he was turned down by Professor Dippet for a teaching position at Hogwarts. HP 20, p. 431. One of the items in the shop was a Vanishing Cabinet that was a mate to the one in the Room of Requirement at Hogwarts. HP 27, p. 587. DH 15, p. 288.

Boris the Bewildered. A wizard who had a statue honoring him on the fifth floor of Hogwarts. The prefects' bathroom was located four doors to the left of it. GF 23, p. 431. The statue portrayed Boris as being lost and wearing gloves on the wrong hands. GF 25, p. 459.

Borneo. The natural habitat of the Acromantula. FB, pp. xviii, 1 and fn. 1. (Borneo is an island in the Malay Archipelago.)

Bottom Bridge. A bridge near the residence of Xenophilius Lovegood. DH 20, p. 404.

Bouncing Bulbs. A plant that Harry Potter's Herbology class repotted during Harry's fourth year at Hogwarts. This event occurred after Harry was selected as a school champion for the Triwizard Tournament. The members of the Hufflepuff house, especially Ernie Macmillan and Justin Finch-Fletchley, were upset that Harry was chosen, in addition to Cedric Diggory, to represent Hogwarts and, as a result, refused to talk to Harry afterwards. GF 18, p. 293.

Bowtruckle. A magical beast. FB, pp. xvii, 5. Professor Grubbly-Plank demonstrated bowtruckles to Harry Potter's Care of Magical Creatures class during Harry's fifth year at Hogwarts. Bowtruckles were tree-guardians and usually lived in wand-trees. They liked to eat wood lice and especially fairy eggs. OP 13, pp. 258-59. They also liked doxy eggs. DH 28, p. 560.

Boxing Day. (The first weekday following Christmas, which is observed in Great Britain as a legal holiday.) GF 24, p. 433.

Boy Who Lived, The. An informal title given to Harry Potter to acknowledge the fact that he survived an attack upon his life, as an infant, at the hands of Lord Voldemort. DH 10, p. 208.

Bozo. A photographer from the *Daily Prophet* who accompanied Rita Skeeter into the Three Broomsticks during Harry Potter's fourth year at Hogwarts. GF 24, p. 450.

Bradley. A student at Hogwarts who was a member of the Ravenclaw house and a chaser on its quidditch team during Harry Potter's fifth year there. OP 30, p. 684; 31, p. 704.

Bragga Broomfleet. A quidditch team from Portugal. QA 8, p. 41.

Bragge, Barberus. A wizard who was Chief of the Wizards' Council in 1269. Bragge attended a quidditch match that year. During the match, the sport of Snidget-hunting crossed paths with quidditch for the first time. QA 4, pp. 11-12.

Brain Room. A room in the Department of Mysteries that contained a tank with brains inside it. OP 34, p. 772; 35, p. 797.

Braithwaite, Betty. A reporter for the *Daily Prophet.* During year seven, she interviewed Rita Skeeter about the later's book *The Life and Lies of Albus Dumbledore.* The interview was published on page 13. DH 2, p 23.

Brand, Rudolf. The captain of the Heidelberg Harriers during a famous match against the Holyhead Harpies. At the end of the game, Rudolf proposed marriage to Gwendolyn Morgan, a player on the other team. QA 7, p. 35.

Brankovitch, Maximus (III). A seeker who played for the Fitchburg Finches. Maximus was the captain when the team went to the World Cup two times. QA 8, p. 45.

Branstone, Eleanor. A student sorted by the Sorting Hat during Harry Potter's fourth year at Hogwarts. Eleanor was a member of the Hufflepuff house. GF 12, p. 178.

Brazil. The natural habitat of a boa constrictor that Harry Potter talked to in a muggle zoo. This incident occurred on Dudley Dursley's eleventh birthday prior to Harry's first year at Hogwarts. SS 2, p. 28. According to Ron Weasley, Bill Weasley had a penfriend from Brazil who sent Bill a cursed hat, to make one's ears shrivel up, because Bill could not afford to take an exchange trip to Brazil. GF 7, p. 84. Quidditch was played in Brazil and the Brazilian team made it to the quarter-finals of the World Cup in the last century. QA 8, p. 45.(Brazil is a country located in South America.)

Break with a Banshee. The title of a book written by Gilderoy Lockhart. The book was required reading for Harry Potter in his second-year at Hogwarts. CS 4, p. 43. DH 6, p. 100.

Bristol. One of the towns that Rubeus Hagrid flew over in a magic motorcycle that he borrowed from Sirius Black. Hagrid used the vehicle to escort the infant Harry Potter to safety after Voldemort's failed attempt to kill Harry. SS 1, p. 15. (Bristol is a seaport in Avon, which is located in Southwest England on the Avon River.)

Britain, Great. The general location for the events in the life of Harry Potter. SS 1, p. 6. DH 7, p. 112. (Great Britain is an island in Northwest Europe that is separated from the mainland by the English Channel and the North Sea and that consists of the following divisions: England, Scotland and Wales.)

British and Irish Quidditch League Headquarters. An organization located on level seven of the Ministry of Magic. OP 7, p. 129.

British Youth Representative to the Wizengamot. A position of distinction that Albus Dumbledore achieved while a student at Hogwarts. DH 18, p. 353.

Broadmoor, Karl. A world-famous beater of the Falmouth Falcons who played, along with his brother Kevin, for the team from 1958 to 1969. QA 7, p. 34.

Broadmoor, Kevin. A world-famous beater of the Falmouth Falcons who played, along with his brother Karl, for the team from 1958 to 1969. QA 7, p. 34.

Brockdale Bridge. A ten-year-old bridge in England that split cleanly into two pieces sending a dozen cars into the river below. This event occurred prior to Harry Potter's sixth year at Hogwarts. HP 1, p. 4.

Brocklehurst, Mandy. A student who was sorted by the Sorting Hat during Harry Potter's first year at Hogwarts. Mandy was a member of the Ravenclaw house. SS 7, p. 119.

Broken Balls: When Fortunes Turn Foul. The title of a book relating to Divination that Harry Potter observed in Flourish and Blotts. This event occurred during the summer prior to Harry's third year at Hogwarts. PA 4,p.53.

Brookstanton, Rupert 'Axebanger.' A reasonably well-known wizard who had the initials R.A.B. Another such wizard was Rosalind Antigone Bungs. Hermione Granger tried to identify the person with those initials at the end of Harry Potter's sixth year at Hogwarts. HP 30, p. 636.

Broom Compass. A magical device that Harry Potter gave to Ron Weasley as a Christmas present during Harry's fifth year at Hogwarts. OP 23, p. 501.

Broom Regulatory Control. An office in the Department of Magical Transport located on level six of the Ministry of Magic. OP 7, p. 129.

Broomstick Servicing Kit. A kit for servicing magic broomsticks that Hermione Granger gave to Harry Potter as a thirteenth birthday present. The kit included Fleetwood's High-Finish Handle Polish, a pair of shiny silver Tail-Twig Clippers, a tiny brass compass and a copy of *Handbook of Do-It-Yourself Broomcare.* This event occurred during Harry's third year at Hogwarts. PA 1, p. 12.

Brown, Lavender. A student sorted by the Sorting Hat during Harry Potter's first year at Hogwarts. Lavender was the first student that year to be sorted into the Gryffindor house. SS 7, p. 119. She had a pet rabbit, named Binky, that died around October 16 during Harry's third year at Hogwarts. PA 8, p. 148. During the following year, Lavender was repulsed by the bubotubors that her classmates handled in a Care of Magical Creatures class taught by Rubeus Hagrid. GF 13, pp. 196-97. Lavender was Seamus Finnigan's date to the Yule Ball. GF 22, p. 401. This event occurred during Harry's fourth year at the school. Two years later, she was observed kissing Ronald Weasley after the Gryffindor quidditch match against Slytherin. HP 14, p. 300. Her pet name for Ron was Won-Won. HP 17, p. 351. DH 7, p. 113; 32, p. 646.

Bryce, Frank. The muggle gardener for the Riddle family of Little Hangleton. Frank fought in an unspecified war and returned to take on the quiet duties of a gardener. He was arrested for the murder of the Riddles but was later released when medical examiners determined that the Riddles had not been murdered. Frank proclaimed his innocence and insisted that a dark-haired, pale, teenage boy performed the crime. During Harry Potter's fourth year at Hogwarts, Frank was, at the age of seventy-six years old, still the gardener at the property and was killed later that year. at GF 1, pp. 2-5, 15.

Bubble-Head Charm. A charm used by Fleur Delacour and Cedric Diggory to breathe underwater as part of the second task of the Triwizard Tournament. GF 26, p. 506.

Bubotubor. A plant that was thick, black and had the appearance of a giant slug. During his fourth year at Hogwarts, Harry Potter learned about this plant in Herbology class. Bubotubors contained extremely valuable pus. The pus smelled like petrol and was an excellent remedy for acne. One extracted the pus by putting on dragon-hide gloves and squeezing the plant. GF 13, pp. 194-195.

Buckbeak. A hippogriff that Rubeus Hagrid held in captivity for the Care of Magical Creatures class he taught at Hogwarts during Harry Potter's third year at Hogwarts. PA 6, p. 115. Draco Malfoy was injured by

Buckbeak and the incident eventually lead to a death sentence against Buckbeak. PA 6, p. 118; PA 16, p. 325. Buckbeak was very useful to Sirius Black. PA 21, p. 396; GF 27, p. 521. DH 36, p. 733.

Budleigh Babberton. A charming village that included the residence of Horace Slughorn. Harry Potter visited the village with Albus Dumbledore during Harry's sixth year at Hogwarts. HP 4, p. 59.

Building Society. A muggle financial institution from which Hermione Granger withdrew all of her savings during year seven. DH 9, p. 165.

Bulbadox Powder. A substance that Fred Weasley placed in Kenneth Towler's pajamas that made Kenneth suffer boils. This event occurred during Fred's fifth year at Hogwarts. OP 12, p. 226.

Bulgaria. A national team from Bulgaria played Ireland in the Quidditch World Cup during the summer prior to Harry Potter's fourth year at Hogwarts. GF 3, p. 35. The team's star player was Viktor Krum. GF 5, p. 63. The team's color was scarlet and its mascot was the Veela. GF 8, pp. 102-103. The Vratsa Vultures was a quidditch team from Bulgaria. QA 8, p. 40. (Bulgaria is a country in Southeast Europe.)

Bulgarian National Quidditch Team. The national team from Bulgaria that played in the Quidditch World Cup during the summer prior to Harry Potter's fourth year at Hogwarts. The members of the team, in order of their introduction at the match, were as follows: Dimitrov (chaser), Ivanova (chaser), Zograf (keeper), Levski (chaser), Vulchanov (beater), Volkov (beater) and Viktor Krum (seeker). GF 8, pp. 104, 107-08.

Bulgarian National Team Mascot. The title given to the Veela as the mascot of the quidditch team from Bulgaria that played in the Quidditch World Cup during the summer prior to Harry Potter's fourth year at Hogwarts. GF 8, p. 102.

Bulstrode, Millicent. A student sorted by the Sorting Hat during Harry Potter's first year at Hogwarts. Millicent was the first student that year to be sorted into the Slytherin house. SS 7, p. 119. She was Hermione Granger's dueling partner in the first meeting of the Dueling Club the following year. CS 11, p. 191. Millicent's name appeared on the list of borrowers found inside the cover of *Quidditch Through the Ages*. QA, p. i.

Bumphing. The name of one of the ten most common fouls committed in quidditch. QA 6, p. 29.

Bundimun. A magical beast removed from a house with a Scouring Charm. Diluted bundimun secretion was used in certain magical cleaning fluids. FB, pp. 5-6.

Bundy, K. A student at Hogwarts whose name appeared on the list of borrowers found inside the cover of *Quidditch Through the Ages*. QA, p. i.

Bungs, Rosalind Antigone. A reasonably well-known wizard who had the initials R.A.B. Another such wizard was Rupert 'Axebanger' Brookstanton. Hermione Granger tried to identify the person with those initials at the end of Harry Potter's sixth year at Hogwarts. HP 30, p. 636.

Bungy. A budgie who lived, according to a report by Mary Dorkins of the muggle news, at the Five Feathers in Barnsley and learned how to water ski. This event occurred during the summer prior to Harry Potter's fifth year at Hogwarts. OP 1, p. 4.

Burbage, Charity. A witch who was the professor of Muggle Studies at Hogwarts before year seven. DH 1, p. 11.

Burke, Caractacus. A wizard who founded Borgin and Burkes. Caractacus purchased Slytherin's locket from Merope Gaunt Riddle for ten galleons. HP 13, p. 261.

Burkins Faso. A small country in Africa that was the natural habitat of the Runespoor. FB, pp. 36-38.

Burning Day. The day on which a phoenix burst into flames and was reborn. Albus Dumbledore explained the significance of Burning Day and the nature of the phoenix in his office to Harry Potter during Harry's second year at Hogwarts. CS 12, p. 207.

Burrow, The. The name of the Weasley residence which was located a short distance outside the village of Ottery St. Catchpole. Harry Potter first visited the Burrow prior to his second year at Hogwarts. CS 3, pp 31-32. The residence had once been a large stone pigpen, but extra rooms were added until the structure was several stories high. The Burrow was so crooked that magic appeared to hold it up. CS 3, p. 32. Among the unusual items in the house was a clock with only one hand and no numbers. Instead, around the edge were phrases like "Time to make tea," "Time to feed the chickens" and "You're late." CS 3, p. 34. There was also a grandfather clock with nine golden hands, one for each family member. The hands rested on words on the dial like "home," "school," "work," "traveling," "lost," "hospital" or "prison." GF 10, p. 151. At the beginning of year seven, the Burrow was connected by portkey to the Tonks residence. DH 4, p. 48.

Butterbeer. A foaming beverage sold by the mugful in the wizarding world The Three Broomsticks in Hogsmeade sold Butterbeer. PA 8, p. 158. Harry Potter ventured into the Three Broomsticks and sampled Butterbeer during his third year at Hogwarts. PA 10, p. 200. The following year Harry drank Butterbeer during the celebration in the Gryffindor house common room to honor Harry's selection as a school champion in the Triwizard Tournament. GF 17, p. 285. Barny the Fruitbat, the mascot of the Ballycastle Bats, was well-known for his appearance in Butterbeer advertisements. QA 7, p. 33. The bartender at Hog's Head charged Harry six sickles for three bottles of Butterbeer. This event occurred during Harry's fifth year at Hogwarts. OP 16, p. 337. DH 8, p. 146.

CADMUS - CRYSTAL GAZING

Cadmus. A wizard who may have been one of the legendary Three Brothers who owned the Deathly Hallows. DH 21, p. 412-13. See **Peverell.**

Cadogan, Sir. A short, squat knight who lived in a painting on the seventh floor of Hogwarts. PA 6, pp. 99-101; 14, p. 269. Sir Cadogan rode a fat, dapple-gray pony. He assisted Harry Potter, Ron Weasley and Hermione Granger with finding their Divination classroom during Harry's third year at Hogwarts. PA 6, pp. 99-101. He also replaced the Fat Lady at the entrance to the Gryffindor house after the Fat Lady's canvas was damaged by Sirius Black. PA 9, p. 167. Sir Cadogan established the following passwords for entry to the Gryffindor house: Scurvy cur, PA 11, p. 230; and Oddsbodikins, PA 12, p. 249. These events occurred during Harry's third year at Hogwarts. DH 31, p. 621.

Cadwallader. A student at Hogwarts who was a member of the Hufflepuff house and a chaser on its quidditch team during Harry Potter's sixth year at Hogwarts. HP 19, p. 414.

Caerphilly Catapults. A quidditch team from Wales formed in 1402. The Catapults' most famous player was "Dangerous" Dai Llewellyn. QA 7, p. 33.

Cairo. The place where an International Alchemical Conference was held and at which Albus Dumbledore was the winner of a Gold-Medal while Albus was a student at Hogwarts. DH 18, p. 353. (Cairo is the capital and largest city in Egypt.)

Callisto. One of the moons of the planet Jupiter that Ron Weasley mistakenly thought was the largest of Jupiter's moons. This information was part of an Astronomy essay written by Ron during Harry Potter's fifth year at Hogwarts. OP 14, p. 295.

Calming Draught. A potion that Madam Pomfrey gave to Hannah Abbott to calm her distress over the upcoming O.W.L.s. This event occurred during Harry Potter's fifth year at Hogwarts. OP 27, p. 606.

Canada. The home country for three important quidditch teams: the Moose Jaw Meteorites, the Haileybury Hammers and the Stonewall Stormers. QA 8, p. 43. (Canada is the country directly north of the United States of America.)

Canary Creams. Magical custard creams that Fred and George Weasley hexed as a joke. A person who ate one of these creams turned into a canary. Neville Longbottom ate one and was transformed into a large canary after Harry Potter completed the first task of the Triwizard Tournament. This event occurred during Harry's fourth year at Hogwarts. GF 21, p. 366.

Canary Islands. A vacation destination visited by a muggle family that lived in Budleigh Babberton. While the family was away from their home, Horace Slughorn moved into the home. This event occurred the summer prior to Harry Potter's sixth year at Hogwarts. HP 4, p. 68. (The Canary Islands are a group of mountainous islands in the Atlantic Ocean near the northwest coast of Africa.)

Capper, S. A student at Hogwarts whose name appeared on the list of borrowers found inside the cover of *Quidditch Through the Ages*. QA, p. i.

Caput Draconis. A password that was used to gain access to the Gryffindor house of Hogwarts during Harry Potter's second year at the school. CS 5, p.84.

Care of Magical Creatures. A subject that was taught at Hogwarts. Fred and George Weasley took the Care of Magical Creatures class during Harry Potter's second year at the school. CS 8, p. 130. The class was not offered to first-year or second-year students. CS 14, p. 252. Harry took the class during his third year, at which time Rubeus Hagrid was the professor. Hagrid replaced Professor Kettleburn who had retired. PA 5, p. 93. Hagrid also taught the class during part of the following year until he became ashamed over an article Rita Skeeter wrote for the *Daily Prophet.* The event caused Hagrid to go into hiding and Professor Grubbly-Plank took over the instructor's position for the class. GF 24, p. 437.

Carmichael, Eddie. A student at Hogwarts who was a member of the Ravenclaw house and who was one year ahead of Harry Potter. During Harry's fifth year, Eddie offered Harry's classmates Baruffio's Brain Elixir to help them study for O.W.L.s. Eddie claimed that it helped him to get nine "Outstanding" O.W.L.s. OP 31, p. 708.

Carrow. A family of Death Eaters who failed to search for Lord Voldemort after he disappeared. Other Death Eaters who failed to do so were: Avery, Yaxley, Fenrir Greyback and Lucius Malfoy. HP 2, p. 26.

Carrow, Alecto. A witch and Death Eater who was appointed as professor of Muggle Studies at Hogwarts during year seven. Her brother was Amycus Carrow. DH 12, p. 226.

Carrow, Amycus. A wizard and Death Eater who was appointed as professor of Defense Against the Dark Arts during year seven. His sister was Alecto Carrow. DH 12, p. 226.

Cartomancy. The power of a Seer to sense the distant vibrations of a coming catastrophe. Sibyll Trelawney had this power. HP 25, p. 544.

Catcher. The old term for a chaser on a quidditch team. QA 3, p. 9.

Caterwauling Charm. A charm used by Death Eaters in Hogsmeade to alert them of anyone or anything moving in the streets after curfew. This event occurred during year seven. DH 28, p. 558.

Cattermole, Alfred. One of three children of Mary and Reg Cattermole during year seven. DH 13, p. 259.

Cattermole, Ellie. One of three children of Mary and Reg Cattermole during year seven. DH 13, p. 259.

Cattermole, Maisie. One of three children of Mary and Reg Cattermole during year seven. DH 13, p. 259.

Cattermole, Mary Elizabeth. A witch and wife of Reg Cattermole. She was the mother of Alfred, Maisie and Ellie Cattermole. Mary was on trial at the Ministry of Magic during year seven. Her parents, probably muggles, were greengrocers. DH 13, pp. 258-61.

Cattermole, Reg. A wizard who was Head of the Office of Magical Maintenance in the Ministry of Magic during year seven. Ron Weasley used Polyjuice Potion to turn himself into Reg that year. DH 12, pp. 240, 244.

Cauldron Cakes. Pastries that were sold in the wizarding world. Harry Potter was introduced to Cauldron Cakes on the Hogwarts Express prior to his first year at Hogwarts. SS 6, p. 101. DH 11, p. 217.

Cauldron Full of Love and Hate, A. The title of a song that Ron Weasley heard on a wizarding radio during year seven. DH 22, p. 439.

Cauldwell, Owen. A student who was sorted by the Sorting Hat during Harry Potter's fourth year at Hogwarts. Owen was a member of the Hufflepuff house. GF 12, p. 179.

Cave Inimicum. The magic words used by Hermione Granger to invoke one of several protective enchantments over her camping area during year seven. DH 14, p. 272.

Centaur. A half-man, half-horse creature that liked to stargaze. The following centaurs lived in the Forbidden Forest: Ronan, Bane and Firenze. Harry Potter encountered the centaurs during his first year at

Hogwarts. SS 15, pp. 252-253,256-257. Centaurs were regarded as Beings under Madam Elfrida Clagg's definition of "being" in the fourteenth century because they could speak the human tongue. Centaurs refused to attend Wizards' Council meetings because the definition excluded the merpeople. FB, pp. xii, 6. DH 36, p. 728.

Centaur Liaison Office. A special office established in the Beast Division of the Ministry of Magic to assist centaurs in communicating with magical creatures labeled as "beings." The centaurs never communicated with the office because they disagreed with the label attached to them. FB, p. xiii, fn. 3.

Challenges in Charming. A periodical in the Wizarding World. Albus Dumbledore had some of his papers published in *Challenges in Charming.* DH 2, p. 17.

Chamber of Secrets. A legendary chamber that was built by Salazar Slytherin and hidden within Hogwarts. Salazar purportedly sealed the chamber until his true heir arrived at Hogwarts to open it. It was believed that when opened, the chamber would release horrors into the school to purge it of students who were unworthy to study magic. CS 8, p. 139; 9, pp. 150-51. DH 22, p. 426; 31, p. 622.

Chambers. A student at Hogwarts who was a member of the Ravenclaw house and chaser on that house's quidditch team during Harry Potter's fifth year at the school. OP 31, p. 704.

Chameleon Ghoul. An unidentified creature that Hermione Granger suggested as the possible monster of the Chamber of Secrets. She was prevented by Ron Weasley from discussing the creature. This event occurred during Harry Potter's second year at Hogwarts. CS 11, p. 184.

Championship. The title given to the house quidditch team that had the best season during the school year at Hogwarts. During Harry Potter's sixth year at the school, the final game of the year for the title was between Gryffindor and Ravenclaw. Going into the game, Gryffindor needed to win by 300 points. If the Gryffindor team came in last, it would have been its first bottom-of-the-table defeat in two centuries. HP 24, p. 520.

Chancellor of the Exchequer. A public official in England who tried to help the Prime Minister remove a "magical" painting from a wall in the Prime Minister's office. HP 1, p. 7.

Chang, Cho. A student of Hogwarts who was a member of the Ravenclaw house. Cho was the seeker on the Ravenclaw quidditch team and rode on a Comet Two Sixty during Harry Potter's third year at Hogwarts. She was one year ahead of Harry. PA 13, p. 254. Harry saw Cho at the Quidditch World Cup during the summer prior to his fourth year at the school. GF 7, p. 84. Cho was Cedric Diggory's date to the Yule Ball that year. GF 22, p. 397. She supported the Tutshill Torndados quidditch team since she had been six years old and wore the team badge on her school robes. OP 12, p. 230. At the end of Harry Potter's fifth year at Hogwarts, Cho dated Michael Corner. OP 38, p. 866. DH 29, p. 582.

Charing Cross Road. A road that the Knight Bus flew over when Harry Potter rode the bus. This event occurred after Harry ran away from the Dursley residence prior to his third year at Hogwarts. PA 3, p. 41. Charing Cross Road was the street on which the Leaky Cauldron was located. HP 6, p. 109. DH 9, p. 164.

Charm Club. A club at Hogwarts to which Vicky Forbisher belonged during Harry Potter's fifth year at Hogwarts. OP 13, p. 276.

Charm to Cure Reluctant Reversers, A. The title of a book that Harry Potter owned. Harry tried to remember page 12 of the book when Marge Dursley insulted him on the last day of her visit to the Dursley home. This event occurred during the summer prior to Harry's third year at Hogwarts. PA 2, p. 27.

Charm Your Own Cheese. The title of a book located on the mantelpiece of the Burrow. Two other books on the mantelpiece were: *Enchantment in Baking* and *One Minute Feasts–It's Magic.* Harry Potter observed these books during the summer prior to his second year at Hogwarts. CS 3, p. 34.

Charms. Magic spells invoked by speaking magic words and waving magic wands. Charms was a subject taught by Professor Flitwick at Hogwarts. SS 8, p. 133.

Chaser. One of three players on a quidditch team who passed between themselves a bright red ball, known as a quaffle. SS 10, p. 167. If the chasers passed the quaffle through one of their opponents' three hoops, their team scored ten points. SS 10, p. 167. The chaser was the oldest quidditch position. Beginning in 1884, only one chaser was permitted to enter the scoring area at a time. QA 6, pp. 20, 25-26. Dragomir Gorgovitch was a chaser for the Chudley Cannons. He was the record holder for most quaffles dropped in a season. DH 7, p. 112.

Chaser Hawkshead Attacking Formation. A famous quidditch play invented by Darren O'Hare of the Kenmare Kestrels. QA 7, p. 35. See also **Hawkshead Attacking Formation**.

Cheering Charm. A charm taught by Professor Flitwick to his Charms class during Harry Potter's third year at Hogwarts. The charm had the effect of cheering up the person on whom it was placed. PA 15, p. 294.

Chief Warlock. Part of Albus Dumbledore's official title. SS 4, p. 51. The Chief Warlock was the head of the Wizengamot and Albus was removed from that position during the summer prior to Harry Potter's fifth year at Hogwarts. OP 15, p. 308. DH 2, p. 20.

Chimera. A rare Greek monster. FB, p. 6. A Chimera from Mykonos, Greece ate "Dangerous" Dai Llewellyn. QA 7, p. 33. After graduating from Hogwarts, Elphias Doge escaped from a chimera in Greece. DH 2, p. 18.

China. The natural habitat of the Chinese Fireball dragon and one of the locations where the Phoenix was found. FB, pp. 11-12, 32. (China refers to either The People's Republic of China or the Republic of China, which consists mostly of the island of Taiwan. Both countries are located in East Asia.)

Chinese Chomping Cabbage. Hermione Granger copied a diagram of a Chinese Chomping Cabbage during Harry Potter's fifth year at Hogwarts. OP 16, p. 332.

Chinese Fireball. A type of red dragon used in the first event of the Triwizard Tournament hosted at Hogwarts. Charlie Weasley was part of the team that controlled the dragons. The event occurred during Harry Potter's fourth year at Hogwarts. GF 19, pp. 326-327. Viktor Krum fought a Chinese Fireball in the tournament and went third in order of the champions who competed for that task. GF 19, p. 350. The Chinese Fireball was one of ten pure-bred dragons sometimes known as Liondragon and the only dragon from the Orient. The Chinese Fireball was more tolerant of its own species than other dragons. FB, pp. 11-12.

Chipolatas. An item of food that Albus Dumbledore offered to Derek, a student at Hogwarts, during a Christmas feast. This event occurred during Harry Potter's third year at Hogwarts. PA 11, p. 230.

Chizpurfle. A magical beast. FB, pp. xviii, 6.

Chocoballs. A candy sold at Honeydukes in Hogsmeade. Chocoballs were full of strawberry mousse and clotted cream. Ron Weasley described Chocoballs to Harry Potter during Harry's third year at Hogwarts. PA 5, p. 77.

Chocolate Frogs. A candy sold in the wizarding world. Each package of Chocolate Frogs included a Famous Witches and Wizards Collectors Card. Harry Potter purchased some Chocolate Frogs on the Hogwarts Express and received the card with Albus Dumbledore on it. This event occurred as Harry traveled to his first year at Hogwarts. SS 6, pp. 101-102. During his fourth year at the school, Harry observed Ernie Macmillan and Hannah Abbot trading Chocolate Frog cards in the Three Broomsticks. GF 19, p. 320. Rubeus Hagrid gave Harry a box of candy, including this treat, as a Christmas present during Harry's fourth year at Hogwarts. GF 23, p. 410. DH 2, p. 24.

Chorley, Herbert. A Junior Minister to the Prime Minister of England who brought attention to himself by acting like a duck during the summer prior to Harry Potter's sixth year at Hogwarts. HP 1, pp. 2, 17. Herbert was scheduled to be transferred to St. Mungo's Hospital for Magical Maladies and Injuries at that time. HP 1, p. 10.

Chosen One. The title of the wizard destined to overcome Lord Voldemort. Dean Thomas stated that he believed the Chosen One was Harry Potter during year seven. DH 15, p. 299.

Christmas. In the southern United States of America, some muggles wondered whether glowing Clabbert pustules that hung from trees were in fact Christmas lights still on display in July. FB, p. 8. There were usually twelve Christmas trees in the Great Hall of Hogwarts during the holiday season. HP 15, p. 303. DH 15, p. 307.

Christmas Day. Harry Potter and Hermione Granger fled Bathilda Bagshot's residence on Christmas Day. DH 17, p. 342.

Christmas Eve. During year seven, Harry Potter and Hermione Granger apparated into Godric's Hollow on Christmas Eve. DH 16, p. 323.

Chubb, Agatha. A witch who was an expert in ancient wizarding artifacts. Agatha was known for her identification of twelve lead bludgers from the early sixteenth century. QA 6, p. 22.

Chudley Cannons. The name of Ron Weasley's favorite quidditch team. Before the start of Harry Potter's second year at Hogwarts, Ron looked at a full set of Chudley Cannon robes in the window of Quality Quidditch Supplies. CS 4, p. 58. The team color was orange and it was ninth in the league during Harry's second year at the school. Posters of the Chudley Cannons covered the walls of Ron's bedroom at the Burrow that same year. CS 3, p. 40; GF 5, p. 56. According to Albus Dumbledore's foreword to *Quidditch Through the Ages,* the Chudley Cannons brought its fans together for moments of despair. QA, p. vii. The Cannons experienced a lackluster record for over a century. QA 7, pp. 33-34. Dragomir Gorgovitch was a chaser for the Chudley Cannons. He was the record holder for most quaffles dropped in a season. DH 7, p. 112.

Cinderella. A story that was read by muggles. DH 7, p. 135.

Circe. A famous witch featured on the collectors cards inside packages of Chocolate Frogs. Harry Potter obtained the Circe card on the Hogwarts Express. This event occurred as Harry traveled to Hogwarts for his first year. SS 6, p. 102.

Clabbert. A magical beast that originated in the southern United States of America. FB, p. 8.

Clagg, Madam Elfrida. The Chief of the Wizards' Council who succeeded Burdock Muldoon. FB, p. xi. Madam Clagg presided as Chief during the mid-1300's and was responsible for enacting a law that made snidgets a protected species, thus prohibiting them from being used for sport in quidditch. QA 4, p. 14.

Clankers. A magical device used by goblins at Gringotts Wizarding bank to gain access to secure vaults. The metallic object, when shaken, sounded like miniature hammers on anvils. DH 26, pp. 531, 536.

Clapham. The location where, at 2 Laburnum Gardens, Sturgis Podmore lived. OP 14, p. 287. Stan Shunpike also lived in Clapham. HP 11, p. 221.

Class A Nontradable Goods. The Department for the Regulation and Control of Magical Creatures designated certain goods that could not be traded as Class A Nontradable Goods. Among the items with this designation were: Acromantula eggs, FB, p. 1; Chimera eggs, FB, p. 7; and Dragon eggs, FB, p. 10.

Class B Tradeable Material. A magical material deemed dangerous and subject to strict control. FB, p. 16. The golden horn of the Romanian Longhorn was classified as a Class B Tradeable Material and highly valued as an ingredient for potions. FB, p. 14. The Erumpent horn, tail and its Exploding Fluid were also used in potions and received the same classification. FB, p. 16. DH 20, p. 401.

Class C Non-Tradeable Substance. The shriveled black seed pods of the *Venomous Tentacula* were classified as a Class C Non-Tradeable Substance. OP 9, p. 171.

Classroom Eleven. Classroom eleven was located on the ground-floor corridor that lead off the entrance hall on the opposite side of the Great Hall at Hogwarts. The classroom had the appearance of a forest clearing. Firenze taught Divination in Classroom Eleven during Harry Potter's fifth year at Hogwarts. OP 27, p. 600.

Clauricorn. Another name for the Leprechaun. FB, p. 25. See **Leprechaun**.

Cleansweep Broom Company. A quidditch broom company formed in 1926 by three brothers: Barnaby, Bill and Bob Ollerton. The company's first model was the Cleansweep One. QA 9, p. 49.

Cleansweep One. The first quidditch broom made by the Cleansweep Broom Company, probably in 1926. QA 9, p. 49.

Cleansweep Two. The second quidditch broom made by the Cleansweep Broom Company in 1934. The Cleansweep Two was an improvement over its predecessor. It was marketed during an intense competition with the Comet Trading Company models of the period. QA 9, p. 50.

Cleansweep Three. The third quidditch broom made by the Cleansweep Broom Company in 1937. The Cleansweep Three was an improvement over its predecessor. It was marketed during an intense competition with the Comet Trading Company models of the period. QA 9, p. 50.

Cleansweep Five. A type of broom used to play quidditch. Oliver Wood suggested a Cleansweep Five when Minerva McGonagell introduced Harry as the new seeker of the Gryffindor house team. Fred and George Weasley both used this broom during Harry's second year at Hogwarts. Cleansweep brooms were much slower than the Nimbus Two Thousand and Nimbus Two Thousand and One brooms. CS 7, p. 111. Gwendolyn Morgan rode on a Cleansweep Five during a famous quidditch match in 1953. Gwendolyn gave a concussion to the captain of the other team, Rudolf Brand, and it caused Rudolf to propose marriage to her at the end of the match. QA 7, p. 35.

Cleansweep Six. The model of broom on which a wizard rode to the moon and back. This claim was reported in *the Quibbler*. OP 10, p. 193.

Cleansweep Seven. A type of broom used to play quidditch. SS 9, p. 152. The Ravenclaw team used the Cleansweep Seven during Harry Potter's third year at Hogwarts. PA 12, p. 251. Cleansweep brooms were much slower than the Nimbus Two Thousand and Nimbus Thousand and One brooms. CS 7, p. 111.

Cleansweep Eleven. During the summer prior to Harry Potter's fifth year at Hogwarts, the new Cleansweep Eleven broom was announced. The handle was made of Spanish oak and the broom was equipped with anti-jinx varnish and in-built vibration control. Molly Weasley purchased one for Ron Weasley as a reward for being made prefect that school year. OP 9, pp. 164, 170, 173; 13, p. 271.

Clearwater, Penelope. A fifth-year student of Hogwarts who was a prefect and member of the Ravenclaw House. Ron Weasley and Harry Potter asked her for directions to the Slytherin common room while they were under the effects of a Polyjuice Potion. This incident occurred during Harry's second year at Hogwarts. CS 12, p. 219. Penelope became the third petrified muggle, followed by Hermione Granger, when the Chamber of Secrets was reopened that year. CS 14, p. 258. She was Percy Weasley's girlfriend. CS 18, p. 341; PA 5, p. 69. Hermione Granger attempted to use Penelope's name as an alias during year seven. DH 23, p. 448.

Cliodna. A druidess featured on some of the collectors cards inside packs of Chocolate Frogs. Harry Potter obtained the card on the Hogwarts Express. This event occurred during the summer prior to Harry's first year at Hogwarts. SS 6, p. 102.

Cloak of Invisilibility, The. An invisibility cloak that, according to wizard legend, was able to hide one from even Death. It was one of the Deathly Hallows and its origin was from The Tale of the Three Brothers. The tale appeared in *The Tales of Beedle the Bard.* Three brothers received gifts from Death: the Elder Wand, a wand more powerful than any other; the Resurrection Stone, a stone that could help bring back the dead; and the Cloak of Invisibility. In contrast to other inferior cloaks, the Cloak of Invisibility was eternal, and provided constant and impenetrable concealment, even with spells cast against it. DH 21, pp. 406-09, 411. The current, true owner of the Cloak was revealed near the end of year seven. DH 35, p. 714.

Cobbing. The name of one of the ten most common fouls committed in quidditch. QA 6, p. 29.

Cockatrice. A creature that the contestants in the Triwizard Tournament of 1792 were supposed to catch, but that went on a rampage and injured three of the judges on the panel instead. Hermione Granger learned this information from reading *Hogwarts A History* during Harry Potter's fourth year at Hogwarts. GF 15, p. 238.

Cockroach Clusters. A candy sold at Honeydukes in Hogsmeade. Harry Potter observed Cockroach Clusters at Honeydukes during his third year at Hogwarts. PA 10, p. 197. During his fourth year, Harry unsuccessfully tried to use the password "sherbet lemon" to open the secret passageway to Albus Dumbledore's office. He then tried several candy names on the door, until "Cockroach Clusters" opened it. GF 29, p. 579.

Code of Wand Use. Clause three of this law prohibited any non-human creature from carrying or using a magic wand. The Ministry of Magic wizards who investigated the appearance of the Dark Mark after the Quidditch World Cup that Harry Potter attended, accused Winky of breaking the Code of Wand Use. This event occurred during the summer prior to Harry's fourth year at Hogwarts. GF 9, p. 132.

Cokeworth. The place where Vernon Dursley temporarily moved his family and Harry Potter after dozens of letters were delivered for Harry at the Dursley residence on Privet Drive. The Dursleys and Harry stayed at the Railview Hotel, Room 17 in Cokeworth. This event occurred during the summer prior to Harry's first year at Hogwarts. SS 3, p. 42.

Cole, Mrs. A woman in charge of an orphanage in London where Tom Riddle lived during his childhood. HP 13, p. 263. One of the other women who worked at the orphanage was Martha. In addition to Tom Riddle, other orphans there were: Billy Stubbs, Eric Whalley, Amy Benson and Dennis Bishop. HP 13, pp. 264, 268.

Colloportus. A magic word used to invoke a charm that sealed doors. Hermione Granger invoked this charm in the Department of Mysteries during Harry Potter's fifth year at Hogwarts. OP 35, p. 788.

Color-Change Charm. A charm that Harry Potter invoked as part of the practical examination of the O.W.L.s during his fifth year at Hogwarts. OP 31, p. 713.

Come and Go Room. A special room in Hogwarts, also referred to as the Room of Requirement, that magically appeared when someone had a real need for it. Dobby the House Elf made Harry Potter aware of the Come and Go Room and used it to hide Winky from time to time. The room was located on the seventh floor opposite the tapestry of Barnabas the Barmy. Dumbledore's Army assembled in the Come and Go Room for meetings. These events occurred during harry's fifth year at the school. OP 18, pp. 386-88.

Comet 140. The first quidditch broom manufactured by the Comet Trading Company, probably in 1929. QA 9, p. 49.

Comet 180. A broom manufactured by the Comet Trading Company in 1938. The Comet 180 was an improvement over its predecessor. It was marketed during an intense competition with the Cleansweep Broom Company models of the period. QA 9, p. 50.

Comet Trading Company. A quidditch broom company formed by Randolph Keith and Basil Horton in 1929. Its first broom was the Comet 140. The Comet Trading Company competed directly against the Cleansweep Broom Company. Its founders patented a breaking charm for the company's broomsticks. QA 9, p. 49.

Comet Two Sixty. A specific make and model of broom used in quidditch. The Comet Two Sixty was flashy but not in the same league as the Nimbus. SS 10, p. 165. Draco Malfoy rode a Comet Two Sixty to play quidditch at home before his first year at Hogwarts. SS 10, p. 165. Cho Chang rode on a Comet Two Sixty during Harry Potter's third year at Hogwarts. PA 13, p. 254. Nymphadora Tonks rode a Comet Two Sixty the evening that Harry was rescued by an advance guard of the Order of the Phoenix. This event occurred during the summer prior to Harry's fifth year at Hogwarts. OP 3, p. 53.

Comet Two Ninety. During Harry Potter's fifth year at Hogwarts, the Comet Two Ninety was the newest model of quidditch broomstick made by the Comet Trading Company. It could accelerate from zero to sixty in ten seconds, but was outdone by the new Cleansweep Eleven model. OP 9,p. 170.

Committee for the Disposal of Dangerous Creatures. A committee within the Ministry of Magic that conducted a hearing into Lucius Malfoy's complaint against the hippogriff that injured his son, Draco. This event occurred during Harry Potter's third year at Hogwarts. The committee sent notice of the hearing, scheduled for April 2 of that year to Rubeus Hagrid. The members of the committee consisted of the Board of Governors at Hogwarts. PA 11, p. 218. During the aftermath that followed the Quidditch World Cup that Harry attended, a young wizard boasted to a Veela that he worked for this committee as a dragon killer and was compensated at a rate of one hundred sacks of galleons per year. The young wizard's own friend accused him of being a dishwasher at the Leaky Cauldron. This event occurred during the summer prior to Harry's fourth year at Hogwarts. GF 9, p. 125.

Committee on Experimental Charms. An office within the Ministry of Magic. The committee placed into custody a wizard named Mortlake who was questioned for his extremely odd ferrets. CS 3, p. 38. Gilbert Wimple was employed by the committee. Arthur pointed out Gilbert to Harry Potter and Hermione Granger at the camp on the grounds of the Quidditch World Cup. This event occurred during the summer prior to Harry's fourth year at Hogwarts. GF 7, p. 86.

Common Apparition Mistakes and How to Avoid Them. The title of a leaflet that the Ministry of Magic distributed to students in order to prepare them for the apparition test during Harry Potter's sixth year at Hogwarts. HP 22, p. 469.

Common Magical Ailments and Afflictions. The title of a book that Harry Potter imagined Hermione Granger would probably consult for information on the pain he experienced at his forehead scar. This event occurred during the summer prior to Harry's fourth year at Hogwarts. GF 2, p. 21.

Common Welsh Green Dragon. One of only two types of wild dragon that existed in Britain; the other was the Hebridean Black. Ron Weasley explained the types of dragons to Harry Potter during Harry's first year at Hogwarts. SS 14, p. 231. This type of dragon was used in the first event of the Triwizard Tournament hosted at Hogwarts. Charlie Weasley was part of the team that controlled the dragons. This event occurred during Harry's fourth year at Hogwarts. GF 19, pp. 326-327. Fleur Delacour fought a Common Welsh Green Dragon in the tournament and went second in order of the champions who competed in that task. GF 19, p. 350. The Common Welsh Green dragon was one of ten pure-bred dragons and one of only two native dragons in Great Britain; the other was the Hebridean Black. FB, p. 12.

Compendium of Common Curses and Their Counter-Actions, A. The title of a book found inside the Room of Requirement during Harry Potter's fifth year at Hogwarts. OP 18, p. 390.

Concealment and Disguise. A course of training took by aurors. Nymphadora Tonks received top marks in Concealment and Disguise without studying because she was a Metamorphmagus. OP 3, p. 52.

Confringo. The magic word for a curse that Harry Potter invoked in year seven to explode the side car of Sirius Black's motorcycle. Hermione

Granger also used the curse, known as the Blasting Curse, in Bathilda Bagshot's residence that year. DH 4, p. 59; 17, p. 342.

Confronting the Faceless. The title of a book that was used in Defense Against the Dark Arts during Harry Potter's sixth year at Hogwarts. HP 9, p. 177.

Confusing Draught. A potion that caused inflammation of the brain. Harry Potter studied the Confusing Draught during his fifth year at Hogwarts. The ingredients for the potion included scurvy-grass, lovage and sneezewort. The potion was similar to the Befuddlement Draught. OP 18, p. 383.

Confundus Charm. A charm that Severus Snape suspected Sirius Black of placing on Harry Potter, Ron Weasley and Hermione Granger, thus clouding their judgement when he confronted them at the Shrieking Shack in Hogsmeade. This event occurred during Harry's third year at Hogwarts. PA 21, p. 386. The following year, Mad-Eye Moody suspected that a powerful witch or wizard used the Confundus Charm to make the Goblet of Fire believe that there were more than three schools competing in the Triwizard Tournament so that Harry Potter's name could be slipped in under a fourth school's name. GF 16, p. 279. During year seven, Severus, stated that Dawlish, the auror, was susceptible to the Confundus Charm. DH 1, p. 4.

Confusing Concoction. A potion that students were supposed to produce for their final exam in Potions class during Harry Potter's third year at Hogwarts. PA 16, p. 318.

Congo. One of the natural habitats of the Tebo. FB, p. 40. (Congo refers to either the People's Republic of the Congo or the Democratic Republic of the Congo, formerly known as Zaire. Both countries are located in Central Africa.)

Conjunctivitus Curse. A curse that Sirius Black intended to recommend to Harry Potter for subduing a dragon in the first task of the Triwizard Tournament. GF 23, p. 406. Sirius' secret meeting with Harry was interrupted, so he never got the opportunity to finish explaining the curse to Harry. In a letter addressed to Harry after the first task, Sirius stated that the curse worked on a dragon's eyes, which were the beast's weakest point. Hermione Granger informed Harry that Viktor Krum used this spell in the tournament against the dragon assigned to him. GF 23, p. 406. Madam Maxine used the curse against giants during Harry's fifth year at Hogwarts. OP 20, p. 430.

Connolly. A member of the Irish National Quidditch Team who played in the Quidditch World Cup that Harry Potter attended during the summer prior to his fourth year at Hogwarts. Connolly was a beater. The other members of the team were as follows: Ryan, Troy, Mullet, Moran, Quigley and Lynch. GF 8, p. 105.

Coote, Ritchie. A student at Hogwarts who was a member of Gryffindor house and who Harry Potter chose to be a beater on the house quidditch team during Harry's sixth year at the school. HP 11, p. 225.

Cork. The location that had a team of warlocks who played quidditch against an Irish team in 1385. The match was played in Lancashire. QA 8, p. 38. (Cork is a county in the Munster Province of the Republic of Ireland.)

Corner, Michael. A student at Hogwarts who was a member of the Ravenclaw house. Michael appeared at Hog's Head, along with several other students, to discuss formation of a club to study Defense Against the Dark Arts. Michael dated Ginny Weasley at that time. OP 16, pp. 338, 347. By the end of that school year, Michael dated Cho Chang. These events occurred during Harry Potter's fifth year at Hogwarts. OP 38, p. 866. During year seven, Michael was severely disciplined at Hogwarts for releasing a first-year student that had been chained up by the Carrows. DH 29, p. 575.

Cornish Pixies. Mischievous creatures that Gilderoy Lockhart released into the first Defense Against the Dark Arts class he taught during Harry Potter's second year at Hogwarts. CS 6, p. 101. The creatures were electric blue, approximately eight inches long and had pointed faces and shrill voices. CS 6, p. 101.

Cornwall. A location in which pixies were mostly found. FB, p. 32. In 1884, a Golden Snitch evaded capture in Cornwall and was never caught. The local wizards claimed that the Golden Snitch continued to run wild. QA 6, p. 23. One of the villages in Cornwall was Tinworth. DH 16, pp. 318-19. (Cornwall is a county in Southwest England.)

Council of Magical Law. A council of prominent wizards and witches that acted as both judge and jury in trials of witches and wizards charged with violating magical laws. During his fourth year at Hogwarts, Harry Potter witnessed an important trial of the council through the pensieve in Albus Dumbledore's office. GF30, p. 592.

Courtroom Ten. The courtroom in the Ministry of Magic where Harry Potter's hearing was convened during the summer prior to Harry's fifth year at Howarts. The courtroom was located down so low at the Ministry of Magic that the elevators did not extend there. OP 7, pp. 134-35.

Cousin Barny. The name of a fictitious Weasley relative assigned to Harry Potter at the wedding of Bill Weasley and Fleur Delacourt during year seven in order to keep Harry's real identity secure. DH 8, p. 137.

Crabbe. A wizard who was a Death Eater and responded to the summons of Lord Voldemort during Harry Potter's fourth year at Hogwarts. GF 33, p. 651. Crabbe was present in the Department of Mysteries when Harry Potter retrieved the prophecy relating to himself and Lord

Voldemort. This event occurred during Harry's fifth year at Hogwarts. OP 35, p. 788.

Crabbe, Vincent. A student of Hogwarts who was a friend of and bodyguard, along with Gregory Goyle, for Draco Malfoy. SS 6, p. 108; PA 5, p. 79. Vincent became a beater on the Slytherin quidditch team during Harry Potter's fifth year at Hogwarts; Vincent and Gregory replaced Derrick and Bole on the team. OP 19, 405. DH 4, p. 50; 31, p. 628. Vincent met his fate in the Room of Requirement during year seven. DH 31, p. 634.

Cragge, Elfrida. A witch who was featured in a painting at the Ministry of Magic. OP 22, p. 471.

Crapaud. One of two characters in the early 1400's play, *Alas, I've Transfigured My Feet,* by the French wizard Malecrit. The other character was Grenouille. QA 8, p. 39.

Creaothceann. A broomstick game that originated in Scotland and was regarded as the most dangerous of all broomstick games. In 1762 Creaothceann was prohibited by law. The Ministry of Magic refused to lift the ban in the 1960's, despite a lobbying effort by Magnus "Dent-Head" Macdonald. QA 2, pp. 5-6.

Creevey, Colin. A student at Hogwarts who was a fan of Harry Potter, liked to follow him around and took his photograph repeatedly. Colin was a member of the Gryffindor house. His father was a milkman and probably a muggle. CS 6, p. 96. Colin sat next to Ginny Weasley in Charms class. CS 11, p. 185. He was the first person attacked when the Chamber of Secrets was reopened during Harry's second year at Hogwarts. CS 10, p. 180. Colin was a member of Dumbeldore's Army during Harry's fifth year at the school. OP 16, pp.337-40. DH 31, p. 611. Colin's fate was observed by Harry during year seven. DH 34, p. 694.

Creevey, Dennis. The brother of Colin Creevey who began to attend Hogwarts during Harry Potter's fourth year at Hogwarts. GF 12, p. 174. Dennis was a member of the Gryffindor house. GF 12, p. 179. He was a member of Dumbeldore's Army during Harry's fifth year at the school. OP 16, pp.337-40. DH 31, p. 611.

Cresswell, Dirk. A student at Hogwarts who was one year behind Lily (Evans) Potter's class and a favorite student of Horace Slughorn. Dirk was born to muggle parents. During the summer prior to Harry Potter's sixth year at Hogwarts, Dirk was the Head of the Goblin Liaison Office within the Ministry of Magic and was familiar with the activities inside Gringotts Bank. HP 4, p. 71. Dirk held the same position the following year and was sent to Azkaban for falsifying his family tree. He was married and had sons. DH 12, p. 245; 13, p. 255.

Dirk's fate was announced during a broadcast of *Potterwatch.* DH 22, p. 439.

Cribbage's Wizarding Crackers. Large piles of these items were displayed in the Great Hall during the Christmas lunch at Hogwarts. This event occurred during Harry Potter's fourth year at Hogwarts. GF 23, p. 410. See also **Wizard Crackers**.

Croaker. A wizard who worked as an Unspeakable for the Department of Mysteries. Arthur Weasley had no idea what Croaker did in that position but knew that it was top secret. GF 7, p. 86.

Crockford, Doris. A patron of the Leaky Cauldron in London who met Harry Potter on his first trip to the pub. This event occurred during the summer prior to Harry's first year at Hogwarts. SS 5, p. 69.

Crookshanks. A large orange cat that Hermione Granger purchased as a pet from the Pet Menagerie before the commencement of Harry Potter's third year at Hogwarts. Crookshanks did not like Ron Weasley's pet rat, Scabbers. PA 4, pp. 59-60. Crookshanks was present at the Burrow before Bill Weasley married Fleur Delacourt during year seven. DH 6, p. 93.

Cross-Species Switches. The task of transforming an animal of one species into an animal of another species. This task required adaptation of Transforming Spells. In a Transfiguration class during Harry Potter's fourth year at Hogwarts, the class was asked to transform a guinea fowl into a guinea pig. GF 22, p. 385.

Crouch, Barty (Bartemius). The head of the Department of International Magical Cooperation during the summer prior to Harry Potter's fourth year at Hogwarts. Prior to holding that position, Barty was Head of the Department of Magical Law Enforcement and in that position issued the order to send Sirius Black to Azkaban without a trial. Many people hoped Barty would become the head of the Ministry of Magic. Barty imprisoned his own son who was accused of being a Death Eater so as not to ruin his chances of being promoted in the Ministry. GF 27, pp. 526-529. According to Percy Weasley, who worked for Barty during Harry's fourth year at Hogwarts, Barty could speak over two-hundred different languages, including Mermish, Gobbledegook and Troll. GF 5, p. 57; 7, p. 88. Percy idolized Barty, in part, because he dressed so much like a muggle that he looked like a bank manager. Barty had a house elf named Winky. GF 7, 90; 9, p. 132. He was one of the five judges on the panel for the Triwizard Tournament at Hogwarts during Harry's fourth year at the school. GF 16, p. 254. Barty was killed that school year. GF 35, p. 690. DH 6, p. 94.

Crouch, Barty (Master). The son of Barty Crouch. Harry Potter observed Master Crouch's trial in front of the Council of Magical Law in Albus

Dumbledore's pensieve. Master Crouch was accused of being a Death Eater and despite his pleas of innocence, was imprisoned in Azkaban. GF 30, pp. 594-96. Master Crouch made a revelation to Harry Potter and another to Albus Dumbledore. GF 35, pp. 674-78, 682-90. He also murdered someone. These events occurred during Harry's fourth year at Hogwarts. GF 35, p. 690.

Cruciatus Curse. An illegal curse invoked with the magic word "*crucio.*" The Cruciatus Curse had the effect of causing pain in the person on whom it was placed. Mad-Eye Moody demonstrated the curse, through the use of a spider, in a Defense Against the Dark Arts class that Harry Potter attended during Harry's fourth year at Hogwarts. GF 14, p. 214. It was classified as one of the three Unforgivable Curses; the other two curses were the Imperius Curse and the Killing (or "*Avada Kedarva*") Curse. GF 14, p. 217. DH 10, p. 206.

Crucio. The magic word used to invoke the illegal Cruciatus Curse. During a Divination class in his fourth year at Hogwarts, Harry Potter had a dream that he heard the voice of Lord Voldemort casting the curse on Wormtail. GF 29, p. 577. That same year, Viktor Krum attempted to place the curse on Cedric Diggory in the third task of the Triwizard Tournament. GF 31, p. 626. Lord Voldemort also uttered the curse that year. GF 33, p. 648.

Crumple-Horned Snorkack. A magical beast that Luna Lovegood believed existed, but Hermione Granger was not convinced was real. OP 13, p. 262. Luna insisted the Snorkack lived in Sweden and stated that she and her father were going there to catch one the summer after Harry Potter's fifth year at Hogwarts. OP 38, p. 849. DH 8, p. 149. According to Xenophilius Lovegood, the Snorkack was a shy and highly magical creature. DH 20, p. 401. It had little ears like a hippo's and was purple and hairy. The Snorkback could be summoned by humming a waltz. DH 25, p. 511.

Crup. A magical beast. FB, pp. xviii, 8. The owner of a Crup was legally required to remove its tail with a painless Severing Charm while the crup was six to eight weeks old. FB, p. 9. The owner was also required to have a licence for the beast. FB, p. 25. The subject of crups was often tested on O.W.L.'s. OP 15, p. 323.

Cuaditch. An alternative spelling for the game of quidditch. Madam Modesty Rabnott used the word in a 1269 letter sent to her sister Prudence. QA 4, p. 12.

Cuffe, Barnabas. Editor of the *Daily Prophet* during the summer prior to Harry Potter's sixth year at Hogwarts. Barnabas was a former student of Horace Slughorn and continued to listen to Horace's take on the news. HP 4, p. 71.

Curse. A magical incantation that had the effect of inflicting negative power or harm to someone or something. FB, p. viii. See **Thief's Curse.**

Cushioning Charm. A charm invented by Elliot Smethwyck in 1820. The Cushioning Charm was used to make broomsticks more comfortable to ride. QA 9, p. 47. Hermione Granger used the charm in the caverns of Gringotts Wizarding Bank during year seven. DH 26, p. 534.

Crystal Gazing. A particularly refined art, according to Sibyll Trelawney, that was taught using crystal balls. Harry Potter learned about Crystal Gazing in his Divination class during his third year at Hogwarts. PA 15, p. 297.

D.A. – DWARFS

D.A. See **Dumbledore's Army**.

D.A.D.A. The acronym for Defense Against the Dark Arts. HP 12, p. 239.

Dagworth-Granger, Hector. A wizard who founded the Most Extraordinary Society of Potioneers. HP 9, p. 185.

Daily Mail. A muggle newspaper read by Vernon Dursley during the summer prior to Harry Potter's fourth year at Hogwarts. GF 3, p. 26.

Daily Prophet. A daily newspaper in the wizarding world. Harry Potter was introduced to this newspaper when Rubeus Hagrid read it prior to Harry's first year at Hogwarts. SS 5, p. 64. The other edition of the newspaper was called the *Evening Prophet.* CS 5, p 79. During Harry's fourth year at Hogwarts, one of the *Daily Prophet's* special correspondents was Rita Skeeter. GF 13, p. 202. Every Wednesday the *Daily Prophet* had a zoological column. Rita suggested to Hagrid that she could feature his Blast-Ended Skrewts in that edition. GF 21, p. 370. The *Daily Prophet* was delivered to Harry at Privet Drive about 5:00 a.m. OP 1, p. 8. Hermione paid a barn owl one knut for an edition of the *Daily Prophet.* OP 12, p. 225. These events occurred during the summer prior to and during Harry's fifth year at Hogwarts. Barnabas Cuffe was the editor of the *Daily Prophet* during the following year. HP 4, p. 71. Prior to year seven, Charity Burbage wrote an impassioned defense of Mudbloods in an article that appeared in the *Daily Prophet.* DH 1, p. 12. Death Eaters took over control of the *Daily Prophet* during year seven. DH 11, p. 207.

Dangerous Dai Commemorative Medal. An annual quidditch award, named after "Dangerous" Dai Llewellyn. The medal was presented at the end of the season to the league player who took the most exciting and foolhardy risks during a quidditch game. QA 7, p. 33.

Dark Arts. A collective term used for the various types of dark magic. Harry Potter discovered that the shops on Knockturn Alley were devoted to the Dark Arts prior to his second year at Hogwarts. CS 4, p. 53. Rita Skeeter claimed in her book, *The Life and Lies of Albus Dumbledore*, that in his youth, Albus dabbled in the Dark Arts. DH 2, p. 25.

Dark Arts Outsmarted, The. The title of a book found inside the Room of Requirement during Harry's fifth year at Hogwarts. OP 18, p. 390.

Dark Detectors. A collective term for a group of magical devices, among them Sneakoscopes and Foe-Glass, that showed when Dark wizards or enemies were around. OP 18, p. 391. Mad-Eye Moody kept the devices in his office at Hogwarts. He had used them when he was an auror for the Ministry of Magic. The devices were: a Sneakoscope, a Secrecy Sensor and Foe-Glass. This event occurred during Harry Potter's fourth year at Hogwarts. GF 19, pp. 342-43.

Dark Force Defense League. A member of the Dark Force Defense League was quoted in a *Daily Prophet* article as stating that any wizard who could speak parseltongue was worthy of investigation. The statement was made in connection with Rita Skeeter's report that Harry Potter was disturbed and dangerous. The article appeared the day of the third event of the Triwizard Tournament during Harry's fourth year at Hogwarts. GF 31, p. 612.

Dark Forces: A Guide to Self-Protection, The. The title of a book written by Quentin Trimble and required for first-year students at Hogwarts. SS 5, p. 66. Harry Potter read this book in his first Defense Against the Dark Arts class with Mad-Eye Moody during Harry's fourth year at Hogwarts. GF 14, p. 210.

Dark Mark. The term for a symbol that represented Lord Voldemort. The symbol consisted of a large skull with a serpent hanging from its mouth like a tongue. During the aftermath of the Quidditch World Cup that Harry Potter attended, the Dark Mark floated in green smoke in the sky and appeared to be made of emerald stars. It was conjured by someone who spoke the magic word "*morsmordre*," and was witnessed by Harry, Ron Weasley and Hermione Granger. The appearance of the Dark Mark caused many wizards to scream and flee in panic. This event occurred during the summer prior to Harry's fourth year at Hogwarts. GF 9, pp. 128-29. For the identity of the person who conjured the Dark Mark, see GF 35, p. 687. Prior to that event, the appearance of the Dark Mark had not occurred for thirteen years. GF 9, p. 141. The Dark Mark was used by Death Eaters to signal that they had entered a building and committed a murder. HP 27, p. 581. Although Fenrir Greyback wore Death Eater robes, he did not have the Dark Mark during year seven. DH 23, p. 453.

Dark Side. The side of magic that involved evil and darkness. Rubeus Hagrid first mentioned the Dark Side to Harry Potter when he explained the death of Harry's parents at the hands of Lord Voldemort. SS 4, p. 55.

Davies, Roger. The student who was captain of the Ravenclaw quidditch team at Hogwarts during Harry Potter's third and fourth years at the school. PA 13, p. 259; GF 23, p. 413. Roger took Fleur Delacour to the Yule Ball during Harry's fourth year. GF 23, pp. 412-13. Roger took a blond-haired girl on a date to Madam Pudfoot's on Valentine's Day. This event occurred during Harry fifth year at Hogwarts. OP 25, p. 559. DH 33, p. 680.

Dawlish. A wizard who was an auror for the Ministry of Magic. Dawlish was present with Cornelius Fudge at Hogwarts when Harry Potter was accused of forming Dumbledore's Army. Albus Dumbledore remembered Dawlish as a Hogwarts student who achieved "outstanding" in all of his N.E.W.T.s. These events occurred during Harry's fifth year at the school. OP 27, p. 620. Dawlish was stationed at Hogwarts to provide the school with extra security during Harry's sixth year there. Dawlish was joined by Nymphadora Tonks, Proudfoot and Savage. HP 8, p. 158. During year seven, Dawlish inadvertently let it be known that the Order of the Phoenix was going to move Harry from the Dursley's home on July 30. According to Severus Snape, Dawlish was susceptible to a Confundus Charm and had been subjected to it before. DH 1, p. 4.

Dearborn, Caradoc. A wizard who was a member of the Order of the Phoenix. Caradoc was killed fighting for the Order, but his body was never found. OP 9, p. 174.

Death Chamber. A room in the Department of Mysteries that contained an ancient archway into which Sirius Black fell and disappeared. This event occurred during Harry Potter's fifth year at Hogwarts. OP 34, p. 773; 35, pp. 805-06; 36, p. 817.

Death Eaters. The title for certain followers of Lord Voldemort who tortured and murdered muggles for sport. Arthur Weasley suspected that Death Eaters appeared during the aftermath of the Quidditch World Cup that Harry Potter attended. During that event a hooded procession of wizards levitated four terrified muggles, the Roberts family, high in the air. Some of the Death Eaters managed not to get imprisoned in Azkaban. GF 9, pp. 142-43. Professor Karkaroff was a Death Eater. GF 19, p. 332. Other Death Eaters were: Avery, the Lestranges, Rosier and Wilkes. According to Sirius Black, Severus Snape was considered by some wizards to be a Death Eater. GF 27, p. 531. Death Eaters were identifiable by a red tattoo-like mark on their left arm that was in the shape of the Dark Mark. The Dark Mark reappeared on the arms of the Death Eaters when Lord

Voldemort regained his power during Harry's fourth year at Hogwarts. GF 27, p. 519; GF 33, p 645. Two other Death Eaters who appeared during Harry's sixth year at Hogwarts were Alecto and Amycus, who were sister and brother. HP 27, p. 593; DH 3, p. 35.

Death Omens: What to Do When You Know the Worst is Coming. The title of a book that Harry Potter observed in Flourish and Blotts. The cover of the book had a large black dog with gleaming eyes on it, presumably a Grim. This event occurred during the summer prior to Harry's third year at Hogwarts. PA 4, p. 54.

Death Stick, The. An extra-powerful wand that, according to historical accounts, was owned by a Dark wizard. DH 21, p. 415.

Deathday. The day on which a person died and, in the case of a ghost, the anniversary of that ghost's death. Nearly Headless Nick celebrated his five-hundredth Deathday on Halloween during Harry Potter's second year at Hogwarts. The tar-like icing on his gray cake, which was shaped like a tombstone, listed Nick's date of death as October 31, 1492. CS 8, pp. 129, 133.

Deathly Hallows. A sign that Xenophilius Lovegood wore on a necklace during year seven. The symbol was worn to reveal one's belief in the Deathly Hallows. The Hallows were actually three magical objects from wizarding legend: the Elder Wand, the Resuurection Stone; and the Cloak of Invisibility. If the objects were united they gave the person who yielded them the master over Death itself. DH 20, pp. 404, 409, 410.

Decoy Detonators. A magic joke device invented by Fred and George Weasley. When dropped, this device ran off and made a loud noise out of sight, giving the user a diversion. HP 6, p. 119. DH 12, p. 236.

Decree for Justifiable Confiscation. A decree that provided the Ministry of Magic with the purported right to confiscate the contents of a Last Will and Testament. Rufus Scrimgeour cited this law as his authority for examining a certain will during year seven. The decree was originally intended to prevent wizards from passing on Dark artifacts and could be used to seize possessions of a deceased person only if there was powerful evidence that the deceased possessions were illegal. Once seized, the possessions had to be relinquished within 30 days, unless they were proven to be dangerous. DH 7, pp. 123-24.

Decree for the Reasonable Restriction of Underage Sorcery. A decree that was issued in 1875. Paragraph C of the decree prohibited underage wizards from performing spells outside of their schools. A violation of the decree resulted in expulsion from school. Mafalda Hopkirk made Harry Potter aware of the decree after Dobby used a Hover Charm on Petunia Dursley's violet pudding. This event occurred during the summer prior to Harry's second year at

Hogwarts. CS 2, p. 21. Clause seven of the decree provided an exception and allowed the use of magic in life-threatening situations. OP 2, pp. 26-27; 4, p. 62; 8, p. 148. Paragraph C of the decree forbade the use of magic by certain underage wizards. It was this provision that Harry was charged with violating on August 2 at 9:23 p.m. during the summer prior to his fifth year at Hogwarts. OP 8, p. 140.

Decree for the Restriction of Underage Wizardry. A law recited by Severus Snape, perhaps the same as the Decree for the Reasonable Restriction of Underage Sorcery, as having been violated by Harry Potter and Ron Weasley when they flew an automobile into the Whomping Willow. This event occurred when Harry arrived for his second year at Hogwarts. CS 5, p. 81; PA 3, p. 31.

Defense Against the Dark Arts. A subject that was taught at Hogwarts. SS 8, p. 134. A different professor taught the subject each year. For various reasons Hogwarts had difficulty retaining a professor to teach the subject. The wizards who taught this subject while Harry Potter attended the school were, in order: Professor Quirrell, SS 8, p. 134; Gilderoy Lockhart, CS 4, p. 60; Remus J. Lupin, PA 5, p. 74; Mad-Eye Moody, who agreed to serve only for one year as a special favor to Albus Dumbledore. GF 12, p. 185; 14, p. 211; and Dolores Umbridge, OP 11, p. 211. During Harry's fourth year at the school, Mad-Eye felt that the students in Harry's class were behind in studying curses, so he spent the whole year on curses. The Ministry of Magic decided that the curriculum for fourth-year students should include countercurses and not Dark curses. GF 14, p. 211. The classroom was located four floors beneath the Gryffindor common room. HP 9, p. 176. The acronym for Defense Against the Dark Arts was D.A.D.A. HP 12, p. 239. Harry learned during his sixth year at Hogwarts that the school could not keep a teacher in the position of Defense Against the Dark Arts professor for more than one year after Albus Dumbledore refused the position to Tom Riddle. HP 20, p. 446. DH 10, p. 204.

Defense Association. A name suggested by Cho Chang, but rejected, for the group of Hogwarts students that referred to itself as Dumbledore's Army. This event occurred during Harry Potter's fifth year at Hogwarts. OP 18, p. 391.

Defensive Magical Theory. The title of a book written by Wilbert Slinkhard. The book was required reading during Harry Potter's fifth year Divination class at Hogwarts. OP 9, p. 160. The title for Chapter three of the book was: "The Case for Non-Offensive Responses to Magical Attack." OP 17, p. 267. DH 6, p. 100.

Deflagration Deluxe. Some of the magical fireworks invented by Fred and George Weasley, collectively referred to as Weasleys' Wildfire Whiz-Bangs. They cost twenty galleons. The other type of fireworks, Basic Blaze, sold for five galleons. This event occurred during Harry Potter's fifth year at Hogwarts. OP 28, p. 634.

Deflating Draft. A potion that counteracted the effects of Swelling Solution. CS 11, p. 187. Severus Snape applied this draft on students who were accidentally splashed by Swelling Solution from Gregory Goyle's cauldron. This event occurred during Harry Potter's second year at Hogwarts. CS 11, p. 187.

Defodio. The magic word used by Hermione Granger to enlarge a passageway in the caverns of Gringotts Wizarding Bank during year seven. DH 26, p. 542.

De-gnome. To remove gnomes from an area by swinging them around in the air and letting them go when they were dizzy. This activity did not injure the gnomes. The Weasley family de-gnomed their garden to temporarily rid themselves of the gnomes. Harry Potter helped to de-gnome the Weasley garden prior to his second year at Hogwarts. CS 3, pp. 35-37. DH 6, p. 89.

Delacour, Apolline. The mother of Fleur and Gabrielle Delacour. Apolline and her husband arrived at the Burrow to attend the wedding of Fleur and Bill Weasley during year seven. DH 6, pp. 92, 107.

Delacour, Fleur Isabelle. A Veela-girl who was a student of the Beauxbatons Academy of Magic. Fleur was selected as her school's champion for the Triwizard Tournament held at Hogwarts during Harry Potter's fourth year at Hogwarts. GF 16, p. 269. Ron Weasley was particularly taken with Fleur's beauty. GF 16, p. 252. Fleur's magic wand was made of rosewood and contained a strand of hair from the head of a Veela. GF 18, p. 308. Ron asked Fleur to the Yule Ball and ran away in humiliation when she did not answer him. GF 22, p. 399. Fleur went with Roger Davies to the event. GF 23, pp. 412-13. She got a job at the Gringotts bank to improve her English during the summer prior to Harry's fifth year at Hogwarts. OP 4, p. 70. During the summer prior to Harry's sixth year at Hogwarts, Fleur worked part-time at Gringotts Wizarding bank and announced that she was going to marry Bill Weasley the following summer. Ginny Weasley nicknamed her "Phlegm." HP 6, pp. 92-93. At the beginning of year seven, Fleur Delacourt, who had taken Polyjuice Potion to look with Harry, was escorted by Bill Weasley on a thestral from the Dursley residence. Fleur was not fond of riding brooms. DH 4, pp. 45, 52. Her middle name was revealed at her wedding to Bill Weasley during year seven. DH 8, p. 145.

Delacour, Gabrielle. The sister of Fleur Delacour who was one of the four hostages placed underwater for the second task of the Triwizard Tournament. This event occurred during Harry Potter's fourth year at Hogwarts. GF 26, pp. 498, 504. During year seven, Gabrielle was eleven years old. DH 6, p. 108.

Delacour, Monsiuer. The father of Fleur and Gabrielle Delacour. Monsiuer Delacour was married to Apolline Delacour. He and his wife attended the wedding of Fleur and Bill Weasley at the Burrow during year seven. DH 6, pp. 92, 107.

Delaney-Podmore, Sir Patrick. A ghost who was leader of the Headless Hunt. Sir Patrick sent Nearly Headless Nick a letter that denied Nick membership in the Headless Hunt during Harry Potter's second year at Hogwarts. Nick referred to the leader of the Headless Hunt as "Sir Properly Decapitated-Podmore." CS 8, p. 124.

Deletrius. The magic word used to extinguish the charm invoked with the magic words "*prior incantato.*" Amos Diggory invoked this charm to determine the last spell cast by Harry Potter's wand during the aftermath of the Quidditch World Cup that Harry attended. This event occurred during the summer prior to Harry's fourth year at Hogwarts. GF 9, pp. 135-36.

Deluminator. A magical device in the shape of a silver cigarette lighter that was designed by Albus Dumbledore. The device removed light from a light source and could restore the light again with a simple click. Ronald Weasley obtained a Deluminator during year seven. DH 7, p. 125. That same year, Ron was able to use it to locate Harry Potter and Hermione Granger. It acted like a radio and produced an external light that entered Ron's chest and assisted him in finding Harry and Hermione in the Forest of Dean. DH 19, pp. 383-84.

Dementor. A magical creature that served as one of the prison guards at Azkaban. PA 5, pp. 83, 85. Dementors were hooded, cloaked figures who were not fooled by tricks, disguises or invisibility cloaks. PA 5, p. 92. They drained peace, hope and happiness out of the air around them and even muggles felt their presence. They were evil and had no souls. PA 10, p. 187. Dementors lowered their hoods only when they were going to inflict the Dementor's Kiss, their last and worst weapon, on a person. A common remedy for a person who became unconscious at the sight of a Dementor was chocolate. PA 5, p. 86. When Harry Potter first encountered Dementors he became unconscious and was revived with chocolate. PA 5, pp. 84-85. Dementors were positioned around the grounds of Hogwarts on suspicion that the Azkaban escapee, Sirius Black, would find and kill Harry. This event occurred during Harry's third year at Hogwarts. PA 5, p. 92. The following year, Lord Voldemort stated his belief that the

Dementors were natural allies to himself and the Death Eaters. GF 33, p. 651. A Dementor was capable of attacking a muggle in the muggle world. OP 1, p. 19. Dementors were sent to Little Whinging by a witch during the summer prior to Harry's fifth year at Hogwarts. OP 32, p. 747. The Dementors revolted from service to the Ministry of Magic at Azkaban during that school year and aligned themselves with Lord Voldemort. OP 38, p. 845. DH 3, p. 35; 13, p. 257.

Dementor's Kiss. The last and final weapon that a Dementor could inflict on a person. The Dementor's Kiss had the effect of sucking the soul out of its victim. PA 12, p. 247. The Ministry of Magic authorized the Dementors to inflict this weapon on Sirius Black after he was suspected of lingering around Hogwarts to kill Harry Potter. This event occurred during Harry's third year at the school. PA 12, p. 247. During Harry's fourth year at Hogwarts, a Dementor gave the fatal kiss to a Death Eater. GF 35, p. 703. DH 13, p. 258.

Demiguise. A magical beast native to the Far East. The pelt of the Demiguise was prized for its silvery hair, which was capable of being spun into Invisibility Cloaks. FB, pp. xvii, 9.

Dennis. A member of Dudley Dursley's gang who liked to tease Harry Potter by playing "Harry Hunting." The other members of the gang, in addition to Dudley, were Piers, Malcolm and Gordon. SS 3. p. 31.

Densaugeo. The magic word used by Draco Malfoy in a charm that he intended to throw on Harry Potter after Draco called Hermione Granger a Mudblood in a Potions class. However, the light from Draco's wand hit one from Harry's wand and the charm landed on Hermione. The charm caused Hermione's front teeth to grow at an alarming rate and looked like they belonged to a beaver. This event occurred during Harry's fourth year at Hogwarts. GF 18, p. 299.

Department for the Regulation and Control of Magical Creatures. A department located within the Ministry of Magic. Amos Diggory worked for this department during the summer prior to Harry Potter's fourth year at Hogwarts. GF 6, p. 71. Winky expressed concern to Dobby that his unusual behavior would cause him to be brought before the department like a common goblin. GF 8, p. 98. The department also closely observed the creation of new breeds of magical creatures. GF 24, p. 438. It was comprised of the following divisions: Beast Division; Being Division; and Spirit Division. FB, p. xii, fn. 2. The divisions were established by Grogan Stump. FB, p. xii, fn 2. Newt Scamander was employed in the department after graduating from Hogwarts. FB, p. vi. The department was the second largest in the Ministry of Magic. FB, p. xviii, fn. 9. The following administrative units were also located in the department: Ghoul Task Force; Goblin Liason Office; Pest Sub-Division; and Pest Advisory

Bureau. FB, pp. 6, 17-18, 31; OP 7, p. 130. Quintapeds resisted capture by the department. FB, p. 35. The department was located on level four of the Ministry of Magic. OP 7, p. 130. DH 12, p. 245.

Department of International Magical Cooperation. A department located within the Ministry of Magic. After graduating from Hogwarts, Percy Weasley was employed by the department. GF 3, p. 36. One of Percy's assignments involved the standardization of cauldron thickness. The assignment was in response to the fact that some foreign import cauldrons were a shade too thin and caused leaks. GF 5, p. 56. At that time, Barty Crouch was the head of the department. GF 27, p. 526-529. These events occurred during the summer prior to Harry Potter's fourth year at Hogwarts. GF 3, p. 36. The department and the Department of Magical Games and Sports authorized the resumption of the Triwizard Tournament during that year. GF 12, p. 187. The department was located on level five of the Ministry of Magic and included the following offices within itself: International Confederation of Wizards, British Seats; International Magical Office of Law; and International Magical Trading Standards Body. OP 7, p. 130.

Department of Magical Accidents and Catastrophes. A department located on level three of the Ministry of Magic that included the following offices: Accidental Magic Reversal Squad; Obliviator Headquarters; and Muggle-Worthy Excuse Committee. OP 7, p. 130. Harry Potter attempted to create an alias of a Ministry official named Dudley who worked in the Department of Magical Accidents and Catastrophes during year seven. DH 23, p. 450.

Department of Magical Catastrophes. A department located within the Ministry of Magic. Cornelius Fudge was the Junior Minister of the department when Sirius Black purportedly murdered Peter Pettigrew and twelve muggles outside the Potter home. Harry Potter learned this information from eavesdropping on a conversation between Cornelius and Minerva McGonagell in the Three Broomsticks during Harry's third year at Hogwarts. PA 10, p. 208.

Department of Magical Games and Sports. A department located within the Ministry of Magic. Arthur Weasley obtained tickets to the Quidditch World Cup through the department. The sporting event occurred during the summer prior to Harry Potter's fourth year at Hogwarts. GF 3, p. 30. At that time, the department was headed by Ludo Bagman. GF 5, p. 61. The department and the Department of International Magical Cooperation authorized the resumption of the Triwizard Tournament during Harry's fourth year at Hogwarts. GF 12, p. . The department was formed in the British Ministry of Magic in response to the International Statute of Wizarding Secrecy of 1692 rule that made each ministry of a country responsible for the consequences of magical sports occurring in its own territory. QA 5, p. 16. The department also had the duty to select quidditch referees, after they took rigorous flying tests and a written exam on the rules of the game. QA 6, p. 31. The following offices were included in the department: British and Irish Quidditch League Headquarters; Ludicrous Patents Office; and Official Gobstones Club. The department was located on level seven of the Ministry of Magic. OP 7, p. 129.

Department of Magical Law Enforcement. A department in the Ministry of Magic. It was the largest of the seven departments. All of the other departments were in some way answerable to this department, with the exception of the Department of Mysteries. Wizards from the Department of Magical Law Enforcement were called to dispel the crowd that was angry over the new Stooging Penalty established by the Department of Magical Games and Sports. QA 6, p. 26. Amelia Bones was head of the department during the summer prior to Harry Potter's fifth year at Hogwarts. Amelia's office was located on the same floor as Arthur Weasley's office. OP 7, p. 123. The department included the following offices: Auror Headquarters. OP 7, p. 130; Auror Office. DH 1, p. 4; Improper use of Magic Office. OP 7, p. 130; and Wizengamot Administration Services. OP 7, p. 130. During year seven, the department was headed by Pius Thicknesse. DH 1, p. 5.

Department of Magical Transport. A department located on level six of the Ministry of Magic that incorporated the following offices: Apparation Test Center; Broom Regulatory Control; Floo Network Authority; and Portkey Office. OP 7, p. 129. During year seven, the department was infiltrated by Death Eaters. DH 1, p. 6. See **Department of Magical Transportation**.

Department of Magical Transportation. A department located within the Ministry of Magic. The purpose of this department was to issue licenses for wizards and witches who wanted to apparate. A couple of people were fined by this department for apparating without a license and splinching themselves. They had to be sorted out by the Accidental Magic Reversal Squad. This event occurred during the summer prior to Harry Potter's fourth year at Hogwarts. GF 6, pp. 66-67.

Department of Mysteries. A department located within the Ministry of Magic. Its business was conducted by Unspeakables, two of whom were Bode and Croaker. Arthur Weasley identified the two wizards for Harry Potter and Hermione Granger, but admitted that he did not know what they did; it was top secret. This event occurred during the summer prior to Harry Potter's fourth year at Hogwarts. GF 7, p. 86. Augustus Rookwood was an employee of the department during the time period when aurors apprehended Death Eaters. GF 30, p. 590. The department was the only one of seven departments in the Ministry of Magic not answerable to the Department of Magical Law Enforcement. FB, p. xviii, fn. 9. It was located on the ninth floor of the Ministry and opened into a circular room. OP 34, p. 769. In one of the adjoining rooms were rows of shelves containing prophecies, including a prophecy relating to Harry and Lord Voldemort (located on row ninety-seven). The label on the glass ball containing Harry's prophecy read: "S.P.T. to A.P.W.B.D. Dark Lord and (?) Harry Potter." Only the person to whom a prophecy applied could retrieve it; anyone else who attempted it became mad. OP 34, p. 779-80, 786. The room was known as the Hall of Prophecy. OP 35, p. 789. The contents of Harry's prophecy were stored inside the glass ball. OP 37, p. 841. DH 13, p. 256.

Deprimo. The magic word used by Hermione Granger to invoke a charm that destroyed the floor on which she was standing in the home of Xenophilius Lovegood during year seven. DH 21, p. 422.

Derek. A student who attended Hogwarts. Derek was asked by Albus Dumbledore during a Christmas feast whether he wanted any chipolatas. This event occurred during Harry Potter's third year at Hogwarts. PA 11, p. 230.

Derrick. A student of Hogwarts who was a member of the Slytherin house. Derrick played the position of beater on the Slytherin house's quidditch team during Harry Potter's third year at Hogwarts. The other beater on that team was Bole. PA 15, p. 308. Derrick graduated from Hogwarts during Harry's fourth year at the school. Derrick's replacement on the Slytherin quidditch team was either Vincent Crabbe or Gregory Goyle. OP 19, p. 405.

Dervish and Banges. A shop located in Hogsmeade. Dervish and Banges repaired magical instruments and sold wizarding equipment. Ron Weasley suggested that Harry Potter take his Pocket Sneakoscope to this shop for repair. This event occurred during Harry's third year at Hogwarts. PA 5, p. 76; 8, p. 158.

Derwent, Dilys. A witch who was a celebrated headmaster at Hogwarts prior to Albus Dumbledore. Dilys was the subject of a painting in Albus' office and was sent by him to look for an injured Arthur Weasley during Harry Potter's fifth year at the school. Dilys was so revered that there were paintings of her in other important wizarding institutions. She was a healer at St. Mungo's Hospital for Magical Maladies and Injuries from 1722-1741 and headmistress at Hogwarts from 1741-1768. OP 22, pp. 468-69, 485. DH 36, p. 747.

Descendo. The magic word for a charm invoked by Ron Weasley to open a hatch in the ceiling at the Borrow and to have a ladder slide down. The event occurred during year seven. DH 6, p. 97. Vincent Crabbe used the charm to force a tower of old furniture and other objects in the Room of Requirement to crumble. Harry Potter invoked a counter charm, *finite*, to stop it. DH 31, p. 629.

Despard, Dragomir. An alias that Ron Weasley used during year seven. Dragomir was supposedly a Transylvanian wizard sympathetic to Lord Voldemort's cause. DH 26, p. 528.

Detachable Cribbing Cuff. A magical device banned from the O.W.L. examination hall during Harry Potter's fifth year at Hogwarts. OP 31, p. 709.

Deverill, Barnabas. One of the reputed owners of the Elder Wand. Deverill was killed by Loxias who obtained the Elder Wand from him. DH 21, p. 412.

Devil's Snare. A plant that liked damp, darkness and strangled persons with its snakelike tendrils. Devil's Snare was repelled by light. Harry Potter, Ron Weasley and Hermione Granger encountered this plant during Harry's first year at Hogwarts. SS 16, pp. 277-78. A cutting of Devil's Snare killed Broderick Bode while he was a patient at St Mungo's Hospital for Magical Maladies and Injuries. This event occurred during Harry's fifth year at Hogwarts. OP 25, p. 547. Professor Sprout intended to use Devil's Snare as a defense against Death Eaters during year seven. DH 30, p. 600.

Devon. The location where Nicolas Flamel, the alchemist, and his wife Perenelle resided. SS 13, p. 220. The game of Shuntbumps was popular in Devon. QA 2, p. 6. (Devon is a county in Southwest England.)

Diagon Alley. A cobblestoned street in London, not far from the Leaky Cauldron, where wizards shopped in numerous stores. Diagon Alley was accessed by tapping on a brick wall three times until the wall magically opened and then by stepping through an archway into the alley. SS 5, p. 71. DH 11, p. 222.

Didsbury. The location of Warlock D.J. Prod's residence. Prod took the Kwikspell course and afterward was able to use a charm to turn his wife into a yak. This information was listed on a piece of parchment that advertised the Kwikspell course and that Harry Potter read in Argus Filch's office during Harry's second year at Hogwarts. CS 8, p. 127.

Diffindo. The magic word used by Harry Potter to invoke a charm that caused Cedric Diggory's book bag to split open. This event occurred during Harry's fourth year at Hogwarts. GF 19, p. 340. DH 9, p. 166.

Diggle, Dedalus. A wizard who Minerva McGonagell suspected of shooting stars in Kent on the day that Voldemort disappeared. SS 1, p. 10. Dedalus was one of the patrons who met Harry Potter on his first visit to the Leaky Cauldron. This event occurred during the summer prior to Harry's first year at Hogwarts. SS 5, p. 69. Dedalus was a member of the Order of the Phoenix and the advance guard that rescued Harry from the Dursley home during the summer prior to Harry's fifth year at Hogwarts. OP 3, pp. 47-49. At the beginning of year seven, Harry suggested to Vernon Dursley that Dedalus and Hestia Jones would be more up to the job of protecting the Dursleys than Kingsley Shacklebolt. DH 3, pp. 34, 36. Dedalus' house was burned down by Death Eaters during year seven. DH 10, p. 206.

Diggory, Amos. The father of Cedric Diggory who worked for the Department for the Regulation and Control of Magical Creatures. Amos and Cedric appeared at the portkey on Stoatshead Hill the same time as the Weasley family, Harry Potter and Hermione in order to travel to the Quidditch World Cup. This event occurred during the summer prior to Harry's fourth year at Hogwarts. GF 6, p. 71.

Diggory, Cedric. A student and member of the Hufflepuff house at Hogwarts. Cedric was captain and seeker of the Hufflepuff quidditch team during Harry Potter's third and fourth years at the school. PA 9, p. 168; GF 6, p. 71. At those times, Cedric was in his fifth and sixth years, respectively. PA 9, p. 174. During Harry's fourth year, Cedric was a prefect. GF 15, p. 236. Cedric was chosen as the school champion for Hogwarts in the Triwizard Tournament hosted by Hogwarts. GF 16, p. 270. His magic wand was made of ash and contained a single hair from the tail of a fine male unicorn. Cedric took Cho Chang to the Yule ball during Harry's fourth year at Hogwarts. GF 18, 309; 22, p. 397. He died after the third event of the Triwizard Tournament. GF 37, p. 638. Cedric's name appeared on the list of borrowers found inside the cover of *Quidditch Through the Ages*. QA, p. i. During year seven, Harry still had in his trunk an old badge that flickered between "Support Cedric Diggory" and "Potter Stinks." DH 2, p. 14.

Dijon. A city in France that Hermione visited. Rubeus Hagrid and Madam Maxine lost the person who trailed them in Dijon. This event occurred during Harry Potter's fifth year at Hogwarts. OP 20, p. 427. (Dijon is a city and the capital of Côte d'Or in East Central France.)

Dilligrout. A secret password used by the Gryffindor students to enter their house through the portrait of the Fat Lady during Harry Potter's sixth year at Hogwarts. HP 12, p. 256.

Dillonsby, Ivor. A wizard who, as claimed by Rita Skeeter in her book *The Life and Lies of Albus Dumbledore*, already discovered eight uses of dragon's blood when Albus Dumbledore "borrowed" his papers. He also commented on the mental condition of Bathilda Bagshot. DH 2, p. 26; 18, p. 355.

Dimitrov. A member of the Bulgarian National Quidditch Team who played at the Quidditch World Cup that Harry Potter attended during the summer prior to his fourth year at Hogwarts. Dimitrov was a chaser. The other members of the team were: Ivanova, Zograf, Levski, Vulchanov, Volkov and Viktor Krum. GF 8, pp. 104, 108.

Dingle, Harold. A student at Hogwarts from whom Hermione Granger confiscated powdered dragon claw during Harry Potter's fifth year at Hogwarts. Harold offered to sell students firewhisky that same year. OP 31, p. 708; 32, p. 738.

Dint and Mildewe. The publishers of *The Philosophy of the Mundane: Why the Muggles Prefer Not to Know* by Professor Mordicus Egg. FB, p. xvii, fn. 8.

Dippet, Armando. The headmaster of Hogwarts at the time that Tom Riddle was in his fifth year at Hogwarts. Harry Potter learned this information from Tom Riddle's diary during Harry's second year at the school. CS 13, pp. 241-42; CS 17, p. 311. A picture of Armando, who was Albus Dumbledore's immediate predecessor as headmaster at Hogwarts, hung on the wall of Albus's office at Hogwarts. Like the other headmasters in the portraits there, Armando was duty bound to provide the current headmaster with assistance when called on to do so. OP 22, p. 472.

Diricawl. A magical beast that originated in Mauritius. Muggles were once aware of the Diricawl and referred to it as the "Dodo" bird. FB, pp. xi, 9. The Diricawl was capable of disappearing and reappearing at will. FB, p. 32.

Dirigible Plums. A fruit that grew on Xenophilius Lovegood's property, north of Ottery, St. Catchpole. A sign on the property stated: "Keep off the Dirigible Plums." The fruit, which were orange and radish-like, were worn by Luna Lovegood as earrings. DH 20, p. 398. Her father believed that they enhanced one's ability to accept the extraordinary. DH 20, p. 404.

Disapparate. The opposite action of apparate. PA 22, p. 419; GF 4, p. 45. DH 3, p. 37. See **Apparate**.

Disarming Charm. A charm invoked with the magic word "*expelliarmus*" and used to remove a magic wand from the hand of a wizard. CS 11, p. 190. The charm was demonstrated by Severus Snape against Gilderoy Lockhart during a Dueling Club meeting. This event occurred during Harry Potter's second year at Hogwarts. CS 11, p. 190. The

Disarming Charm was the first skill that Harry taught other students in Dumbledore's Army. This event occurred during Harry's fifth year at the school. OP 18, p. 392. At the beginning of year seven, Harry attempted to disarm Stan Shunpike with the charm. DH 5, p. 70.

Disillusionment Charm. A charm that owners of a hippogriff were required by law to invoke in order to distort the vision of any muggle who might see the creature. The charm did not last long and needed to be invoked on a daily basis. FB, p. xix. Owners of winged horses were also required to use the Disillusionment Charm. FB, p. 42. Alastor "Mad Eye" Moody cast the charm on Harry Potter during the summer prior to Harry's fifth year at Hogwarts and it gave Harry the appearance of a human chameleon. OP 3, p. 54. At the beginning of year seven, members of the Order of the Phoenix used the charm as they appeared at the Dursley residence. DH 4, p. 45; 31, p. 629.

Dissendium. A magic word used to open a secret door behind a one-eyed witch on the third floor of Hogwarts. The door opened an underground passageway that led to Honeydukes in Hogsmeade. Harry Potter learned this spell from the Marauder's Map during his third year at Hogwarts. PA 10, p. 195.

Dittany. A word that appeared in *One Thousand Magical Herbs and Fungi.* Harry Potter searched for this word while working on a homework assignment during his first year at Hogwarts. SS 14, p. 229.

Divination. A class taught by Sibyll Trelawney in the top of the North Tower at Hogwarts and that was first offered to third-year students. CS 14, p. 252; PA 6, pp. 99-101. Percy Weasley recommended Divination class and Muggle Studies to Harry Potter during Harry's second year at Hogwarts. CS 14, p. 252. Harry elected to take the Divination in his third year. PA 4, p. 52. According to Professor Trelawney, Divination was the most difficult of all Magical Arts and if a student did not have the "Sight" she could not teach the subject to that student. Divination included instruction in reading tea leaves, palmistry, fire omens and crystal balls. PA 6, pp. 103-04. Minerva McGonagell viewed the class with suspicion. She stated that Divination was one of the most imprecise branches of magic and true seers were very rare. PA 6, p. 109. Next to Potions class, Divination class was Harry's least favorite class because Sibyll kept predicting Harry's death. While he took the class in his fourth year, Hermione Granger dropped out of the class that year in order to take Arithmancy. GF 13, pp. 193-94. Dream interpretation was very probably on the O.W.L. for Divination. Op 12, p. 237. When Firenze taught Divination, it was held in Classroom Eleven of Hogwarts because he was unable to climb the ladder up to the North Tower. Classroom Eleven was located on the ground-floor corridor that lead off the entrance hall on the opposite side of the Great Hall. OP 27, p. 600.

Dobbs, Emma. A student sorted by the Sorting Hat during Harry Potter's fourth year at Hogwarts. Emma's placement into a house was not specified. GF 12, p. 179.

Dobby. A house-elf who worked for the Malfoy family and tried to prevent Harry Potter from attending Hogwarts during Harry's second year at the school. Harry freed Dobby from his life of servitude to the Malfoy family at the end of that school year. CS 2, p. 12; 18, p. 338. During Harry's fourth year at Hogwarts, Dobby was given a job by Albus Dumbledore and worked in the school's kitchen for one galleon per week. GF 21, pp. 375-76, 379. Dobby apparated into the cellar prison cell in which Harry and Ron Weasley were imprisoned at Malfoy Manor during year seven. Dobby's fate was connected with the escape from Malfoy Manor. DH 23, pp. 467, 475-76.

Doge, Elphias. A wizard who was a member of the Order of the Phoenix and the advance guard that rescued Harry Potter from the Dursley home during the summer prior to Harry's fifth year at Hogwarts. OP 3, pp. 47-49. He wrote an obituary for an important wizard that appeared in the *Daily Prophet* at the beginning of year seven. DH 2, p. 16. Elphias was a classmate of Albus Dumbledore. DH 2, p. 16. During year seven, Elphias was Special Advisor to the Wizengamot. DH 2, p. 24. Doge attended the Fleur Delacourt and Bill Weasley wedding that year. DH 8, p. 151. His nickname was reportedly "Dogbreath." DH 18, p. 353.

Dolohov, Antonin. A wizard who served Lord Voldemort as a Death Eater and was caught by an auror shortly after Igor Karkaroff was captured. During his fourth year at Hogwarts, Harry Potter learned this information from the pensieve in Albus Dumbledore's office. GF 30, p. 589. Antonin was known for having brutally murdered Gideon and Fabian Prewett. OP 25, p. 543. Antonin was present in the Department of Mysteries when Harry retrieved the prophecy relating to himself and Lord Voldemort. This event occurred during Harry's fifth year at Hogwarts. OP 35, p. 788. During year seven, Dolohov attended a meeting of the Death Eaters and Voldemort at the Malfoy manor house. DH 1, p. 3. Dolohov was one of three Death Eaters who followed Harry, Ron Weasley and Hermione Granger into a muggle cafe that year. DH 9, p. 166. Antonin's fate was revealed at the end of year seven. DH 36, p. 735.

Dom. The name for a gallbladder of a goat used to play Aingingein in Ireland. QA 2, p. 5.

Dopplebeater Defence. A widely-known quidditch move. QA 10, p. 52.

Dorkin, Mary. A muggle news reporter who covered the story about Bungy the budgie who learned how to water-ski. This event occurred during the summer prior to Harry Potter's fifth year at Hogwarts. OP 1, p. 4.

Dorney, J. A student at Hogwarts whose name appeared on the list of borrowers found inside the cover of *Quidditch Through the Ages*. QA, p. i.

Dorset. The location where Newt Scamander and his wife, Porpentina, resided with three Kneazles named Hoppy, Milly and Mauler. Dorset was also the home of the Porlock. FB, pp. vi, 33. (Dorset, also known as Dorcetshire, is a county in South England.)

Dott. A villager in Little Hangleton who was in the Hanged Man and discussed the murders of the Riddle family. Dott reported that Frank Bryce was known for having a horrible temper and believed that Frank was responsible for the Riddle family deaths even after Frank was released from custody. GF 1, p. 3.

Double Eight Loop. A widely known quidditch move. QA 10, p. 52.

Double-Ended Newts. A creature mentioned in a dispute between the witch who owned Magical Menagerie and a wizard. Harry Potter, Ron Weasley and Hermione Granger overheard the dispute prior to Harry's third year at Hogwarts. PA 4, p. 58.

Downing Street. The location where Kingsley Shacklebolt went after the Order of the Phoenix escorted Harry Potter to the Burrow at the beginning of year seven. DH 5, p. 77. (Downing Street is the address and residence of the Prime Minister of England.)

Doxy. A magical beast, also known as the biting fairy, found in Northern Europe and America. FB, p. 10. Doxies lived in the curtains at Number Twelve, Grimmauld Place, London. OP 5, p. 85. Fred and George Weasley intended to use doxy venom in their Skiving Snackboxes. OP 6, p. 104. The bowtruckle liked to eat doxy eggs. DH 28, p. 560.

Doxycide. A product used by wizards to rid a place of doxies. Mrs. Weasley used Doxycide at Number Twelve, Grimmauld Place during the summer prior to Harry Potter's fifth year at Hogwarts. OP 6, p. 102.

Dr. Filibuster's Fabulous Wet-Start, No-Heat Fireworks. Fireworks that Fred and George Weasley and Lee Jordan purchased from the Gambol and Japes Wizarding Joke Shop at Diagon Alley. CS 4, p. 58. The Weasley twins set off the fireworks in the Burrow kitchen the evening before the children left for the start of Harry Potter's second year at Hogwarts. CS 5, p. 65. Fred's trunk sprang open and some of the fireworks exploded, causing a muggle taxi driver to scream. This event occurred during the summer prior to Harry's fourth year at Hogwarts. GF 11, p. 162.

Dr. Ubbly's Oblivious Unction. A magical healing ointment that Madam Pomfrey applied to the wounds Ron Weasley sustained from the tentacles of the brains in the Department of Mysteries. This event occurred during Harry Potter's fifth year at Hogwarts. OP 38, p. 847.

Dragon. A large, fire-breathing creature that came in many different types. Charlie Weasley studied dragons in Romania after graduating from Hogwarts. SS 6, p. 99, 107. A dragon was extremely difficult to kill because of the ancient magic imbued in its thick hide. GF 19, p. 338. The dragon was the most famous of all magical beasts. The ten pure-bred types of dragons were as follows: Antipodean Opaleye; Chinese Fireball; Common Welsh Green; Hebridean Black; Hungarian Horntail; Norwegian Ridgeback; Peruvian Vipertooth; Romanian Longhorn; Swedish Short-Snout; and Ukranian Ironbelly. FB, pp. 10-15. Albus Dumbledore discovered twelve uses of dragon's blood. However, Ivor Dillonsby claimed that he had already discovered eight of them when Albus "borrowed" his papers on the subject. DH 2, pp. 20, 26. Female dragons were more vicious than male dragons, and this characteristic assisted with identifying the gender of a dragon. DH 7, p. 120.

Dragon Research and Restraint Bureau. A division in the Ministry of Magic, probably in the Department for the Regulation and Control of Magical Creatures. Newt Scamander worked for a while in the Dragon Research and Restraint Bureau. FB, p. vi.

Dragon Breeding for Pleasure and Profit. A book in the library of Hogwarts used by Rubeus Hagrid to hatch a black dragon's egg he won from a stranger in a card game. This event occurred during Harry Potter's first year at Hogwarts. SS 14, p. 233.

Dragon Pox. A contagious disease suffered by Elphias Doge shortly before his arrival at Hogwarts as a student. The disease caused one's face to become pockmarked with a greenish hue. DH 2, p. 16.

Dragon Species of Great Britain and Ireland: From Egg to Inferno, A Dragon Keeper's Guide. A book in the library of Hogwarts that Rubeus Hagrid consulted during Harry Potter's first year at Hogwarts. Rubeus did not want Harry and Ron Weasley to know that he was searching for books in the dragon section of the library on that occasion. SS 14, p. 230.

Draught of Living Death. A powerful sleep potion made with powdered asphodel root and an infusion of wormwood. Severus Snape quizzed Harry Potter about this potion during the first Potions class Harry attended in his first year at Hogwarts. SS 8, pp. 137-38.

Draught of Peace. A potion used to calm anxiety and soothe agitation. Severus Snape taught the Draught of Peace to his fifth year students, in part because the potion needed to be learned for the O.W.L.s.

Powdered moonstone and syrup of hellebore were two of the potion's ingredients. OP 12, pp. 232-34.

Dreadful Denizens of the Deep. A book that Harry Potter consulted in order to find a way to breathe underwater in the second task of the Triwizard Tournament. This event occurred during Harry's fourth year at Hogwarts. GF 26, p. 488.

Dream Oracle, The. A book written by Inigo Imago and used by Sibyl Trelawney in her Divination Class with fifth-year students. The book was also referred to as *Dream Oracles*. OP 12, p. 237; 15, p. 312.

Drear, Isle of. See **Isle of Drear**.

Drooble's Best Blowing Gum. A candy sold in the wizarding world. SS 6, p. 101. The candy filled a room with bluebell-colored bubbles that failed to pop for days. It was sold at Honeydukes in Hogsmeade. Harry Potter observed the candy during his third year at Hogwarts. PA 10, p. 197. Rubeus Hagrid gave Harry a box of candy, including , Drooble's Best Blowing Gum as a Christmas present during Harry's fourth year at the school. GF 23, p. 410.

Drought Charm. A charm used to dry up puddles and ponds. Ron Weasley mentioned the charm to Harry Potter for the second task in the Triwizard Tournament. This event occurred during Harry's fourth year at Hogwarts. GF 26, p. 486.

Dueling Club. A club in Hogwarts that taught students how to duel using their magic wands and spells. It was formed during Harry Potter's second year at Hogwarts. Gilderoy Lockhart was the club's instructor and Severus Snape provided him with assistance. CS 11, pp. 188-89.

Dugbog. A marsh-dwelling magical beast found in Europe, North Amercia and South America. The Dugbog's favorite food was the mandrake. FB, p. 15.

Dumbledore. A wizarding family that moved into Godric's Hollow after Pervical Dumbledore was imprisoned. They were neighbors to Bathilda Bagshot. DH 8, p. 158. A photograph of the Dumbledore family was printed in the *Daily Prophet* during year seven. DH 11, p. 216.

Dumbledore, Aberforth. The younger brother of Albus Dumbledore who was prosecuted for practicing inappropriate charms on a goat and although it was reported in the press, Aberforth did not hide. Albus shared this family history with Rubeus Hagrid in order to bring Rubeus out of hiding after a negative article appeared about Rubeus in the *Daily Prophet*. This event occurred during Harry Potter's fourth year at Hogwarts. GF 24, p. 454. Aberforth was a member of the Order of the Phoenix. OP 9, p. 174. His parents were Percival and Kendra Dumbledore. Aberforth was three years younger than his brother, Albus. DH 2, pp. 16, 18. Rita Skeeter claimed in her book,

The Life and Lies of Albus Dumbledore, that Aberforth was convicted by the Wizengamot for misuse of magic and that the event caused a minor scandal fifteen years prior to year seven. DH 2, p. 25. During year seven, Aberforth was the barman of Hog's Head Inn. His patronus took the form of a goat. DH 28, pp. 558-59.

Dumbledore, Albus Percival Wulfric Brian. The headmaster of Hogwarts during Harry Potter's lifetime. SS 1, p. 8. Albus' full title was "Order of Merlin, First Class, Grand Sorc., Chf. Warlock, Supreme Mugwump, International Confed. of Wizards." SS 4, p. 51. A short biography of Albus was found on the collectors' card Harry received from purchasing Chocolate Frogs on the Hogwarts Express. SS 6, p. 102. Albus was regarded as the best headmaster Hogwarts ever had and his powers were believed to rival those of Lord Voldemort at the height of his strength. SS 4, p. 58; CS 2, p. 17. Albus' office was accessed from a rotating spiral staircase. CS 12, pp. 205-06. During the years that Rubeus Hagrid attended Hogwarts as a student, Albus was the professor of the Transfiguration class. CS 17, p. 313. When Albus was a student at the school, he was a member of the Gryffindor house. SS 6, p. 106. Albus wrote forewords for the special editions of *Fantastic Beasts and Where to Find Them* and *Quidditch Through the Ages* that were marketed to the muggle world. FB, pp. vii-viii; QA, pp. vii-viii. Albus was voted out of the Chairmanship of the International Confederation of Wizards because he announced the return of Lord Voldemort and was demoted from Chief Warlock on the Wizengamot. These events occurred during the summer prior to Harry Potter's fifth year at Hogwarts. OP 5, p. 95. Albus' full name was announced at Harry Potter's disciplinary hearing of the Wizengamot as: Albus Percival Wulfric Brian Dumbledore. OP 8, p. 139. During Harry's fifth year at Hogwarts, the magic password to gain access to the staircase that led to Albus' office was "Fizzing Whizbee." OP 22, p. 466. Educational Decree Twenty-eight replaced Albus as headmaster at Hogwarts with Dolores Umbridge. OP 28, p. 624. The *Daily Prophet* formerly announced Albus' "reinstatement" as headmaster at the end of Harry's fifth year. OP 38, p. 846. His favorite flavor of jam was raspberry and he enjoyed reading about knitting patterns in muggle magazines. HP 4, pp. 62, 73. His parents were Percival and Kendra Dumbledore. DH 2, pp. 16, 18. Albus discovered twelve uses of dragon's blood. DH 2, p. 20. As a student at Hogwarts, Albus earned the following prizes and distinctions: the Barnabus Finkley Prize for Exceptional Spell-Casting; British Youth Representative to the Wizaengamot; and Gold Medal-Winner for Ground-Breaking Contribution to the International Alchemical Conference in Cairo. DH 18, p. 353. During year seven, the magic word to gain access to Albus' office was "Dumbledore." DH 33, p. 662. For an important promise Albus asked from Severus Snape during Harry's sixth year, which was revealed to Harry in the pensieve the following year, see DH 33, p. 683.

Dumbledore, Ariana. The daughter of Percival and Kendra Dumbledore. Ariana was younger than her brother, Albus. DH 2, p. 19. Auntie Muriel claimed that Ariana had been a squib and had never attended Hogwarts. DH 8, pp. 154-155. A detailed account of Ariana's life story was explained by Aberforth Dumbledore during year seven. DH 28, pp. 564-67.

Dumbledore, Kendra. The wife of Percival Dumbledore. Kendra died shortly after her son, Albus, graduated from Hogwarts. DH 2, p. 18. Auntie Muriel claimed that Kendra was muggle-born. DH 8, p. 154. Kendra died before her daughter, Ariana. DH 8, p. 157. On her gravestone in Godric's Hollow was this inscription: "Where your treasure is, there will your heart be also." DH 16, p. 325.

Dumbledore, Percival. The father of Aberforth and Albus Dumbledore, who committed a savage attack on three muggles the year before Albus attended the Hogwarts School of Witchcraft and Wizardy as a student. Percival was sentenced to Azkaban for the conduct and died there. DH 2, p. 16. Perzival was also charged in Aberforth's conduct over fiddling with goats, which incident caused a minor scandal. DH 2, p. 25.

Dumbledore's Army (D.A.). An unofficial club formed by students at Hogwarts to study Defense Against the Dark Arts during Harry Potter's fifth year at the school. The members included: Harry, Ron Weasley, Hermione Granger, Fred Weasley, George Weasley, Ginny Weasley, Neville Longbottom, Dean Thomas, Lavender Brown, Parvati Patil, Padma Patil, Cho Chang, Marietta Edgecombe, Luna Lovegood, Katie Bell, Alicia Spinnet, Angelina Johnson, Colin Creevy, Dennis Creevy, Ernie Macmillan, Justin Finch-Fletchley, Hannah Abbott, Anthony Goldstein, Michael Corner, Terry Boot, Lee Jordan, Susan Bones and Zacharias Smith. There were twenty-eight students in the club. While Ginny Weasley originated the name for the club, other names were considered and rejected as follows: Anti-Umbridge League (suggested by Angelina Johnson); Ministry of Magic Are Morons Group (suggested by Fred Weasley); and Defense Association, or D.A. (suggested by Cho Chang). OP 16, pp. 337-40; 17, p. 372; 18, pp. 392, 394. The D.A. members held fake galleons that revealed, through a Protean Charm that Hermione invoked, the date and time of the next meeting. OP 19, p. 398. Seamus Finnigan joined the D.A. later in the school year. OP 27, pp. 606-07. The D.A.

was reformed during year seven by Ginny Weasley, Neville Longbottom and Luna Lovegood. DH 16, p. 314.

Dundee. One of three muggle towns that reported a downpour of shooting stars on the day Lord Voldemort disappeared after murdering James and Lily Potter. The other two towns were Kent and Yorkshire. SS 1, p. 6. (Dundee is a seaport in East Scotland on the Firth of Tay.)

Dungbomb. A joke device that Fred and George Weasley detonated in a corridor of Hogwarts during their first year at the school. The incident got them into trouble with Argus Filch and helped them to discover and steal the Marauder's Map from Filch's office. PA 10, p. 191. Dungbombs were sold at Zonko's Joke Shop in Hogsmeade, where Harry Potter and Ron Weasley bought some during Harry's third year at Hogwarts. PA 14, p. 278. The following year, Hermione Granger was prepared to drop a bag of dungbombs in the Gryffindor common room in order to clear the room for Harry's secret meeting with Sirius Black on November 22. GF 18, p. 312, 19, p. 314. DH 2, p. 26.

Dungeon Five. A dungeon in Hogwarts. During Harry Potter's second year at the school, some third-year students accidentally plastered frog brains all over the ceiling of Dungeon Five and Argus Filch cleaned up the mess. Nearly Headless Nick warned Harry that the work put Filch in a terrible mood. CS 8, p. 125.

Dunstan, B. A student at Hogwarts whose name appeared on the list of borrowers found inside the cover of *Quidditch Through the Ages*. QA, p. i.

Durmstrang Institute. A wizarding school that, according to Hermione Granger, had a horrible reputation and placed a heavy emphasis on teaching the Dark Arts. GF 11, p. 165; GF 31, p. 621. Draco Malfoy bragged that his father considered sending him to Durmstrang Institute, but his mother said that it was too far away. The remark was made on the Hogwarts Express immediately prior to Harry Potter's fourth year at Hogwarts. Durmstrang's location was a mystery so that its secrets could not be stolen. It was unplottable on maps. Durmstrang students wore fur cape uniforms. GF 11, pp. 165-67. The school consisted of a castle with four floors and its grounds were larger than those at Hogwarts. During winter months there was little daylight at Durmstrang. GF 23, p. 417. During Harry Potter's fourth year at Hogwarts, the head of Durmstrang was Igor Karkaroff. Karkaroff accompanied his school's contestants to the Triwizard Tournament at Hogwarts on a ship that surfaced out of the black lake on the school grounds. GF 15, pp. 246-47. Durmstrang sent twelve contestants to the tournament. GF 27, p. 554. The students at Durmstrang wore blood red robes as their school uniform. GF 16, p. 251. These events occurred during Harry's fourth year at Hogwarts. The infamous wizard, Gellert Grindelwald, was a student at Durmstrand, where he carved his symbol, a triangular eye, into the walls before he was expelled. DH 8, p. 148; 18, p. 356.

Duro. The magic word used by Hermione Granger to act as a counter charm to *glisseo* during year seven. The charm had the effect of eliminating a slide she had created out of a staircase at Hogwarts. DH 32, p. 643.

Dursley. The muggle family, consisting of Vernon, Petunia and Dudley, that Harry Potter lived with at Number Four Privet Drive, Little Whinging, Surrey. SS 1, p. 1; 3, p. 34. Petunia was the sister of Harry's mother. SS 1, p. 7. Vernon was the head of the household. SS 2, p. 20.

Dursley, Dudley. Harry Potter's muggle cousin who was the same age as Harry. SS 1, pp. 1-2. Petunia called her son by the following pet names: Duddy, SS 2, p. 19; Popkin and Sweetums, SS 2, p. 21; Dinky Duddydums, SS 2, p. 23; Ickle Dudleykins, SS 3, p. 32; Dudders, PA 2, pp. 19, 22; and Diddy, GF 3, p. 26. Dudley attended Smeltings for school when Harry started his wizarding education at Hogwarts. SS 3, p. 32. Dudley was the Junior Heavyweight Inter-School Boxing Champion of the Southeast during the summer prior to Harry's fifth year at Hogwarts. Piers Polkiss, called Dudley "Big D" and Harry teased Dudley about his nickname "Ickle Diddykins." OP 1, pp. 11-13. DH 2, p. 13; 3, p. 30. During year seven, Petunia called him "Diddy," "Popkin" and "Dudders" and Harry called him "Big D." DH 3, pp. 38, 41, 42.

Dursley, Marge. Vernon Dursley's muggle sister who was commonly referred to as Aunt Marge. SS 2, p. 21; 3, p. 34. Marge was not a blood-relative of Harry Potter's, but he was forced to call her Aunt Marge. PA 2, p. 18. Marge bred bulldogs and had twelve of them. She came to a few of Dudley Dursley's birthday parties. PA 2, pp. 18, 22, 26.

Dursley, Petunia. Harry Potter's muggle aunt who was the sister of Harry's mother, Lily Potter. Petunia was married to Vernon Dursley and mother of Dudley Dursley. She lived with her family and Harry Potter at Number Four Privet Drive, Little Whinging, Surrey. SS 1, pp. 1, 7. During the summer prior to Harry's fifth year at Hogwarts, Petunia received a howler from Albus Dumbledore reminding her of a promise she had made to him. OP 2, p. 39; 37, p. 836. DH 2, p. 29; 3, p. 30. Petunia as a young girl was part of an episode that Harry watched in the pensieve during year seven. Lily Potter called her "Tuney" as a nickname. DH 33, p. 663.

Dursley, Vernon. Harry Potter's muggle uncle who was the husband of Petunia Dursley and father of Dudley Dursley. SS 2, p. 20. Vernon lived with his family and Harry Potter at Number Four Privet Drive, Little Whinging, Surrey. Vernon was employed by Grunnings, a drill-making firm. SS 1, p. 1; 2, p. 20. DH 3, p. 30.

Dusty. The playful name given by Ron Weasley to the moving form of Mad-Eye Moody that was placed in Number Twelve Grimmauld Palace to scare Severus Snape if he ventured into the property during year seven. DH 9, p. 172.

Dwarfs. A dozen of these creatures, wearing golden wings and carrying harps, were paraded by Gilderoy Lockhart as cupids into the Great Hall of Hogwarts on Valentines' Day. This event occurred during Harry Potter's second year at Hogwarts. CS 13, p. 236.

EASTER – EXTINGUISHING SPELL

Easter. During year seven, Draco Malfoy was at home during the Easter holidays. DH 23, p. 457.

Edgecombe, Madam. A witch who worked for the Floo Network in the Department of Magical Transportation and was the mother of Marietta Edgecombe. Madam Edgecombe policed the fireplaces at Hogwarts during Harry Potter's fifth year at the school. OP 27, p. 612.

Edgecombe, Marietta. A student at Hogwarts who was Cho Chang's friend. Marietta attended the D.A. meetings with Cho and was an informant for Dolores Umbridge regarding the D.A.'s activities. These events occurred during Harry Potter's fifth year at Hogwarts. OP 27, p. 612.

Edible Dark Marks. A joke or gag device sold at Weasleys' Wizarding Wheezes during the summer prior to Harry Potter's sixth year at Hogwarts. An advertisement for the product claimed that "they'll make anyone sick." HP 6, p. 118.

Educational Decree Twenty-Two. A law passed by the Ministry of Magic giving the Minister of Magic the authority to appoint an appropriate person to fill a teaching vacancy at Hogwarts if the current headmaster was unable to do so. Cornelius Fudge used this law to appoint Dolores Umbridge as professor of Defense Against the Dark Arts during Harry Potter's fifth year at Hogwarts. OP 15, p. 307.

Educational Decree Twenty-Three. A law passed by the Ministry of Magic establishing the position of "Hogwarts High Inquisitor." This event occurred during Harry Potter's fifth year at Hogwarts. OP 15, p. 307.

Educational Decree Twenty-Four. A law cited as the authority for Dolores Umbridge, as High Inquisitor, to disband all student organizations, societies, teams, groups and clubs. This event occurred during Harry Potter's fifth year at Hogwarts. OP 17, pp. 351-52.

Educational Decree Twenty-Five. A law that provided the Hogwarts High Inquisitor with the authority to punish, sanction and remove the privileges of students and alter the punishments, sanctions and removal of privileges made by professors. The law was signed by Cornelius Fudge and Dolores Umbridge used it to impose a lifetime ban on Harry Potter and Fred and George Weasley from playing quidditch. This event occurred during Harry's fifth year at Hogwarts. OP 19, p. 415.

Educational Decree Twenty-Six. A law that provided the Hogwarts High Inquisitor with the right to prohibit professors from giving students any information not strictly related to the subjects the professors were paid to teach. This event occurred during Harry Potter's fifth year at Hogwarts. OP 25, p. 551.

Educational Decree Twenty-Seven. A law that provided the Hogwarts High Inquisitor with the right to expel any student who possessed a copy of *The Quibbler*. This event occurred during Harry Potter's fifth year at Hogwarts. OP 26, p. 581.

Educational Decree Twenty-Eight. A law that provided the Ministry of Magic with the right to remove Albus Dumbledore as headmaster of Hogwarts and replace him with Dolores Umbridge. OP 28, p. 624.

Eeylops Owl Emporium. A shop that sold owls and was located on Diagon Alley. The types of owls listed on the shop's sign included tawny, screech, barn, brown and snowy owls. Harry Potter observed this shop during the summer prior to his first year at Hogwarts. SS 5, p. 72. The shop sold owl nuts, which Harry and Ron Weasley purchased for their owls during the summer prior to Harry's sixth year at Hogwarts. HP 6,p. 115.

Egbert the Egregious. One of the reputed owners of the Elder Wand. Egbert killed Emeric the Evil in order to obtain the Elder Wand. DH 21, p. 412.

Egg, Mordicus (Professor). The author of *The Philosophy of the Mundane: Why the Muggles Prefer Not to Know*. The book was published in 1963 by Dint and Mildewe. FB, p. xvii, fn. 8.

Egypt. The location where Bill Weasley worked as a curse breaker for the Gringotts Wizarding Bank. CS 12, p. 211; PA 1, p. 8. Hassan Mostafa, an Egyptian, was the Chairwizard of the International Association of Quidditch and the referee of the Quidditch World Cup that Harry Potter attended during the summer prior to his fourth year at Hogwarts. GF 8, p. 106. Egypt was one of the natural habitats of the Phoenix. FB, p. 32. After graduating from Hogwarts, Elphias Doge experimented with the work of Egyptian alchemists. DH 2, p. 18. (Egypt is a country in Northeast Africa.)

Elder Wand. A magic wand that, according to wizard legend, was more powerful than any other. It was one of the Deathly Hallows and its origin was from The Tale of the Three Brothers. The tale appeared in *The Tales of Beedle the Bard.* Three brothers received gifts from Death: the Elder Wand, a wand more powerful than any other; the Resurrection Stone, a stone that could help bring back the dead; and the Cloak of Invisibility. DH 21, pp. 406-09. Some of the owners of the Elder Wand, who had to kill the previous owner to master it, were: Egbert the Egregious, Emeric the Evil, Godelot, Hereward, Loxias, Barnabas Deverill and perhaps Arcus or Livius. DH 21, p. 412. Harry Potter deduced the true whereabouts of the Elder Wand during year seven. DH 24, pp. 499-500. He then publicly announced the true owner of the Elder Wand. DH 36, p. 743.

Elephant and Castle. A location where a regurgitating public toilet was reported to the Ministry of Magic. This event occurred during the summer prior to Harry Potter's fifth year at Hogwarts. OP 7, p. 133. Elephant and Castle was also the location of a nasty backfiring jinx during the following year. HP 5, p. 87.

Elf. See **House Elf**.

Elfric the Eager. The person responsible for a historical uprising. Elfric's name appeared on the final examination for the History of Magic class during Harry Potter's first year at Hogwarts. SS 16, p. 263.

Elixir of Life. A magic liquid produced from the Sorcerer's Stone. The Elixir of Life made the person who drank it immortal. The only wizard ever known to have produced the Elixir of Life was Nicolas Flamel. SS 13, pp. 219-20. The elixir had to be drunk regularly, for all eternity, if the drinker was to maintain immortal. HP 23, p. 502.

Ellerby and Spudmore. A company located in the Black Forest and that manufactured quidditch brooms such as the Tinderblast and Swiftstick. QA 9, p. 50.

Emeric the Evil. A famous wizard who was studied by Harry Potter in a History of Magic class during his first year at Hogwarts. Students frequently confused Emeric the Evil with Uric the Oddball. SS 8, p. 133. Emeric was one of the reputed owners of the Elder Wand. He was killed by Egbert the Egregious in order to obtain the Elder Wand. DH 21, p. 412.

Enchantment in Baking. A book found on the mantelpiece of the Weasley residence. Two other books on the mantelpiece were *Charm Your Own Cheese* and *One Minute Feasts–It's Magic.* Harry Potter observed these books during the summer prior to his second year at Hogwarts. CS 3, p. 34.

Encyclopedia of Toadstools. A book that hit Lucius Malfoy in the eye during his brawl with Arthur Weasley in Flourish and Blotts. This event occurred during the summer prior to Harry Potter's second year at Hogwarts. CS 4, p. 63.

Engorgement Charm. A charm used to enlarge objects. CS 7, pp. 117-18. It was invoked with the magic word "*engorgio*" and its effects were reversed by the magic word "*reducio.*" GF 14, p. 214. Rubeus Hagrid used the charm to enlarge pumpkins for the Halloween feast at Hogwarts. This event occurred during Harry Potter's second year at the school. CS 7, p. 117. Fred Weasley applied the charm to some toffee as a joke. When the Weasley's arrived at the Dursley residence to take Harry to the Quidditch World Cup, Dudley Dursley ate the toffee and immediately his tongue swelled to one foot in length. Arthur Weasley tried to help Dudley before leaving for the game. Mad-Eye Moody demonstrated the Cruciatus Curse by invoking the Engorgement Charm on a spider. These two events occurred during the summer prior to and during Harry's fourth year at Hogwarts. GF 14, pp. 214-15. Harry used this charm during year seven to enlarge a spider. DH 20, p. 392.

Enlargement Charm. A charm that Fred and George Weasley placed on the front cover of an edition of *The Quibbler*, which edition featured an interview with Harry Potter. This event occurred during Harry's fifth year at Hogwarts. OP 26, p. 584.

Ennervate. The magic word used by Amos Diggory to place a charm on Winky. The charm compelled Winky to answer questions about her involvement in the appearance of the Dark Mark during the aftermath of the Quidditch World Cup. This event occurred during the summer prior to Harry's fourth year at Hogwarts. GF 9, p. 133. Albus Dumbledore also used the charm on Viktor Krum to determine how Barty Crouch had escaped from him near the Forbidden Forest that same year. GF 27, p. 560.

Entrail-Expelling Curse. A curse invented by Urquhart Rackharrow. OP 22, p. 487.

Entrancing Enchantment. An enchantment that Gilderoy Lockhart claimed Professor Flitwick knew more about than any other wizard. This event occurred on Valentine's Day of Harry Potter's second year at Hogwarts. CS 13, p. 236.

Episkey. The magic word used to invoke a Healing Spell capable of repairing a broken nose. HP 8, p. 157.

Erecto. The magic word used by Hermione Granger to invoke a charm that assembled a tent during year seven. DH 14, p. 273.

Eric. The security guard in the Atrium of the Ministry of Magic who held wands of witches and wizards for safekeeping. OP 7, p. 128.

Erised, Mirror of. See **Mirror of Erised**.

Erkling. An elfish creature that originated in the Black Forest of Germany. The German Ministry of Magic placed strict controls over the erkling in order to prevent them from killing and attacking people. FB, p. 15.

Errol. An ancient owl owned by the Weasley family. Ron Weasley used Errol to deliver letters to Harry Potter at the Dursley residence during the summer prior to Harry's second year at Hogwarts. The Weasley's other owl was named Hermes. Hermes was given to Percy as a present from his parents. CS 3, p. 30. Prior to Harry's fourth year at Hogwarts, Ron Weasley acquired a tiny gray owl who Ron nicknamed Pig. GF 3, p. 35.

Erumpent. A magical beast native to Africa. The Erumpent's horn, tail and Exploding Fluid were used in potions. FB, p. 16. Xenophilius Lovegood mounted one of the horns on a wall of his residence. According to Hermione Granger, an Erumpent's horn was a Class B Tradeable Material and very dangerous to have in a house because it could explode at the slightest touch. DH 20, p. 401.

Essence of Dittany. A potion for healing a splinch that was used by Hermione Granger to help Ron Weasley during year seven. A few drops of the potion poured directly on the skin, healed it on contact. DH 14, pp. 269-70.

Ethiopia. The Gimbi Giant-Slayers, a quidditch team, was from Ethiopia. QA 8, p. 43. (Ethiopia is a country in East Africa formerly known as Abyssinia.)

Eton. A school, unidentified as a wizarding school and probably a muggle school, that Justin Finch-Fletchley almost attended rather than Hogwarts. Justin informed Harry Potter of this fact while they replanted mandrakes in a Herbology class during Harry's second year at Hogwarts. CS 6, p. 94.

Euphoria. A potion that Harry Potter produced during his sixth year at Hogwarts. Based on the Half-Blood Prince's instructions, Harry added a sprig of peppermint, that tended to counterbalance the occasional side effects of excessive singing and nose-tweaking. HP 22, p. 475.

Europa. One of the moons around the planet Jupiter covered in ice. Europa was mentioned in an Astronomy essay that Harry Potter wrote during his fifth year at Hogwarts. OP 14, p. 300.

European Cup. The prize awarded to the best quidditch team in Europe. QA 7, p. 38. The event started in 1652 and was played every three years. QA 8, p. 40.

Evanesco. The magic word of a charm invoked by Bill Weasley to make scrolls vanish. This event occurred during the summer prior to Harry Potter's fifth year at Hogwarts. OP 5, p. 80. Severus Snape also used the charm to make Harry's failed Draught of Peace disappear that same year. OP 12, p. 234.

Evans, Lily. A student at Hogwarts who was a member of thr Gryffindor house and who later married James Potter. She was a mudblood. OP 28, pp. 647, 648. Horace Slughorn was one of her professors at Hogwarts and he considered her to be one of his brightest students. HP 4, p. 70. See **Potter, Lily.**

Evans, Mark. A ten-year old boy bullied by Dudley Dursley during the summer prior to Harry Potter's fifth year at Hogwarts. OP 1, p. 13.

Evening Prophet. The title of a late edition newspaper published in the wizarding world. The flight of Harry Potter and Ron Weasley in Arthur Weasley's Ford Anglia was reported in the *Evening Prophet.* This event occurred during Harry's second year at Hogwarts. CS 5, p 79. The other edition was known as the *Daily Prophet.* SS 5, p. 64.

Everard. A wizard and celebrated headmaster at Hogwarts prior to Albus Dumbledore's tenure as headmaster. Everard was the subject in one of the paintings in Albus' office and was sent by Albus to look for an injured Arthur Weasley. Everard was so revered that there were paintings of him in other important wizarding institutions. This event occurred during Harry Potter's fifth year at Hogwarts. OP 22, pp. 468-69. While he was the subject of a painting in Albus' office, Everard served as a messenger to the Ministry of Magic. HP 29, p. 627.

Ever-Bashing Boomerang. A magic boomerang included on Argus Filch's list of objects that were forbidden within Hogwarts. The list contained approximately 437 items and during Harry's fourth year the list was expanded to include not only Ever-Bashing Boomerangs, but Fanged Frisbees and Screaming Yo-yos as well. GF 12, p. 183.

Everlasting Elixirs. A subject that Harry Potter studied from reading *Advanced Potion-Making* during his sixth year at Hogwarts. HP 15, p. 305.

Everlasting Ink. Magical ink that did not fade with time. Everlasting Ink was used by witches and wizards to place short messages on the sign that sprang up on the Potter residence in Godric's Hollow. DH 17, p. 333.

Every Flavor Beans. DH 21, p. 406. See **Berty Botts Every Flavor Beans.**

Expecto patronum. The magic words used to invoke the Patronus Charm and produce a patronus. Remus Lupin taught Harry Potter this difficult charm during Harry's third year at Hogwarts. PA 12, p. 238. DH 13, p. 262.

Expelliarmus. The magic word used to invoke the Disarming Charm. The charm knocked someone off of his feet and removed his wand or other object from his hands. Severus Snape demonstrated this charm to the Dueling Club during Harry Potter's second year at Hogwarts. CS 11, p. 190; 13, p.239. During the third task of the Triwizard Tournament, Harry used the charm to subdue a huge spider. This event occurred during Harry's fourth year at the school. GF 31, p. 632. During year seven, Harry invoked thes charm against Stan Shunpike who chased him and Rubeus Hagrid as they fled from the Dursley residence. DH 4, p. 59. This was one of the last three charms invoked at the end of year seven; the others were Avada Kedavra and Reparo. DH 36, pp. 743, 749.

Experimental Charms. An office within the Ministry of Magic. During year seven, pamphlet-makers in Dolores Umbridge's office at the Ministry suspected the Decoy Detonator as having been carelessly let go by the Experimental Charms office. Apparently the office had previously let go a poisonous duck. DH 13, p. 253.

Exploding Snap. A game that Harry Potter looked forward to playing in Gryffindor house after most of the other students of Hogwarts left for Christmas during Harry's second year at Hogwarts. CS 12, pp. 210-211; CS 15, p. 271. The Weasley children also played the game aboard the Hogwarts Express on its return trip to Platform Nine and Three Quarters after the end of Harry's second and fourth years at Hogwarts. CS 18, p. 340; GF 37, p. 730. During his third year at the school, Neville Longbottom asked Harry to play this game when Harry attempted to run off to Hogsmeade. PA 14, p. 276. At the end of the fall term the following year, Ron Weasley built a card castle out of his pack of Exploding Snap and preferred it over muggle cards because it could explode at any time. GF 22, p. 392.

Expulso. The magic word for a charm used to explode an object. A Death Eater used the charm, which had the effect of exploding a table, during year seven. DH 9, p. 165.

Extendable Ear. A magical device invented by Fred and George Weasley that allowed a person to eavesdrop. An Extendable Ear looked like a piece of very long, flesh colored string. This event occurred during the summer prior to Harry Potter's fifth year at Hogwarts. OP 4, pp. 67-68. DH 12, p. 236.

Extension Charm. An undetectable charm used to place multiple large objects into a small container. Hermione Granger invoked the charm to deposit numerous items into a fragile-looking bag during year seven. DH 9, p.162.

Extinguishing Spell. A spell that the wizards who controlled the dragons for the first event of the Triwizard Tournament were prepared to use in order to subdue the dragons, presumably to put out any fire they caused. This event occurred during Harry Potter's fourth year at Hogwarts. GF 19, p. 328.

FABIAN - FWOOPER

Fabian. The wizard brother of Molly Weasley. During year seven, Mrs. Weasley gave Fabian's watch to Harry Potter on his seventeenth birthday, since that gift was traditional. The watch was gold with stars that circled around the face instead of hands. DH 7, p. 114.

Fainting Fancies. One of the chews invented by Fred and George Weasley that collectively were referred to as Skiving Snackboxes. Fred and George developed the candies during the summer prior to Harry Potter's fifth year at Hogwarts. Two of the other chews were Nosebleed Nougat and Puking Pastilles. OP 6, pp. 104-05.

Fairy. A magical beast that inhabited woodlands and glades. Fairies were preyed upon by augureys. FB, pp. 16-17.

Falmouth Falcons. A quidditch team in the league known for its rough play. QA 7, p. 34. Two of its players, Randolph Keitch and Basil Horton, founded the Comet Trading Company. QA 9, p. 49.

Fang. The name of Rubeus Hagrid's pet dog which was an enormous, black boarhound. SS 8, p. 140. DH 31, p. 618.

Fanged Frisbee. A magic frisbee included on Argus Filch's list of objects that were forbidden within Hogwarts. The list consisted of approximately 437 items and during Harry Potter's fourth year the list was expanded to include not only Fanged Frisbees but Ever-Bashing Boomerangs and Screaming Yo-yos as well. GF 12, p. 183. Fanged Frisbees continued to be banned during Harry's sixth year and Hermione Granger confiscated one that she found on a fourth year student. HP 8, p. 172.

Fanged Geranium. A plant that Harry Potter received a small bite from during the O.W.L. examination for Herbology. This event occurred during Harry's fifth year at Hogwarts. OP 31, p. 714.

Fantastic Beasts and Where to Find Them. The title of a book written by Newt Scamander. The book was required for first-year students during Harry Potter's first year at Hogwarts. SS 5, p. 66. Between Harry's fourth and fifth years at Hogwarts, the book was published in its fifty-second edition for the muggle world; it was first published for the wizarding world in 1927. The fifty-second edition of the book listed 75 different species of magical beasts. FB, pp. vi, ix and xxi. DH 20, p. 401.

Far East. The native habitat of the demiguise and the occamy. FB, pp. 9, 31.

Fat Friar. A resident ghost of Hogwarts who was affiliated with the Hufflepuff house. Harry Potter first observed the Fat Friar before the Sorting Ceremony commenced during Harry's first year at Hogwarts. SS 7, p. 115. At a ghost's council held during Harry's fourth year at Hogwarts, the Fat Friar voted to allow Peeves the opportunity to join the rest of the school in the feast that followed the Sorting Ceremony. However, the Bloody Baron opposed the idea and in retaliation Peeves wreaked havoc in the school's kitchen. GF 12, p. 181.

Fat Lady. A woman dressed in a pink dress who lived within a painting and allowed persons access through the painting, that opened like a door, to the Gryffindor house of Hogwarts. SS 7, p. 129. Access was gained through the use of a secret password that periodically changed. Passwords used to open the door were: Caput Draconis, SS 7, p. 130; Pig Snout, SS 9, p. 156; Wattlebird, CS 5, p. 84; and Fortuna Major, PA 5, p. 94. When Sir Cadogan took over the post during the Fat Lady's absence, he invented the following passwords: Scurvy Cur, PA 11, p. 230, and Oddsbodikins, PA 12, p. 249. Later, the Fat Lady used the following words: Flibbertigibbet, PA 15, p. 295; Balderdash, GF 12, p. 191; Fairy Lights, GF 22, p. 398; and Banana Fritters, GF 24, p. 459. At the beginning of Harry Potter's fifth year at Hogwarts, the magic words to gain entrance to the Gryffindor tower were "Mimbulus mimbletonia." OP 11, p. 216. The following school year, the students used "Dilligrout," and "Baubles" as the secret passwords. HP 12, p. 256; 15, p. 308. After the Christmas vacation that year, the new password was abstinence. HP 17, p. 351. During March the password was "tapeworm." HP 23, p. 493. Another password later that year was "quid agis." HP 24, p. 533. DH 33, p. 675.

Father Christmas. Statues of Father Christmas and his reindeer were part of the decorations for the Yule Ball. The decorations also included hundreds of fairies sitting in conjured rosebushes. The scene was displayed in a grotto on the lawn in front of Hogwarts. This event occurred during Harry Potter's fourth year at Hogwarts. GF 23, p. 413. DH 14, p. 279. See also **Santa Claus**.

Fawcett, Miss S. A student of Hogwarts who attended the first meeting of the Dueling Club and received the encouragement of the club's instructor, Gilderoy Lockhart, to pinch something to make one of her body part's stop bleeding. CS 11, p. 192. Miss Fawcett was a member of the Ravenclaw house. GF 16, p. 260. During Harry Potter's fourth year at Hogwarts, Miss Fawcett attempted to use an Aging Potion in order to qualify for the Triwizard Tournament and failed. Other students who tried the same trick and failed as well were Fred and George Weasley and Mr. Summers of Hufflepuff. GF 16, p. 260. At the Yule Ball, Severus Snape took ten points away from the Ravenclaw house because he caught Miss Fawcett in the rosebushes with Mr. Stebbins. This event occurred during Harry's fourth year at Hogwarts. GF 23, p. 426. Miss Fawcett's name appeared on the list of borrowers found inside the cover of *Quidditch Through the Ages.* QA, p. i.

Fawcetts. A family of wizards who lived in the vicinity of Stoatshead Hill and could not get tickets for the Quidditch World Cup. This event occurred during the summer prior to Harry Potter's fourth year at Hogwarts. GF 6, p. 73.

Fawkes. A phoenix that was Albus Dumbledore's pet and that was kept in the headmaster's office at Hogwarts. Fawkes was instrumental in saving Harry Potter from the Chamber of Secrets. CS 12, p. 206; 17, p. 315. The magic wands of Harry Potter and Lord Voldemort each contained a feather from Fawkes. GF 35, p. 697. Like other birds of its kind, Fawkes' tears had special healing powers. GF 35, p. 698. Fawkes left Hogwarts at the end of Harry's sixth year. HP 29, p. 632. DH 33, p. 683.

Felix Felicis. A power that made a wizard lucky. If taken too often, it caused the wizard to feel giddy, reckless and dangerously overconfident. HP 9, p. 187.

Fenwick, Benjy. A wizard who was a member of the Order of the Phoenix. Benjy was killed fighting for the Order and only bits of him were ever found. OP 9, p. 174.

Ferrari. A make of car manufactured in the muggle world. Harry Potter doubted that Vernon Dursley would have liked the Weasleys even if they came to pick him up for the Quidditch World Cup in a Ferrari. GF 4, p. 41.

Ferula. A magic word that Remus Lupin used to conjure bandages for Ron Weasley's broken leg. This event occurred during Harry Potter's third year at Hogwarts. PA 19, p. 376.

Fever Fudge. A trick food that Fred and George Weasley invented during Harry Potter's fifth year at Hogwarts. The formula was not perfected, however, because in addition to raising one's temperature, it also produced boils on one's bottom. OP 18, pp. 378-79.

Fidelius Charm. A complex charm used to store a secret in someone who was known as a secret-keeper. The secret could not be wrenched out of the secret-keeper unless he chose to tell it. When James and Lilly Potter found out that Lord Voldemort was after them, Dumbledore suggested the Fidelius Charm to them. PA 10, p. 205. Dumbledore was the secret-keeper for the location of the Order of the Phoenix. The strength of the charm was diluted if the secret was split among too many wizards. DH 6, p. 90.

Fiendfyre. A fire caused by a curse that was capable of following a person and acted like an animal. Vincent Crabbe invoked the curse in the Room of Requirement during year seven. Fiendfyre was one of only a few substances that was capable of destroying a Horcrux. DH 31, p. 635.

Figg, Mrs. Arabella Doreen. A mad old lady who lived two streets away from the Dursley household. The Dursleys forced Harry Potter to stay with Mrs. Figg while the Dursley's celebrated Dudley's birthday each year. Mrs. Figg's cats were named Tibbles, Snowy, Mr. Paws and Tufty. SS 2, p. 22. Harry also had to stay with her while the Dursleys went on trips. GF 7, p. 79. Albus Dumbledore referred to Mrs. Figgs as one of the "old crowd." She was a friend of Albus and Sirius Black. Albus mentioned her name after Cornelius Fudge refused to believe that Lord Voldemort was back and there was a parting of the ways between Albus and Fudge. GF 36, p. 713. This event occurred during Harry's fourth year at Hogwarts. Mrs. Figg was a squib. OP 2, p. 20. Her full name was stated at Harry's disciplinary hearing at the Wizengamot. This event occurred during the summer prior to Harry's fifth year at Hogwarts. OP 8, p. 143.

Fiji. The native habitat of the Firecrab. A stretch of coast on Fiji was made into a reservation for the protection of Firecrabs. FB, p. 17. (Fiji is an independent archipelago consisting of about 800 islands in the South Pacific Ocean, north of New Zealand.)

Filch, Argus. The caretaker of Hogwarts. Filch owned a cat named Mrs. Norris who patrolled the corridors of the school looking for students who broke the rules. SS 7, p. 127; 8, p. 132. Filch had his own office at Hogwarts. He admitted to being a squib during Harry Potter's second year at the school. CS 8, p. 125; 9, p. 142. He maintained a list of forbidden objects within the school. The list consisted of 437 items and during Harry's fourth year the list was expanded to include Screaming Yo-yos, Fanged Frisbees and Ever-Bashing Boomerangs.

GF 12, p. 183. Filch's predecessor was Apollyon Pringle. GF 31, p. 616. DH 13, p. 251; 30, p. 602.

Filibuster, Dr. The name associated with Dr. Filibuster's Fabulous, Wet-Start, No-Heat Fireworks. CS 4, p. 58. Fred and George Weasley and Lee Jordan purchased some of the fireworks from the Gambol and Japes Wizarding Joke Shop on Diagon Alley. This event occurred during the summer prior to Harry Potter's second year at Hogwarts. CS 4, p. 58.

Filibuster's Fabulous No-Heat, Wet-Start Fireworks. Fireworks that Fred Weasley hid in his suitcase prior to the start of Harry Potter's fourth year at Hogwarts. The suitcase was placed in a muggle taxi and the fireworks accidentally exploded. GF 11, p. 162. See also **Dr. Filibuster's Fabulous, Wet-Start, No-Heat Fireworks**.

Filius. A witch or wizard who was a member of the Order of the Phoenix and probably was Professor Flitwick. Minerva McGonagall sent Filius to get Severus Snape to help fight Death Eaters who had entered Hogwarts at the end of Harry Potter's sixth year at the school. HP 29, p. 616.

Finch-Fletchley, Justin. A student sorted by the Sorting Hat during Harry Potter's first year at Hogwarts. Justin was a member of the Hufflepuff house. SS 7, p. 120. He almost attended the Eton school and was muggle-born. CS 6, p. 94; 11, p. 198. Justin became frightened of Harry after Harry spoke parseltongue in an effort to save him from a snake at the Dueling Club meeting. CS 11, pp. 198-99. Justin was the second person attacked after the Chamber of Secrets was reopened. CS 11, p. 202. These events occurred during Harry's second year at Hogwarts. During Harry's fourth year, Justin refused to talk to Harry in Herbology class as a result of Harry being selected as a school champion for the Triwizard Tournament. GF 18, p. 293.

Fingal the Fearless. A champion aingingein player who lived in Ireland. QA 1, pp. 4-5.

Finite. The magic word for a charm that stopped another charm from working. Remus Lupin invoked the charm to assist Neville Longbottom in the Department of Mysteries during Harry Potter's fifth year at Hogwarts. OP 36, p. 808. Harry invoked the charm to stop a tower of furniture and other objects from collapsing in the Room of Requirement during year seven. DH 31, p. 629.

Finite Incantatem. The magic words for a charm that Hermione Granger suggested Ron Weasley use to stop rain from falling inside a room at the Ministry of Magic, if the source of the rain was a hex or curse. DH 12, p. 244.

Finkley, Barnabus. The wizard for whom a certain prize, named the Barnabus Finkley Prize for Exceptional Spell-Casting, was awarded to Albus Dumbledore when he was a student at Hogwarts. DH 18, p. 353.

Finnigan, Fergus. A cousin of Seamus Finnigan who was older than Seamus and apparated just to annoy Seamus who was too young to learn the skill yet. HP. 17, p. 355.

Finnigan, Mrs. The mother of Seamus Finnigan. Mrs. Finnigan was a witch, but didn't tell her husband until after they were married. SS 4, p. 125. She accompanied Seamus to the Quidditch World Cup and was annoyed that the Ministry of Magic did not like the fact that her tent was decorated with shamrocks to show pride for the quidditch team from Ireland. This event occurred during the summer prior to Harry Potter's fourth year at Hogwarts. GF 7, p. 82.

Finnigan, Seamus. A student sorted by the Sorting Hat during Harry Potter's first year at Hogwarts. Seamus was a member of the Gryffindor house. He was a mudblood because his father was a muggle and his mother a witch. SS 7, pp. 120, 125. During a Defense Against Dark Arts class in which the students were asked to repel a bogart in a wardrobe, Seamus revealed that his greatest fear was a banshee. This event occurred during Harry's third year at Hogwarts. PA 7, p. 137. DH 29, p. 571. Seamus' patronus took the form of a silver fox. DH 32, p. 649.

Firebolt. A state-of-the-art racing broom that had a streamlined, superfine ash handle and was treated with a diamond-hard polish. The Firebolt had its own registration number and each birch twig in the tail was individually selected. It was billed as aerodynamically perfect, with unsurpassable balance and pinpoint precision. It could reach 150 miles per hour in ten seconds and incorporated an unbreakable Braking Charm. PA 4, p. 51. Harry Potter first observed the Firebolt in Quality Quidditch Supplies before the start of his third year at Hogwarts. PA 4, p. 51. That same school year he received a Firebolt as a Christmas present from an anonymous person who was later revealed to him. PA 11, p. 223; 22, p. 432. The Firebolt was an international standard broomstick. OP 3, p. 53. Harry still had the Firebolt with him at the beginning of year seven. DH 4, p. 43.

Fire-Crab. A creature that, when crossed with a manticore, made a blast-ended skrewt. This information was conveyed in a *Daily Prophet* article written by Rita Skeeter during Harry Potter's fourth year at Hogwarts. GF 24, p. 438. The firecrab was native to Fiji. FB, p. 17.

Firenze. A palomino centaur who lived in the Forbidden Forest and saved Harry Potter from a beast that was drinking the blood of a dead unicorn. This event occurred during Harry's first year at Hogwarts.

SS 15, pp. 256-57. Albus Dumbledore appointed Firenze as the professor to teach the Divination classes after Dolores Umbridge fired Sibyl Trelawney. This event occurred during Harry's fifth year at Hogwarts. OP 26, p. 598. Firenze split the classes of Divination the following school year, and Sibyl took the sixth-year class. HP 9, p. 174. DH 31, p. 608.

Firewhisky. A beverage that Harold Dingle offered to sell students firewhisky during Harry Potter's fifth year at Hogwarts. OP 31, p. 708; 32, p. 738. It was also used to toast the death of a member of the Order of the Phoenix during year seven. DH 5, p. 79.

Fitchburg Finches. A quidditch team from Massachusetts that won the U.S. League seven times. Maximus Brankovitch, III was the Finches' well-known seeker. QA 8, p. 45.

Fizzing Whizbees. Levitating sherbet balls that were filled with strawberry mousse and clotted cream and sold at Honeydukes in Hogsmeade. Harry Potter observed Fizzing Whizbees at Honeydukes during his third year at Hogwarts. PA 10, p. 197. Rubeus Hagrid gave Harry a box of candy, including Fizzing Whizbees, as a Christmas present during Harry's fourth year at Hogwarts. GF 23, p. 410. During Harry's fifth year at the school, "Fizzing Whizbee" was the magic password to gain access to the staircase leading to Albus Dumbledore's office at Hogwarts. OP 22, p. 466; 27; p. 609.

Flacking. The name of one of the ten most common fouls committed in quidditch. QA 6, p. 30.

Flagrante Curse. One of two curses, the other being the Gemino Curse, used by goblins at Gringotts Wizarding Bank to prevent treasure from being stolen. When applied to an object, the curse caused an object to burn the person who touched it and the object multiplied itself into worthless copies. DH 26, p. 537.

Flagrate. The magic word for a charm that Hermione Granger used to place a fiery "X" on a door in the Department of Mysteries. This event occurred during Harry Potter's fifth year at Hogwarts. OP 34, p. 772.

Flame Freezing Charm. A charm used by witches from the fourteenth century to pretend that they were being burned when subjected to witch burning. It actually tickled. Harry Potter learned about the charm when he worked on a homework assignment prior to his third year at Hogwarts. PA 1, p. 2.

Flamel, Nicolas. The alchemy partner of Albus Dumbledore. Nicolas was also the only known maker and owner of the Sorcerer's Stone. SS 6, p. 103; 13, p. 219. During Harry Potter's first year at Hogwarts, Nicolas was 665 years old and lived with his wife Perenelle, herself 658 years old, in Devon. Nicolas was an opera lover. SS 13, p. 220. Albus and Nicolas shared regular correspondence. DH 2, p. 17.

Flamel, Perenelle. The wife of Nicolas Flamel, who lived with Nicolas in Devon. During Harry Potter's first year at Hogwarts, Perenelle was 658 years old. SS 13, p. 220.

Flanders. The home country of a quidditch team that played in the final match of the first Quidditch World Cup held in 1473. QA 9, pp. 39-40. The other team was from Transylvania. (Flanders was a medieval country in Western Europe that extended along the North Sea from the Strait of Dover to the Scheldt River. In modern times, the region is found in part of West Belgium.)

Fleet, Angus. A person who lived in Peebles and observed a flying car. Angus' account of the incident was reported in the *Evening Prophet.* The vehicle was driven by Ron Weasley with his passenger, Harry Potter. Another person who witnessed the same incident was Hetty Bayliss. This event occurred during the summer prior to Harry's second year at Hogwarts. CS 5, p. 79.

Fleetwood's High-Finish Handle Polish. An item included in the Broomstick Servicing Kit given by Hermione Granger to Harry Potter as a thirteenth birthday present. The kit also included a pair of shiny silver Tail-Twig Clippers, a tiny brass compass and a copy of *Handbook of Do-It-Yourself Broomcare.* This event occurred during Harry's third year at Hogwarts. PA 1, p. 12.

Flesh Memory. See **Snitch, Golden**.

Flesh-Eating Trees of the World. A book that Hermione Granger used to study the Snargaluff during Herbology Class. This event occurred during Harry Potter's sixth year at Hogwarts. HP 14, p. 283.

Fletcher, Mundungus (Dung). A wizard who attempted to put a hex on Arthur Weasley while Arthur was on an assignment for the Ministry of Magic. This event occurred during the summer prior to Harry Potter's second year at Hogwarts. CS 3, p. 38. Mundungus attended the Quidditch World Cup and submitted a claim to the Ministry of Magic for the cost to replace a twelve-bedroom tent with an en-suite jacuzzi that was damaged during the aftermath of the sporting event. Percy Weasley stated that this claim was a fraud because Mundungus slept under a cloak propped on sticks. This event occurred during the summer prior to Harry's fourth year at Hogwarts. GF 10, p. 151. Albus Dumbledore referred to Mundungus as one of the "old crowd" who was a friend to Sirius Black and himself. Albus mentioned Mundungus' name after Cornelius Fudge refused to believe that Lord Voldemort was back and there was a parting of the ways between Albus and Cornelius. GF 36, p. 713. This event occurred during Harry's fourth year at the school. Mundungus was derelict in his duty to watch over Harry in Little Whinging during the summer prior to Harry's fifth year at Hogwarts. OP 1, p. 19. Mundungus was an unreliable member of the Order of the Phoenix and knew all the crooks because he was one himself. OP 5, pp. 81, 86. During Harry's sixth year at Hogwarts, Mundungus was arrested by the Ministry of Magic and sent to Azkaban. HP 21, p. 457. By the beginning of year seven, Mundungus was free and appeared with other members of the Order of the Phoenix to escort Harry from the Dursley residence. DH 4, p. 46. At that time, Mundungus took Polyjuice Potion to look like Harry and left the residence on a broomstick with Mad-Eye Moody. DH 4, p. 52.

Flesh-Eating Slug Repellent. A product that repelled slugs. Rubeus Hagrid attempted to purchase the product on Knockturn Alley in order to prevent slugs from eating the cabbages at Hogwarts. This event occurred during Harry Potter's second year at Hogwarts. CS 4, p. 55.

Flibbertigibbet. A password used to gain access to the Gryffindor house during Harry Potter's third year at Hogwarts. The password was spoken to the Fat Lady. PA 15, p. 295.

Flint, Marcus. A student who was captain of the Slytherin quidditch team at Hogwarts during Harry Potter's first year there. Marcus was a sixth year student that year. SS 10, p. 185. He was also captain of that team during Harry's second and third years at the school. CS 7, p. 110; PA 13, p. 263. Marcus's name appeared on the list of borrowers found inside the cover of *Quidditch Through the Ages*. QA, p. i.

Flitterbloom. A harmless plant that Broderick Bode thought he was looking after at St. Mungo's Hospital for Magical Maladies and Injuries. However, the plant was actually Devil's Snare and killed him. OP 25, p. 547.

Flitwick, Professor (Filius). The professor of the Charms class at the time Harry Potter attended Hogwarts. Professor Flitwick was a tiny little wizard who had to stand on a pile of books to see over his desk. SS 8, p. 133. His office was located on the seventh floor of the school and the office's window was thirteenth from the right of the West Tower. Sirius Black was locked in the office after being captured on the school grounds during Harry's third year at Hogwarts. PA 21, p. 393. Professor Flitwick was the Head of House of Ravenclaw. HP 18, p. 382. He was injured during a battle with Death Eaters at the end of Harry's sixth year at Hogwarts. HP 29, p. 612. Professor Flitwick's first name was probably Filius. HP 29, p. 618. DH 29, p. 584; 30, p. 598.

Flobberworm. A magical creature that Rubeus Hagrid demonstrated to his Care of Magical Creatures class during Harry Potter's third year at Hogwarts. PA 6, p. 121. Harry considered the flobberworm to be the most boring creature in existence. Its diet included shredded lettuce. PA 8, p. 142. Draco Malfoy was quoted in the *Daily Prophet* as saying that Vincent Goyle received a bad bite from a flobberworm, even though the creatures had no teeth. GF 24, pp. 438, 440.

Floo Network. The network of interconnected magic chimney flues that wizards and witches used for transportation. Arthur Weasley connected the Dursley fireplace flue to the network just for an afternoon through the help of a friend at the Floo Regulation Panel so that the Weasleys could pick up Harry Potter for the Quidditch World Cup. This event occurred during the summer prior to Harry's fourth year at Hogwarts. GF 4, p. 45. Two years later, the Ministry of Magic convinced the Floo Network to allow a one-off connection for Harry, Rn and Ginny to together be transported to Hogwarts. This event occurred as their Christmas vacation ended that year. HP 17, p. 549. During year seven, Pius Thicknesse made it an imprisonable offense to connect the Dursley residence to the Floo Network. DH 4, p. 46.

Floo Powder. Magic powder used by wizards and witches to travel from one fireplace to another. CS 4, p. 47. One threw the powder into a fire, waited until it turned emerald green, stepped into the fire and then shouted the name of the destination fireplace. Harry Potter first used floo powder on his way to Diagon Alley prior to his second year at Hogwarts. CS 4, pp. 47-49. The Weasley family used floo powder to pick up Harry at the Dursley home for the Quidditch World Cup. This event occurred during the summer prior to Harry's fourth year at Hogwarts. GF 4, p. 42.

Floo Network Authority. An office in the Department of Magical Transport located on level six of the Ministry of Magic. OP 7, p. 129.

Floo Network Regulator. A witch or wizard who worked for the Floo Network Authority. OP 28, p. 631.

Floo Regulation Panel. A panel presumably located within the Ministry of Magic. Arthur Weasley connected the Dursley fireplace flue to the Floo Network just for an afternoon through the help of one of Arthur's friends at the Floo Regulation Panel so that the Weasleys could pick up Harry Potter for the Quidditch World Cup. This event occurred during the summer prior to Harry's fourth year at Hogwarts. GF 4, p. 45.

Florean Fortescue's Ice Cream Parlor. An ice cream parlor located on Diagon Alley. Harry Potter frequented the shop and received free sundaes every half-hour from its owner. This event occurred when Harry was temporarily housed at the Leaky Cauldron during the summer prior to his third year at Hogwarts. PA 4, p. 50.

Florence. A student of Hogwarts who attended the school at the same time as Bertha Jorkins. According to Albus Dumbledore's pensieve, Bertha complained that someone placed a hex on her because she teased that person about kissing Florence behind the greenhouse at the school. Harry Potter learned this information during his fourth year at Hogwarts GF 30, p. 599.

Flourish and Blotts. A bookstore on Diagon Alley where wizard students purchased their school books. SS 5, p. 80. Harry Potter first visited the bookstore during the summer prior to his first year at Hogwarts. DH 8, p. 153.

Fluffy. The name given by Rubeus Hagrid to a three-headed dog that guarded a trapdoor on the third floor of Hogwarts. Hagrid purchased the animal from a Greek man he met in a pub. Fluffy was fierce, but was easily lulled to sleep with music. These events occurred during Harry's first year at Hogwarts. SS 9, p. 160; 11, p. 192; 16, p. 266.

Flume, Ambrosius. An employee of Honeydukes during the summer prior to Harry Potter's sixth year at Hogwarts. Ambrosius was a former student of Horace Slughorn and sent Horace a hamper every birthday as appreciation for having gotten him an interview with Ciceron Harkiss. HP 4, p. 71.

Flutterby Bush. A plant that Hermione Granger pruned in a Herbology class before the first event of the Triwizard Tournament. This event occurred during Harry Potter's fourth year at Hogwarts. GF 19, p. 345. DH 6, p. 106.

Fluxweed. A plant used as an ingredient in Polyjuice Potion, provided that the fluxweed was picked at the full moon. Hermione Granger read the ingredients of the potion from *Most Potent Potions* to Harry Potter and Ron Weasley. This event occurred during Harry's second year at Hogwarts. CS 10, pp. 165-66.

Flying with the Cannons. The title of a book that Ron Weasley gave as a Christmas present to Harry Potter. This event occurred during Harry's second year at Hogwarts. The book contained interesting facts about Ron's favorite quidditch team, the Chudley Cannons. CS 12, p. 212. Around the Christmas season of his fourth year at Hogwarts, Harry read this book for the tenth time. GF 22, p. 392.

Flying Charm. The charm applied to broomsticks in order to make them fly. OP 14, p. 290.

Flyte and Barker. A quidditch company that manufactured the Twigger 90 in 1990. The Twigger 90 had such features as the Warning Whistle and Self-Straightening Brush. QA 9, p. 51.

Foe-Glass. A magic device, considered a Dark Detector, that Mad-Eye Moody kept in his office at Hogwarts. Foe-Glass looked like a mirror, except that rather than reflect the objects of the room it was in, it revealed moving, shadowy figures that were out of focus. If they came into focus, it was a warning sign to the owner of the device.

Harry Potter observed a foe-glass in Mad-Eye's office during his fourth year at Hogwarts. GF 19, p. 343.

Ford. The make of an automobile that Arthur Weasley drove and modified with magic so that it could fly. The model of the Ford was an Anglia and it was capable of holding many pieces of luggage in its trunk. Harry Potter rode in the Ford with seven members of the Weasley family prior to his second year at Hogwarts. CS 5, p. 66.

Forbidden Forest. The forest around Hogwarts. It was dangerous and generally considered off limits to students because of the creatures that lived in it. SS 15, p. 248. DH 14, p. 268; 32, p. 639.

Forbisher, Vicky. A student at Hogwarts who was a member of the Gryffindor house and tried out for the keeper position on the Gryffindor team that Ron Weasley finally won. Vicky was involved in all sorts of societies, including the Charms Club. This event occured during Harry Potter's fifth year at Hogwarts. OP 13, p. 276.

Forest of Dean. A forest that Hermione Granger and her parents once camped in and in which she and Harry Potter also camped during year seven. A frozen pool in the forest held the Sword of Gryffindor. DH 19, p. 364. (The Forest of Dean is located in Gloucestershire, England.)

Fortescue, Dexter. One of the former headmasters of Hogwarts, who had a distinctive ear-trumpet. His portrait hung on the wall of the headmaster's office. DH 36, p. 747.

Fortescue, Florean. The owner of Florean Fortescue's Ice Cream Parlor that was located on Diagon Alley. Florean helped Harry Potter on his witch-burning essays. This event occurred when Harry was temporarily housed at the Leaky Cauldron during the summer prior to his third year at Hogwarts. PA 4, p. 50. Florean was dragged off by Death Eaters during the summer prior to Harry's sixth year at Hogwarts. HP 6, p. 106.

Fortuna Major. A password used to gain access to the Gryffindor house of Hogwarts during Harry Potter's third year at Hogwarts. It was the first password used by the Fat Lady that school year. PA 5, p. 94.

Four-Point Spell. A spell that made a wand point to true north. Harry Potter learned this spell and used it against a blast-ended skrewt in the third task of the Triwizard Tournament during his fourth year at Hogwarts. GF 31, p. 608; 31, p. 626.

Fountain of Magical Brethren. The title of the fountain in the center of the Atrium of the Ministry of Magic. The fountain included golden, larger than life-size figures of a wizard, witch, centaur, goblin and a house-elf. Coins thrown into the fountain were given to St. Mungo's Hospital for Magical Maladies and Injuries. OP 7, p. 127.

Fowl or Foul? A Study of Hippogriff Brutality. The title of a book that Ron Weasley consulted. Ron hoped the book would help in the appeal, on behalf of Buckbeak, that he prepared for the Committee for the Disposal of Dangerous Creatures. This event occurred during Harry Potter's third year at Hogwarts. PA 15, p. 300.

France. The Quiberon Quafflepunchers, a frequent League winner in quidditch, was from France. QA 8, p. 40. Fleur Delacourt had originally decided to marry Bill Weasley in France, but changed her mind during year seven. DH 5, p. 82.

Freshwater Plimpies. A fish that was found in a stream near Xenophilius Lovegood's residence. DH 20, p. 402.

Fridwulfa. The mother of Rubeus Hagrid who was a giant and left Hagrid when he was only three years old. GF 27, pp. 427-28, 439. It was reported that Fridwulfa fled to a foreign mountain range after many of the giants in Britain who joined Lord Voldemort were killed off by aurors. Harry Potter learned this information during his fourth year at Hogwarts. GF 24, p. 439.

Frog Spawn Soup. A joke device sold at Zonko's Joke Shop in Hogsmeade. Harry Potter and Ron Weasley purchased the device from Zonko's during Harry's third year at Hogwarts. PA 14, p. 278.

Fubster, Colonel. A friend of Marge Dursley who watched Marge's bulldogs, except for Ripper, when Marge came to visit the Dursley family. This event occurred during the summer prior to Harry Potter's third year at Hogwarts. PA 2, p. 23.

Fudge, Cornelius Oswald. A wizard who was the head of the Ministry of Magic. SS 5, p. 65; CS 14, pp. 260-61; PA 3, p. 43. Cornelius usually wore a green bowler hat and a pin-stripped cloak. He was the Junior Minister of the Department of Magical Catastrophes when Sirius Black purportedly murdered Peter Pettigrew and twelve muggles outside the Potter home. Harry Potter learned this information while eavesdropping on a conversation between Cornelius and Minerva McGonagell in the Three Broomsticks during Harry's third year at Hogwarts. PA 10, p. 208. Cornelius was an interrogator during Harry Potter's disciplinary hearing held at the Wizengamot. This event occurred during the summer prior to Harry's fifth year at Hogwarts. OP 8, p. 138. *The Quibbler*, quoting an unnamed source, reported that Cornelius' nickname among his friends was "Goblin-Crusher" because of his hatred of goblins. OP 10, pp. 192-93. Part of Cornelius' official title was Order of Merlin First Class. OP 19, p. 415. Cornelius was removed from office the summer prior to Harry's sixth year at Hogwarts, and was replaced by Rufus Scrimgeour. HP 1, p. 15. DH 35, p. 717.

Fudge Flies. Candy that the students of the Gryffindor house ate during the celebration of the house quidditch team's victory over the Ravenclaw house. This event occurred during Harry Potter's third year at Hogwarts. PA 13, p. 265.

Furnunculus. The magic word used by Harry Potter in a charm that he intended to throw on Draco Malfoy after Draco called Hermione Granger a mudblood during a Potions class. The light from Harry's wand hit light from Draco's wand and Harry's charm landed on Gregory Goyle instead. The charm caused great ugly boils to appear on Goyle's nose. This event occurred during Harry's fourth year at Hogwarts. GF 18, p. 299.

Furnunculus Charm. A charm that, when mixed with the Jelly-Legs Jinx, caused a person's face to sprout little tentacles. Harry Potter invoked this charm against Vincent Crabbe at the same time that George Weasley invoked the Jelly-Legs Jinx. This event occurred on the Hogwarts Express on the way home from Harry's fourth year at Hogwarts. GF 37, p. 730.

Fwooper. An African bird whose song eventually drove the listener of it insane. FB, pp. xi; 18. Owners of fwoopers were required to have a licence. The birds were sold with Silencing Charms that needed to be reinforced each month. FB, p. 18. Uric the Oddball unsuccessfully tried to convince the Wizards' Council that the fwooper song was healthy. FB, p. 18, fn. 8.

GADDING WITH GHOULS - GWENOG

Gadding with Ghouls. The title of a book written by Gilderoy Lockhart. The book was required for second-year students during Harry Potter's second year at Hogwarts. CS 4, p. 43.

Gaddley. A place in Great Britain where a muggle family of five was found dead. The muggle authorities suspected a gas leak as the cause of death, but members of the Order of the Phoenix suspected that the muggles were murdered by the Killing Curse. DH 22, p. 439.

Galleon. A gold coin used in the wizarding world. Seventeen silver sickles equaled a galleon and 29 knuts equaled a sickle. SS 5, p. 75. Arthur Weasley won a prize of 700 galleons from the *Daily Prophet* during the summer prior to Harry Potter's third year at Hogwarts. PA 1, p. 8. During the Quidditch World Cup, Arthur bet Ludo Bagman a galleon that Ireland would win. Fred and George Weasley also bet Ludo Bagman 37 galleons, 15 sickles and three knuts (plus one of their fake wands) that not only would Ireland win but that Viktor Krum would get the snitch. Ludo was so impressed with the quality of the fake wand that he said it was worth five galleons. These events occurred during the summer prior to Harry's fourth year at Hogwarts. GF 7, p. 88. A pair of omniocculars at the Quidditch World Cup cost ten galleons. GF 7, p. 93. The personal prize money offered to the champion of the Triwizard Tournament was 1,000 galleons. GF 12, p. 188. At the time that Albus Dumbledore wrote his foreword for *Quidditch Through the Ages*, 34,000,000 galleons were equivalent to $250,000,000 or £174,000,000. QA, p. vii. At a quidditch match conducted in 1269, Bartemus Bragge offered to award 150 galleons to the wizard who caught a snidget placed on the field. Madam Modesty Rabnott was fined ten galleons for saving the snidget from the game. QA 4, pp. 12-13. The Ministry of Magic promised to pay a 10,000 galleon bounty for the capture of Sirius Black. OP 5, p. 94. Harry promised to throw ten galleons into the Fountain of Magical Brethren if he was acquitted at his disciplinary hearing. This event occurred during the summer prior to Harry's fifth year at Hogwarts. OP 7, p. 128. Fred and George paid ten galleons for a handful of Venomous Tentacula seeds from Mundungus Fletcher. OP 9, p. 171. Fred and George sold their Headless Hats for two galleons each. OP 24, p. 540. A Metamorph-Medal sold for ten galleons during the summer prior to Harry's sixth year at Hogwarts. HP 5, p. 87. That same summer a new copy of the text book *Advanced Potion-Making* cost nine galleons. HP 11, p 220. Twelve apparation lessons, offered by the Ministry of Magic to Hogwarts students, were 12 galleons. HP 17, p. 354. A suit of goblin-made armor owned by Hepzabah Smith was worth at least 500 galleons. HP 20, p. 435. A pint of acromantula venom was worth about 100 galleons. HP 22, p. 480. A single strand of unicorn hair was worth ten galleons. HP 22, p. 487. DH 2, p. 24. The Ministry of Magic placed a bounty of 10,000 galleons on Harry Potter during year seven. DH 12, p. 231.

Gambol and Japes Wizarding Joke Shop. A joke shop located on Diagon Alley. CS 4, p. 58. In the shop, Fred and George Weasley and Lee Jordan purchased Dr. Filibuster's Fabulous Wet-Start, No-Heat Fireworks. This event occurred during the summer prior to Harry Potter's second year at Hogwarts. CS 4, p. 58.

Ganymede. The largest moon around the planet Jupiter. Ganymede was part of an Astronomy essay written by Ron Weasley during Harry Potter's fifth year at Hogwarts. OP 14, p. 295.

Gargoyle. A magical creature. A large and extremely ugly stone gargoyle led to Dumbledore's office at Hogwarts. Harry Potter discovered the passageway during his second year at Hogwarts. CS 11, p. 204. Lemon Drop was a password for opening the secret passageway. Two years later, Harry tried to use the password "sherbet lemon" on the passageway, thinking it was the password he had used before. He assumed that the password must have been changed when the door did not open. GF 27, p. 557. Harry then tried several candy names on the door until "cockroach cluster" finally worked as the password. GF 29, p. 579. During his sixth year, "toffee eclairs" was the password. HP 20, p. 426.

Garroting Gas. A joke device that Fred and George Weasley intended to use at Hogwarts, but never did so. Ginny Weasley used the fictitious release of garroting gas as a means to divert students away from a corridor in the school. These events occurred during Harry Potter's fifth year at Hogwarts. OP 31, p. 737.

Gaunt. A very ancient wizarding family noted for a vein of instability and violence that flourished for generations due to their habit of marrying their own cousins. Several generations before Marvolo Gaunt was born, the family squandered their gold and Marvolo lived in poverty. HP 10, p. 212. The Gaunt shack was the hiding place of one of the Horcruxes formed by Voldemort. DH 27, p. 550.

Gaunt, Marvolo. A wizard who lived near Little Hangleton. Marvolo was the father of Merope and Morfin Gaunt and the grandfather of Lord Voldemort. Marvolo spoke Parseltongue and was a pure-blood wizard. HP 10, pp. 199, 200. He and his two children, Merope (who was Voldemort's mother) and Morfin, were the last living relatives of Salazar Slytherin. HP 10, pp. 208, 212. Marvolo was sentenced to six months in Azkaban for injuring several Ministry of Magic employees, including Bob Ogden. HP 10, p. 212. Marvolo was descended from the Peverell wizarding family. DH 22, p. 428.

Gaunt, Merope. The daughter of Marvolo Gaunt and the mother of Lord Voldemort. Merope was a squib. HP 10, p. 205. She and her father and brother were the last living relatives of Salazar Slytherin. HP 10, pp. 208, 212.

Gaunt, Morfin. The son of Marvolo Gaunt who had a history of attacking muggles. HP 10, pp. 202-03. Morfin and his father and sister were the last living relatives of Salazar Slytherin. HP 10, p. 208. For his attack on Tom Riddle, Morfin was imprisoned in Azkaban for three years. HP 10, p. 211. He later confessed to having murdered Tom Riddle and Tom's parents and spent the remainder of his life in Azkaban. Actually, Lord Voldemort committed the crimes against the Riddles and placed a false memory in Morfin's mind so that he would take the blame. HP 17, p. 366.

Geminio. The magic word for a charm invoked by Hermione Granger to duplicate a locket during year seven. DH 13, p. 263.

Gemino Curse. One of two curses, the other being the Flagrante Curse, used by goblins at Gringotts Wizarding Bank to prevent treasure from being stolen. When applied to an object, the curse caused the object to burn the person who touched it and the object multiplied itself into worthless copies. DH 26, p. 537.

German Ministry of Magic. The German Ministry of Magic placed tight controls on the erkling population in order to prevent them from killing and attacking wizards. FB, p. 15.

Germany. One of three locations, specifically southern Germany, that served as the natural habitat for the bowtruckle. The other two locations were the west of England and certain Scandinavia forests. FB, p. 5. Germany was also the native habitat of the erkling. FB, p. 15. An illuminated manuscript from Germany dated around A.D. 962

showed warlocks on broomsticks. QA 1, p. 2. From as early as 1105, wizards in Germany played stichstock. QA 2, p. 4. (Germany is a country in Central Europe that is officially known as the Federal Republic of Germany.)

Gernumbli gardensi. According to Luna Lovegood, another name for gnomes. DH 8, p. 140.

Gernumbli magic. Magic relating to *gernumbli gardensi*, or gnomes, according to Luna Lovegood. DH 8, p. 140.

Ghost. According to Sir Nicholas de Mimsy-Porpington, only wizards could be ghosts after they died, but very few wizards chose that path. They formed ghosts by leaving an imprint of themselves on the earth to walk palely where their living selves once walked. Sir Nicholas chose to become a ghost because he was afraid of death. OP 38, pp. 860-61.

Ghoul. A creature that lived in the attic of the Burrow. CS 3, p. 29. The ghoul was heard groaning above Ron Weasley's bedroom and banging on the pipes. CS 3, p. 41. There was a Ghoul Task Force in the Department for the Regulation and Control of Magical Creatures. The Task Force removed ghouls from muggle dwellings. FB, pp. 18-19. DH 6, p. 98.

Ghoul Task Force. A special task force in the Department for the Regulation and Control of Magical Creatures that removed ghouls from muggle dwellings. FB, pp. 18-19.

Giant. Ron Weasley informed Harry Potter at the Yule Ball that giants no longer existed in Britain because they had been dying out and then were killed off by aurors. Giants had a reputation for being vicious and for killing things. Giants were believed to live outside Britain. GF 23, p. 430. Rubeus Hagrid was a half-giant and kept that fact a secret throughout Harry's first three years at Hogwarts. GF 23, pp. 428-30. Rita Skeeter wrote an article in the *Daily Prophet* that disclosed Hagrid's background and summarized the history of giants in Britain. The article stated that many giants served Lord Voldemort and that their affiliation with him was the reason why they were killed by aurors. GF 24, p. 439. Lord Voldemort tried to recruit the giants to join his army after he returned to power. During Harry's fifth year at Hogwarts there were only about 70 or 80 giants remaining. Their chief was called Gurg. OP 20, pp. 426-27.

Gibbon. A wizard who was a Death Eater. Gibbon died as a result of being hit by a Killing Curse during the fight between Death Eaters and member s of the Order of the Phoenix at the end of Harry Potter's sixth year at Hogwarts. HP 29, pp. 618-19.

Gilderoy Lockhart's Guide to Household Pets. The title of a book written by Gilderoy Lockhart that Mrs. Weasley consulted for information on how to de-gnome a garden. This event occurred during the summer prior to Harry Potter's second year at Hogwarts. CS 3, p. 35.

Gillyweed. A plant that helped one to breathe underwater. GF 26, p. 491. The uses of gillyweed were discussed in *Magical Water Plants of the Mediterranean.* GF 35, p. 677. When rolled into a ball, Gillyweed looked like slimy, grayish green rat tails. Dobby offered a ball of gillyweed to Harry Potter in order to help him with the second task of the Triwizard Tournament. This event occurred during Harry's fourth year at Hogwarts. GF 26, pp. 491, 494.

Gimbi Giant-Slayers. A quidditch team from Ethiopia. The Giant-Slayers won the All-Africa Cup twice. QA 8, p. 43.

Ginevra. A witch that Auntie Muriel mistook Ronald Weasley for, given his long hair at the wedding of Fleur Delacourt and Bill Weasley during year seven. DH 8, p. 141.

Ginger. The root of the ginger plant was one of the ingredients in Wit-Sharpening Potion. The other ingredients were powdered scarab beetles and armadillo bile. Harry Potter worked on this potion during his fourth year at Hogwarts. GF 27, pp. 513-14, 518.

Ginger Newt. A biscuit that Minerva McGonagall offered to Harry Potter in her office during Harry's fifth year at Hogwarts. OP 12, p. 248.

Gladrags Wizardwear. A wizard clothes store located in London, Paris and Hogsmeade. The store was advertized on the flashing advertisement in the stadium at the Quidditch World Cup. This event occurred during the summer prior to Harry Potter's fourth year at Hogwarts. GF 8, p. 96. Harry, Ron Weasley and Hermione Granger visited the store in Hogsmeade in the spring of Harry's fourth year at Hogwarts in order to purchase socks for Dobby. Harry bought several pairs, including one pair that had flashing silver and gold stars and another that screamed when they got too smelly. GF 27, p. 520.

Glisseo. The magic word used by Hermione Granger to invoke a charm that flattened a staircase at Hogwarts and converted it into a slippery slide during year seven. The counter charm was "*duro.*" DH 32, p. 643.

Glumbumble. A magical insect that produced melancholy-inducing treacle and ate nettles. The treacle was used as an antidote to hysteria caused by the consumption of alihotsy leaves. FB, p. 19.

Gnome. A creature that lived around the Burrow and liked to play in the garden. CS 3, p. 29. A gnome was not the same as a garden gnome found on muggle lawns. Muggle garden gnomes were described as fat little Santa Clauses with fishing rods. CS 3, p. 36. The creature was small and leathery in appearance and had a large, knobby head exactly like a potato. Its feet were horny. CS 3, p. 37. While some wizards used a jarvey to rid their gardens of gnomes, other wizards believed the method too brutal. FB, p. 19. Gnomes considered the Horklump a delicacy. FB, p. 22. DH 6, p. 107. According to Xenophilius Lovegood, the correct name of the gnome was "*gernumbli gardensi*" and their saliva was enormously beneficial. He referred to them as "grenumblies." DH 8, p. 140.

Gobbledegook. According to Percy Weasley, one of two-hundred languages that Barty Crouch could speak. GF 7, p. 88. Gobbledegook was the language spoken by goblins. In the Three Broomsticks, Ludo Bagman stated to Harry Potter that the only word in Gobbledegook that he knew was "bladvak," which meant pickax. GF 24, p. 446. DH 15, p. 296.

Goblet of Fire. A magic, roughly made, wooden goblet that determined the champions to compete in the Triwizard Tournament. The goblet was stored in a casket and when taken out of the casket, was full to the brim with dancing blue-white flames. Students who were eligible to be considered for the school champions were instructed to place their names in the goblet. Albus Dumbledore drew a magical age line around the goblet so that underage students could not submit their names for consideration. Once selected by the goblet, the student was required to compete to the end of the tournament. GF 16, pp. 255-56. At the appointed time on Halloween, the goblet turned red and a tongue of flame shot out a piece of parchment bearing the names of the selected champions. During Harry Potter's fourth year at Hogwarts, the champions were Viktor Krum, Fleur Delacour, Cedric Diggory and Harry. GF 16, pp. 269-71.

Goblin. Gringotts Wizarding Bank was operated by goblins. On their way to the bank before the start of Harry Potter's first year at Hogwarts, Rubeus Hagrid advised Harry never to play around with goblins. SS 5, p. 63. During Harry's fourth year at Hogwarts, he studied the Goblin Rebellions of the eighteen century in his History of Magic class. GF 15, p. 234. The *Daily Prophet* reported that Griselda Marchbanks had alleged links to subversive goblin groups. The report was published during Harry's fifth year at Hogwarts. OP 15, p. 308. Griphook and Gornuk were goblins. Goblins were not interested in the "wizards' war" that occurred during year seven and did not take sides in it. DH 15, pp. 295, 296. Griphook admitted that Harry Potter was famous even among goblins. DH 24, p. 486.

Goblin Liaison Office. An office located within the Ministry of Magic and headed by Cuthbert Mockbrudge during Harry Potter' lifetime. Arthur Weasley pointed out Cuthbert to Harry and Hermione Granger at the camp on the grounds of the Quidditch World Cup. This event occurred during the summer prior to Harry's fourth year at Hogwarts. GF 7, p. 86. The office was located on level four of the Ministry of Magic. OP 7, p. 130. During the summer prior to Harry's sixth year at Hogwarts, the head of the office was Dirk Cresswell. HP 4, p. 71. DH 12, p. 245.

Gobstones. A game similar to marbles, except that the playing stones of the game squirted a bad smelling liquid into the face of the player who lost a point. Harry Potter stopped himself from buying a set of solid gold gobstones during the summer prior to his third year at Hogwarts. PA 4, p. 50.

Gobstones Club. A wizard club to which Flavius Belby belonged. Flavius was the president of the Gobstones Club and used the happiness he felt from being elected to that position as his happy memory for a Patronus Charm aimed at a lethifold in 1782. FB, p. 27. A Gobstones Club existed at Hogwarts during Harry Potter's fifth year at the school. OP 17, 352. See also **Official Gobstones Club**.

Godelot. One of the reputed owners of the Elder Wand. Godelot died in his own cellar after his son, Hereward, took the Elder Wand from him. DH 21, p. 412.

Godric's Hollow. The location of James and Lily Potter's residence and the place where Lord Voldemort killed them. SS 1, p. 12. Godric's Hollow was also the residence of Bowman Wright who invented the Golden Snitch. QA 4, p. 14. At the end of his sixth year at Hogwarts, Harry Potter decided that he needed to go to Godric's Hollow, the site of his parents grave. HP 30, p. 650. DH 6, p. 100. Bathilda Bagshot also resided there and the Dumbledore family moved into Godric's Hollow after Pervical Dumbledore was imprisoned. DH 8, p. 158. A number of wizarding families lived there. DH 11, p. 217. It was also the birthplace of Godric Gryffindor and was located in the West Country. DH 16, p. 319.

Gold Medal-Winner for Ground-Breaking Contribution to the International Alchemical Conference. Part of the title earned by Albus Dumbledore while a student at Hogwarts. The conference took place in Cairo, Egypt. DH 18, p. 353.

Golden Egg. A magic egg that each school champion obtained from a dragon in the first task of the Triwizard Tournament. GF 20, p. 356. The egg contained a clue to the second task of the tournament. GF 20, p. 261; GF 25, pp. 463-64.

Golden Snidget. See **Snidget, Golden**.

Golden Snitch. See **Snitch, Golden**.

Goldstein, Anthony. A student at Hogwarts who was a member of the Ravenclaw house and in Harry Potter's class. During Harry's fifth year at Hogwarts, Anthony was a prefect, along with Padma Patil. OP 10, p. 188. Anthony appeared at Hog's Head, along with several other students, to discuss the formation of a club to study Defense Against the Dark Arts. OP 16, p. 338. DH 29, p. 578.

Golgomath. A giant who killed Karkus in order to become the Gurg. This event occurred during Harry Potter's fifth year at Hogwarts. OP 20, p. 430.

Golpalott's Third Law. A law of potions that stated: "the antidote for a blended poison will be equal to more than the sum of the antidotes for each of the separate components." HP 18, p. 374.

Gordon. A member of Dudley Dursley's gang who liked to tease Harry Potter by playing "Harry Hunting." The other members of the gang, in addition to Dudley, were Piers, Dennis and Malcolm. SS 3, p. 31.

Gornuk. A goblin that along with Griphook and Ted Tonks, fled from Death Eaters during year seven. DH 15, p. 295. Gornuk's fate was announced during a broadcast of *Potterwatch*. DH 22, p. 439.

Gorodok Gargoyles. A quidditch team from Lithuania. QA 8, p. 46.

Gorgovitch, Dragomir. A chaser in quidditch who was transferred to the Chudley Cannons for a record fee two years before year seven. Dragomir was the record holder for most quaffles dropped in a season. DH 7, p. 112.

Goshawk, Miranda. The author of *The Standard Book of Spells (Grade 1)*. The book was required for first-year students at Hogwarts. SS 5, p. 66. Miranda was also the author of *The Standard Book of Spells, Grade 2* and *The Standard Book of Spells, Grade 4*. These other books were required for second-year and fourth-year students at Hogwarts. CS 4, p. 43; GF 10, p. 155. Miranda was also the author of *The Standard Book of Spells, Grade 5*. Harry Potter was required to read this book during his fifth year at Hogwarts. OP 9, p. 160.

Goyle. A wizard who was a Death Eater and responded to the summons of Lord Voldemort during Harry Potter's fourth year at Hogwarts. GF 33, p. 651.

Goyle, Gregory. A student of Hogwarts who was a friend of and bodyguard, along with Vincent Crabbe, for Draco Malfoy. SS 6, p. 108; PA 5, p. 79. Gregory was a beater on the Slytherin quidditch team during Harry Potter's fifth year at Hogwarts. Gregory and Vincent replaced Derrick and Bole. OP 19, p. 405. DH 4, p. 50; 31, p. 628.

Grand Prize Galleon Draw. A contest sponsored by the *Daily Prophet* that Arthur Weasley won. Arthur used the prize money of 700 galleons to take his family to Egypt and visit Bill Weasley. This event occurred during the summer prior to Harry Potter's third year at Hogwarts. PA 1, p. 8.

Grand Sorcerer. Part of Albus Dumbledore's official title. SS 4, p. 51.

Granger. A family of muggles that included Hermione Granger. SS 6, pp. 105-06. Mr. and Mrs. Granger were dentists. GF 3, p. 28; 23, p. 405. They accompanied Hermione Granger to Diagon Alley and met the Weasleys in front of Gringotts Wizarding Bank during the summer prior to Harry Potter's second year at Hogwarts. CS 4, pp. 56-57. During year seven, Hermione modified their memories so that they believed their names were Wendell and Monica Wilkins. They moved to Australia, not realizing that they had a daughter. DH 6, pp. 88, 96.

Granger, Hermione Jean. A Hogwarts student who had bushy brown hair. Hermione had magical abilities even though both of her parents were muggles. SS 6, pp. 105-06. She was a member of the Gryffindor house. SS 7, p. 120. Hermione was an excellent student and placed at the top of her class at Hogwarts. CS 2, p. 15. She was one of Harry Potter's classmates and best friends. CS 1, p. 7. Her birthday was in September. PA 4, p. 57. Victor Krum escorted Hermione to the Yule Ball during Harry's fourth year at the school. GF 23, p. 414. Hermione informed Viktor Krum that her name was pronounced: "Her-my-oh-nee." GF 23, p. 419. Hermione's name appeared on the list of borrowers found inside the cover of *Quidditch Through the Ages*. QA, p. i. She was a prefect for the Gryffindor house, along with Ron Weasley, during Harry Potter's fifth year at Hogwarts. OP 9, p. 162. DH 2, p. 14; 4, p. 45. At the beginning of year seven, Hermione, who had taken Polyjuice Potion to look with Harry, was escorted by Kingsley Shacklebolt on a thestral from the Dursley residence. Hermione lacked confidence riding a broomstick. DH 4, p. 53. Hermione's middle name, Jean, was not revealed until year seven. DH 7, p. 125. She withdrew all of her savings from the Building Society during that same year. DH 9, p. 165. The only spell Hermione had trouble with was the Patronus Charm and when she was able to invoke it, it produced a silver otter. DH 13, p. 263.

Granian. A breed of winged horse that was grey and particularly fast. FB, p. 42.

Graphorn. A magical beast found in mountainous European regions and ridden by trolls. The horn of the graphorn, when made into powder, was an expensive ingredient for potions. The hide of a graphorn was tougher than dragon hide and repelled most spells. FB, p. 20.

Gray Lady. The ghost of Ravenclaw Tower at Hogwarts. She was the daughter of Rowena Ravenclaw. Harry Potter had seen but not spoken to the Gray Lady prior to year seven. The Bloody Baron had loved her and when she refused his advances he stabbed her to death and then committed suicide. DH 31, pp. 613-16.

Grawp. A small, sixteen foot giant who was Rubeus Hagrid's half-brother. After leaving his father, Rubeus' mother lived with a giant and gave birth to Grawp. Rubeus brought Grawp to the Forbidden Forest to protect him during Harry Potter's fifth year at Hogwarts. OP 30, pp. 690-91. The following year Grawp lived in a cave in the mountains near Hogwarts. Dumbledore helped with the living arrangements. HP 8, p. 170. DH 3, p. 39; 32, p. 648.

Great Grays. A type of owl used in the wizarding world for the delivery of mail. Harry Potter and Ron Weasley observed great grays in the Hogsmeade owl post office during Harry's third year at Hogwarts. PA 14, p. 278.

Great Hall. The dining hall of Hogwarts. The Great Hall was the place where special ceremonies and events took place. SS 7, p. 114. DH 16, p. 324.

Great Hangleton. The neighboring town to Little Hangleton. The police station in Great Hangleton was the location where Frank Bryce was questioned about the Riddle murders. This event was explained during the summer prior to Harry's fourth year at Hogwarts. GF 1, p. 3.

Great Wizards of the Twentieth Century. The title of a book located in the library at Hogwarts. Harry Potter, Ron Weasley and Hermione Granger consulted the book regarding the identity of Nicolas Flamel, only to discover that he was not discussed in the book. SS 12, p. 197.

Great Wizarding Events of the Twentieth Century. The title of a book read by Hermione Granger and that listed Harry Potter. Hermione mentioned this fact to Harry when she first met him on the Hogwarts Express. This event occurred during the summer prior to Harry's first year at Hogwarts. SS 6, p. 106.

Greece. The country in which Harpo the Foul resided. Greece was believed to be the country of origin for centaurs and griffins. FB, pp. 3, 6. In Mykonos, Greece, "Dangerous" Dai Llewellyn was eaten by a Chimera. QA 7, p. 33. After graduating from Hogwarts, Elphias Doge escaped from a chimera in Greece. DH 2, p. 18. (Greece is a country in Southern Europe that is at the southern end of the Balkan Peninsula.)

Green Dragon. An inn where Janus Thickey was discovered after faking his abduction by a lethifold in 1973. FB, p. 27, fn. 9.

Greenhouse Three. One of the greenhouses located on the grounds of Hogwarts. Greenhouse Three contained more interesting and dangerous plants than Greenhouse One, where first-year students met for Herbology class. Second-year students had their classes in Greenhouse Three and Harry Potter experimented with mandrakes in it during his second year at Hogwarts. CS 6, pp. 90-91. During his fourth year at the school, Harry learned about bubotubors in Greenhouse Three. GF 13, p. 194.

Greenland. Bill Weasley teased Harry Potter that Alistor "Mad Eye" Moody brought Harry to the headquarters of the Order of the Phoenix via Greenland. OP 5, p. 80. (Greenland is a self-governing island located northeast of North America that belongs to Denmark. It is the largest island in the world.)

Greengrass, Daphne. A student at Hogwarts who was called to take the practical examination of O.W.L.s along with Hermione Granger during Harry Potter's fifth year at Hogwarts. OP 31, p. 713.

Gregorovitch. During year seven, Harry Potter first mentioned this name in his sleep, not knowing the identity of the person. DH 7, p. 111. Gregorovitch was a famous wandmaker in the wizarding world. Viktor Krum claimed to have been one of the last wizards to have purchased a wand from Gregorovitch, before the wandmaker retired a few years prior to year seven. DH 8, pp. 149-50; 14, p. 279. Harry had a vision of the fate of Gregorovitch that year. DH 25, p. 469.

Gregory the Swarmy. A wizard whose likeness was carved into a statue placed at Hogwarts. A secret passageway out of the school was located behind the statue. Fred and George Weasley informed Harry Potter during his first year at Hogwarts that they found the passageway during their first week there. SS 9, p. 153. Fred and George caused a diversion in Gregory the Swarmy's cooridor, which was in the East Wing of Hogwarts, in order for Harry to secretly get into Dolores Umbridge's office. This event occurred during Harry's fifth year at Hogwarts. OP 29, p. 659.

Grenouille. One of two characters in the early 1400's play, *Alas, I've Transfigured My Feet,* by the French wizard Malecrit. The other character was Crapaun. QA 8, p. 39.

Greyback, Fenrir. A Death Eater who failed to search for the Dark Lord after he disappeared. Other Death Eaters who failed to do so were: Avery, Yaxley, the Carrows, Greyback and Lucius Malfoy. He was a friend of the Malfoys. HP 2, p. 26; 6, p. 125. Fenrir was the most savage werewolf alive. HP 16, p. 334. It was rumored that he attacked a five-year old boy, with the last name of Montgomery, and the boy later died at St. Mungo's Hospital. HP 22, p. 473. Fenrir developed a thirst for human flesh more often than once a month. HP 27, p. 593. DH 8, p. 144. He was permitted to wear Death Eater robes the following year for his assistance to Lord Voldemort's cause, but did not have the Death Mark. DH 23, p. 447. Fenrir's fate was revealed at the end of year seven. DH 36, p. 735.

Griffin. A magical beast that originated in Greece. Griffins were often employed by wizards to guard treasure. FB, p. 20. The claw of the griffin, when made into a powder, was an ingredient in Strengthening Solution. OP 17, p. 368.

Griffiths, Glynnis. A witch who played the position of seeker for the Holyhead Harpies during a famous quidditch match that occurred in

1953. Glynnis ended the seven-day match by catching the snitch. QA 7, p. 34.

Grim. A giant, spectral dog that haunted churchyards and was an omen of death. Sibyll Trelawney observed a grim when she read the tea leaves in Harry Potter's cup. This event occurred during Harry's third year at Hogwarts. PA 6, p. 107.

Grimmauld Place. The London street on which the headquarters of the Order of the Phoenix was secretly located. The specific location on the street was Number Twelve. OP 3, p. 58. Sirius Black owned the property during Harry Potter's fifth year at Hogwarts. OP 5, p. 79. DH 9, pp. 163, 169.

Grimmauld Square. The city square that the Knight Bus rumbled around after leaving number twelve Grimmauld Place. This event occurred during Harry's fifth year at Hogwarts. OP 24, p. 525.

Grimstone, Elias. A broom-maker from Portsmouth who made the first Oakshaft 79. This event occurred in 1978. The Oakshaft 79 was a broomstick used to play quidditch. QA 9, p. 47.

Grindelvald. See **Grindelwald**.

Grindelwald, Gellert. A dark wizard who was defeated by Albus Dumbledore in 1945. Harry Potter read this information on the back of a collectors' card from Chocolate Frogs. This event occurred during the summer prior to Harry's first year at Hogwarts. SS 6, pp. 102-103. DH 2, p. 20. Gellert killed many people, including the grandfather of Viktor Krum, and attended Durmstrang as a student. His symbol was a triangular eye. DH 8, p. 148. Gellert stole a wand from the shop of Gregorovitch during year seven. DH 17, p. 353. Gellert was the great-nephew of Bathilda Bagshot and lived with her for a while in Godric's Hollow, where he befriended Albus Dumbledore. DH 18, p. 355.

Grindylow. A water demon that was sickly green with sharp little horns and long, spindly fingers. Remus Lupin demonstrated a grindylow in his Defense Against the Dark Arts class. This event occurred during Harry Potter's third year at Hogwarts. PA 8, p. 153. Harry encountered a grindylow in the lake as part of the second task of the Triwizard Tournament that occurred during his fourth year at Hogwarts, GF 26, p. 495. The grindylow was found in lakes throughout Great Britain and Ireland. Merpeople were able to domesticate the grindylow. FB, p. 20.

Gringotts' Charm Breakers. The title given to certain employees of the Gringotts Wizarding Bank who broke charms. Bill Weasley was employed in this capacity and was upset that Rita Skeeter referred to these people as "long-haired pillocks." GF 10, p. 152.

Gringotts Wizarding Bank. The only bank for wizards that existed in the wizarding world. Gringotts was operated by goblins and its vaults were located hundreds of miles under London. The high security vaults were guarded by dragons and in one of the vaults Harry Potter's parents left a wealth of money for their son. SS 5, pp. 63-64, 72-73. The contents in vault number 713 belonged to Hogwarts. SS 5, p. 73. Bill Weasley was employed as a curse breaker for the bank in Egypt. SS 6, p. 107; PA 1, p. 8. He was also described as a Gringotts' charm breaker. GF 10, p. 152. Dirk Cresswell, head of the Goblin Liaison Office during the summer prior to Harry's sixth year at Hogwarts, was very knowledgable about the activities of the bank. HP 4, p. 71. Fleur Delacourt worked part-time at the bank that summer. HP 5, p. 92. During year seven, Severus Snape moved the Gryffindor sword to Gringotts for protection after several students attempted to steal it. DH 15, pp. 290, 298. The goblins who worked at Gringotts agreed to a code that they would not speak of the secrets contained in the bank. DH 24, p. 489. The Lestrange family had one of the most ancient vaults at Gringotts. DH 25, p. 509. The Thief's Downfall was one of the protective devices inside the bank's caverns. DH 26, p. 534.

Griphook. A goblin who worked at the Gringotts Wizarding Bank and escorted Harry Potter and Rubeus Hagrid to the vaults. This event occurred during the prior to Harry's first year at Hogwarts. SS 5, p. 73. DH 15, p. 293.

Gripping Charm. A charm discovered in 1875. The Gripping Charm eliminated the need for quaffles to have straps and finger holes. QA 6, p. 20.

Grodzisk Goblins. A quidditch team from Poland. Josef Wronski played for the Grodzisk Goblins and was the most innovative seeker in history. QA 8, p. 41.

Grow-Your-Own-Warts Kit. A prize that Harry Potter found inside a wizard cracker. This event occurred during Harry's first-year Christmas day dinner at Hogwarts. SS 12, p. 204.

Growth Charm. A charm that Harry Potter invoked as part of the practical examination of the O.W.L.s during his fifth year at Hogwarts. OP 31, p. 713.

Grubbly-Plank, Wilhelmina. An elderly witch with closely cropped gray hair and a very prominent chin who served as the temporary professor for the Care of Magical Creatures class at Hogwarts. GF 24, p. 435. Wilhelmina filled in for Rubeus Hagrid who was so ashamed over the article Rita Skeeter wrote for the *Daily Prophet* that he hid. GF 24, p. 437. These events occurred during Harry's fourth year at Hogwarts. Wilhelmina greeted the first-year students when they arrived at Hogsmeade Station during the summer prior to Harry Potter's fifth year at Hogwarts and served as the Care of Magical Creatures instructor that year. OP 10, p. 196; 12, p. 211. Minerva McGonagall was on a first name basis with Wilhelmina. OP 17, p. 359.

Grunnings. The drill making firm where Vernon Dursley worked. SS 1, p.1. Vernon's office was located on the ninth floor. SS 1, p. 3.

Grunnion, Alberic. A wizard who was featured on the collectors cards inside packs of Chocolate Frogs. Harry Potter obtained the Grunnion card on the Hogwarts Express. This event occurred during the summer prior to Harry's first year at Hogwarts. SS 6, p. 102.

Gryffindor. One of the four dormitory houses at Hogwarts. SS 6, p. 106. It was named after Godric Gryffindor. CS 9, p. 150. In addition to Harry Potter, Albus Dumbledore, the members of the Weasley family and Hermione Granger belonged to the Gryffindor house. SS 6, p.106. Minerva McGonagell was head of the house during Harry's years at the school. SS 8, p. 135. Gryffindor's house colors were scarlet and gold and the mascot was the Gryffindor lion. SS 17, p. 306. During Harry's fourth year at the school, a red banner bearing a gold lion for Gryffindor decorated the Great Hall for the Triwizard Tournament. GF 15, p. 237. There were six floors between the Gryffindor common room and the top of the marble staircase that led down to the entrance hall of Hogwarts. GF 21, p. 374. The entrance to the Gryffindor tower was located on the seventh floor of Hogwarts castle. OP 18, p. 396. The hourglass for the Gryffindor house in the entrance hall contained rubies. OP 38, p. 853.

Gryffindor, Godric. One of the four great witches and wizards who established Hogwarts. Godric believed that the school should accept children of muggles if they showed signs of magic. CS 9, p. 150. He had a serious disagreement with Salazar Slytherin over this subject, which caused Salazar to leave the school. Professor Binns explained these events to the History of Magic class that Harry Potter attended during his second year at Hogwarts. CS 9, p. 150. According to remarks of the Sorting Hat made at the sorting ceremony during Harry's fourth year at Hogwarts, Godric looked for students who had bravery as their virtue. Godric created the Sorting Hat. GF 12, p. 177. During year seven, a historical artifact was attributed to Godric; the "sword of Godric Gryffindor." The sword had a ruby-encrusted hilt and had appeared out of the Sorting Hat to Harry. Albus Dumbledore believed the sword was the only weapon that could kill the Heir of Slytherin. DH 7, p. 129. During year seven, Severus Snape moved a fake copy of the Gryffindor sword to Gringotts for protection after several students attempted to steal it. Goblin silver, like that in the real sword, repelled dirt; it imbibbed only that which strengthened it. DH 15, pp. 290, 298, 303. Godric's birthplace was Godric's Hollow. DH 16, p. 319. Harry discovered the Sword of Gryffindor in a frozen pool within the Forest of Dean. DH 19, p. 367.

Gryffindor Sword. See **Gryffindor, Godric**.

Gryffindor Tower. One of the three tallest towers at Hogwarts, in which the Gryffindor students resided. DH 31, p. 613.

Gubraithian fire. Magical fire that was everlasting. Rubeus Hagrid offered gubraithian fire to Kerkus as a gift. This event occurred during Harry Potter's fifth year at Hogwarts. OP 20, p. 428.

Gudgeon, Davey. A student of Hogwarts who attended the school, along with Rubin Lupin, the year the Whomping Willow was planted. Davey ventured too close to the tree and it almost gouged his eye. The administrators of the school forbid any other student from going near the tree as a result of the incident. PA 10, p. 186.

Gudgeon, Gladys. A person who Gilderoy Lockhart claimed was a fan of his. Harry Potter wrote a reply to Gladys as part of his detention for being in the flying car that injured the Whomping Willow. This event occurred during Harry's second year at Hogwarts. CS 7, p. 120. Gladys wrote weekly to Gilderoy Lockhart while he was a patient at St. Mungo's Hospital for Magical Maladies and Injuries. This event occurred during Harry Potter's fifth year at Hogwarts. OP 23, p. 511.

Guide to Advanced Transfiguration, A. The title of a book that fell out of Cedric Diggory's book bag when Harry Potter put a charm on it during Harry's fourth year at Hogwarts. Harry invoked the charm so that he could get Cedric alone and have the opportunity to inform him that the first event of the Triwizard Tournament involved dragons. GF 19, p. 340.

Guide to Medieval Sorcery. The title of a book that Harry Potter consulted in order to find a way to breathe underwater in the second task of the Triwizard Tournament. This event occurred during Harry's fourth year at Hogwarts. GF 26, p. 488.

Guidelines for the Treatment of Non-Wizard Part-Humans. A document that Percy Weasley was prepared to cite in defense of the actions of the Ministry of Magic against criticism voiced by Rita Skeeter in the *Daily Prophet.* This event occurred during the summer prior to Harry Potter's fourth year at Hogwarts. GF 10, p. 147.

Gulping Plimpies. A magical beast that could be warded off with gurdyroot, according to Luna Lovegood. HP 20, p. 425.

Gunhilda. The wife of Goodwin Kneen who played the position of catcher on a kwidditch team during the tenth century. QA 3, p. 9.

Gunther the Violent. The subject of a famous painting titled "Gunther the Violent is the Winner" from 1105. The painting demonstrated the ancient German game of stichstock. QA 2, p. 4.

Gurdyroot. A part of a plant that was used to ward off gulping plimpies, according to Luna Lovegood. HP 20, p. 425. DH 8, p. 146. It could be made into a beverage, with a purple hue as deep as beetroot juice. DH 20, p. 404.

Gurg. The title for the chief of the giants. Karkus, and later Golgomath, were the Gurg during Harry Potter's fifth year at Hogwarts. OP 20, p. 427.

Gwenog. A witch who visited Gertie Keddle for nettle tea. Gwenog joined Gertie as she watched warlocks throw a ball around on broomsticks at Queerditch Marsh. Gwenog admitted that she often played the game herself. This event occurred during the eleventh century. QA 3, pp. 7-8.

HAG – HURLING HEX

Hag. A creature, along with vampires, that Professor Quirrell reportedly encountered in the Black Forest. According to Rubeus Hagrid, the encounter changed Professor Quirrell from a person with a brilliant mind to someone who was extremely nervous and scared of everything. SS 5, p. 71. Because they were not skilled at putting on disguises like wizards, many hags avoided the muggle world and lived in Hogsmeade, which was known as a haven for hags. GF 19, p. 319.

Hagrid, Rubeus. The Keeper of Keys and Grounds at Hogwarts during the time that Harry Potter attended the school. SS 1, pp. 13-14; 4, p. 48. Because only one of his parents was a giant, Hagrid was a half-giant. His mother was one of the last giants in Britain and she left home when Hagrid was three years old. GF 23, pp. 427-28. Her name was Fridwulfa and she reportedly fled to foreign mountain ranges where giants still dwelled. GF 24, p. 439. Hagrid's father, who was not a giant (but a wizard) raised him, but then died during Hagrid's second year as a student at Hogwarts. GF 23, pp. 427-28; GF 24, p. 455. Hagrid was expelled from Hogwarts during his third year and kept his broken wand concealed in a flowery pink umbrella. SS 4, p. 59; CS 7, p. 117. He carried Harry to safety after Lord Voldemort killed Harry's parents and unsuccessfully tried to murder Harry as well. SS 1, p. 14. Hagrid was the professor of Care of Magical Creatures during Harry's third year at Hogwarts. PA 5, p. 93. Cornelius Fudge referred to Hagrid's interest in unusual creatures as a "monster fixation." GF 29, p. 580. Hagrid had a romantic relationship with Madam Maxime that ended during Harry's fifth year at Hogwarts. OP 30, p. 692. DH 2, p. 15; 4, p. 45. During year seven, Hagrid was in hiding from Death Eaters after hosting a "Support Harry Potter" party at his hut on the Hogwarts grounds. DH 22, p. 442; 31, p. 618.

Hagrid was commanded by Voldemort to carry Harry to the base of Hogwarts at the end of year seven. DH 36, p. 727.

Haileybury Hammers. A quidditch team from Canada. QA 8, p. 43.

Hair-Raising Potion. A potion that included rat tails as one of its ingredients. Ron Weasley considered making the potion in order to remove hair from his face that was left after a Polyjuice Potion wore off. This event occurred during Harry Potter's second year at Hogwarts. CS 13, p. 228.

Hair-Thickening Charm. A charm that Severus Snape accused Alicia Spinnet of inflicting on herself when her eyebrows grew so thick and fast that her vision was obscured. This event occurred during Harry Potter's fifth year at Hogwarts. OP 19, p. 400.

Hairy Snout, Human Heart. The title of a book written by an anonymous author and published by Whizz Hard Books in 1975. FB, p. 41.

Half-Blood. A name given to describe someone who had one muggle parent. During Harry Potter's lifetime, most wizards were half-bloods. If wizards had not married muggles, wizards would have died out. CS 7, p. 116. A wizard who had both a witch and wizard as parents was known as a "pure-blood" and a wizard who had two muggle parents was sometimes referred to, in a derogatory fashion, as a "mudblood." See also **Mudblood** and **Pureblood**.

Half-Blood Prince. The former owner of a copy of the book *Advanced Potion-Making*, which book was given to Harry Potter by Horace Slughorn during Harry's sixth year at Hogwarts. HP 9, p. 193. Severus Snape admitted to Harry that he was the Half-Blood Prince. HP 28, p. 604.

Half-Giant. A person who had only one giant parent. At the Yule Ball, Rubeus Hagrid admitted to Madam Maxime that he was a half-giant. This event occurred during Harry Potter's fourth year at Hogwarts. GF 23, p. 428.

Hall of Prophecy. A room in the Department of Mysteries that contained glass jars with prophecies inside. OP 35, p. 789.

Hand of Glory. An enchanted, withered hand that was sold in Borgin and Burkes on Knockturn Alley. A candle inserted into the Hand of Glory produced light for the holder of the device. The Hand of Glory was marketed as a friend of thieves and plunderers. Draco Malfoy was interested in the object during the summer prior to Harry Potter's second year at Hogwarts. CS 4, pp. 52-53. By the end of Harry's sixth year at the school, Draco actually had possession of the Hand of Glory. HP 29, p. 618.

Handbook of Do-It-Yourself Broomcare. The title of a book included in the Broomstick Servicing Kit given by Hermione Granger to Harry Potter as a thirteenth birthday present. The kit also included,

Fleetwood's High-Finish Handle Polish, a shiny pair of silver Tail-Twig Clippers and a tiny brass compass. This event occurred during Harry's third year at Hogwarts. PA 1, p. 12.

Handbook of Hippogriff Psychology, The. The title of a book that Ron Weasley consulted regarding the appeal of the Committee for the Disposal of Dangerous Creatures decision against Buckbeak. This event occurred during Harry Potter's third year at Hogwarts. PA 15, p. 300.

Hanged Man, The. A pub located in Little Hangleton. The pub was very busy the night that the three Riddle family members were murdered in their manor house. GF 1, p. 2.

Harkiss, Ciceron. A person who knew Horace Slughorn, probably as a former student, and interviewed Ambrosius Flume for his first job. HP 4, p. 71.

Harper. A student at Hogwarts who, during Harry Potter's sixth year there, was a substitute seeker on the Slytherin quidditch team. Draco Malfoy did not play in the game against Gryffindor that year. HP 14, pp. 296-97.

Harris, Warty. A witch or wizard who was cheated out of his or her toads by Bill Weasley, according to Mundungus Fletcher. OP 5, p. 86.

Hawkshead Attacking Formation. A famous quidditch play invented by Darren O'Hare of the Kenmare Kestrels. QA 7, p. 35; 10, p. 52.

Haversacking. The name of one of the ten most common fouls committed in quidditch. QA 6, p. 30.

Hawkshead Attacking Formation. One of the plays recorded by the omnioculars Harry Potter looked through during the Quidditch World Cup. Three Irish team chasers executed the play. Another play was the Porskoff Ploy. This event occurred during the summer prior to Harry's fourth year at Hogwarts. GF 8, p. 106.

He Flew Like a Madman. The title of a book written by Kennilworthy Whisp. The book was a biography of "Dangerous" Dai Llewellyn. QA, p. v.

He-Who-Must-Not-Be-Named. A euphemism for Lord Voldemort. SS 5, p. 85. Lord Voldemort was also referred to as "You-Know-Who." SS 1, p. 5.

Head Boy. A prestigious title given to the most accomplished male student at Hogwarts. Students were selected for the honor. PA 4, p. 61. They were given a badge and fez to wear on their heads. PA 1, p. 10. Bill Weasley was Head Boy when he attended Hogwarts. SS 6, p. 99. A list of the Head Boys was displayed in the trophy room at the school and it included the name of T.M. Riddle. CS 13, p. 234. James Potter was Head Boy when he attended Hogwarts. SS 4, p. 55. Percy

Weasley received the honor at the beginning of Harry Potter's third year at the school. PA 1, p. 10.

Head Girl. A prestigious title given to the most accomplished female student at Hogwarts. Lily Potter was Head Girl when she attended the school. SS 4, p. 55.

Head Hockey. A game using the heads of ghosts that was played by the Headless Hunt during Nearly Headless Nick's five hundredth deathday party. This event occurred during Harry Potter's second year at Hogwarts. CS 8, p. 124.

Head of House. The title for the professor who was in charge of one of the four student houses at Hogwarts. GF 13, p. 206. The head of house for Gryffindor was Minerva McGonagell and for Slytherin was Severus Snape. After two students were attacked at the same time by the monster from the Chamber of Secrets, Minerva McGonagell canceled the quidditch final match and ordered the students to their houses for safety. She announced that the heads of houses would provide further instructions to the students. These events occurred during Harry Potter's second year at Hogwarts. CS 14, p. 256. Minerva McGonagell informed Mad-Eye Moody that if Draco Malfoy had misbehaved, instead of punishing him by transfiguring him into a ferret, Mad-Eye should have reported him to the Slytherin head of house. GF 13, p. 206. This event occurred during Harry's fourth year at Hogwarts. In addition to Minerva and Severus, the other two heads of house were Professors Flitwick, for Hufflepuff, and Sprout, for Ravenclaw. GF 18, p. 293; HP 18, p. 382. DH 30, p. 596.

Head Polo. A sporting event engaged in by the Headless Hunt. Nearly Headless Nick received a rejection letter from the Headless Hunt stating that it would not be possible to play head polo if one's head was not parted from one's body. This event occurred during Harry Potter's second year at Hogwarts. CS 8, p. 124.

Headless Hat. A joke device that Fred and George Weasley invented during Harry Potter's fifth year at Hogwarts. When the hat was placed on one's head, the hat and head disappeared. The hat cost two galleons. OP 24, p. 540.

Headless Hunt. An association of ghosts whose heads had departed company with their bodies. The association engaged in such activities as horseback head-juggling and head polo. The Headless Hunt refused to allow Nearly Headless Nick to join its ranks because he had not completely lost his head. This event occurred during Harry Potter's second year at Hogwarts. CS 8, pp. 123-24. DH 31, p. 634.

Healer. A witch or wizard who was able to heal the illnesses or diseases of other witches and wizards. Healers worked at St. Mungo's Hospital for Magical Maladies and Injuries. They wore green coats with a wand and bone emblem on them. Dilys Derwent was a healer at St. Mungo's from 1722 through 1741. OP 22, p. 484. Auntie Muriel claimed that her brother, Launcelot, had been a healer at St. Mungo's, which explained her knowledge as to whether Ariana Dumbledore was ever a patient there. DH 8, p. 156.

Healer's Helpmate, The. A book owned and used by Molly Weasley. HP 5, p. 100.

Healing Spells. A general name for the group of magic spells used to heal or repair a bodily injury. For example, the magic word "*episkey*" repaired a broken nose. HP 7, p. 157.

Hebridean Black Dragon. One of only two types of wild dragons in Britain. The other type was the Common Welsh Green. Ron Weasley explained the types of dragons to Harry Potter during Harry's first year at Hogwarts. SS 14, p. 231. The MacFusty wizard clan of the Hebrides took care of the Hebridean Black dragons for centuries. FB, p. 12. The Banchory Bangers, a quidditch team, was forced to disband after attempting to catch a Hebridean Black for its team mascot. This event occurred in 1814. QA 5, pp. 16-17.

Hedwig. A female, snowy white owl that Harry Potter purchased at Eeylops Owl Emporium prior to his first year at Hogwarts. SS 5, p. 81. Harry selected Hedwig as a name from *A History of Magic*. SS 6, p. 88. Snowy owls were not native birds to Britain. GF 15, p. 240. DH 2, p. 15. For an important episode with Hedwig that occurred during year seven, see DH 4, p. 56.

Heidelberg Harriers. A quidditch team defeated by the Holyhead Harpies in 1953. The match was widely agreed as one of the finest ever played. Rudolf Brand was captain of the Harriers for that match. QA 7, pp. 34-35; 8, pp. 40-41.

Heir of Slytherin. According to legend, a person who was the heir of Salazar Slytherin and capable of controlling the monster of the Chamber of Secrets. CS 9, p. 151. The heir was later identified. CS 17, p. 317. This event occurred during Harry Potter's second year at Hogwarts. DH 7, p. 129.

Heliopath. A spirit of fire that galloped across the ground and burned everything in its path. Luna Lovegood claimed that Cornelius Fudge had an entire army of heliopaths. She made her claim during Harry Potter's fifth year at Hogwarts. OP 16, p. 345.

Hellebore. A substance that, when made into a syrup, was one of the ingredients required for the Draught of Peace. Harry Potter forgot to include syrup of hellebore in the Draught of Peace he made during his fifth year at Hogwarts. OP 12, p. 234. (Hellebore is any of the several plants of the genus, *Helleborus*, of the buttercup family, having basal leaves and clusters of flowers. Its substances are poisonous and medicinal.)

Hengist of Woodcroft. A witch or wizard who was featured on the collectors cards inside packages of Chocolate Frogs. Harry Potter obtained the Hengist card on the Hogwarts Express. This event occurred during the summer prior to Harry's first year at Hogwarts. SS 6, p. 103.

Heptomology. A magical art. Dolores Umbridge repeatedly asked questions of Sybil Trelawney about heptomology and ornithomancy. This event occurred during Harry Potter's fifth year at Hogwarts. OP 25, p. 552.

Herbology. A class taught at Hogwarts by Professor Sprout. Herbology involved the care of all strange plants and fungi. SS 8, p. 133. During Harry Potter's second year at Hogwarts, he learned about the Mandrake in the class. CS 6, pp. 91-93. First year students had the class in Greenhouse One and other students had it in Greenhouse Three. During his fourth year at Hogwarts, Harry learned about bubotubors in herbology. GF 13, p. 194.

Herefordshire. The location in England where swivenhodge was played as a popular sport. QA 2, p. 6. (Herefordshire is a former county in Western England and is now part of Hereford and Worcester.)

Hereward. One of the reputed owners of the Elder Wand. Hereward took the Elder Wand from his father, Godelot. DH 21, p. 412.

Hermes. The name of the owl owned by Percy Weasley. Hermes was a gift from the Weasleys' to Percy when he became prefect at Hogwarts. The Weasleys' other owl was named Errol. CS 3, p. 30. Prior to Harry Potter's fourth year at Hogwarts, Ron Weasley acquired a tiny gray owl, that he named Pig. GF 3, p. 35. Hermes was a handsome screech owl. OP 14, p. 296.

Herpo the Foul. A Greek dark wizard and Parselmouth who bred the first Basilisk. FB, p. 3.

Hiccup Sweets. A joke candy sold at Zonko's Joke Shop in Hogsmeade. Harry Potter and Ron Weasley purchased Hiccup Sweets during Harry's third year at Hogwarts. PA 14, p. 278.

Hiccuping Solution. A potion that Draco Malfoy attempted to produce in a Potions Class during Harry Potter's sixth year at Hogwarts. Horace Slughorn declared that Draco's potion was merely passable. HP 22, p. 475.

Higgs, Bertie. A wizard who joined Damocles McLaggen and his nephew Cormac McLaggen, along with Rufus Scrimgeour, on a nogtail hunting trip to Norfolk. HP 7, p. 144.

Higgs, Terence. The seeker for the Slytherin quidditch team during Harry Potter's first year at Hogwarts. SS 11, p. 187. Draco Malfoy replaced Terence as seeker the following year. CS 7, p. 111.

High Inquisitor. The title given to a witch or wizard by appointment of the Ministry of Magic to oversee certain activities and have certain powers over matters at Hogwarts, including the inspection of professors. The position was established by Educational Decree Twenty-Three during Harry Potter's fifth year at Hogwarts. Dolores Umbridge was appointed to the position by Cornelius Fudge. OP 15, pp. 306-307.

High Street. The name of a street located in Hogsmeade. Harry Potter walked down High Street during his third and fourth years at Hogwarts. PA 14, p. 278; GF 24, p. 444. Scrivenshaft's Quill Shop was located on High Street. OP 16, p. 348. DH 28, p. 554.

High Table. The table in the Great Hall of Hogwarts on which the professors ate their meals. SS 7, p. 122.

Hinkypuff. A little, one-legged creature that appeared to be made of wisps of smoke and that lured travelers into bogs by dangling a lantern from its hands. PA 10, p. 186. Remus Lupin intended to teach his Defense Against the Dark Arts class about the creature immediately after the unit on grindylows. Severus Snape took over the class due to Remus' illness and abandoned the material on hinkypuffs in favor of werewolves. These events occurred during Harry Potter's third year at Hogwarts. PA 9, p. 171.

Hippocampus. A magical aquatic beast that originated in Greece and was usually found in the Mediterranean Sea. Merpeople off the coast of Scotland discovered a hippocampus in 1949. FB, pp. 20-21.

Hippogriff. A magical creature that Rubeus Hagrid demonstrated during the first Care of Magical Creatures class that he taught during Harry Potter's third year at Hogwarts. A hippogriff had the hind legs and tail of a horse, but its front legs, wings and head resembled those of a giant eagle with brilliant orange eyes. A hippogriff was extremely proud and easily offended; it attacked if insulted. Rubeus instructed the students in his class to approach a hippogriff with a bow of their heads and if the creature bowed its head in return, it was safe to move closer. PA 6, pp. 113-115. A hippogriff's wingspan was about twelve feet and it could be ridden into the air. PA 6, p. 117. Buckbeak was one of the hippogriffs demonstrated in the Care of Magical Creatures class. PA 6, p. 115. The hippogriff was native to Europe. FB, p. 21. Madam Modesty Rabnott owned a hippogriff. QA 4, p. 13. DH 2, p. 24; 36, p. 733.

History of Magic. A class taught at Hogwarts by Professor Binns who was the only ghost professor at the school. SS 8, p. 133. History of Magic was considered to be the dullest subject. CS 9, p. 148. Remus Lupin used the History of Magic classroom to give Harry Potter a lesson in conjuring a patronus during Harry's third year at Hogwarts. PA 12, p. 235.

History of Magic, A. The title of a book written by Bathilda Bagshot. The book was required for first-year students during Harry Potter's first year at Hogwarts. SS 5, p. 66. The book included a full account of a famous wizard retreat into hiding from muggles during the Middle Ages. FB, p. xv, fn. 4. DH 16, p. 318.

Hit Wizards. Special wizards who were employed by the Ministry of Magic in the Magical Law Enforcement Squad. These wizards were trained to handle such situations as Sirius Black's attack on Peter Pettigrew and a group of muggle bystanders. Cornelius Fudge informed Rubeus Hagrid in the Three Broomsticks that only Hit Wizards could have apprehended Sirius. This conversation occurred during Harry Potter's third year at Hogwarts. PA 10, p. 208.

Hobgoblins, The. A popular singing group in the wizarding world. Its lead singer was Stubby Boardman. Doris Polkiss was reported in *The Quibbler* as believing that Sirius Black was actually Stubby Boardman. The article appeared during Harry Potter's fifth year at Hogwarts. OP 10, p. 192.

Hog's Head. The name of the pub that was frequented by Rubeus Hagrid. Hog's Head was located down in the village below Hogwarts, presumably Hogsmeade. Hagrid won a dragon egg from a stranger in a card game at Hog's Head. This event occurred during Harry Potter's first year at Hogwarts. SS 16, p. 265. Hermione Granger organized a meeting of students at Hog's Head to discuss the formation of a club to be taught Defense Against the Dark Arts by Harry. This event occurred during Harry's fifth year at Hogwarts. OP 16, p. 335. The bartender of the Hog's Head banned Mundungus Fletcher from the pub 20 years prior to Harry's fifth year at Hogwarts. OP 17, p. 370. It was one of only two pubs in Hogsmeade; the Three Broomsticks was the other one. HP 12, p. 245.

Hog's Head Inn. An inn in Hogsmeade where the barman was Aberforth Dumbledore. DH 28, pp. 557, 559. See **Hog's Head.**

Hogsmeade. The village near Hogwarts where third-year and older students of the school were allowed to visit, provided that they had written permission slips from their parents or guardians. PA 1, p. 14. Hogsmeade was the only entirely non-muggle settlement in Britain. PA 5, p. 76. The village was a haven for hags. GF 19, p. 319. There was wild countryside around Hogsmeade and the settlement lay in the shadow of a mountain. GF 27, p. 520. The first weekend in October was one of several ocassions during which Hogwarts students were permitted to visit Hogsmeade. A list of all the

Hogsmeade weekends was posted in the Gryffindor house common room. OP 16, p. 332; 17, p. 351. DH 15, p. 305.

Hogsmeade Station. The railroad station where the Hogwarts Express stopped to drop off students who attended Hogwarts. PA 5, p. 86. Most of the students were transported from the station to the school grounds by stagecoaches that had no visible horses. This event occurred during Harry Potter's third year at Hogwarts. PA 5, p. 87. First-year students reached the school by sailing across the school's black lake with Rubeus Hagrid in little boats that held up to four passengers at one time. SS 6, p. 111; GF 11, p. 170.

Hogwartian. A general descriptive name for any student who attended Hogwarts. DH 32, p. 646.

Hogwarts. See **Hogwarts School of Witchcraft and Wizardry**.

Hogwarts, A History. The title of a book that was read by Hermione Granger for information about Hogwarts before she attended the school. SS 7, p. 117. The book was over a thousand pages in length. GF 15, p. 238. The book stated that Hogwarts was hidden so that its secrets could not be stolen from persons who attended other wizarding schools. When muggles looked at Hogwarts, it appeared to be a smoldering ruin with a sign over the entrance that read: "Danger, Do Not Enter, Unsafe." GF 11, p. 166. *Hogwarts, A History* also contained information about the Triwizard Tournament of 1792 in which tournament a cockatrice went on a rampage and injured three of the judges. Hermione was upset that the book did not mention Hogwarts' use of house-elf labor. GF 15, p. 238. DH 6, p. 96.

Hogwarts Express. The name given to a scarlet, steam engine-driven train that arrived at Platform Nine and Three-quarters of the King's Cross station and that transported passengers, mainly students, to Hogwarts at Hogsmeade Station. The train left the station at 11:00 a.m. SS 6, p. 93. Harry Potter was prevented from reaching the Hogwarts Express on the way to his second year at Hogwarts. CS 5, p. 68. One of the carriages on the train was reserved exclusively for prefects. OP 10, p. 184. DH 12, p. 227; 33, pp. 669-70.

Hogwarts Four. The title for the four founding wizards of Hogwarts. CS 17, p. 317. They were Godric Gryffindor, Helga Hufflepuff, Rowena Ravenclaw and Salazar Slytherin. CS 9, p. 150.

Hogwarts High Inquisitor. See **High Inquisitor.**

Hogwarts School of Witchcraft and Wizardry. A private school for the instruction of witches and wizards. SS 4, pp. 48, 51. Many people considered it to be the best school for teaching witchcraft. SS 4, p. 58; 6, p. 105. Hogwarts was founded over a thousand years before Harry Potter's lifetime by the four greatest witches and wizards of that age: Godric Gryffindor, Helga Hufflepuff, Rowena Ravenclaw and Salazar Slytherin. CS 9, p. 150. Its coat of arms had a lion (for Gryffindor), eagle (for Ravenclaw), badger (for Hufflepuff) and a snake (for Slytherin) that surrounded a large letter H. SS 3, p. 34. Hogwarts stood high on a cliff over a black lake, which lake was located south of the school. SS 6, p. 111; CS 5, p. 73; PA 6, p. 99. A giant squid lived in the lake, as well as merpeople and grindylows. SS 16, p. 263; GF 25, p. 464; GF 26, p. 495. The school building was a castle and had 142 staircases. SS 8, p. 131. Its main building was at least seven stories tall. GF 21, p. 374. There were many tricks throughout the building that contained false steps. Most of the students knew to jump the steps, but Neville Longbottom was forgetful and fell in them. GF 12, p. 190. Albus Dumbledore was surprised to find a secret room full of chamber pots at 5:30 a.m. on Christmas day during Harry Potter's fourth year at the school. GF 23, pp. 417-18. The Hogwarts kitchen was accessed through a painting of a bowl of fruit. When the pear was tickled, it giggled and opened to the kitchen. GF 21, p. 366. The entrance to the school grounds consisted of a pair of gates with winged boars on either side. GF 24, p. 452. The school castle was constructed with enchantments so that no one could apparate into or out of it. PA 9, p. 164. In addition, Hogwarts's location was a mystery so that its secrets could not be stolen. GF 11, p. 166. Hogwarts students sang the school song with whatever tune each person wished to sing to it, all at the same time. SS 7, p. 127-28. The students wore black robes as their school uniform. GF 16, p. 251. Two talking, stone gargoyles flanked the door to the staff room. OP 17, p. 357. The points in the Inter-House Championship were displayed in giant hourglasses within the school. SS 14, p. 244. The hourglasses were located in niches of the entrance hall. The one for the Slytherin house had emeralds; for the Gryffindor house, rubies; and for the Ravenclaw house, sapphires. OP 28, p. 626; 38, p. 853. DH 2, p. 27. During year seven, the Ministry of Magic made attendance by young wizards and witches mandatory, for the first time in the school's history. In addition, students were not admitted unless they had blood status, meaning they had proven their wizard descent to the satisfaction of the Ministry. DH 11, p. 210. The three tallest towers of the school were: Astronomy, Gryffindor and Ravenclaw. DH 31, p. 611.

Hokey. A female house elf of Hepzibah Smith. HP 20, pp. 430-33. Hokey was convicted of poisoning and killing her mistress. HP 20, p. 436.

Holidays with Hags. The title of a book written by Gilderoy Lockhart. The book was required for second-year students during Harry Potter's second year at Hogwarts. CS 4, p. 43.

Holyhead Harpies. A quidditch team in the league from Wales. The Harpies was a unique team because only witches were permitted to play on it. QA 7, pp. 34-35. During the summer prior to Harry Potter's sixth year at Hogwarts, the captain of the team was Gwenog Jones, a former student of Horace Slughorn. HP 4, p. 71. Ginny Weasley had a picture of Gwenog on her bedroom wall during year seven. DH 7, p. 115.

Home Life and Social Habits of British Muggles. The title of a book that Hermione Granger read during the celebration in the Gryffindor common room after Gryffindor's quidditch victory over Ravenclaw. PA 13, p. 264. This event occurred during Harry Potter's third year at Hogwarts. The book was written by Wilhelm Wigworthy and published by Little Red Books in 1987. FB, p. 7, fn. 6.

Homenum revelio. The magic words for a spell to detect human presence in a room. Hermione Granger invoked this spell at Number Twelve Grimmauld Place during year seven. DH 9, pp. 171-72.

Homorphus Charm. An immensely complex charm, according to Gilderoy Lockhart, that turned a werewolf back into a human being again. In a Defense Against the Dark Arts class that Harry Potter attended during his third year at Hogwarts, Lockhart claimed to have used the charm on a werewolf and became a hero to a village because of it. PA 10, p. 162.

Honeydukes. A candy shop located in Hogsmeade. Honeydukes sold: Pepper Imps; Chocoballs; massive sherbert balls that caused levitation, known as Fizzing Whizbees; Toothflossing Stringmints; Jelly Slugs; Droobles Best Blowing Gum; Ice Mice; fragile sugar-spun quills, exploding bonbons, Cockroach Clusters, Acid Pops and Peppermint Toads. Harry Potter visited the shop during his third year at Hogwarts. PA 5, p. 77; 10, pp. 190, 196, 197, 200; 11, p. 213. Hermione Granger and Ron Weasley purchased chocolates at Honeydukes for Harry's birthday during the summer prior to Harry's fifth year at Hogwarts. OP 1, p. 8. Ambrosius Flume worked at Honeydukes during the following year and was a former student of Horace Slughorn. HP 4, p. 71.

Hooch, Madam. The professor at Hogwarts who coordinated and refereed the quidditch matches during the time that Harry Potter attended the school. SS 7, p. 127. Madam Hooch provided broom flying lessons to the students as well. SS 9, p. 146.

Hooper, Geoffrey. A student at Hogwarts who was member of the Gryffindor house and tried out for the open keeper position on the Gryffindor team that Ron Weasley finally won. In Angelina Johnson's opinion, Geoffrey was a real whiner. This event occurred during Harry Potter's fifth year at Hogwarts. OP 13, p. 276.

Hopkirk, Mafalda. An employee of the Improper Use of Magic Office, Ministry of Magic, who sent an owl letter to Harry Potter warning him about his violation of two wizard laws. The letter arrived after Dobby performed a Hover Charm on Petunia Dursley's violet pudding. This event occurred during the summer prior to Harry's second year at Hogwarts. CS 2, p. 21. Mafalda, as the official of the Improper Use of Magic Office, sent Harry a notice that he violated a wizarding law during the summer prior to his fifth year at Hogwarts. OP 2, p. 27. During year seven, Mafalda was an assistant in the Improper Use of Magic Office. DH 12, p. 237.

Hoppy. One of the names of the kneazles that were owned as pets by Newt Scamander. The other two kneazles were named Mauler and Milly. FB, p. vi.

Horcrux. A subject about which Tom Riddle asked Horace Slughorn when Tom attended Hogwarts. HP 17, p. 370. The only reference to horcruxes in the Hogwarts library was in the introduction of *Magick Moste Evile.* The book stated that the horcrux was the wickedest of magical instruments. HP 18, p. 381. A horcrux was an object in which a person concealed part of his soul. Without the destruction of the horcrux , the wizard could not die. In order to split the soul, which was an evil act against nature, a wizard had to commit murder. It was possible to have more than one horcrux, perhaps as many as six. Together with the portion remaining in the wizard, the soul would have been in seven pieces, a magical number. The subject of horcruxes was banned at Hogwarts when Dumbledore was headmaster. Tom Riddle's diary was a horcrux and was destroyed by Harry Potter during his second year at Hogwarts. HP 23, pp. 497-500. Another horcrux was Marvolo's ring. Albus Dumbledore removed the horcrux after much effort that left him injured during Harry's sixth year at Hogwarts. HP 23, p. 503. For a summary of the six suspected horcuxes see HP 23, p. 507. Ron Weasley casually referred to the horcruxes during year seven as the "You-Know-Whats." DH 6, p. 86. The method of creating and destroying a horcrux was described in *Secrets of the Darkest Art.* The soul was reassembled if the wizard who invoked it was remorseful, but it was very painful and perhaps fatal to attempt to do so. A horcrux could only be destroyed if it was beyond magical repair. It depended on the container into which it was placed for survival. It could not exist or transfer itself to another container. DH 6, pp. 102-04. Nagini was the last horcrux that Voldemort knew he had made. DH 27, p. 550. Fiendfyre was one of only a few substances capable of destroying a horcrux. DH 31, p. 635. A final horcrux with a portion of Voldemort's soul was identified at DH 35, p. 709.

Horklump. A magical beast that originated in Scandinavia, but was widespread throughout Europe. The horklump was a favorite delicacy of gnomes. FB, pp. vii, 21. The venom of the streeler was used in a few substances to kill horklumps. FB, p. 40.

Hornby, Olive. A female student at Hogwarts who teased Moaning Myrtle about her glasses the night that Moaning Myrtle died. Harry Potter learned about this incident during his second year at Hogwarts. CS 16, p. 299.

Horseback Head-Juggling. A sporting event engaged in by the Headless Hunt. CS 8, p. 124.

Horton, Basil. One of the two co-founders of the Comet Trading Company, which was established in 1929. QA 9, p. 49. Randolph Keitch was the other co-founder.

Horton-Keitch Breaking Charm. A charm patented by the co-founders of the Comet Trading Company. The charm made quidditch players less likely to overshoot goals or fly offside. QA 9, pp. 49-50.

House Cup. A ceremonial cup awarded each year to the student house at Hogwarts that had the most points accumulated by its students over the course of the school year. SS 7, p. 114. The competition for points was known as the Inter-House Championship. GF 12, p. 180. Points were earned and deducted by the professors based on the achievements, conduct and misconduct of the students. SS 7, p. 114. The point totals for each house were displayed in giant hourglasses within the school. SS 14, p. 244. The hourglasses were located in niches of the entrance hall. The one for the Slytherin house had emeralds; for the Gryffindor house, rubies; and for the Ravenclaw house, sapphires. OP 28, p. 626; 38, p. 853.

House-Elf. A little creature that had bat-like ears and bulging green eyes the size of tennis balls. CS 2, p. 12. A house-elf was bound as a servant to a wizard house and wizard family forever, unless the family set the elf free. CS 2, p. 14. A house-elf's master was usually from an old-wizarding family and very wealthy. CS 3, p. 29. A house-elf had powerful magic of his own, but could not use it without his master's permission. CS 3, p. 28. Part of a house-elf's enslavement was to keep his master's secrets, to be silent and to uphold his master's honor. GF 21, p. 380. A master could only free a house-elf by giving the house-elf real clothes. CS 10, p. 177. The bizarre clothes worn by a house-elf, typically a pillowcase, were a mark of the house-elf's enslavement. CS 10, p. 177. If a master of a house-elf dismissed the house-elf from service, the master provided the house-elf with normal clothes. GF 9, p. 138. Dobby and Winky were house elves. CS 2, p. 12; GF 8, pp. 97-98. According to Nearly Headless Nick, the largest group of house-elves that worked in one building in Britain worked in the kitchen at Hogwarts. There were over one hundred house-elves who worked there. GF 12, pp. 181-82. DH 6, p. 106. Elf magic did not operate like wizard magic. For example, an elf was capable of apparating or disapparating from an area where wizards could not. DH 10, p. 195; 36, p. 734.

House-Elf Liberation Front. Ron Weasley teased Hermione Granger about changing the name of her club from S.P.E.W. to the House-Elf Liberation Front. He made the comment before Hermione led Harry Potter and him into the kitchen at Hogwarts during Harry's fourth year at the school. GF 21, p. 374.

Hover Charm. A magical charm that allowed an object to float in the air. Dobby used the charm to levitate Petunia Dursley's violet pudding for a dinner party. This event occurred during the summer prior to Harry Potter's second year at Hogwarts. CS 2, pp. 19-20; DH 17, p. 346.

Howler. A letter in a red envelope that when opened screamed the message to the recipient in the voice of the person who sent it. If the recipient refused to open the envelope, the howler smoked. Ron Weasley received a howler from his mother for flying and wrecking Arthur Weasley's Ford Anglia. CS 6, p. 87. Neville Longbottom received a howler from his grandmother after he foolishly lost a piece of paper that had the Gryffindor passwords on it, which list was discovered by Sirius Black. PA 14, pp. 271-72. Percy Weasley received many howlers from wizards who complained about the Ministry of Magic's handling of security at the Quidditch World Cup that Harry Potter attended. GF 10, p. 151. Hermione Granger received howlers after *Witch Weekly* reported that she was Harry's unfaithful girlfriend. These last two events occurred prior to and during Harry's fourth year at Hogwarts. GF 27, p. 546. Petunia Dursley received a howler during the summer prior to Harry's fifth year at Hogwarts. OP 2, p.39. It was sent by Albus Dumbledore. OP 37, p. 836.

Hufflepuff. One of the four student houses at Hogwarts. SS 5, p. 77. It was named after Helga Hufflepuff. CS 9, p. 150. Hufflepuff's quidditch team color was canary yellow. CS 14, p. 255. Its mascot was a badger. SS 3, p. 34. Professor Sprout was the head of the house. GF 18, p. 293. During Harry's fourth year at Hogwarts, a yellow banner bearing a black badger for Hufflepuff decorated the Great Hall for the Triwizard Tournament. GF 15, p. 237. Cedric Diggory was a member of the house. PA 9, p. 168. The other students in the house were thrilled when Cedric was chosen as a school champion for the Triwizard Tournament during Harry's fourth year at Hogwarts, because it gave the Hufflepuff House a chance to earn the type of glory that it had not had in centuries. GF 31, p. 634. The Hufflepuff dormitory was accessed by the basement corridor, which corridor also led to the kitchens. OP 18, p. 396.

Hufflepuff, Helga. One of the four great witches and wizards who established Hogwarts. CS 9, p. 150. Professor Binns explained her role in the formation of the school in a History of Magic class that Harry Potter attended during his second year at Hogwarts. CS 9, p. 150. According to the Sorting Hat at the sorting ceremony during Harry's fourth year at Hogwarts, Helga looked for students who had a hard working nature as their virtue. GF 12, p. 177. Helga's golden cup had passed into the possession of Hepzibah Smith and then it was stolen by Tom Riddle. During year seven, it was located in the Lestrange vault at Gringotts Wizarding Bank. DH 26, p. 538.

Humberto, The Great. The host of a television program that Dudley Dursley liked to watch on Mondays. When the Dursley family fled from their residence to avoid the letters that were arriving for Harry Potter, Dudley wanted to make sure that the room they stayed in had a television. He didn't want to miss The Great Humberto. This event occurred during the summer prior to Harry's first year at Hogwarts. SS 3, p. 43.

Hungarian Horntail. A type of dragon used in the first event of the Triwizard Tournament hosted at Hogwarts. The Hungarian Horntail was black and looked more like a lizard than the other dragons used for the event. Charlie Weasley was part of the team that controlled the dragons. This event occurred during Harry Potter's fourth year at Hogwarts. GF 19, pp. 326-27. Harry fought this dragon in the tournament and went fourth in order of the champions who competed. GF 19, p. 350. The Hungarian Horntail was considered the most dangerous of all dragon breeds. FB, pp. 12-13.

Hunter. The original name given to a seeker. A hunter had the task of catching the golden snidget. QA 4, p. 13.

Huton-on-the-Rock. A broken down house located along the sea where Vernon Dursley and his family, along with Harry Potter, finally rested after attempting to escape from many letters delivered to Number Four Privet Drive for Harry. The letters invited Harry to attend his first year at Hogwarts. SS 4, p. 51.

Hurling Hex. A hex that Professor Flitwick suspected was placed on Harry Potter's Firebolt by Sirius Black. This event occurred during Harry's third year at Hogwarts. PA 12, p. 245.

ICE MICE - IVANOVA

Ice Mice. Candy sold at Honeydukes in Hogsmeade. Harry Potter and Ron Weasley purchased Ice Mice from Honeydukes during Harry's third year at Hogwarts. PA 10, p. 197.

Ignotus. The name on a tombstone in Godric's Hollow. Ignotus may have been one of the legendary Three Brothers who owned the Deathly Hallows. DH 16, p. 327. See **Peverell**.

Ilfracombe Incident of 1932. In 1932, a Welsh Green Dragon swooped down on a crowded beach of muggles sunbathing in Ilfracombe. A wizarding family performed the largest batch of Memory Charms in that century on the muggles. FB, pp. xvi, 12.

Imago, Inigo. The author of *The Dream Oracle.* The book was used by Sibyl Trelawney in her Divination Class for fifth-year students. This occurred during Harry Potter's fifth year at Hogwarts. OP 12, p. 237.

Imp. A magical beast found only in Great Britain and Ireland. Imps were often confused with pixies. FB, p. 22.

Impediment Curse. A curse that Harry Potter attempted to learn for the third task of the Triwizard Tournament. The curse had the effect of slowing down anything that tried to attack the wizard who invoked the curse. This event occurred during Harry's fourth year at Hogwarts. GF 29, p. 574. The curse was invoked with the magic word "*impedimenta.*" Harry used the curse against a blast-ended skrewt and a large spider in the third task of the tournament. GF 31, pp. 626, 631. He also invoked the curse against inferius in a cave during his sixth year at Hogwarts. HP 26, p. 575.

Impediment Hex. A hex that Flavius Belby unsuccessfully invoked against a Lethifold in 1782. FB, p. 26.

Impediment Jinx. A jinx that Colin Creevy mastered after only three meetings of Dumbledore's Army. This event occurred during Harry

Potter's fifth year at Hogwarts. OP 19, p. 397. During year seven, Hagrid used the hex against a Death Eater who tried to hurl a curse at Harry Potter as they fled the Dursley residence. DH 4, p. 58. See **Impediment Curse**.

Impedimenta. The magic word for a curse. See **Impediment Curse**.

Imperio. The magic word used to invoke the Imperius Curse. GF 14, pp. 212-13. The illegal curse was invoked by Lord Voldemort during Harry Potter's fourth year at Hogwarts. GF 33, p. 661. See **Imperius Curse**.

Imperius Curse. An illegal curse that was invoked with the magic word "*imperio*." A wizard who invoked the curse was subject to severe punishment under wizarding law. The curse had the effect of totally controlling the will of the person onto whom it was placed, unless the person had real strength of character to resist it. The Imperius Curse was the first curse that Mad-Eye Moody taught Harry Potter and his Defense Against the Dark Arts classmates during Harry's fourth year at Hogwarts. GF 14, pp. 212-13. The Imperius Curse was classified as one of the three Unforgivable Curses; the other two curses were the Cruciatus Curse and the Killing (or "Avada Kedarva") Curse. GF 14, p. 217. Madam Rosmerta was placed under the Imperius Curse by Draco Malfoy during Harry's sixth year at Hogwarts. HP 27, p. 588. The following year, Yaxley reportedly placed the Imperius Curse on Pius Thicknesse. DH 1, p. 5; 11, p. 208. Harry actually used the curse for the first time in his life at Gringotts Wizarding Bank during year seven. DH 26, p. 531.

Imperturbable Charm. A charm that protected the surface on which it was placed. Molly Weasley placed the charm on the kitchen door at the headquarters of the Order of the Phoenix so that her children could not overhear the voices at a meeting in the room behind the door. OP 4, p. 69.

Impervius. The magic word used in a charm by Hermione Granger to make Harry Potter's glasses repel rain water. The charm helped Harry to see through his rain-streaked glasses in a quidditch game during his third year at Hogwarts. PA 9, p. 177. DH 12, p. 244.

Impervius Charm. The Gryffindor quidditch team used this charm during a practice session to keep rain out of their eyes. This event occurred during Harry Potter's fifth year at Hogwarts. OP 18, p. 378.

Important Modern Magical Discoveries. The title of a book that was located in the library at Hogwarts. Harry Potter, Ron Weasley and Hermione Granger consulted the book for the identity of Nicolas Flamel, but Flamel was not mentioned in it. SS 12, p. 197.

Improper Use of Magic Office. An office located within the Ministry of Magic. CS 2, p. 21. Harry Potter received a letter from the office when Dobby performed a Hover Charm on Petunia Dursley's violet pudding. This event occurred during the summer prior to Harry's second year at Hogwarts. CS 2, p. 21. Molly Weasley expressed her concern to Harry that Fred and George Weasley's pranks and jokes would end up getting them in trouble with the Improper Use of Magic Office. This conversation occurred during the summer prior to Harry's fourth year at Hogwarts. GF 5, p. 58. The office, incorporated in the Department of Magical Law Enforcement, was located on level two of the Ministry of Magic. OP 7, p. 130. During year seven, Mafalda Hopkirk was an assistant in the office. DH 12, p. 237.

Inanimatus Conjurus. A spell and the subject of an essay assigned by Minerva McGonagall during Harry Potter's fifth year at Hogwarts. OP 14, pp. 289, 295.

Incarcerous. The magic word for a charm that produced ropes out of thin air, which ropes wrapped themselves around the person or object on which the charm was cast. Dolores Umbridge cast the charm on Magorian in the Forbidden Forest during Harry Potter's fifth year at Hogwarts. OP 33, p. 755. Harry invoked the charm against inferius in a cave during his sixth year at Hogwarts. HP 26, p. 575.

Incendio. The magic word for a charm used by Arthur Weasley to conjure a fire in the Dursley fireplace so that the Weasleys and Harry Potter could leave the residence by floo powder. This event occurred during the summer prior to Harry's fourth year at Hogwarts. GF 4, p. 47.

India. One of the natural habitats of the occamy and the phoenix. FB, pp. 31, 32. The Ministry of Magic in India regarded quidditch with some suspicion. QA 8, p. 46. (India is a country in South Asia.)

Indian Ocean. The natural habitat of the Ramora. FB, p. 36.

Inner Eye. The part of a true seer that can "see" the future. OP 15, p. 314.

Inferi. Dead bodies that are bewitched to do a Dark wizard's bidding. Inferi had not seen since prior to Voldemort's disappearance from his attack on the infant Harry Potter. HP 4, p. 62. Inferi were solid, as opposed to ghosts, which were transparent. Inferi were merely used like a puppet to do as commanded by the Dark Wizard that animated them. A ghost, in contrast, was the imprint of a departed soul left on the earth. HP 21, p. 460. Inferi were afraid of fire. HP 26, p. 576. DH 3, p. 35.

Inquisitorial Squad. A group of students who were faithful to the Ministry of Magic and selected by Dolores Umbridge, as head of Hogwarts, to perform certain duties. The squad had the power to dock points awarded to students. Draco Malfoy was selected for the squad. This event occurred during Harry Potter's fifth year at Hogwarts. OP 28, p. 626.

Instant Darkness Powder. A magic joke device that Fred and George Weasley imported from Peru for Weasleys Wizard Wheezes during Harry Potter's sixth year at Hogwarts. HP 6, p. 119.

InterCity 125. A muggle train that arrived on Platform Nine at King's Cross and that Arthur Weasley pretended to be interested in when the Weasley children were attempting to go to Platform Nine and Three-Quarters. This event occurred during the summer prior to Harry's third year at Hogwarts. PA 5, p. 71.

Inter-House Championship. The official name of the competition conducted each year between the four houses at Hogwarts. GF 12, p. 180. The students earned or lost points for their houses based on academic achievement or misconduct. The professors assigned the points and determined the point values. GF 12, p. 180. The point totals for each house were displayed in giant hourglasses at the school. SS 14, p. 244. Gryffindor won the championship the first three years that Harry Potter attended Hogwarts. GF 12, p. 180. The hourglasses were located in niches of the entrance hall. The one for the Slytherin house had emeralds; for the Gryffindor house, rubies; and for the Ravenclaw house, sapphires. OP 28, p. 626; 38, p. 853.

Inter-House Quidditch Cup. The official name of the quidditch competition conducted each year between the four houses at Hogwarts. During Harry Potter's fourth year at the school, the competition was cancelled due to the demands placed on the staff for the Triwizard Tournament. GF 12, pp. 183-84.

Intermediate Transfiguration. The title of a book that Harry Potter purchased in Flourish and Blotts for his third year at Hogwarts. PA 4, p. 54.

International Alchemical Conference. A conference that was held in Cairo, Egypt, during which Albus Dumbledore was the Gold Medal-Winner for Ground-Breaking Contribution to the International Alchemical Conference. The conference occurred in Cairo, Egypt when Albus was a student at Hogwarts. DH 18, p. 353.

International Association of Quidditch. An association for international quidditch matches involved with the Quidditch World Cup that Harry Potter attended during the the summer prior to his fourth year at Hogwarts. The chairwizard of the association was Hassan Mostafa. GF 8, p. 106.

International Ban on Dueling. A law that Percy Weasley proudly announced to Ludo Bagman he was going to discuss with the Transylvanians. Percy hoped they would sign the law in the upcoming year. This discussion occurred during Harry's fourth year at Hogwarts. GF 23, p. 425.

International Code of Wizarding Secrecy. A law that Harry Potter was afraid of violating if he used a Summoning Charm to propel aqua-lungs from the muggle world to the site of the second task of the Triwizard Tournament. This event occurred during Harry Potter's fourth year at Hogwarts. GF 26, p. 482. In 1750, Clause 73 was added to this law for the purpose of increasing the list of magical creatures hidden from the muggle world. FB, p. xvi. See also **International Statute of Wizarding Secrery** and **Statute of Secrecy**. Compare to **International Confederation of Warlocks' Statute of Secrecy**.

International Confederation of Warlocks' Statute of Secrecy. Section 13 of this law made it a offense to conduct any magical activity that might risk notice by members of the nonmagical community. Mafalda Hopkirk made Harry Potter aware of this law after Dobby used a Hover Charm on Petunia Dursley's violet pudding. This event occurred during the summer prior to Harry's second year at Hogwarts. CS 2, p. 21. Compare to **International Code of Wizarding Secrecy**.

International Confederation of Wizards. An organization of wizards that included Albus Dumbledore. SS 1, p. 8. Igor Karkaroff vowed to file a complaint with this organization concerning the Goblet of Fire's selection of four school champions (two of which were Hogwarts students) when the Triwizard Tournament was hosted at Hogwarts. This event occurred during Harry Potter's fourth year at the school. GF 17, p. 278. In 1692, the organization met to discuss the issue of how to conceal magical creatures from muggles. Its members finally agreed to hide 27 species, ranging from dragons to budimuns. FB, p. xv. The confederation also observed the abilities of the largest known kelpie in Loch Ness, Scotland and enacted laws to protect the ramora. FB, pp. 24, 36. In 1692, the Confederation established the right of wizards to carry a wand at all times. QA 6, p. 28, fn. 1. The Quidditch Committee in the Confederation frowned upon the Japanese practice of ceremonially setting quidditch broomsticks on fire when a Japanese team was defeated. QA 8, p. 46. Albus had the chairmanship of the confederation until he was voted out of that seat by Ministry of Magic wizards. This event occurred during the summer prior to Harry's fifth year at Hogwarts. OP 5, p. 95. The wizards of Liechtenstein refused to join the confederation and the first Supreme Mugwump of the Confederation was Pierre Bonaccord. The first meeting of the confederation was in France. OP 31, pp. 725-26.

International Confederation of Wizards, British Seats. An office located in the Department of International Magical Cooperation on level five of the Ministry of Magic. OP 7, p. 130.

International Confederation of Wizards' Conference. A conference held during the summer prior to Harry Potter's fourth year at Hogwarts. Rita Skeeter of the *Daily Prophet* reported on the convention and called Albus Dumbledore an "obsolete dingbat" in her story. GF 18, p. 307.

International Federation of Warlocks. An association of warlocks openly critical of Cornelius Fudge's efforts to inform the muggle Prime Minister of Sirius Black's escape from Azkaban. The criticism was reported in a *Daily Prophet* article that Harry Potter read on the Knight Bus. This event occurred during the summer prior to Harry's third year at Hogwarts. PA 3, p. 37.

International Magical Office of Law. An office located in the Department of International Magical Cooperation on level five of the Ministry of Magic. OP 7, p. 130.

International Magical Trading Standards Body. An office located in the Department of International Magical Cooperation on level five of the Ministry of Magic. OP 7, p. 130.

International Statute of Secrecy. See **International Statute of Wizarding Secrecy**.

International Statute of Wizarding Secrecy. A law in the wizarding world. Long before the law was enacted in 1692, witches and wizards kept themselves away from muggles. QA 1, p. 2. The law made each Ministry of Magic responsible for the consequences of magical sports played in each of their own territories. QA 5, p. 16. See also **International Code of Wizarding Secrecy.** The law was also referred to as the **International Statute of Secrecy**. DH 2, p. 20.

International Warlock Convention of 1289. A convention featured in a deadly dull lecture given by Professor Binns during a History of Magic class at Hogwarts. This event occurred during Harry Potter's second year at Hogwarts. CS 9, p. 148.

Intruder Charm. A magical charm invoked to make a wizard aware that an intruder had entered a building. HP 4, p. 67.

Invigoration Draught. A potion that Harry Potter made in a Potions Class during his fifth year at Hogwarts. OP 29, p. 660.

Invisibility Booster. A special device that Arthur Weasley added to his Ford Anglia in order to make it invisible while it flew in the air. Harry Potter and Ron Weasley flew the car on their way to Hogwarts for the beginning of their second year at Hogwarts. CS 5, p. 67.

Invisibility Cloak. A magic cloak that made the wearer of it invisible. Harry Potter received his father's invisibility cloak as an anonymous

Christmas present during his first year at Hogwarts. SS 12, p. 201. Albus Dumbledore later admitted to giving Harry the gift. SS 17, p. 299. Mad-Eye Moody was able to see through the cloak. GF 19, p. 322. This event occurred during Harry's fourth year at Hogwarts. The silvery hair of the demiguise was spun into invisibility cloaks. FB, p. 9. DH 21, p. 411. Mundungus Fletcher possessed an invisibility cloak. OP 2, p. 22. Alastor "Mad-Eye" Moody lent his best invisibility cloak to Sturgis Podmore during the summer prior to Harry Potter's fifth year at Hogwarts. OP 9, p. 173. DH 2, p. 15. Invisibility cloaks were typically traveling cloaks imbued with a Disillusionment Charm, or carrying a Bedazzling Hex or woven from demiguise hair. The cloaks faded over time and eventually no longer worked. DH 21, pp. 410-11. See also **Cloak of Invisibility**.

Invisibility Marquee. A magical device that was larger than an invisibility cloak and could cover several people at once. Hermione suggested that the members of Dumbledore's Army needed an invisibility marquee in order to hide themselves. OP 17, p. 372.

Invisibility Spell. A spell that made an object invisible. Fred and George Weasley applied an Invisibility Spell to their Headless Hat. OP 24, p. 540.

Invisible Book of Invisibility. The title of a book on invisibility. The owner of Flourish and Blotts ordered two hundred copies of the book and then never found them after they arrived. This event occurred during the summer prior to Harry Potter's third year at Hogwarts. PA 4, p. 53.

Io. A moon around the planet Jupiter that had volcanos. This information was included in an Astronomy essay written by Ron Weasley during Harry Potter's fifth year at Hogwarts. OP 14, p. 295.

Iran. The Ministry of Magic in Iran regarded quidditch with some suspicion. QA 8, p. 46. (Iran is a republic in Southwest Asia.)

Ireland. A national team from Ireland played Bulgaria in the Quidditch World Cup during the summer prior to Harry Potter's fourth year at Hogwarts. GF 3, p. 35. The game of aingingein was played in Ireland. QA 2, p. 4. The earliest recorded quidditch match involving a team from Ireland occurred in 1385. The game was played in Lancashire against a team from Cork. QA 8, p. 38. (Ireland is an island nation to the west of Great Britain and is part of the United Kingdom.)

Irish International. A quidditch team on which Barry Ryan was keeper. OP 19, p. 400. See **Irish National Quidditch Team**.

Irish International Side. A quidditch team that ordered seven Firebolts; the brooms were some of the first to be sold after the Firebolt went on the market, according to a statement made by the owner of Quality

Quidditch Supplies. The statement was made during the summer prior to Harry Potter's third year at Hogwarts. PA 4, p. 51.

Irish National Quidditch Team. The name given to the national team from Ireland that played the national team from Bulgaria in the Quidditch World Cup during the summer prior to Harry Potter's fourth year at Hogwarts. According to Charlie Weasley, the national quidditch team from Ireland flattened the team from Peru in the semifinal games that led to the World Quidditch Cup. These events occurred during the summer prior to Harry Potter's fourth year at Hogwarts. GF 5, p. 63. The following were members of the team, in order of their introduction at the match: Connolly (beater), Ryan (keeper), Troy (chaser), Mullet (chaser), Moran (chaser), Quigley (beater) and Aiden Lynch (seeker). GF 8, pp. 105-07. The Irish players rode on Firebolts during the game. GF 8, p. 105. Mrs. Finnigan and her son Seamus attended the Quidditch World Cup and Mrs. Finnigan was annoyed that the Ministry of Magic did not like the fact that her tent was decorated with shamrocks to show pride for the quidditch team from Ireland. GF 7, p. 82.

Irish National Team Mascots. The title given to the leprechauns who served as the mascots for the quidditch team from Ireland that played in the Quidditch World Cup during the summer prior to Harry Potter's fourth year at Hogwarts. GF 8, p. 102.

Isle of Drear. An island off the northernmost tip of Scotland where the quintaped was found. FB, pp. 34-36.

Isle of Skye. An island in Scotland from which came the quidditch team, Pride of Portree. QA 7, p. 36.

Isle of Wright. The place where Marge Dursley vacationed. She sent Dudley Dursley a postcard from the Isle of Wright during the summer prior to Harry's first year at Hogwarts. SS 3, p. 34. (The Isle of Wight is an island off the southern coast of England and forms an administrative division of Hampshire, a county in South England.)

Ivanova. A member of the Bulgarian National Quidditch Team who was introduced at the Quidditch World Cup that Harry Potter attended during the summer prior to his fourth year at Hogwarts. Ivanova was a chaser. The other members of the team were: Dimitrov, Zograf, Levski, Vulchanov, Volkov and Viktor Krum. GF 8, pp. 104, 107.

JACK RUSSELL TERRIER - JUPITER

Jack Russell Terrier. The crup closely resembled the Jack Russell Terrier, except for its forked tail. FB, p. 8.

Japan. The natural habitat of the Kappa. FB, p. 23. Unlike other countries in Asia, quidditch was a popular sport in Japan. Japan's best known team was the Toyohasi Tengu. QA 8, p. 46. (Japan is a constitutional monarchy on a chain of islands off the coast of Asia.)

Jarvey. A magical beast found in Great Britain, Ireland and North America. The jarvey had the appearance of an overgrown ferret and pursued gnomes underground. FB, pp. xii, 22.

Jelly Slugs. Candy sold at Honeydukes in Hogsmeade. Harry Potter and Ron Weasley purchased Jelly Slugs at Honeydukes during Harry's third year at Hogwarts. PA 10, p. 196.

Jelly-Legs Jinx. A jinx that Hermione Granger placed on Harry Potter while Harry practiced for the third task of the Triwizard Tournament. GF 31, p. 608. When mixed with the Furnunculus Curse, the jinx caused a person's face to sprout little tentacles. Harry invoked the Furnunculus Curse against Vincent Crabbe at the same time that George Weasley invoked the Jelly-Legs Jinx. This event occurred on the Hogwarts Express on the way home from Harry's fourth year at Hogwarts. GF 37, p. 730.

Jenkins, Joey. A player on the Chudley Cannons who played the position of beater. Harry Potter read about Joey in *Flying with the Cannons* during Harry's fourth year at Hogwarts. GF 22, p. 393.

Jewkes, Leonard. The inventor of the Silver Arrow. The Silver Arrow was the true forerunner of the quidditch racing broom. QA 9, p. 49.

Jigger, Arsenius. The author of *Magical Drafts and Potions*. The book was required for first-year students during Harry Potter's first year at Hogwarts. SS 5, p. 66.

Jinx. A spell to invoke bad luck or a misfortune on a person. Minerva McGonagell confiscated Harry Potter's Firebolt, which he received as a Christmas present from an anonymous person, in order to have Madam Hooch and Professor Flitwick check it for jinxes. Minerva was concerned that the Firebolt had been sent from Sirius Black. This event occurred during Harry's third year at Hogwarts. PA 11, p. 232. Some jinxes went in and out of fashion. HP 16, p. 336.

Jinxes for the Jinxed. The title of a book found inside the Room of Requirement. OP 18, p. 390.

Jobberknoll. A magical bird found in Northern Europe and America. Jobberknoll feathers were used in truth serums and memory potions. FB, pp. 22-23.

Johnson, Amanda. Amanda Johnson's name appeared on the list of borrowers found inside the cover of *Quidditch Through the Ages*. QA, p. i.

Johnson, Angelina. A black student who attended Hogwarts. Angelina was a chaser on the Gryffindor quidditch team during Harry Potter's first, second and third years at the school. SS 11, p. 185; CS 7, p. 108; PA 8, p. 144; GF 16, p. 261. The other two chasers on the team were Katie Bell and Alicia Spinnet. During Harry's fourth year at Hogwarts, Angelina placed her name in the Goblet of Fire to be considered for the Hogwarts champion in the Triwizard Tournament. She turned seventeen years of age one week before Halloween of that year, so was old enough to qualify. GF 16, p. 261. Angelina was Fred Weasley's date to the Yule Ball held as part of the Triwizard Tournament. GF 22, p. 394. Angelina became captain of the Gryffindor quidditch team during Harry Potter's fifth year at Hogwarts. OP 12, p. 224. She refused to date Lee Jordan. OP 19, p. 406. Angelina was one year ahead of Harry at Hogwarts. OP 26, p. 575. DH 30, p. 603.

Jones, Gwenog. The captain of the Holyhead Harpies during the summer prior to Harry Potter's sixth year at Hogwarts. Gwenog was a former student of Horace Slughorn. HP 4, p. 71. Ginny Weasley had a picture of Gwenog on her bedroom wall during year seven. DH 7, p. 115.

Jones, Hestia. A witch who was a member of the Order of the Phoenix and the advance guard that rescued Harry Potter from the Dursley home during the summer prior to Harry's fifth year at Hogwarts. OP 3, pp. 47-49. At the beginning of year seven, Harry suggested to Vernon Dursley that Hestia and Dedalus Diggle would be more up to the job of protecting the Dursleys than Kingsley Shacklebolt. DH 3, pp. 34, 36.

Jordan, Lee. A student who attended Hogwarts. Lee was a member of the Gryffindor House. SS 6, pp. 94, 98. He was a friend of Fred and George Weasley and was the announcer for the quidditch matches at Hogwarts. SS 9, p. 153; 10, p. 186. During Harry Potter's fourth year at Hogwarts, Lee joined in Fred and George's plan of taking Aging Potion in order to meet the age requirement and qualify for the Triwizard Tournament. GF 16, p. 259. Lee was interested in dating Angelina Johnson, but she refused to date him. He was responsible for putting nifflers in Dolores Umbridge's office after Fred and George Weasley left the school. These events occurred during Harry Potter's fifth year at Hogwarts. OP 19, p. 406; 31, pp. 723-24. Lee attended the wedding of Fleur Delacourt and Bill Weasley during year seven. DH 8, p. 151. Lee was the announcer for *Potterwatch* and his code name on the program was River. DH22, p. 438.

Jorkins, Bertha. An employee of the Department of Magical Games and Sports who disappeared while on vacation in Albania prior to Harry Potter's fourth year at Hogwarts. Wormtail was responsible for her disappearance and she was eventually killed. GF 1, pp. 10-11; 5, p. 61. Bertha attended Hogwarts a few years ahead of Sirius Black and James Potter and was considered by Sirius to be an idiot. GF 19, p. 334. The full story of Bertha's disappearance was explained later that school year. GF 33, p. 655; 35, pp. 685-86.

Jugson. A Death Eater for Lord Voldemort who was present in the Department of Mysteries when Harry Potter retrieved the prophecy relating to himself and Lord Voldemort. This event occurred during Harry's fifth year at Hogwarts. OP 35, p. 788.

Junior Minister. A subordinate public official who reported to the Prime Minister of England. Herbert Chorley was one of the Junior Ministers during Harry Potter's sixth year at Hogwarts. HP 1, p. 2.

Jupiter. Harry Potter studied a map that included Jupiter during his first year at Hogwarts. SS 15, p. 247. Overcome by a villa after the Quidditch World Cup that Harry attended, Ron Weasley bragged that he invented a broomstick that reached to Jupiter. This event occurred during the summer prior to Harry's fourth year at Hogwarts. GF 9, p. 126. Harry wrote an essay for Professor Sinistra on the moons of Jupiter. Hermione Granger corrected Ron Weasley's essay that Ganymede was the largest moon, not Callisto, and that Io had volcanos and Europa had ice. These events occurred during Harry's fifth year at Hogwarts. OP 14, pp. 295, 300. (Jupiter is the fifth planet from the sun in the solar system that includes Earth.)

KAPPAS - KWIKSPELL

Kappas. Creepy water-dwellers that looked like scaly monkeys and had webbed hands. Kappas strangled persons who waded into their ponds. Harry Potter studied these creatures in his Defense Against the Dark Arts class during his third year at Hogwarts. PA 8, p. 141. Kappas were generally found in Mongolia. Severus Snape mentioned Mongolia as he criticized the work that students performed for Remus Lupin in their Defense Against the Dark Arts class. This event occurred during Harry's third year at Hogwarts. PA 9, p. 172. A kappa was a Japanese water demon. FB, p. 23.

Karasjok Kites. A quidditch team from Norway. The Karasjok Kites were defeated by the Caerphilly Catapults in the European Cup final of 1956. QA 7, p. 33.

Karkaroff, Igor. The wizard who was head of the Durmstrang Institute and accompanied his school's contestants to the Triwizard Tournament at Hogwarts. GF 15, pp. 244, 247; 23, p. 417. This event occurred during Harry Potter's fourth year at Hogwarts. Sirius Black informed Harry that Igor was a Death Eater who was caught by Mad-Eye Moody and imprisoned in Azkaban, but who was later released. GF 19, p. 332. Igor was killed by Death Eaters the summer prior to Harry's sixth year at Hogwarts. HP 6, p. 106. DH 33, p. 680.

Karkus. The gurg of the giants during Harry Potter's fifth year at Hogwarts. OP 20, p. 427.

Keddle, Gertie. A witch who lived during the eleventh century and wrote in a diary about the earliest version of quidditch that was played on Queerditch Marsh. Gertie's diary was maintained in the Museum of Quidditch. QA 3, p. 7.

Keeper. The player on a quidditch team who had the duty to keep the quaffle from going through the three hoops that he defended for his team.

SS 10, p. 168. The following persons were keepers on various teams: Ryan, Oliver Wood and Zograf. The earliest known date for the use of the term "keeper" in a game of quidditch was 1269. The event was recorded in a letter written by Madam Modesty Rebnott. QA 4, p. 12; 6 p. 23.

Keitch, Randolph. One of the two co-founders of the Comet Trading Company, which was established in 1929. Randolph played for the Falmouth Falcons. Basil Horton was the other co-founder. QA 9, p. 49.

Kelpie. A creature that lived in wells. CS 7, p. 114. Gilderoy Lockhart gave Rubeus Hagrid advice on how to remove a kelpie from his well. Hagrid informed Harry Potter that he did not need the advice. This event occurred during Harry's second year at Hogwarts. CS 7, p. 114. A kelpie was a British and Irish water demon. A wizard was able to subdue a kelpie by throwing a bridle over its head using a Placement Charm. The largest kelpie was found in Loch Ness, Scotland. FB, pp. 23-24.

Kenmare Kestrels. A quidditch team in the League from Ireland. The Kestrels' mascot was the leprechaun. QA 7, p. 35. Seamus Finnigan had a poster of the Kenmare Kestrels in his room at Hogwarts. This occurred during Harry Potter's fifth year at Hogwarts. OP 11, p. 217.

Kent. One of three towns that reported a downpour of shooting stars on the day Lord Voldemort disappeared. The other two towns were Dundee and Yorkshire. SS 1, p. 6. Kent was also the residence of the Wailing Widow, a ghost, who came to Nearly Headless Nick's five hundredth deathday party. This event occurred during Harry Potter's second year at Hogwarts. CS 8, p. 135. Kent was the location of Madam Modesty Rabnott's residence. QA 4, p. 12. (Kent is a county in Southeast England.)

Kettleburn, Professor. A wizard who was the professor of the Care of Magical Creatures class at Hogwarts. Professor Kettleburn retired after Harry Potter's second year at Hogwarts. PA 5, p. 93. Rubeus Hagrid replaced him the following year. PA 5, p. 93.

Kevin. A little boy who played with his father's wand and inflated a slug outside a large pyramid-shaped tent on the camp grounds outside the Quidditch World Cup. This event occurred during the summer prior to Harry Potter's fourth year at Hogwarts. GF 7, p. 81.

Killing Curse. An illegal curse invoked with the magic words "*avada kedavra.*" Hermione Granger gave the name of this charm as an answer to a question posed by Mad-Eye Moody in a Defense Against the Dark Arts class. This event occurred during Harry Potter's fourth year at Hogwarts. There was no countercurse to the Killing Curse and Harry was the only known person to have survived it. GF 14, p. 215. The

Killing Curse was classified as one of the three Unforgivable Curses; the other two curses were the Cruciatus Curse and the Imperius Curse. GF 14, p. 217. During year seven, Death Eaters directed the curse at Harry as he fled the Dursley residence. DH 4, p. 57.

King's Cross. The train station where students boarded the Hogwarts Express to travel to Hogwarts. SS 5, p. 87. The Hogwarts Express left the station from Platform Nine and Three-quarters, which was a magical gateway concealed between two muggle train platforms. It was accessed by running through a wall between those platforms. SS 6, p. 93. Harry Potter was prevented from passing through the gateway on the way to his second year at Hogwarts. CS 5, p. 68. During year seven, Harry appeared in a mystical place that looked very much like King's Cross, although he was not sure. DH 35, pp. 712, 722.

Kingsley. DH 3, p. 32. See **Shacklebolt, Kingsley**.

Kirke, Andrew. A student at Hogwarts who was a member of the Gryffindor house and became a beater for the house team, along with Jack Sloper, when Fred and George Weasley were banned from the team by Dolores Umbridge. This event occurred during Harry Potter's fifth year at Hogwarts. OP 21, p. 453.

Knarl. A magical beast usually mistaken for a hedgehog. FB, p. 24. Fred and George Weasley purchased knarl quills from Mundungus Fletcher for six sickles. OP 9, p. 171. The subject of nifflers was often tested on O.W.L.'s. OP 15, p. 323.

Kneazle. A magical beast originally bred in Great Britain. The Kneazle looked very similar to a cat. FB, p. 24. Newt Scamander owned three kneazles as pets. FB, pp. vi. A wizard was required to have a licence for a kneazle. FB, p. 25. The subject of kneazles was often tested on O.W.L.'s. OP 15, p. 323.

Kneen, Goodwin. A wizard who lived in Yorkshire during the tenth century and wrote a letter to his Norwegian cousin, Olaf, about playing the sport of "kwidditch." Goodwin's wife was Gunhilda. QA 3, pp. 8-9; 8, p. 39.

Knight Bus. A violently purple, triple decker bus that could fly. It served as an emergency transport for stranded witches and wizards. The driver of the Knight Bus was Ernie Prang and the conductor was Stan Shunpike. PA 3, pp. 33, 35. It cost eleven sickles to go from Magnolia Crescent to London–fourteen sickles if chocolate was added; fifteen sickes if a water bottle and toothbrush were added. Harry Potter rode the Knight Bus after running away from the Dursley residence. This event occurred during the summer prior to Harry's third year at Hogwarts. PA 3, p. 35. Hermione Granger rode the Knight Bus from Hogwarts to twelve Grimmauld Place, London in order to spend Christmas with Harry and the Weasley family. Harry, Hermione and the Weasleys rode the Knight Bus back to Hogwarts together; it was Ron Weasley's first time on the bus. It cost eleven sickles to ride the bus from London to Hogwarts. These events occurred during Harry's fifth year at Hogwarts. OP 23, p. 498; 24, pp. 524-25.

Knockturn Alley. A dingy alleyway that was comprised of shops devoted exclusively to the Dark Arts. Knockturn Alley was located near Diagon Alley. CS 4, p. 53. Borgin and Burkes was located on Knockturn Alley. Harry Potter accidentally landed in the shop after using flu powder for the first time. This event occurred during the summer prior to Harry's second year at Hogwarts. CS 4, p. 53.

Knotgrass. An ingredient used in Polyjuice Potion. Hermione Granger read the ingredients for the potion from *Most Potent Potions* to Harry Potter and Ron Weasley during Harry's second year at Hogwarts. CS 10, p. 165.

Knut. A bronze coin used for currency in the wizarding world. Seventeen silver sickles equaled one galleon and 29 knuts equaled a sickle. According to Rubeus Hagrid, one was obligated to give five knuts to a post owl for delivering a newspaper. SS 5, pp. 62, 75. While on the Hogwarts Express en route to his first year at Hogwarts, Harry Potter bought one of each candy for sale and paid for the candy with eleven sickles and seven knuts. SS 6, p. 101. Hermione Granger paid one knut for an edition of the *Daily Prophet* during Harry Potter's fifth year at Hogwarts. OP 12, p. 225. DH 21, p. 416.

Kopparberg. A location in Sweden that served as the beginning point of an annual broom race which dated from the tenth century. The fliers raced from Kopparberg to Arjelog. The course went through a dragon reservation. QA 2, p. 4.

Kreacher. The house-elf who lived at Number Twelve, Grimmauld Place, London. OP 4, pp. 75-76. Kreacher served the Black family and slept under a boiler in a cupboard off of the kitchen. OP 5, p. 83; 6, p. 107; 23, p. 503. DH 10, pp. 189-90; 36, p. 734.

Krum, Viktor. The star player of the Bulgaria quidditch team who played in the Quidditch World Cup during the summer prior to Harry Potter's fourth year at Hogwarts. GF 5, p. 63. Victor played the position of seeker and was only about eighteen years old at the time. His grumpy face was plastered on posters all over the Bulgarian camp site at the Quidditch World Cup. GF 7, p. 83. The other members of the team were: Dimitrov, Ivanova, Zograf, Levski, Vulchanov, and Volkov. GF 8, p. 104. Viktor was selected as the Durmstrang Institute champion for the Triwizard Tournament hosted by Hogwarts. His wand was a Gregorovitch creation and contained a hornbeam and dragon heartstring. GF 18, p. 309. Viktor escorted Hermione Granger to the Yule Ball. GF 23, p. 414. These events occurred during Harry Potter's fourth year at Hogwarts. Viktor attended the wedding of Fleur Delacourt and Bill Weasley during year seven. DH 8, p. 143.

Kwidditch. A game that Goodwin Kneen discussed in a letter addressed to his cousin, Olaf. This event occurred during the tenth century. QA 3, p. 9.

Kwikspell. The title of a correspondence course that involved beginner's magic. Harry Potter discovered information about Kwikspell on a piece of parchment in Argus Filch's office. This event occurred during Harry's second year at Hogwarts. CS 8, p. 127.

LABRADOR – LYNCH, AIDEN

Labrador. Cedric Diggory transfigured a Labrador retriever from a rock during the first event of the Triwizard Tournament. Cedric intended to distract the Swedish short-snout dragon with a dog so that the dragon would leave her nest unguarded and Cedric could steal the golden egg in the nest. This event occurred during Harry Potter's fourth year at Hogwarts. GF 19, p. 359.

Lacewing Flies. An ingredient for Polyjuice Potion that needed to be stewed for 21 days. Hermione Granger read the ingredients for the potion from *Most Potent Potions* to Harry Potter and Ron Weasley during Harry's second year at Hogwarts. CS 10, pp. 165-66.

Lachlan the Lanky. A statue of Lachlan the Lanky was positioned to the right of the top of the stairs leading to the Gryffindor tower at Hogwarts. OP 13, p. 271.

Lake Windermere. A lake. Rita Skeeter once interviewed Elphias Doge about the rights of merpeople and he believed the interview was taking place under Lake Windermere. DH 2, p. 24. (Lake Windermere is England's largest lake and is located in the Cumbrian Mountains of Northwest England.)

Lancashire. A location in Britain where the earliest recorded quidditch match involving a team from Ireland was played in 1385. The British team was from Cork. Zacharias Mumps recorded the match. QA 8, p. 38. (Lancashire is a county in Northwest England.)

Lancelot. A wizard who was the brother of Auntie Muriel and was a Healer at St. Mungo's Hospital, according to Auntie Muriel. DH 8, p. 156.

Langlock. The magic word for a hex that Harry Potter invoked to glue Peeve's tongue to the roof of his mouth during Harry's sixth year at Hogwarts. Harry learned the hex from the Half Blood Prince's instructions in a Potion's book. HP 19, p. 420.

Latin World Cup. The name of the official quidditch championship that occurred in South America. QA 8, p. 45.

Law Fifteen B. A law relating to attacks by magical creatures who were deemed to have near-human intelligence. Dolores Umbridge attempted to explain the provisions of the law to the centaurs in the Forbidden Forest when they cornered her. This event occurred during Harry Potter's fifth year at Hogwarts. OP 33, p. 754.

League. The name for the Great Britain and Ireland quidditch league that was established in 1674. The League consisted of the thirteen best quidditch teams at the time. All other teams in the region were asked to disband. Each year the thirteen teams competed for the League Cup. QA 7, p. 32. The league consisted of the following teams or clubs: Appleby Arrows; Ballycastle Bats; Caerphilly Catapults; Chudley Cannons; Falmouth Falcons; Holyhead Harpies; Kenmare Kestrels; Montrose Magpies; Pride of Portree; Puddlemere United; Tutshill Tornados; Wigtown Wanderers; Wimbourne Wasps. QA 7, pp. 32-38.

League Cup. The prize awarded annually to the best quidditch team in the league. QA 7, p. 32.

Leaky Cauldron. A tiny, grubby-looking pub frequented by wizards in London. The Leaky Cauldron was magically concealed from the view of muggles between a big book shop and a record shop. The bartender and innkeeper's name was Tom. SS p. 5, pp. 68-69. Harry Potter stayed in Room Eleven of the pub when he arrived in Diagon Alley during the summer prior to his third year at Hogwarts. PA 3, p. 46. The mirror in that room talked to him. PA 4, pp 55, 68. Percy and Ron Weasley occupied Room Twelve on that same occasion. PA 4, pp. 64, 67. During the aftermath that followed the Quidditch World Cup that Harry attended, a young wizard boasted to a villa that he worked for the Committee for the Disposal of Dangerous Creatures as a dragon killer and was compensated at a rate of one hundred sacks of galleons a year. The young wizard's own friend accused him of being a dishwasher at the Leaky Cauldron. This event occurred during the summer prior to Harry's fourth year at Hogwarts. GF 9, p. 125. The Leaky Caultdron was located on Charing Cross Road. HP 6, p. 109. DH 9, p. 163.

Leanne. A student of Hogwarts who was a friend of Katie Bell. HP 112, p. 248.

Leaping Toadstools. Toadstools that Ernie Macmillan asked Harry Potter to pass to him in a Herbology class. This event occurred during Harry's second year at Hogwarts. CS 14, p. 251.

Leaving Feast. The meal served at the end of the school year at Hogwarts when the winner of the Inter-House Championship was announced.

This event occurred during Harry Potter's fourth year at Hogwarts. GF 37, p. 720.

Leeches. An ingredient used to make Polyjuice Potion. Hermione Granger read the ingredients of the potion from *Most Potent Potions* to Harry Potter and Ron Weasley during Harry's second year at Hogwarts. CS 10, p. 165.

Leg-Locker Curse. A curse that caused a person's legs to stick together, making it impossible for the person to walk normally. The magic words "*locomotor mortis*" were used to invoke the curse. Neville Longbottom had this curse placed on him by Draco Malfoy and Neville was forced to hop around like a rabbit until Hermione Granger performed the countercurse. This event occurred during Harry Potter's first year at Hogwarts. SS 13, pp. 217, 222.

Legilimency. The magical ability to extract feelings and memories from another person's mind. Lord Voldemort was highly skilled at legilimency. The opposing magical art to legilimency was occlumency. In order for legilimency to operate there needed to be eye contact. OP 24, p. 531. DH 7, p. 128.

Legilimens. The magic word used to intrude into someone else's mind or thoughts. OP 24, p. 534. According to Severus Snape, Lord Voldemort was the most accomplished legilimens the world had ever seen. HP 2, p. 26.

Lemon Drop. A muggle candy that Albus Dumbledore enjoyed. SS 1, p.10. Lemon Drop was a password for opening the secret passageway behind a large and extremely ugly stone gargoyle that led to Dumbledore's office at Hogwarts. Harry Potter discovered the passageway during his second year at Hogwarts. CS 11, p. 204. Two years later, he tried to use the password "sherbet lemon" on the passageway, thinking it was the password he had used before. He assumed that the password must have been changed when the door did not open. GF 27, p. 557. Harry then tried several candy names on the door until Cockroach Cluster finally worked as the password. GF 29, p. 579. During his sixth year, toffee eclairs worked. HP 20, p. 426.

Leprechaun. A little, bearded person who wore a red vest. Leprechauns were the Irish National Team Mascots at the Quidditch World Cup that Harry Potter attended during the summer prior to his fourth year at Hogwarts. The leprechauns arrived at the game on a comet, formed a shamrock that floated in the air and threw down heavy gold coins to the spectators. GF 8, p. 104. Leprechauns were found exclusively in Ireland. FB, p. 25. They were the only "little people" who were able to speak, but never requested reclassification as "Beings." They were also known as clauricorns. FB, p. 25. The Kenmare Kestrels selected the leprechaun as the club mascot. QA 7, p. 35. DH 26, p. 530.

Leprechaun Gold. Gold coins of leprechauns that disappeared after being exposed for a few hours. Rubeus Hagrid used leprechaun gold in a niffler demonstration for Harry Potter's Care for Magical Creatures class. This event occurred during Harry's fourth year at Hogwarts. GF 27, p. 544. Leprechaun gold fell from the air during the Quidditch World Cup that occurred during the summer prior to Harry's fourth year at Hogwarts. GF 8, p. 104.

Lestrange. A married couple of wizards who were Death Eaters and, according to Sirius Black, were imprisoned in Azkaban. Sirius shared this information with Harry Potter during Harry's fourth year at Hogwarts. GF 27, p. 531. The Lestrange family had one of the most ancient vaults at Gringotts Wizarding Bank. DH 25, p. 509.

Lestrange, Bellatrix (Black). A Death Eater convicted of torturing and permanently incapacitating Frank and Alice Longbottom. Bellatrix was Sirius Black's cousin and Rodolphus Lestrange's wife. OP 25, pp. 544, 545. She considered herself to be Lord Voldemort's most faithful servant. OP 36, p. 811. During year seven, Bellatrix attended a meeting between Lord Voldemort and Death Eaters at the Malfoy manor home. She was the aunt to Nymphadora Tonks. DH 1, pp. 8-10. Her magic wand was made out of walnut and dragon heartstring. It was twelve and three-quarter inches long and unyielding. DH 24, p. 493. Bellatrix' fate was revealed at the end of year seven. DH 36, pp. 736-37.

Lestrange, Rabastan. The brother of Rodolphus Lestrange. Rabastan was a prisoner at Azkaban during Harry Potter's fifth year at Hogwarts. OP 6, p. 114.

Lestrange, Rodolphus. The husband of Bellatrix Black. Rodolphus, his wife and brother, Rabastan, were prisoners at Azkaban. OP 6, p. 114. Rodolphus was present in the Department of Mysteries when Harry Potter retrieved the prophecy relating to himself and Lord Voldemort. This event occurred during Harry's fifth year at Hogwarts. OP 35, p. 788. Rodolphus was one of the Death Eaters that chased Harry, after Harry left the protection of the Dursley residence during year seven. DH 5, p. 76.

Lethifold. A magical beast that lived exclusively in tropical climates. The earliest known attack by a lethifold was in 1782. The only spell that worked to repel a lethifold was the Patronus Charm. FB, pp. 25-27.

Levicorpus. A spell that Harry Potter discovered was difficult for the Half Blood Prince to perform. HP 12, p. 238. It had the effect of raising a person by the ankle, upside down, on an invisible hook. The counterjinx was "*liberacorpus*." HP 12, p. 239. Hermione Granger invoked the charm during year seven to raise Harry into the air. DH 26, p. 539.

Levitation Charm. A charm that Harry Potter invoked as part of the practical examination of the O.W.L.s during his fifth year at Hogwarts. OP 31, p. 713.

Levski. A member of the Bulgarian National Quidditch Team who played at the Quidditch World Cup that Harry Potter attended during the summer prior to his fourth year at Hogwarts. Levski was a chaser. The other members of the team were: Dimitrov, Ivanova, Zograf, Vulchanov, Volkov and Viktor Krum. GF 8, pp. 104, 107.

Liberacorpus. The counter jinx to the *levicorpus* charm. HP 12, p. 239. DH 26, p. 540.

Licorice Wands. Special candy sold in the wizarding world. Harry Potter purchased Licorice Wands on the Hogwarts Express as he traveled to his first year at Hogwarts. SS 6, p. 101.

Liechtenstein. A country, the warlocks of which, refused to join the International Confederation of Wizards. This historical fact appeared in a question of the History of Magic O.W.L. that Harry Potter took during his fifth year at Hogwarts. OP 31, p. 725. (Liechtenstein is a small principality in Central Europe located between Austria and Switzerland.)

Life and Lies of Albus Dumbledore, The. During year seven, Rita Skeeter authored the 900-page book *The Life and Lies of Albus Dumbledore*. She marketed the book as an explosive biography of the wizard. DH 2, pp. 22-23.

Liondragon. See **Chinese Fireball**.

Lithuania. The home country of the Gorodok Gargoyles. QA 8, p. 46. (Lithuania is a country in Northern Europe on the Baltic Sea.)

Little Hangleton. The village in which the Riddle House was located. GF 1, p. 1. A pub named The Hanged Man was located in Little Hangleton. GF 1, p. 2. During year four, Harry Potter had a duel with Voldemort in the graveyard of Little Hangleton. DH 35, p. 721.

Little Hangletons. The name for the villagers who resided in Little Hangleton. GF 1, p. 1. They congregated in a pub named The Hanged Man that was located in Little Hangleton. GF 1, p. 2.

Little Norton. The location where Doris Polkiss lived, specifically 18 Acanthia Way. OP 10, p. 191.

Little Red Books. The publisher of *A History of Magic* by Bathilda Bagshot. The book was published in 1947. FB, p. xv, fn. 4. Little Red Books also published: *Why I Didn't Die When the Augurey Cried* by Gulliver Pokeby in 1824, FB, p. 3, fn. 4; and *Home Life and Social Habits of British Muggles* by Wilhelm Wigworthy in 1987, FB, p. 7, fn. 6.

Little Whinging. The town where the Dursley family lived with Harry Potter. The family's full address was 4 Privet Drive, Little Whinging, Surrey. SS 3, p. 34.

Livius. One of the reputed owners of the Elder Wand. Either Livius or Arcus may have killed Loxias in order to obtain the Elder Wand. DH 21, p. 412.

Llewellyn, "Dangerous" Dai. A famous quidditch player. Kennilworthy Whisp wrote a biography of "Dangerous" Dai Llewellyn and titled it: *He Flew Like a Madman.* QA, p. v. "Dangerous" Dai was eaten by a chimera while on vacation in Mykonos, Greece. QA 7, p. 33. A ward at St. Mungo's Hospital for Magical Maladies and Injuries was named after him and Arthur Weasley was a patient in that ward during Harry Potter's fifth year at Hogwarts. OP 22, p. 487.

Lobalug. A magical beast that lived at the bottom of the North Sea. The lobalug's venom sac made it an attractive weapon for merpeople. Wizards also extracted the venom for potions, but the practice was strictly controlled. FB, p. 27.

Loch Ness. A location in Scotland where the world's largest kelpie was found. Scotland repeatedly violated Clause 73 of the International Code of Wizarding Secrecy by allowing muggles to view the kelpie in Loch Ness. FB, pp. xvii, 24. (Loch Ness is a lake in Northwest Scotland near Inverness.)

Lochrin, Guthrie. A Scottish wizard who wrote in 1107 that he suffered a splinter-filled buttocks and bulging piles after taking a short broomstick ride from Montrose to Arbroath. QA 1, p. 2.

Lockhart, Gilderoy. A wizard who had the following title: Order of Merlin, Third Class, Honorary Member of the Dark Force Defense League. Gilderoy claimed to have been a five-time winner of *Witch Weekly's* Most-Charming-Smile Award. CS 6, p. 99, CS 13, p. 228. He also claimed to have been seeker for the National Squad. CS 10, p. 163. Gilderoy was the author of several books in the wizarding world. CS 3, p. 35. His books included: *Break with a Banshee,* CS 4, p. 43; *Gadding with Ghouls,* CS 4, p. 43; 10, p. 162 (This was the author's favorite); *Gilderoy Lockhart's Guide to Household Pets,* CS 3, p. 35; *Holidays with Hags,* CS 4, p. 43; *Magical Me,* CS 4, p. 58; *Travels with Trolls,* CS 4, p. 43; *Voyages and Vampires,* CS 4, p. 43; *Wanderings and Werewolves,* CS 4, p. 43; *Year with the Yeti.* CS 4, pp. 43, 59. Gilderoy was the Defense Against the Dark Arts professor at Hogwarts during Harry Potter's second year at the school. CS 4, p. 60. His office was located on the second floor. CS 7, p. 119. Gilderoy was quoted as giving praise to *Quidditch Through the Ages.* QA, p. iv. During Harry's fifth year at Hogwarts, Gilderoy was a patient on the Janus Thickey ward at St. Mungo's Hospital for Magical Maladies and Injuries. OP 23, pp. 508-09.

Locomotor mortis. The magic words used to invoke the leg-locker curse. The curse caused a person's legs to stick together, making it impossible for the person to walk normally. SS 13, p. 217. Neville Longbottom had the curse placed on him by Draco Malfoy and Neville was forced to hop around like a rabbit until Hermione Granger performed the countercurse. This event occurred during Harry Potter's first year at Hogwarts. SS 13, pp. 217, 222.

Locomotor Trunk. The magic words used in a charm to levitate and move a trunk. Nymphadora Tonks used this charm during the summer prior to Harry Potter's fifth year at Hogwarts. OP 3, p. 53.

London. The place where Petunia Dursley took her son Dudley to buy his uniforms for Smeltings. This event occurred during the summer prior to Harry Potter's first year at Hogwarts. SS 3, p. 32. The wizarding world sometimes referred to part of the city as Muggle London. PA 3, p. 46. T.M. Riddle's diary came from a variety store on Vauxhall Road, London. CS 13, p. 231. London was also the place where the Dursleys took Dudley to a private hospital in order to remove a pigtail that Rubeus Hagrid conjured on Dudley's bottom during the summer prior to Harry's first year at Hogwarts. GF 4, p. 40. Gladrags Wizardwear had a store located in London as well. GF 8, p. 97. London was the secret location, at Number Twelve, Grimmauld Place, of the Order of the Phoenix. OP 3, p. 58. DH 27, p. 544.

London Underground. A scar on Rubeus Hagrid's left knee was in the shape of the map of the London Underground. SS 1, p. 15. See also **Muggle Underground.** (The London Underground refers to the subway system in London.)

Londoners. The muggle residents of London, England. DH 12, p. 1223.

Longbottom, Algie. Neville Longbottom's great uncle who pushed Neville off the end of a pier at Black Pool to test whether Neville was muggle or wizard. Algie purchased Neville a toad, who Neville named Trevor. Neville recounted this information to Ron Weasley after they met each other during Harry Potter's first year at Hogwarts. SS 7, p. 125.

Longbottom, Alice. A witch who was a member of the Order of the Phoenix. Alice was Frank Longbottom's wife and Neville's mother. OP 9, p. 173. She was a patient at St. Mungos Hospital for Magical Maladies and Injuries. Alice and Frank had been aurors for the Ministry of Magic and were injured by Bellatrix Lestrange, who used the Cruciatus Curse on them. OP 23, p. 514; 25, p. 544.

Longbottom, Augusta. The grandmother of Neville Longbottom, who was a witch. SS 7, p. 125. According to Professor McGonagell, Augusta failed her Charms O.W.L. HP 9, p. 174. She was in the Room of Requirement at Hogwarts during year seven. DH 31, p. 624.

Longbottom, Enid. Neville Longbottom's great aunt who offered his Great Uncle Algie a meringue while he was holding Neville out a window.

Algie dropped Neville and he bounced instead of becoming injured. This event demonstrated that Neville had wizarding blood. Neville told this event to Ron Weasley after they met each other during Harry Potter's first year at Hogwarts. SS 7, p. 125.

Longbottom, Frank. Neville Longbottom's father. GF 30, p. 602. Frank was an auror for the Ministry of Magic and was subjected to a Cruciatus Curse by four Death Eaters, one of whom was Barty Crouch's son. The Death Eaters believed that Frank had information on the whereabouts of Lord Voldemort and when he was not forthcoming with the information, they used the same curse on Frank's wife. The Death Eaters were tried before the Council of Magical Law and sentenced to life terms in prison at Azkaban. Harry Potter learned this information from the pensieve in Albus Dumbledore's office during Harry's fourth year at Hogwarts. GF 30, p. 595. Frank and his wife became insane after the Cruciatus Curse was placed on them and were admitted to the St. Mungo's Hospital for Magical Maladies and Injuries. GF 30, p. 602. Frank was a member of the Order of the Phoenix. OP 9, p. 173. He was tortured and permanently incapacitated, through a Cruciatus Curse, by Bellatrix Lestrange. OP 23, p. 514; 25, p. 544.

Longbottom, Neville. A student of Hogwarts who was one of Harry Potter's classmates and friends. He had a toad named Trevor. Neville was a member of the Gryffindor house. He was raised by his grandmother who was a witch. SS 6, pp. 94, 112; 7, pp. 120, 125. Neville shared this information with Ron Weasley after they met each other during Harry Potter's first year at Hogwarts. Neville's grandmother wore a tall hat with a stuffed vulture on top, a long, green dress and carried a big red handbag. PA 7, p. 135. Neville received mail from a barn owl. SS 9, p. 145. Neville's father was Frank Longbottom. GF 30, p. 602. Although he was a pure-blood, Neville had difficulty performing magic. CS 7, p. 116. Neville's best subject was Herbology. GF 14, p. 213. He asked Hermione Granger to the Yule Ball, but she refused him because she had already been asked by someone else whom she did not identify to Neville. Neville then asked Ginny Weasley, who accepted. GF 22, pp. 399, 401. Neville was one of the few students at Hogwarts who could see a thestral, because he had seen his grandfather die. OP 21, p. 449. He was born in July like Harry Potter. OP 37, p. 842. During the summer prior to Harry's sixth year at Hogwarts, Neville purchased a cherry wood and unicorn hair wand from Ollivander's. He believed the wand to be one of the last sold in that shop before it mysteriously closed. HP 7, p. 137. On his O.W.L.s, Neville received only "acceptable" for Transfiguration. HP 7, p. 138. Neville was injured by a Death Eater at the end of Harry's sixth year at Hogwarts. HP 29, p. 612. DH 12, p. 227; 28, p. 570. Nineteen years after the concluding events of year seven, Neville was the professor of Herbology at Hogwarts. DH Epilogue, p. 757.

Loser's Lurgy. A condition that Luna Lovegood believed afflicted Zacharias Smith during the Gryffindor-Hufflepuff quidditch match during Harry Potter's sixth year at Hogwarts. HP 19, p. 415.

Lovage. One of the ingredients in the Confusing Draught and Befuddlement Draught. OP 18, p. 383. (Lovage is a plant in the parsley family, found in Europe, that has coarsely toothed compound leaves.)

Love Potion. A potion that Gilderoy Lockhart suggested that the students of Hogwarts ask Severus Snape to make for them on Valentine's Day. This event occurred during Harry Potter's second year at the school. CS 13, p. 236. According to an article in *Witch Weekly*, Love Potions were banned at Hogwarts. Pansy Parkinson was quoted in *Witch Weekly* as stating that Hermione Granger must have used a love potion. This event occurred during Harry's fourth year at Hogwarts. GF 27, p. 512.

Lovegoods. A family of wizards who, according to Amos Diggory, lived in the vicinity of Stoatshead Hill and who had already been at the location of the Quidditch World Cup for a week when the Weasleys, Harry Potter and Hermione Granger met Amos and Cedric Diggory at the portkey on Stoatshead Hill. This event occurred during the summer prior to Harry's fourth year at Hogwarts. GF 6, p. 73.

Lovegood, Luna. A student at Hogwarts who was in the same year as Ginny Weasley. Luna was a member of the Ravenclaw house. Her father was the editor of *The Quibbler*. Luna's mother was an extraordinary witch who died when one of her spells didn't work properly. At that time Luna was only nine years old. OP 10, pp. 185-186, 193; 38, p. 863. Her father was Xenophilius Lovegood. DH 8, p. 139. During year seven, Luna was captured and taken as a prisoner to the cellar in the Malfoy mansion. DH 23, p. 464. Luna's patronus took the form of a silver hare. DH 32, p. 649.

Lovegood, Xenophilius. The father of Luna Lovegood. A neighbor to the Weasley family, he attended the wedding of Fleur Delacourt and Bill Weasley during year seven. DH 8, p. 139.

Loxias. One of the reputed owners of the Elder Wand. Loxias killed Barnabas Deverill in order to obtain the Elder Wand. DH 21, p. 412.

Ludicrous Patents Office. An office in the Department of Magical Games and Sports of the Ministry of Magic located on level seven of the Ministry. OP 7, p. 129.

Lumos. The magic word used in a charm to produce a light at the end of a wand. CS 15, p. 272. Harry Potter invoked the charm before venturing into the Forbidden Forest with Ron Weasley during Harry's second year at Hogwarts. CS 15, p. 272. He also used the charm to light his wand on Magnolia Crescent after running away from the Dursley residence. PA 3, p. 33. Hermione Granger used the charm to light her wand in the camp ground late at night after the Quidditch World Cup. GF 9, p. 120. Harry used the charm to light the tip of his wand in the library the night before the second task of the Triwizard Tournament and within the maze for the third task. GF 26, p. 489; GF 31, p. 621. Albus Dumbledore used the charm to light the way near the Forbidden Forest. These last three events occurred during Harry's fourth year at Hogwarts. GF 26, p. 489; 31, p. 621; 27, p. 559.

Lunascope. A device that allowed one to dispense with using moon charts. The Lunascope was sold at shops on Diagon Alley. Harry Potter overheard shoppers on Diagon Alley comment about the device. This event occurred during the summer prior to Harry's third year at Hogwarts. PA 4, p. 50. Hermione Granger used a Summoning Charm in a Charms class to propel lunascopes, blackboard erasers and wastepaper baskets across the room. This event occurred during Harry's fourth year at Hogwarts. GF 18, p. 297.

Lupin, Remus John. A wizard who was the professor of the Defense Against the Dark Arts class during Harry Potter's third year at Hogwarts. PA 5, p. 74; PA 18, p. 350. Remus' greatest fear, as revealed during a class demonstration with a bogart, was a silvery-white orb hanging in the air. PA 7, p. 138. Hermione Granger first alluded to knowing a secret about Remus before Harry attended his first patronus lesson with Remus. PA 11, p. 236. Remus' secret was later revealed. PA 17, pp. 345-346; PA 18, pp. 352-353. When he attended the school as a student, Remus' friends called him Moony. PA 17, p. 347. Remus was a member of the Order of the Phoenix and the advance guard that rescued Harry from the Dursley home during the summer prior to Harry's fifth year at Hogwarts. OP 3, p. 46. When he attended Hogwarts as a student, Remus was a prefect. OP 9, p. 170. He became a werewolf as a child after being bitten by Fenrir Greyback. HP 16, p. 335. At the end of Harry's sixth year at the school, it was clear that Nymphadora Tonks was in love with Remus. HP 29, p. 624. Lupin married Tonks immediately prior to the commencement of year seven. DH 1, p. 10; 4, p. 45. At the beginning of year seven, Remus escorted George Weasley, who had taken Polyjuice Potion to look with Harry, on a broomstick from the Dursley residence. DH 4, p. 52. Remus' middle name, John, was not revealed until year seven. DH 10, p. 204. Remus had a serious confrontation with Harry that same year. DH 11, p. 214. He used a code name, Romulus, on *Potterwatch* during year seven. DH 22, p. 441. He was the father of Ted Lupin. DH 25, p. 514. Remus' fate was explained at DH 33, p. 661.

Lupin, Ted. The son of Remus and Nymphadora Lupin who was born during year seven. Ted was named after his maternal grandfather, Ted Tonks. Harry Potter was his godfather. DH 25, p. 514.

Luxembourg. According to Charlie Weasley, the national quidditch team from Luxembourg slaughtered the team from Scotland. This event occurred during the summer prior to Harry Potter's fourth year at Hogwarts. GF 5, p. 63. Luxembourg was the home country of the Bigonville Bombers. QA 8, p. 41. (Luxembourg is a grand duchy surrounded by France, Germany and Belgium.)

Lynch, Aiden. A member of the Irish National Quidditch Team who played in the Quidditch World Cup that Harry Potter attended during the summer prior to his fourth year at Hogwarts. Lynch was a seeker. The other members of the team were: Connolly, Ryan, Troy, Mullet, Moran and Quigley. GF 8, pp. 105, 108.

MACBOON – MYRTLE, MOANING

MacBoon. A wizarding clan from Scotland that had a feud with the McCliverts. The MacBoons were transfigured into five-legged creatures that became known as quintapeds. FB, pp. 34-36.

MacBoon, Quintius. The chief of the MacBoon clan who killed Dugald McClivert in a drunken, wizarding duel. FB, pp. 34-36.

Macdonald, Magnus "Dent-Head." A wizard who unsuccessfully lobbied the Ministry of Magic in the 1960's to lift the ban on the sport of creaothceann. QA 2, p. 6.

Macdonald, Mary. A student at Hogwarts who attended the school at the same time as James and Lily Potter. Avery and Mulciber, two other students, tried to do something unspeakable to her. DH 33, p. 673.

MacDougal, Morag. A student who was sorted by the Sorting Hat during Harry Potter's first year at Hogwarts. Morag's placement into a house was not identified. SS 7, p. 120.

MacFarlen, Harnish. A famous wizard who was the captain of the Montrose Magpies from 1957 through 1968. QA 7, p. 35. After his career with the team, Harnish became the head of the Department of Magical Games and Sports. QA 7, p. 36.

MacFusty. A wizard clan that lived in the Hebrides for centuries and cared for the Hebridean Black dragons. FB, p. 12.

Mackled Malaclaw. A magical creature found on rocky coastlines around Europe that had a slight resemblance to a lobster. A wizard bitten by a mackled malaclaw experienced bad luck for up to one week. FB, p. 28.

Macmillan, Ernie. A student of Hogwarts who attended the first meeting of the Dueling Club and received the encouragement of the club's instructor, Gilderoy Lockhart. CS 11, p. 192. Ernie was a member of the Hufflepuff house and in the same year as Harry Potter. Harry eavesdropped on a conversation between Ernie and Hannah Abbot about Harry's parseltoungue incident at the first meeting of the Dueling Club during Harry's second year at Hogwarts. CS 11, p. 198-200. Harry encountered Ernie around the camp site at the Quidditch World Cup. This event occurred during the summer prior to Harry's fourth year at Hogwarts. GF 7, p. 84. Ernie's name appeared on the list of borrowers found inside the cover of *Quidditch Through the Ages.* QA, p. i. During Harry's fifth year at Hogwarts, Ernie was a prefect, along with Hannah Abbott, for the Hufflepuff house. OP 10, p. 188. The following year, he had scored high enough in O.W.L.s to take the Potions N.E.W.T. class. HP 9, p. 182. DH 29, p. 578. Ernie's patronus took the form of a silver boar. DH 32, p. 649.

Macnair, Walden. A member of the Committee for the Disposal of Dangerous Creatures who was appointed the executioner for Buckbeak at sundown on June 6 of Harry Potter's third year at Hogwarts. Walden was a friend of Lucius Malfoy. PA 16, p. 328; 21, 400. Harry discovered that Walden was a Death Eater during his fourth year at Hogwarts. GF 33, p. 651. Walden was sent by Lord Voldemort to negotiate with the giants during Harry's fifth year at Hogwarts. OP 20, p. 430. He was present in the Department of Mysteries when Harry retrieved the prophecy relating to himself and Lord Voldemort. This event occurred during Harry's fifth year at Hogwarts. OP 35, p. 788. Walden's fate was revealed at the end of year seven. DH 36, p. 735.

Madam Malkin's Robes for All Occasions. A shop located on Diagon Alley where wizard students got fitted for their school robes. Harry Potter purchased his robes in the shop prior to his first year at Hogwarts. SS 5, p. 76. Another robe shop in Diagon Alley was Twilfitt and Tatting's. HP 6, p. 114. DH 23, p. 459.

Madam Puddifoot's Tea Shop. A small tea shop located in Hogsmeade that Harry Potter and Cho Chang visited on Valentine's Day during Harry's fifth year at Hogwarts. OP 25, p. 559. The shop was described as a haunt for happy couples. HP 12, p. 248.

Madcap Magic for Wacky Warlocks. The title of a book that Harry Potter consulted in order to find a way to breathe underwater in the second task of the Triwizard Tournament. This event occurred during Harry's fourth year at Hogwarts. GF 26, p. 488.

Madley, Laura. A student who was sorted by the Sorting Hat during Harry Potter's fourth year at Hogwarts. Laura was a member of the Hufflepuff house. GF 12, p. 178.

Magical Drafts and Potions, A. The title of a book written by Arsenius Jigger. First-year students were required to have the book during Harry Potter's first year at Hogwarts. SS 5, p. 66.

Magical Hieroglyphs and Logograms. A book that Hermione Granger read during her fifth year at Hogwarts. OP 26, p. 574.

Magical Law. A profession in the wizarding world. DH 7, p. 123.

Magical Law Enforcement Patrol. An office in the Ministry of Magic capable of catching the Anti-Muggle pranksters responsible for regurgitating public toilets. This event occurred during the summer prior to Harry Potter's fifth year at Hogwarts. OP 7, p. 133. See **Magical Law Enforcement Squad**.

Magical Law Enforcement Squad. A squad within the Ministry of Magic that used Hit Wizards. Cornelius Fudge mentioned that this was the only squad capable of handling Sirius Black. Fudge's remarks were overheard by Harry Potter, Ron Weasley and Hermione Granger in the Three Broomsticks. This event occurred during Harry's third year at Hogwarts. PA 10, p. 208. At one time the head of the squad was Bob Ogden. HP 10, p. 207.

Magical Maintenance. An office in the Ministry of Magic responsible for enchanting the windows at the Ministry for different types of weather. OP 7, p. 131. The persons who worked in the office always wore navy blue robes. DH 12, p. 229.

Magical Me. The title of an autobiography written by Gilderoy Lockhart. Gilderoy held a book signing for the book at Flourish and Blotts during the sumer prior to Harry Potter's third year at Hogwarts. CS 4, p. 58.

Magical Menagerie. A shop located on Diagon Alley that sold owls and other items. Ron Weasley took his pet rat Scabbers to the shop for a diagnosis during the summer prior to Harry Potter's third year at Hogwarts. PA 4, p. 58.

Magical Theory. The title of a book, written by Adalbert Waffling. The book was required for first-year students during Harry Potter's first year at Hogwarts. SS 5, p. 66.

Magical Water Plants of the Mediterranean. The title of a book that Neville Longbottom read during Harry Potter's fourth year at Hogwarts. Mad-Eye Moody lent Neville the book after Professor Sprout informed Mad-Eye that Neville was good at the study of Herbology. GF 14, p. 220. The book contained important information about gillyweed. GF 35, p. 677.

Magick Moste Evile. The title of a book that Hermione Granger consulted in the Hogwarts library in an effort to find information on horcruxes. This event occurred during Harry Potter's sixth year at Hogwarts. HP 18, p. 381.

Magizoology. The study of magical beasts. Newt Scamander made important contributions to magizoology. FB, p. vi.

Magnolia Crescent. A street located near Privet Drive in Little Whinging. Harry Potter collapsed onto a low wall along Magnolia Crescent after running away from the Dursley residence. This event occurred during the summer prior to Harry's third year at Hogwarts. PA 3, p. 31. Magnolia Crescent ran parallel to Wisteria Walk and was connected to it by a narrow alley. OP 1, p. 13.

Magnolia Road. A street next to Magnolia Crescent in Little Whinging that Harry Potter took to get to a play park during the summer prior to his fifth year at Hogwarts. OP 1, p. 9.

Magorian. A centaur that lived in the Forbidden Forest. Magorian was angry, along with the other centaurs there, that Firenze turned traitor by agreeing to live with humans and teach at Hogwarts. This event occurred during Harry Potter's fifth year at Hogwarts. OP 30, p. 698. DH 36, p. 734.

Majorca. The place where Yvonne, a friend of the Dursley family, vacationed. As a result of being on vacation, Yvonne was unable to watch Harry Potter on Dudley's eleventh birthday. This event occurred during the summer prior to Harry's first year at Hogwarts. SS 2, pp. 22-23. Majorca was also the place where Vernon Dursley bragged that the Dursleys would buy a vacation home after closing a business deal with Mr. Mason. This event occurred during the summer prior to Harry's second year at Hogwarts. CS 1, p. 7. (Majorca is a Spanish island in the Western Mediterranean Sea. It is the largest of the Balearic Islands.)

Malcolm. A member of Dudley Dursley's gang who liked to tease Harry Potter by playing "Harry Hunting." The other members of the gang, in addition to Dudley, were Piers, Dennis and Gordon. SS 3, p. 31.

Malecrit. A French wizard from around the early 1400's who wrote a play titled "Alas, I've Transfigured My Feet." One of the characters in the play, Grenouille, informed Crapaud that he was the keeper on a quidditch team. QA 8, p. 39.

Malfoy. A wizard family that was one of the first to leave the Dark Side after the disappearance of Voldemort; the Malfoys claimed to have been bewitched. SS 6, p. 110. The Malfoy house had a secret chamber below the drawing-room floor where the family stashed valuable objects relating to the Dark Arts. CS 12, p. 224. The Malfoys had a house-elf named Dobby. CS 2, p. 12. After Dobby was freed, he summoned up the courage to inform Harry Potter that the Malfoys were bad, Dark wizards. GF 21, p. 381. The Malfoy family lived in Wiltshire. OP 15, p. 307.

Malfoy, Abraxas. The grandfather of Draco Malfoy who died of dragon pox. Horace Slughorn knew Abraxas. HP 9, p. 189.

Malfoy, Draco. A student of Hogwarts who was Harry Potter's arch enemy and bullied him, with assistance from his bodyguards Vincent Crabbe and Gregory Goyle. SS 5, p. 77, 6, p. 108; CS 1, p. 8. Draco was a member of the Slytherin house. His mail was delivered by an eagle owl. SS 7, p. 120; 9, p. 144. In his second year at Hogwarts, Draco became the seeker of the Slytherin quidditch team after his father purchased new broomsticks for all of the players. CS 7, p. 111. During Harry's fourth year at the school, Mad-Eye Moody turned Draco into a white ferret, which made Draco fear Mad-Eye from then on. GF 13, p. 204. Draco took Pansy Parkinson to the Yule Ball that year. GF 23, p. 413. During Harry's fifth year at Hogwarts, Draco was a prefect, along with Pansy Parkinson, for Slytherin. Draco was appointed to the Inquisitorial Squad by Dolores Umbridge that same year. OP 10, p. 188; 28, p. 626. The following year he was assigned a very important duty by Lord Voldemort. HP 2, p. 33. During year seven, Draco attended a meeting between Lord Voldemort and Death Eaters at his family's manor home. DH 1, p. 8. Draco's magic wand was made from hawthorn and unicorn hair. It was exactly ten inches long and reasonably springy. DH 24, p. 493; 31, p. 628. Draco was the true master of an important magical device, which fact was revealed at the end of year seven. DH 36, p. 743.

Malfoy, Lucius. The father of Draco Malfoy who was a supporter of Lord Voldemort and a member of Lord Voldemort's inner circle. CS 3, p. 29; 4, p. 50. Lucius was a governor of Hogwarts for a portion of Harry Potter's second year there. CS 12, p. 221; 18, p. 340. He disliked Arthur Weasley immensely and got into a fist fight with him at Flourish and Blotts during the summer prior to Harry's third year at Hogwarts. PA 4, pp. 62-63. Harry discovered in his fourth year at the school that Lucius was a Death Eater. GF 33, p. 650. Lucius was 41years old during the fall term of Harry Potter's fifth year at Hogwarts. The Malfoy family lived in Wiltshire. OP 15, p. 307. During the summer prior to Harry's sixth year at Hogwarts, Lucius was imprisoned in Azkaban. HP 7, p. 130. During year seven, Lucius was asked by Lord Voldemort for Lucius' wand. Lucius' wand was made of elm wood and had a dragon heartstring core. DH 1, pp. 7-8. When Lucius attended Hogwarts, he was a prefect in the Slytherin house during Severus Snape's first year there. DH 33, p. 673.

Malfoy, Narcissa (Black). The wife of Lucius Malfoy and mother of Draco Malfoy. Narcissa sat with her family in the top box at the Quidditch World Cup. This event occurred during the summer prior to Harry Potter's fourth year at Hogwarts. GF 8. Narcissa was one of Sirius Black's cousins. Her two sisters were Andromeda Black and Bellatrix Black. OP 6, p. 113, HP 2, p. 21. Her nickname was Cissy. HP 2, p.

20. During year seven, Narcissa attended a meeting between Lord Voldemort and Death Eaters at her manor home. DH 1, p. 8. Narcissa was the Death Eater that Voldemort asked to determine whether Harry was dead after Voldemort struck him with the Killing Curse at the end of year seven. DH 36, p. 727.

Malfoy Manor. The name of the home occupied by the Malfoy family during year seven. DH 23, p. 466.

Malfoy, Scorpius. The son of Draco Malfoy who attended Hogwarts nineteen years after the concluding events of year seven. DH Epilogue, p. 756.

Malkin, Madam. A witch who owned Madam Malkin's Robes for All Occasions, a shop located on Diagon Alley. Harry Potter purchased his robes from this shop prior to his first year at Hogwarts. SS 5, p. 76.

Mallowsweet. A plant material, along with sage, that Harry Potter burned in the first Divination class taught by Firenze. This event occurred during Harry's fifth year at Hogwarts. OP 27, p. 603.

Mandrake. A powerful restorative plant used to return people who had been transfigured or cursed back to their original state. Mandrakes formed the essential part of most antidotes. In its early stage, a mandrake appeared like a small, muddy and extremely ugly baby with leaves growing out of its head. However, the cry of the fully-grown mandrake was fatal to anyone who heard it. CS 6, pp. 91-93. In order to avoid injury when repotting mandrakes as they grew older, it was advisable to wear earmuffs. Harry Potter's Herbology class experimented with this creature during Harry's second year at Hogwarts. CS 6, p.92. Mandrake was the favorite food of dugbogs, which ate the roots of the plant from underneath the earth. FB, p. 15. DH 31, p. 620.

Mandrake Restorative Draught. A potion that counteracted a petrification curse. CS 9, p. 144. Gilderoy Lockhart offered to make this potion for Mrs. Norris. It was later used for the victims petrified by the monster from the Chamber of Secrets. The potion was made from mature mandrakes, in the form of juice. These events occurred during Harry Potter's second year at Hogwarts. CS 18, p. 330.

Manticore. A dangerous creature that in the year 1296 savaged someone and the Committee on the Disposal of Dangerous Creatures relieved the creature of responsibility because everyone was too afraid to approach it. This incident was reported in a book that Harry Potter, Ron Weasley and Hermione Granger studied in their effort to find Buckbeak a legal defense. This event occurred during Harry's third year at Hogwarts. PA 11, p. 222. A manticore when crossed with a fire-crab made a blast-ended skrewt. This information was conveyed in a *Daily Prophet* article written by Rita Skeeter during Harry's fourth year at Hogwarts. GF 24, p. 438. The manticore's sting caused instant death and its skin repelled almost all charms. FB, p. 28.

Maori art. Carvings and paintings from the seventeenth century in New Zealand that depicted white wizards playing quidditch. QA 8, p. 41.

Marauder's Map. A magical map that Fred and George Weasley stole from Argus Filch's office at Hogwarts during their first year at Hogwarts. The map was made by Messrs. Moony, Wormtail, Padfoot and Prongs, as Purveyors of Aids to Magical Mischief-Makers. The map existed on a piece of old parchment that appeared to be blank until one tapped it with a magic wand and said "I solemnly swear that I am up to no good." The ink lines then magically appeared and revealed every detail of the Hogwarts castle, its grounds and the location of every person in it. In order to conceal the map's details one uttered the words "Mischief managed"and the map went blank again. Fred and George gave the map to Harry Potter as a Christmas present during Harry's third year at Hogwarts. PA 10, pp. 191-94. The following year, the map ended up in the hands of Mad-Eye Moody. GF 25, p. 477. DH 2, p. 15.

Marchbanks, Griselda. A witch who was a member of the Wizengamot. Madam Griselda resigned, together with Tiberius Ogden, in protest on the appointment of a High Inquisitor for Hogwarts. The *Daily Prophet* reported that Griselda had alleged links to subversive goblin groups. Griselda was the head of the Wizarding Examinations Authority and a close friend of Lucius Malfoy and Neville Longbottom's grandmother for many years. These events occurred during Harry Potter's fifth year at Hogwarts. OP 15, p. 308; 31, p. 707. Griselda was the examiner for Albus Dumbledore during his Transfiguration and Charms N.E.W.T.s. OP 31, p. 711.

Marius. A wizard who was one of two security guards at the entrance to Gringotts Wizarding Bank during year seven. DH 26, p. 529.

Mars. During one of Harry Potter's Divination classes in the Spring of his fourth year at Hogwarts, Sibyl Trelawney informed the class that Mars was in a most interesting position to Neptune. GF 29, p. 576. (Mars is the fourth planet from the sun in the solar system that includes Earth.)

Mars Bar. Muggle candy that Harry Potter expected to find, but was not sold, on the Hogwarts Express. This event occurred en route to Harry's first year at Hogwarts. SS 6, p. 101.

Marsh, Madam. A witch who was asleep on the Knight Bus when Harry Potter boarded the bus. Madam Marsh's destination was Abergavenny. This event occurred during the summer prior to Harry's third year at Hogwarts. PA 3, p. 36.

Mason, Mr. and Mrs. A rich builder and his wife who were dinner guests at the Dursley household. CS 1, p. 5. Vernon Dursley hoped to close a drill business deal with Mr. Mason after dinner. This event occurred during the summer prior to Harry Potter's second year at Hogwarts. CS 1, p. 7.

Massachusetts. The home state of the Fitchburg Finches. The Finches won the U.S. League seven times. Its seeker was Maximus Brankovitch III. QA 8, p. 45. (Massachusetts is a state on the northeast coast of the United States of America.)

Mauler. One of the names of the kneazles that were owned as pets by Newt Scamander. The other two kneazles were named Hoppy and Milly. FB, p. vi.

Mauritius. The native habitat of the diricawl. FB, p. 9. (Mauritius is an island in the Indian Ocean, east of Madagascar, and that together with surrounding islands is a republic. It was a former British colony.)

Maxime, Madam (Olympe). A witch who was as tall as Rubeus Hagrid and the head of the Beauxbatons Academy of Magic. Olympe accompanied her school's contestants to the Triwizard Tournament at Hogwarts. GF 9, p. 123; 15, pp. 243-44; 37, p. 718. These events occurred during the summer prior to and while Harry Potter attended his fourth year at Hogwarts. Olympe ended her relationship with Rubeus Hagrid after he started to bring back Grawp to the Forbidden Forest during Harry's fifth year at Hogwarts. OP 30, p. 692.

McClivert. A wizarding clan in Scotland that had a feud with the MacBoons. The McCliverts transfigured the MacBoons into five-legged creatures that became known as quintapeds. Dugald McClivert was chief of the McClivert clan. FB, pp. 34-36.

McClivert, Dugald. The chief of the McClivert clan who was killed in a drunken, wizarding duel by Quintius MacBoon. FB, pp. 34-36.

McCormack, Catriona. A witch who was the most well-known chaser for the Pride of Portree quidditch team. Catriona's daughter, Meaghan, also played for that team, but as keeper. Catriona's son, Kirley, was lead guitarist for The Weird Sisters. QA 7, p. 36.

McCormack, Kirley. A wizard who was the son of Catriona McCormack and lead guitarist for The Weird Sisters. QA 7, p. 36.

McCormack, Meaghan. A witch who was the daughter of Catriona McCormack and played keeper for the Pride of Portree. QA 7, p. 36.

McDonald, Natalie. A student who was sorted by the Sorting Hat during Harry Potter's fourth year at Hogwarts. Natalie was a member of the Gryffindor house. GF 12, p. 180.

McGonagell, Minerva. A witch and the deputy headmistress of Hogwarts. SS 1, p. 9; 4, p. 51. Minerva was an animagus and could transform herself into a tabby cat. SS 1, p. 9; PA 6, p.108. She taught the Transfiguration class at Hogwarts while Harry Potter attended the school. SS 8, pp. 133-134. Her office was located on the first floor. SS 15, p. 242. When the governors of Hogwarts issued an Order of Suspension to remove Albus Dumbledore from his position as head master, Minerva took over the position temporarily. This event occurred during Harry's second year at Hogwarts. CS 14, p. 267. Minerva had taught at Hogwarts for 39 years as of December of Harry's fifth year at the school. OP 15, p. 321. At the end of the following school year, Minerva became the Headmistress. HP 29, p. 625. DH 16, p. 316; 30, p. 591. Minerva's patronus took the form of a silver cat with spectacle markings around its eyes. DH 30, p. 596.

McGuffin, Jim. The meteorologist for a muggle television station who reported on the unusual behavior of owls that was observed on the day Lord Voldemort disappeared. SS 1, p. 6.

McKinnons. A family of witches who, according to Rubeus Hagrid, were some of the best witches and wizards of the age, including the Bones and the Prewetts. These families were killed by Lord Voldemort. SS 4, p. 56; DH 10, p. 180.

McKinnon, Marlene. A witch who was killed, along with her whole family, two weeks after a picture had been taken of her standing with the Order of the Phoenix. Alastor "Mad-Eye" Moody showed the picture to Harry Potter during the summer prior to Harry's fifth year at Hogwarts. OP 9, p. 173.

McLaggen, Cormac. Cormac was one of the privileged students to be invited into Compartment C of the Hogwarts Express to meet Professor Horace Slughorn on the way to Harry Potter's sixth year at Hogwarts. His uncle was Tiberius McLaggen. He was a member of the Gryffindor house. HP 7, pp 143-44, 150. During his seventh year at Hogwarts, Cormac tried out for the position of Keeper on the Gryffindor quidditch team. HP 11, p. 223. Although Ron Weasley got the position of keeper, Cormac substituted for Ron when Ron became ill before the match with Hufflepuff that year. HP 19, p. 413.

McLaggen, Tiberius. A wizard known by Horace Slughorn. Tiberius was an uncle to Cormac McLaggen. HP 7, p. 144.

McMillan, Ernie. A student who attended Hogwarts and was in the same Muggle Studies class as Hermione Granger during Harry Potter's third year at Hogwarts. PA 12, p. 244. See **Macmillan, Ernie**.

Meadowes, Dorcas. A witch who was a member of the Order of the Phoenix. Dorcas was murdered by Lord Voldemort. OP 9, p. 174.

Medal for Magical Merit. The name for a medal awarded to certain students of Hogwarts. The medal was located in the trophy room of the school. T.M. Riddle's name appeared on the medal. Harry Potter,

Ron Weasley and Hermione Granger discovered this information during Harry's second year at Hogwarts. CS 13, p. 234.

Medieval Assembly of European Wizards. The subject of a three-foot long composition assignment that Professor Binns gave to his History of Magic students. This event occurred during Harry Potter's second year at Hogwarts. CS 9, p. 147.

Mediterranean Sea. The sea in which hippocampus were usually found. FB, p. 21. The Mediterranean Sea was one of the natural habitats for sea serpents. FB, p. 38. (The Mediterranean Sea is an inland sea surrounded by Europe, Asia, Asia Minor, the Near East and Africa.)

Mediwizard. The title for a wizard who gave first-aid to injured players on a quidditch field. A mediwizard was instructed to kick the referee, Hassan Mostafa, in the shins during the Quidditch World Cup to arouse him from the spell of the veela. GF 8, p. 110. Viktor Krum was assisted by mediwizards after the match was over. GF 8, p. 114. These events occurred during the summer prior to Harry Potter's fourth year at Hogwarts.

Mega-Mutilation Part Three. A video game that Dudley Dursley played on his PlayStation. In a letter to Sirius Black, Harry Potter reported that Dudley angrily threw his PlayStation out of a window when told by his parents that they would no longer give him pocket money if he did not stop smuggling donuts into his room. Dudley was on a diet, and without his PlayStation, could not play *Mega-Mutilation Part Three.* This event occurred during the summer prior to Harry's fourth year at Hogwarts. GF 2, p. 25.

Meliflua, Araminta. The cousin of Sirius Black's mother who lobbied for a bill at the Ministry of Magic to make Muggle-hunting legal. OP 6, p. 113.

Memory Charm. A charm used by the Misuse of Muggle Artifacts Office to make muggles forget that they observed any muggle-made objects that had become bewitched. CS 3, p. 31. Gilderoy Lockhart stated to Harry Potter on their way to the Chamber of Secrets that the one thing Gilderoy prided himself on was his Memory Charm. CS 16, p. 298. According to Lord Voldemort, only powerful wizards were able to break Memory Charms. Lord Voldemort used this as a reason to murder Bertha Jorkin after he interrogated her. This event occurred during the summer prior to Harry's fourth year at Hogwarts. GF 1, p. 12. During year seven, Hermione Granger invoked the charm, using the magic word "*obliviate*," against Antonin Dolohov to erase his memory. DH 9, p. 167.

Memory Potion. The feathers of jobberknolls were used in Memory Potions. FB, p. 23. See **Memory Charm**.

Men Who Love Dragons Too Much. The title of a book that Harry Potter read in the library of Hogwarts in order to find a spell to subdue a dragon. He needed the spell for the first event of the Triwizard Tournament that was hosted by Hogwarts during his fourth year at the school. GF 19, p 338.

Merchieftainess Murcus. See **Murcus, Merchieftainess**.

Mercury. Harry Potter and Ron Weasley used the planet Mercury to fabricate answers for a Divination class homework assignment involving predictions of the future. They wrote that on the upcoming Tuesday they anticipated losing a treasured possession because of the alignment of Mercury. This event occurred during Harry's fourth year at Hogwarts. GF 14, pp. 221-22. (Mercury is the planet closest to the sun in the solar system that includes Earth.)

Merlin. A famous wizard who was featured on the collectors cards inside packs of Chocolate Frogs. Harry Potter obtained the Merlin card on the Hogwarts Express en route to the start of his first year at Hogwarts. SS 6, p. 102. "Order of Merlin" was part of Albus Dumbledore's official title. SS 1, p. 8. Mad- Eye Moody exclaimed "Merlin's beard" when Harry showed him the Marauder's Map during Harry's fourth year at Hogwarts. GF 25, p. 475. DH 6, p. 92. See also **Order of Merlin.**

Mermish. The language spoken by merpeople. According to Percy Weasley, Mermish was one of two-hundred languages that Barty Crouch could speak. GF 7, p. 88. Mermish sounded screechy above the surface of the water, but underwater was understood as English. Albus Dumbledore spoke Mermish to the chief merperson who lived in the lake on the Hogwarts grounds. This event occurred after the second task of the Triwizard Tournament during Harry Potter's fourth year at Hogwarts. GF 26, p. 505.

Merpeople. Creatures that lived in the lake on the Hogwarts grounds. GF 25, p. 464. Merpeople had grayish skin and long, dark green hair. They had yellow eyes and broken teeth. They wore ropes of pebbles around their necks. Harry Potter encountered merpeople as part of the second task of the Triwizard Tournament. GF 26, p. 497. Harry surmised that merpeople did not know how to perform magic. GF 26, p. 501. Their leader was Merchieftainess Mercus. GF 26, p. 506. This event occurred during Harry Potter's fourth year at Hogwarts. Merpeople were not regarded as beings under Madam Elfrida Clagg's definition of "being" in the fourteenth century because they could not speak the human tongue outside of water. Centaurs refused to attend Wizards' Council meetings because the definition of "being" excluded the Merpeople. FB, p. xii. Merpeople domesticated the grindylow and hippocampus. FB, pp. 20-21. Merpeople were also known as Sirens,

Selkies and Merrows. FB, p. 28. Rita Skeeter once interviewed Elphias Doge about the rights of merpeople. DH 2, p. 24.

Merrows. Another name for the Merpeople who lived in Ireland. See **Merpeople**. FB, pp. 28-29.

Merrythought, Galatea. A wizard who was the Defense Against the Dark Arts professor at Hogwarts when Tom Riddle attended the school. Galatea had been teaching the class for 50 years at the time. HP 17, p. 368; 20, p. 432.

Metamorphmagus. The name given to a witch or wizard who could change his or her appearance at will. A metamorphmagus was very rare and the ability to change one's appearance was innate. Nymphadora Tonks was a metamorphmagus. OP 3, p. 52.

Metamorph-Medal. A magical necklace that was advertised to permit a wizard to change appearance at will when the device was worn around the neck. However, the device was a fraud and only turned its wearer orange and possibly sprout tentacles. The device was sold for ten galleons during the summer prior to Harry's sixth year at Hogwarts. HP 5, p. 87.

Metamorphosing. The act of turning into a metamorphmagus. HP 5, p. 95.

Meteolojinx, Recanto. A charm that, according to Arthur Weasley, Bletchley used to stop rain in a room at the Ministry of Magic. DH 13, p. 255.

Midgen, Eloise. A student of Hogwarts who, according to Hannah Abbot, tried to curse the acne off of her face and lost her nose instead. Madam Pomfrey restored the nose. Hannah shared this gossip in a Herbology class during Harry Potter's fourth year at Hogwarts. GF 13, p. 195. That same year, Ron Weasley refused to ask Eloise as his date to the Yule Ball as part of the Triwizard Tournament. GF 22, p. 394. During Harry Potter's sixth year at Hogwarts, Eloise' parents removed her from the school out of fear of Voldemort's activities. HP 11, p. 222.

Millamant's Magic Marquees. The name of a company that provided the tent for the wedding of Fleur Delacourt and Bill Weasley during year seven. DH 6, p. 109.

Milly. One of the names of the kneazles that were owned as pets by Newt Scamander. The other two kneazles were named Hoppy and Mauler. B, p. vi.

Mimbulus mimbletonia. A plant that Neville Longbottom received as a birthday present and showed to Harry Potter on the Hogwarts Express during the summer prior to Harry's fifth year at Hogwarts. The plant was like a small gray cactus and when probed with a quill, ejected stinksap. Stinksap smelled like rancid manure. OP 10, pp. 186-87.

Mimsy-Porpington, de Sir Nicholas. A resident ghost of Hogwarts who was affiliated with the Gryffindor house. He was commonly referred to as "Nearly Headless Nick." SS 7, p. 124. On October 31, 1492, Nick was nearly decapitated from forty-five strikes to his neck by a blunt axe. CS 8, pp. 123, 133. Because he was not totally decapitated, Nick was denied membership in the Headless Hunt. This event occurred during Harry Potter's second year at Hogwarts. CS 8, pp. 123-124.

Minister of Magic. The witch or wizard who served as the chief administrator of the Ministry of Magic. During harry Potter's lifetime, Cornelius Fudge was the Minister of Magic. SS 5, pp. 64-65. Cornelius was removed from that office the summer prior to Harry's sixth year at Hogwarts. He was replaced by Rufus Scrimgeour. HP 1, p. 15. On June 21, 1884, a crowd of wizards who were angry over the newly-announced Stooging Penalty for quidditch matches, threatened to stooge the Minister of Magic. QA 6, p. 26. During year seven, Rufus Scrimgeour was the Minister of Magic. DH 1, p. 5; 7, p. 121. He was replaced that year by Pius Thicknesse, who was under the Imperius Curse. DH 11, p. 208. The Minister of Magic and Support Staff was located on Level One of the Ministry. DH 12, p. 245.

Ministry of Agriculture and Fisheries. A government ministry of the muggle world that made an announcement on the same day that the muggle television news reported Sirius Black's escape from Azkaban. This event occurred during the summer prior to Harry Potter's third year at Hogwarts. PA 1, pp. 16-17.

Ministry of Magic. The governing body for the wizarding world. During Harry Potter's lifetime, the Ministry of Magic was headed by Cornelius Fudge. Its main purpose was to prevent muggles from learning that witches and wizards existed throughout the country. SS 5, pp. 64-65. This purpose was accomplished by putting spells on muggles who spotted magic things, such as dragons. SS 14, p. 231. The Ministry of Magic was located in London. SS 16, p. 267; 17, p. 290. The departments, offices and entities within the Ministry of Magic are listed in the Appendix. In the 1960's, the Ministry of Magic refused to lift a ban on the sport of creaothceann. QA 1, p. 6. The Ministry of Magic used watch wizards to arrest witches and wizards. OP 14, p. 287. The visitors' entrance to the Ministry of Magic was located on a muggle street in London inside of an old red telephone booth. The Ministry of Magic was accessed by dialing 62442. It was an underground facility and the Fountain of Magical Brethren was located in the center of its Atrium. Eric was the security guard in the Atrium who took wands for safekeeping. OP 6, pp. 125-27. The Ministry of Magic lacked the authority to punish Hogwarts students for misdemeanors committed at school. OP 8, p. 149. During year seven, Pius Thicknesse was Head of the Department of Magical Law Enforcement. DH 1, p. 5. Death Eaters took over control of the Ministry of Magic during year seven. DH 8, p. 159. That same year, Dolores Umbridge's office was located on Level One. DH 12, p. 230. The statue in the Atrium was change to a black stone statue of a witch and wizard siting on ornately carved thrones comprised of muggles. DH 12, pp. 241-42. The Atrium was located on Level Eight. DH 13, p. 265.

Ministry of Magic Are Morons Group. A name suggested by Fred Weasley, but rejected, for the group of Hogwarts students that referred to itself as Dumbledore's Army. This event occurred during Harry Potter's fifth year at Hogwarts. OP 18, p. 391.

Minsk. A city in which Rubeus Hagrid had a slight disagreement with a vampire in a pub. This event occurred during Harry Potter's fifth year at Hogwarts. OP 20, p. 426. (Minsk is a city and the capital of Belarus.)

Mirror of Erised. A magic mirror that was as high as the ceiling in a classroom, had an ornate gold frame and stood on two clawed feet. The following inscription (written in reverse) was carved around the top: "Erised stra ehru oyt ube cafru oyt on wohsi." SS 12, p. 207. Persons who looked into the mirror saw the thing they most wanted to see, in other words, the deepest, most desperate desire of their hearts. SS 12, p. 213. When Harry Potter first looked into the mirror he saw his parents and other members of his family. This event occurred during Harry's first year at Hogwarts. SS 12, pp. 208-09. DH 35, p. 719.

Mistletoe. A plant that grew on Xenophilius Lovegood's property, north of Ottery, St. Catchpole. A sign on the property stated: "Pick your own mistletoe." White-beaded mistletoe grew on each side of the front door. DH 20, p. 398.

Misuse of Muggle Artifacts Office. An office located within the Ministry of Magic. Arthur Weasley worked in this office. CS 3, p. 30. The office responded to muggle-made objects that became bewitched and were returned to muggle hands. Employees within the office often performed Memory Charms on muggles to make them forget that the objects had acted strangely at all. CS 3, p. 31.

Mobiliarbus. The magic word spoken for a charm that Hermione Granger used to move a Christmas tree in front of herself, Ron Weasley and Harry Potter in the Three Broomsticks to conceal themselves from several professors who entered the pub. This event occurred during Harry's second year at Hogwarts. PA 10, p. 201.

Mobilicorpus. The magic word spoken by Remus Lupin to levitate the unconscious body of Severus Snape during Harry Potter's third year at Hogwarts. PA 19, p. 377.

Mockbridge, Cuthbert. The head of the Goblin Liaison Office within the Ministry of Magic. Arthur Weasley pointed out Cuthbert to Harry Potter and Hermione Granger in the camp on the grounds of the Quidditch World Cup. This event occurred during the summer prior to Harry's fourth year at Hogwarts. GF 7, p. 86.

Modern Magical History. The title of a book read by Hermione Granger and that included a listing about Harry Potter. Hermione read the book prior to Harry's first year at Hogwarts. SS 6, p. 106.

Moke. A magical beast found throughout Britain and Ireland. The moke's skin was highly prized for use as moneybags and purses because it contracted at the approach of a stranger. FB, p. 29.

Mokeskin. A magical bag made from the skin of a moke that could not be opened except by the owner. Rubeus Hagrid gave a mokeskin to Harry Potter as a seventeenth birthday present during year seven. DH 7, p. 120.

M.O.M. Classification. The Ministry of Magic Classification for the five types of magical beasts, according to how dangerous they were to the wizarding world. The classification list was as follows: XXXXX = Known wizard killer / impossible to train or domesticate; XXXX = Dangerous / requires specialist knowledge / skilled wizard may handle; XXX = Competent wizard should cope; XX = Harmless / may be domesticated; X = Boring. FB, p. xxii.

Mongolia. The place where kappas were generally found. Severus Snape mentioned this location as he criticized the work of students performed for Remus Lupin's Defense Against the Dark Arts class. This event occurred during Harry Potter's third year at Hogwarts. PA 9, p. 172. The Ministry of Magic in Mongolia regarded quidditch with some suspicion. QA 8, p. 46. (Mongolia is a region in Asia consisting of Inner Mongolia of China and the Mongolian People's Republic.)

Monkshood. Another name for the plant known as aconite or wolfsbane used in potions. Severus Snape quizzed Harry Potter about the plant during Harry's first Potions class at Hogwarts. SS 8, pp. 137-38. See also **Aconite**.

Monster Book of Monsters, The. The title of a book that Rubeus Hagrid gave to Harry Potter as a thirteenth birthday present prior to Harry's third year at Hogwarts. The book had a handsome green cover and was able to snap, bite and walk like a crab. PA 1, p. 13. The only way to open the book safely was to pet and gently stroke it. PA 6, p. 113. During the third task of the Triwizard Tournament the following year, Harry recalled that the book contained a picture of a sphinx. GF 31, p. 628. DH 6, p. 95.

Montague. A student of Hogwarts who was a member of the Slytherin house and played the position of chaser on that house's quidditch team during Harry Potter's third year at Hogwarts. PA 15, pp. 306-07. Montague was the captain of the Slytherin quidditch team during Harry Potter's fifth year at Hogwarts. OP 19, p. 405. His parents came to Hogwarts that year to inquire about their son's inability to recover from his sojourn in the toilet. OP 30, pp. 678-79.

Montgomery. The name of two sisters who were students at Howgarts and whose five-year old brother was attacked by a werewolf and died at St. Mungo's Hospital during Harry Potter's sixth year at the school. The rumor was that Fenrir Greyback had attacked him. HP 22, pp. 472-73.

Montrose. The location to which Guthrie Lochrin rode a broomstick in 1107. Guthrie started his short trip in Arbroath and complained that the broomstick caused him to suffer a splintered buttocks and bulging piles. QA 1, p. 2. Montrose was also the home of the most successful quidditch team of all times, the Montrose Magpies. QA 7, p. 35.

Montrose Magpies. A quidditch team that was in the league. The Magpies were the most successful team of all times. Two of its most famous players were Eunice Murray and Harnish MacFarlan. QA 7, p. 35.

Moody, Alastor "Mad-Eye." A wizard who was an old friend of Albus Dumbledore and worked at the Ministry of Magic as an auror. According to Charlie Weasley, half the cells in Azkaban were full due to the efforts of Mad- Eye Moody but he became paranoid in his old age and saw Dark Wizards everywhere. GF 11, pp. 159, 161. Mad-Eye had very unusual eyes: one of them was small, dark and beady; the other was large, round as a coin and had a vivid electric blue color to it. The blue eye moved around continuously without blinking. Mad-Eye had a carved wooden leg that ended in a clawed foot. He was the professor for the Defense Against the Dark Arts class during Harry Potter's fourth year at Hogwarts. GF 12, pp. 184-86. The only person to call Mad-Eye by his proper first name was Albus Dumbledore. GF 16, p. 280. According to Sirius Black, Made-Eye was the best auror the Ministry of Magic ever had. GF 19, p. 333. Mad-Eye had his own office in Hogwarts. GF 19, p. 342. During Harry's fourth year at the school, someone impersonated Mad-Eye and was later revealed. GF 35, pp. 675-78. Mad-Eye was a member of the Order of the Phoenix and the advance guard that rescued Harry Potter from the Dursley home during the summer prior to Harry's fifth year at Hogwarts. OP 3, p. 46. DH 3, p. 37; 4, p. 45. At the beginning of year seven, Mad-Eye left the Dursley home on a broomstick with Mundungus Fletcher, who had taken Polyjuice Potion to look with Harry. DH 4, p. 52. Mad-Eye's fate was recounted by Bill Weasley during year seven. DH 5, p. 78.

Moon. A student who was sorted by the Sorting Hat during Harry Potter's first year at Hogwarts. Moon's placement into a house was not identified. SS 7, p. 121.

Mooncalf. A magical beast that appeared only during full moon from its burrow. Mooncalf dung was used as a fertilizer on magical plants. FB, pp. xviii, 29-30.

Moonstone. When made into a powder, this substance was an ingredient for the Draught of Peace. Harry Potter attempted to make the potion during his fifth year at Hogwarts. OP 12, p. 234.

Moontrimmer. A broomstick made by Gladys Boothby in 1901. The Moontrimmer became popular for use in quidditch QA 9, p. 48.

Moony. A wizard who was responsible, along with three others, for the creation of the Marauder's Map. The other wizards were nicknamed Wormtail, Padfoot and Prongs. Fred and George Weasley gave the map to Harry Potter as a Christmas present during Harry's third year at Hogwarts. PA 10, pp. 191-94. Remus Lupin was Moony. PA 17, p. 347.

Moose Jaw Meteorites. A quidditch team from Canada. QA 8, p. 43.

Moran. A member of the Irish National Quidditch Team who played in the Quidditch World Cup that Harry Potter attended during the summer prior to his fourth year at Hogwarts. Moran was a chaser. The other members of the team were: Connolly, Ryan, Troy, Mullet, Quigley and Lynch. GF 8, pp. 105-06.

Morgan, Gwendolyn. A witch who played on the Holyhead Harpies during a famous match in 1953. During that event, Gwendolyn hit the captain of the other team, Rudolf Brand, with her Cleansweep Five and the blow caused him to propose to her at the end of the match. QA 7, p. 35.

Morgana. A witch who was featured on the collectors cards inside packs of Chocolate Frogs. Ron Weasley had several cards with Morgana on them. Ron mentioned this fact to Harry Potter on the Hogwarts Express as they traveled to their first year at Hogwarts. SS 6, p. 102.

Morsmordre. The magic word used in a charm to invoke the Dark Mark. Harry Potter, Ron Weasley and Hermione Granger witnessed the conjuring of the Dark Mark during the aftermath of the Quidditch World Cup during the summer prior to Harry's fourth year at Hogwarts. GF 9, p. 128.

Mortlake. A wizard who, according to Arthur Weasley, was taken away for questioning by the Committee on Experimental Charms because of his extremely odd ferrets. Arthur shared this information with Harry Potter during the summer prior to Harry's second year at Hogwarts. CS 3, p. 38.

Mosag. A large spider who was the wife of Aragog. Mosag lived deep within the Forbidden Forest and was brought there by Rubeus Hagrid. Harry Potter encountered this spider during his second year at Hogwarts. CS 15, p. 278.

Most Dangerous Dark Wizards of All Time. The title of a list that included Gellert Grindelwald, who was second only to Lord Voldemort. DH 18, p. 355.

Most Extraordinary Society of Potioneers. A wizard society founded by Hector Dagworth-Granger. HP 9, p. 185.

Most Potente Potions. The title of a book located in the restricted section of the library at Hogwarts. Harry Potter, Ron Weasley and Hermione Granger consulted this book in order to make Polyjuice Potion. This event occurred during Harry's second year at Hogwarts. CS 9, p. 160.

Mostafa, Hassan. An Egyptian who was Chairwizard of the International Association of Quidditch and referee of the Quidditch World Cup that Harry Potter attended during the summer prior to his fourth year at Hogwarts. GF 8, pp. 105-106.

Mould-on-the-Wold. The location where the Dumbledores resided before they moved to Godric's Hollow. DH 11, p. 217.

Moutohora Macaws. A quidditch team from New Zealand that had a phoenix mascot named Sparky. QA 8, p. 42.

Mrs. Skower's All-Purpose Magical Mess Remover. A cleaning product that Argus Filch unsuccessfully used to erase the message that mysteriously appeared on the wall of Hogwarts. This event occurred during Harry Potter's second year at the school. CS 9, p. 146. The product was advertized at the stadium during the Quidditch World Cup that occurred during the summer prior to Harry's fourth year at Hogwarts. GF 8, p. 96. This product was also found in a broom cupboard at Hogwarts. Rita Skeeter interviewed Harry Potter in the closet about his being selected as a school champion for the Triwizard Tournament. GF 18, p. 304.

Mudblood. A derogatory name for someone who was muggle-born, in other words, one who had non-magic parents. Draco Malfoy called Hermione Granger a mudblood during Harry Potter's second year at Hogwarts. The opposite of a mudblood was a pure-blood. CS 7, p. 112-116. Draco's use of the word in a Potions class during Harry's fourth year provoked Harry to throw a charm on Gregory Goyle. GF 18, p. 298. Prior to year seven, Charity Burbage wrote an impassioned defense of mudbloods in an article that appeared in the *Daily Prophet.* DH 1, p. 12.

Mudbloods and the Dangers They Pose to a Peaceful Pure-Blood Society. The title of a pamphlet that witches and wizards were mass-producing in the Ministry of Magic during year seven. DH 13, p. 249.

Muffliato. A charm invented by the Half Blood Prince that filled the ears of anyone nearby with an unidentifiable buzzing. Harry Potter discovered the charm during his sixth year at Hogwarts. HP 12, p. 238. Hermione Granger invoked the charm during year seven. DH 7, p. 132.

Muggle. The name used in the wizarding world for a nonmagic person. SS 1, p. 5; 4, p. 53. DH 3, p. 35.

Muggle Liaison Office. An office within the Ministry of Magic that dealt with muggle memory modification after the Dark Mark appeared at the Quidditch World Cup. HP 1, p. 9.

Muggle Prime Minister. The Prime Minister of the muggle world who was notified by Cornelius Fudge about the escape of Sirius Black from Azkaban. This event was reported in the *Daily Prophet* during the summer prior to Harry Potter's third year at Hogwarts. PA 3, p. 37.

Muggle Protection Act. A law that Lucius Malfoy suspected Arthur Weasley of being involved with enacting. CS 4, p. 51. According to Lucius, it was reported in a *Daily Prophet* story that Arthur was the author of the law. This event occurred during Harry Potter's second year at Hogwarts. CS 12, p. 222.

Muggle Repelling Charms. Charms invoked by the Ministry of Magic around the immense gold walls where the Quidditch World Cup took place. The charms were directed at muggles so that they would stay away from the event and worked by reminding the muggles of urgent appointments they needed to keep. GF 8, p. 95.

Muggle Studies. A subject taught at Hogwarts and that was not offered to a student until the student's third-year. CS 14, p. 252. Percy Weasley recommended the class, along with Divination class, to Harry Potter when Harry was planning classes for his third year at the school. CS 14, p. 252. Hermione Granger took the class in her third year and scored 320% on the final exam. PA 4, p. 57; 22, p. 430. Prior to year seven, the class was taught by Charity Burbage. DH 1, p. 11. During year seven, the class was mandatory for all students and was taught by Alecto Carrow. DH 29, p. 574.

Muggle Underground. Another name for the London Underground. Molly Weasley stated that her children and their luggage would have looked a site on the Muggle Underground. This event occurred during the summer prior to Harry Potter's third year at Hogwarts. PA 4, p. 64. See **London Underground**.

Muggle-born Registration Commission. A commission within the Ministry of Magic, formed during year seven, that interviewed muggle-born wizards and witches to determine how they acquired their magical abilities. DH 11, p. 209. Dolores Umbridge was the head of the commission that year. DH 13, p. 250.

Muggle-born Registry. During year seven, the Ministry of Magic initiated a survey of muggle-borns to determine how they acquired their magical powers. Muggle-born wizards and witches were encouraged to come to the ministry to be interviewed by the newly-appointed Muggle-born Registration Commission. DH 11, p. 209.

Muggles Who Notice. The title of a book written by Blenheim Stalk in 1972. Stalk claimed that some residents of Ilfracombe escaped the batch of Memory Charms that were invoked to make the muggles forget about a Welsh Green Dragon that swooped down on sunbathing muggles there in 1932. FB, p. xvi, fn. 7.

Muggle-Worthy Excuse Committee. An office, incorporated in the Department of Magical Accidents and Catastrophes, located on level three of the Ministry of Magic. OP 7, p. 130.

Mugwump. A title of distinction or acheivement given to certain wizards. Part of Albus Dumbledore's title was "Supreme Mugwump." SS 1, p. 8.

Mulciber. A Death Eater who specialized in the Imperius Curse and made countless people do horrible things. Igor Karkaroff attempted to gain his own release from Azkaban by giving Mulciber's name to the Ministry of Magic. However, the Ministry of Magic already had Mulciber in custody. During his fourth year at Hogwarts, Harry Potter learned this information from the pensieve in Albus Dumbledore's office. GF 30, p. 590. Mulciber was present in the Department of Mysteries when Harry Potter retrieved the prophecy relating to himself and Lord Voldemort. This event occurred during Harry's fifth year at Hogwarts. OP 35, p. 788.

Muldoon, Burdock. Chief of the Wizards' Council during the fourteenth century who first attempted to distinguish beings from beasts. FB, p. x.

Mullet. A member of the Irish National Quidditch Team who played in the Quidditch World Cup that Harry Potter attended during the summer prior to his fourth year at Hogwarts. Mullet was a chaser. The other members of the team were: Connolly, Ryan, Troy, Moran, Quigley and Lynch. GF 8, pp. 105-06, 109.

Mumps, Zacharias. A wizard who wrote the first full description of quidditch in 1398. Mumps emphasized the need for anti-muggle security while playing the game. QA 5, p. 15. Zacharias also recorded a quidditch match between a British team from Cork and the other from Ireland in 1385. The game was played in Lancashire. QA 8, p. 38.

Munch, Eric. A watch-wizard for the Ministry of Magic who arrested Sturgis Podmore on August 31. This event occurred during the summer prior to Harry Potter's fifth year at Hogwarts. OP 14, p. 287.

Murcus, Merchieftainess. The female leader of the merpeople who lived under the lake on the Hogwarts grounds. Murcus discussed the second task of the Triwizard Tournament with Albus Dumbledore in order to determine the winner of that task. This event occurred during Harry Potter's fourth year at Hogwarts. GF 26, p. 506.

Murray, Eunice. A witch who was a well-known seeker for the Montrose Magpies. Eunice died in 1942. QA 7, p. 35.

Murtlap. A rat-like creature found in the coastal areas of Great Britain. A wizard who ate pickled Murtlap became resistant to curses and jinxes. FB, p. 30. Hermione Granger offered Harry Potter a bowl containing a solution of strained and pickled murtlap tentacles to ease the pain in his hand. This event occurred during Harry's fifth year at Hogwarts. OP 15, p. 324.

Museum of Quidditch. A museum located in London that displayed, among other things, a broomstick from 1107. Guthrie Lochrin rode on the broom from Montrose to Arbroath. QA 1, p. 2. The Museum of Quidditch also housed the writings of Gertie Keddle. QA 3, p. 7. A letter written by Madam Modesty in 1269 was also keep there. QA 4, p. 12.

Mykonos. A location in Greece where "Dangerous" Dai Llewellyn was eaten by a chimera. QA 7, p. 33. (Mykonos is a mountainous island in Southeast Greece in the South Aegean Sea.)

Myrtle, Moaning. The ghost who haunted a toilet in an out-of-order, girls' bathroom on the first floor of Hogwarts. CS 8, p. 132. It is possible that the girls' bathroom was actually located on the second floor. The prefects bathroom was located on the fifth floor and the S-bend of the toilet Moaning Myrtle occupied was stated as three floors below that. GF 25, p. 461. Myrtle was prone to have tantrums and flood the bathroom. CS 8, p. 133. She complained that people called her the following names: Fat Myrtle; Ugly Myrtle; Miserable, Moaning, Moping Myrtle. CS 8, p. 135. She was also called Pimply Myrtle. CS 8, p. 135. Harry Potter, Hermione Granger and Ron Weasley made Polyjuice Potion in one of Moaning Myrtle's toilets during Harry's second year at Hogwarts. CS 12, p. 215. The circumstances surrounding Myrtle's death were explained to them later that school year. CS 16, p. 299. Moaning Myrtle assisted Harry in deciphering the golden egg for the second task of the Triwizard Tournament. This event occurred during Harry's fourth year at Hogwarts. GF 25, p. 461.

NAGINI - NURMENGARD

Nagini. A giant snake, at least twelve feet long, that was a pet for Lord Voldemort. Voldemort kept Nagini with him while he stayed at the Riddle House. This event occurred during the summer prior to Harry Potter's fourth year at Hogwarts. GF 1, p. 7. During year seven, Nagini accompanied Voldemort at a meeting between Voldemort and Death Eaters at the Malfoy manor. DH 1, p. 8. Nagini was the one of several horcruxes formed by Voldemort. DH 27, p. 550. At the end of year seven, Nagini's fate was witnessed by many wizards, Death Eaters and Voldemort. DH 36, p. 733.

Nargle. A magical creature that Luna Lovegood claimed was often found in Mistletoe. OP 21, p. 452. DH 22, p. 425.

Nastily Exhausting Wizarding Tests. Special achievement tests, also known as N.E.W.T.S., given as the highest qualification at Hogwarts. Percy Weasley took N.E.W.T.S. during Harry Potter's third year at Hogwarts. PA 16, p. 314. Students elected which N.E.W.T.s to take during their sixth year at Hogwarts. OP 12, p. 228.

National Squad. A quidditch team. Gilderoy Lockhart claimed that he was a seeker and had been asked to try out for this team, but decided to eradicate the Dark Forces instead. Gilderoy informed Harry Potter of this fact after a Defense Against the Dark Arts class during Harry's second year at Hogwarts. CS 10, p. 163.

Nature's Nobility: A Wizarding Genealogy. The title of a book found at Number Twelve, Grimmauld Place, London. OP 6, p. 116. DH 10, p. 190.

Nearly Headless Nick. A resident ghost of Hogwarts who was affiliated with the Gryffindor house. His full name was Sir Nicholas de Mimsy-Porpington. SS 7, p. 124. On October 31, 1492, Nick was nearly decapitated from forty-five strikes to his neck by a blunt axe. CS 8, pp. 123, 133. DH 31, p. 613.

Neptune. In a Divination class during his fourth year at Hogwarts, Harry Potter was confused by the existence of two Neptunes on his piece of parchment. Harry was working on an assignment about the planets that were visible on his date of birth. Ron Weasley, in mocking Sibyl Trelawney, suggested that two Neptunes in the sky was a sure sign that a midget in glasses was being born. GF 13, p. 201. (Neptune is the eighth planet from the sun in the solar system that includes Earth.)

Nettles, Madam Z. A witch from Topsham who was quoted as having taken the Kwikspell course and afterwards became the center of attention at parties for her Scintillation Solution. Harry Potter discovered this information on a piece of parchment in Argus Filch's office during Harry's second year at Hogwarts. CS 8, p. 127.

New Guinea. The location where Flavius Belby vacationed in 1782 when he was attacked by a lethifold. Flavius survived the encounter by invoking the Patronus Charm. FB, pp. 26-27. (New Guinea is a large island north of Australia that is divided into the Indonesian province of Irian Jaya and the independent country of Papua New Guinea.)

New Theory of Numerology. A book that Harry Potter gave as a Christmas present to Hermione Granger during Harry's fifth year at Hogwarts. OP 23, p. 503.

N.E.W.T.s. See **Nastily Exhausting Wizarding Tests**. PA 16, p. 314.

New Zealand. The native habitat of the Antipodean Opaleye dragon. FB, p. 11. Quidditch was not introduced in New Zealand until the seventeenth century. QA 8, p. 41. (New Zealand is a country in the South Pacific Ocean, southeast of Australia.)

New Zealand Ministry of Magic. The New Zealand Ministry of Magic was located in Wellington, New Zealand. The ministry spent much time and money preventing muggles from getting hold of Maori art of the seventeenth century that depicted white wizards playing quidditch. QA 8, p. 41.

Niffler. A fluffy, black creature with a long snout that had flat, front paws like spades. A niffler was commonly found in mines because it was attracted to shiny objects such as treasure. According to Rubeus Hagrid, a niffler made a useful little treasure detector. Hagrid introduced nifflers to Harry Potter's Care for Magical Creature class during Harry's fourth year at Hogwarts. GF 27, pp. 542-43. A niffler's native habitat was Great Britain. Nifflers were kept by goblins to burrow for treasure. FB, p. 30. The subject of nifflers was often tested on O.W.L.s. OP 15, p. 323.

Nigellus, Phineas. The great-great-grandfather of Sirius Black who was, according to Sirius, the least popular headmaster Hogwarts ever had. OP 6, p. 113. A portrait of Phineas hung in Albus Dumbledore's office at Hogwarts and also at 16 Grimmauld Place. Phineas was a member of the Slytherin house when he was a student at the school. OP 9, p. 178; 22, p.472. DH 36, p. 747. See also **Black, Phineas Nigellus**.

Nimbus Racing Broom Company. A company that manufactured quidditch brooms. When it was formed in 1967, Nimbus galvanized the broom world with its first model, the Nimbus 1000. QA 9, pp. 50-51.

Nimbus 1000. The first quidditch broom manufactured by the Nimbus Racing Broom Company in 1967. The Nimbus 1000 was the broom of first choice for professional quidditch players across Europe. Later models were the Nimbus 1001, 1500 and 1700. QA 9, pp. 50-51.

Nimbus Two Thousand. The make and model of a magic broom used for playing quidditch and sold in a shop on Diagon Alley. It was reportedly the "fastest ever" during Harry Potter's first year at Hogwarts. SS 5, p. 72. It was sleek and shiny with a mahogany handle, a long tail of neat, straight twigs and the name was written in gold near the top. SS 10, p. 166. This was the first quidditch broom that Harry used to play the game and was given to him by Minerva McGonagell. SS 10, p. 164. It was destroyed when Harry fainted during a quidditch match against Hufflepuff in Harry's third year at Hogwarts. The broom was blown away in a storm and flew into the Whomping Willow. PA 9, p. 182.

Nimbus Two Thousand and One. The make and model of a magic broom that was used for playing quidditch. All of the members of the Slytherin quidditch team used this broom; the brooms were purchased for them by Lucius Malfoy. This event occurred during Harry Potter's second year at Hogwarts. This broom was the very latest model and claimed to outstrip the old Two Thousand series by a considerable amount. CS 7, p. 111.

Noble Sport of Warlocks, The. A book written by Quintius Umfraville in 1620. The book included a diagram of a seventeenth century quidditch pitch. QA 6, p. 18.

Nogtail. A magical beast found only in rural areas in Europe, Russia and America. If the nogtail was undetected and allowed to suckle a pig, the farm where the pig was located experienced blight. FB, pp. 30-31.

Norbert. The name given by Rubeus Hagrid to a rare dragon, a Norwegian Ridgeback, that Hagrid hatched from an egg. This event occurred during Harry Potter's first year at Hogwarts. SS 14, p. 236. During year seven, Charlie Weasley announced that Norbert was renamed

Norberta, because it was discovered that the dragon was actually a female. DH 7, p. 120.

Norberta. See **Norbert**.

Norfolk. The location where Mrs. Hetty Bayliss observed a flying car driven by Ron Weasley with his passenger, Harry Potter. The incident was reported in the *Evening Prophet* during the summer prior to Harry Potter's second year at Hogwarts. CS 5, p. 79. The quidditch referee Cyprian Youdle resided in Norfolk until he was murdered during a quidditch match in 1357. QA 6, p. 30. Tiberius McLaggen and his nephew, Cormac, hunted nogtails in Norfolk. They were joined by Bertie Higgs and Rufus Scrimgeour. HP 7, p. 144. (Norfolk is a county in East England.)

Norris, Mrs. The cat owned by Argus Filch that patrolled the corridors of Hogwarts looking for students who broke the rules or got into mischief. SS 8, p. 132. Mrs. Norris was the first victim of the monster from the Chamber of Secrets during Harry's second year at the school. CS 9, p. 142. DH 31, p. 621.

North Sea. The bottom of the North Sea was the habitat of the Lobalug. FB, p. 27. The prison of Azkaban was also located in the North Sea. HP 1, p. 8. (The North Sea is a portion of the Atlantic Ocean between Great Britain and the mainland of Europe.)

North Tower. A tower at Hogwarts. Sibyll Trelawney taught Divination class in a circular classroom at the top of the North Tower. It was reached by climbing a tightly spiraling staircase and a silver stepladder led to a circular trapdoor in the ceiling of the classroom. CS 14, p. 252; PA 6, pp. 99-101; GF 13, p. 199.

Northern Ireland. The location that served as the home of the celebrated quidditch team known as the Ballycastle Bats. QA 7, p. 32. (Northern Island is a political division of the United Kingdom in the northeast part of the island of Ireland.)

Norway. Fred and George Weasley admitted that they anonymously sent a sample of dragon dung fertilizer from Norway to the in-box at Percy Weasley's office. Their admission was made during the summer prior to Harry Potter's fourth year at Hogwarts. GF 5, p. 64. The Karasjok Kites, a quidditch team, was from Norway. QA 7, p. 33. Norway adopted the game of quidditch as early as the 1400's. QA 8, p. 39. (Norway is a kingdom in Northern Europe.)

Norwegian Ministry of Magic. The Ministry of Magic in Norway was the location where a tenth century letter from Goodwin Kneen to his cousin Olaf about the sport of "kwidditch" was stored. QA 3, p. 9.

Norwegian Ridgeback Dragon. A rare type of dragon. Rubeus Hagrid won a black egg containing one of these dragons in a card game. SS 14, p. 233. He named the dragon Norbert. This event occurred during

Harry Potter's first year at Hogwarts. SS 14, p. 236. The Norwegian Ridgeback was one of ten pure-bred dragons and one of the rarer dragon breeds during Harry Potter's lifetime. In 1802 a Norwegian Ridgeback carried off a whale calf from the coast of Norway. FB, p. 13. DH 7, p. 120.

Nose-Biting Teacup. A joke device sold at Zonko's Joke Shop in Hogsmeade. Harry Potter and Ron Weasley purchased some of these devices during Harry's third year at Hogwarts. PA 14, p. 278.

Nosebleed Nougat. One of the chews invented by Fred and George Weasley that collectively were referred to as Skiving Snackboxes. Fred and George developed the candies during the summer prior to Harry Potter's fifth year at Hogwarts. Two of the other chews were labeled Fainting Fancies and Puking Pastilles. OP 6, pp. 104-05. DH 12, p. 236.

Notable Magical Names of Our Times. A book in the library at Hogwarts that Harry Potter, Ron Weasley and Hermione Granger consulted regarding the identity of Nicolas Flamel. They discovered that Nicolas was not discussed in the book. This event occurred during Harry's first year at Hogwarts. SS 12, p. 197.

Nott. A student who was sorted by the Sorting Hat during Harry Potter's first year at Hogwarts. Nott's placement into a house was not identified. SS 7, p. 121. Nott was also the name of a wizard who was a Death Eater and who responded to the summons of Lord Voldemort during Harry Potter's fourth year at Hogwarts. GF 33, p. 651.

Nott, T. A student at Hogwarts whose name appeared on the list of borrowers found inside the cover of *Quidditch Through the Ages*. QA, p. i.

Nott, Theodore. Harry Potter identified Theodore Nott's father, along with Draco Malfoy's, as a Death Eater in an interview he gave to Rita Skeeter for *The Quibbler*. This event occurred during Harry's fifth year at Hogwarts. OP 26, p. 583. Nott was apprehended in the Ministry of Magic that same year. HP 7, p. 151.

Nottingham. The location close to where Lord Voldemort murdered a goblin family. This event occurred years prior to Harry Potter's fifth year at Hogwarts. OP5, p. 85. (Nottingham is a southwestern city in Nottinghamshire, in Central England.)

Nottinghamshire. The location where Kennilworthy Whisp resided. QA, p. v. (Nottinghamshire is a county in Central England.)

Nox. A magic word used by Harry Potter and Hermione Granger to extinguish the light at the end of their wands inside the Shrieking Shack. This event occurred during Harry's third year at Hogwarts. PA 17, p. 338. DH 32, p. 652.

Number Seven, Mrs. The woman who lived across the street from the Dursley family at Number Seven Privet Drive. OP 1, p. 5.

Numerology and Gramatica. A book that Hermione Granger used to prepare for her final exams during Harry Potter's third year at Hogwarts. PA 16, p. 315. DH 6, p. 93.

Nundu. A magical beast from East Africa. The nundu was arguably the most dangerous beast in the world because its breath was capable of causing disease in an entire village. It was difficult to subdue a nundu. FB, p. 31.

Nurmengard. The name of a prison that Gellert Grindelwald constructed to house persons who opposed him. After Albus Dumbledore defeated him, Grindelwald was imprisoned there. DH 18, p. 360.

OAKSHAFT 79 – OWLERY TOWER

Oakshaft 79. The make and model number of a quidditch broomstick produced in 1879 by Elias Grimstone of Portsmouth. QA 9, p. 47.

Oblansk (Obalonsk), Mr. A wizard who was the Minister of Magic in Bulgaria. Mr. Oblansk sat in the Top Box during the Quidditch World Cup with Cornelius Fudge. Cornelius was unable to pronounce Mr. Oblansk's name and didn't understand a word that he said. This event occurred during the summer prior to Harry Potter's fourth year at Hogwarts. GF 8, p. 101.

Obliteration Charm. A charm used by Hermione Granger to erase footprints in the snow during Harry Potter's fifth year at Hogwarts. OP 20, p. 440.

Obliviate. The magic word used to invoke the Memory Charm. Gilderoy Lockhart used the charm in the tunnel leading to the Chamber of Secrets. This event occurred during Harry Potter's second year at Hogwarts. CS 16, p. 303. During year seven, Hermione Granger invoked the charm against Antonin Dolohov to erase his memory. DH 9, p. 167.

Obliviator. The title given to a wizard who was a member of the Acccidental Magic Reversal Squad. Arnold Peasegood was an obliviator. Arthur Weasley pointed Arnold out to Harry Potter and Hermione Granger at the camp on the grounds of the Quidditch World Cup. This event occurred during the summer prior to Harry's fourth year at Hogwarts. GF 7, p. 86. The Ministry of Magic sent in a team of obliviators whenever there were severe cases of muggles who noticed magical beasts. FB, p. xx.

Obliviator Headquarters. An office incorporated in the Department of Magical Accidents and Catastrophes and located on level three of the Ministry of Magic. OP 7, p. 130.

Obscuro. The magic word for a charm invoked by Hermione Granger to place a blindfold around the eyes of Phineas Negellus Black during year seven. DH 15, p. 301.

Obscursus Books. A publisher of books in the wizarding world with an address of 18a Diagon Alley, London. Obscursus published *Fantastic Beasts and Where to Find Them.* In 1918, Augustus Worme of Obscurus convinced Newt Scamander to write the book. FB, pp. iii, ix.

Occamy. A magical beast found in the Far East and India. FB, p. 31.

Occlumency. The magical defense of the mind against external penetration and influence. Occlumency was an obscure branch of magic, but a highly useful one. Albus Dumbledore insisted that Severus Snape instruct Harry Potter on occlumency during Harry's fifth year at Hogwarts. OP 24, pp. 518-519. A witch or wizard skilled in this art was known as an occlumens. OP 24, p. 527. The opposing magical art to occlumency was legilimency, which magical art was practiced by Lord Voldemort. OP 24, p. 530. DH 9, p. 173.

Occlumens. A witch or wizard skilled in the art of occlumency. Severus Snape was revered for his skill as an occlumens. OP 24, p. 527.

Odo. A wizard whose death was mentioned in a drinking song that was sung by Rubeus Hagrid and Horace Slughorn. This event occurred during Harry Potter's sixth year at Hogwarts. HP 22, p. 487.

Oddsbodikins. A password used to gain access to the Gryffindor house of Hogwarts during Harry Potter's third year at Hogwarts. PA 12, p.249.

Office for House-Elf Relocation. A division in the Ministry of Magic. Newt Scamander worked for the Office for House-Elf Relocation for two years. FB, p. vi.

Office for the Detection and Confiscation of Counterfeit Defensive Spells and Protective Objects. An office created in the Ministry of Magic by Rufus Scrimgeour during the summer prior to Harry Potter's sixth year at Hogwarts. Arthur Weasley was appointed as the first head of the office and ten people reported to him. HP 5, p. 84.

Office of Misinformation. An office in the Ministry of Magic that cooperated with the muggle Prime Minister to seek a plausible non-magical explanation for a muggle siting of a magical beast. The office was used in only the worst magical-muggle collisions. FB, p. xx. For example, the office was used to deal with a "hurricane" caused by giants and Death Eaters during the summer prior to Harry Potter's sixth year at Hogwarts. HP 1, p. 13.

Official Gobstones Club. A club located on level seven of the Ministry of Magic. OP 7, p. 129.

Ogden, Bob. A wizard who worked for the Ministry of Magic. Bob was Head of the Magical Law Enforcement Squad. HP 10, pp.199, 207.

Ogden, Tiberius. A wizard who was a member of the Wizengamot. Tiberius resigned, together with Griselda Marchbanks, in protest over the appointment of a High Inquisitor for Hogwarts. This event occurred during Harry Potter's fifth year at Hogwarts. OP 15, p. 308. Tiberius was a friend of Professor Tofty. OP 31, p. 714.

Ogden's Old Firewhisky. A beverage that came in a large bottle and that Gilderoy Lockhart stated would be an ideal birthday gift for him. He made the statement to his Defense Against the Dark Arts class. This event occurred during Harry Potter's second year at Hogwarts. CS 6, p. 100. Arthur Weasley poured some of Ogden's Old Firewhisky into a cup of tea that Hermione Granger made for Molly Weasley after the Weasleys returned from the Quidditch World Cup that they attended. This event occurred during the summer prior to Harry Potter's fourth year at Hogwarts. GF 10, p. 147.

Ogg. The gamekeeper of Hogwarts prior to Rubeus Hagrid. When Molly Weasley visited Harry Potter the day of the third task in the Triwizard Tournament, she reminisced about Ogg. This event occurred during Harry's fourth year at Hogwarts. GF 31, p. 617.

O'Hare, Darren. A famous quidditch player for the Kenmare Kestrels. Darren was the keeper and captain of the team. He invented the Chaser Hawkshead Attacking Formation. QA 7, p. 35; 8, p. 41.

Olaf. A Norwegian wizard who was the cousin of Goodwin Kneen and lived during the tenth century. Olaf received a letter from Goodwin who told about his playing a game called "kwidditch." QA 3, pp. 8-9.

Olde and Forgotten Bewitchments and Charmes. A book that Hermione Granger consulted in order to help Harry Potter find a way to breathe underwater in the second task of the Triwizard Tournament. This event occurred during Harry's fourth year at Hogwarts. GF 26, p. 486.

Ollerton, Barnaby. A wizard who, along with his two other brothers, Bill and Bob, started the Cleansweep Broom Company in 1926. QA 9, p. 49.

Ollerton, Bill. A wizard who, along with his two other brothers, Barnaby and Bob, started the Cleansweep Broom Company in 1926. QA 9, p. 49.

Ollerton, Bob. A wizard who, along with his two other brothers, Barnaby and Bill, started the Cleansweep Broom Company in 1926. QA 9, p. 49.

Ollivander's. A magic wand shop located on Diagon Alley. SS 5, p. 81. The shop, known as the best of its kind, was closed during the summer prior to Harry Potter's sixth year at Hogwarts. HP 6, p. 106. During the summer prior to Harry's sixth year at Hogwarts, Neville Longbottom purchased a cherry wood and unicorn hair wand from Ollivander's. He believed the wand to be one of the last sold in that shop before it mysteriously closed. HP 7, p. 137. See **Ollivander, Mr.**

Ollivander, Mr. The owner of a magic wand shop located on Diagon Alley. The sign over the shop door read: "Ollivanders: Makers of Fine Wands since 382 B.C." SS 5, pp. 81, 82. Harry Potter purchased a holly and phoenix feather, 11-inch long wand from Ollivander's prior to his first year at Hogwarts. The "brother" to that wand was sold to Lord Voldemort. SS 5, pp. 84-85. Mr. Ollivander was the official for the Weighing of the Wands Ceremony that occurred at the Triwizard Tournament during Harry's fourth year at Hogwarts. GF 18, p. 307. Mr. Ollivander disappeared during the summer prior to Harry's sixth year at Hogwarts. HP 6, p. 106. However, the following year Mr. Ollivander was interrogated by Lord Voldemort and held as a prisoner in the cellar of the Malfoy manor. DH 5, p. 84; 23, p. 464.

Omniocculars. A brass device that had the appearance of binoculars and was covered with weird knobs and dials. Omnioculars allowed one to replay action, slow down action and flash a play-by-play account of a sporting event. The device was sold at the Quidditch World Cup for ten galleons. Harry Potter purchased three pairs of Omnioculars during the summer prior to his fourth year at Hogwarts. GF 7, p; 93. Some of the plays recorded by Harry's Omnioculars were the Hawkshead Attacking Formation and the Porskoff Ploy. GF 8, p. 106.

One Minute Feasts–It's Magic. A book located on the mantelpiece of the Weasley residence. Two other books on the mantel were *Charm Your Own Cheese* and *Enchantment in Baking*. Harry Potter observed the books during the summer prior to his second year at Hogwarts. CS 3, p. 34.

One Thousand Magical Herbs and Fungi. A book written by Phyllida Spore. The book was required for first-year students during Harry Potter's first year at Hogwarts. SS 5, p. 66. The book was referenced by Harry in connection with Potions Class that year. SS 8, p. 138. Ginny Weasley mended her copy with Spellotape during the summer prior to Harry's fourth year at the school. GF 10, p. 151. Harry read the book in Potions class during his fifth year. OP 17, p. 362.

Oona. A witch from an inn who gave Goodwin Kneen's team barrels to use in Kneen's game of kwidditch. This event occurred during the tenth century. QA 3, p. 9.

Oppugno. The magic word used to invoke a charm that made a little flock of conjured, golden birds attack. Hermione Granger invoked the charm against Ron Weasley during Harry Potter's sixth year at Hogwarts. HP 14, p. 302.

Orchideous. The magic word used by Mr. Ollivander to invoke a charm that caused flowers to burst from the end of Fleur Delacour's wand. Mr. Ollivander used the charm to test the working order of Fleur's wand during the Weighing of the Wands Ceremony as part of the Triwizard Tournament. This event occurred during Harry Potter's fourth year at Hogwarts. GF 18, p. 308.

Order of Merlin. A special commendation bestowed by the Ministry of Magic on certain exemplary wizards and witches. Albus Dumbledore was a recipient of the honor (Order of Merlin, First Class). SS 4, p. 51. Gilderoy Lockhart also claimed to have the honor in his official title (Third Class). CS 6, p. 99. Cornelius Fudge considered Severus Snape for the order (Second Class) based on his assistance with the recapture of Sirius Black. However, Severus' chances of receiving it were nonexistent after Remus Lupin reappeared and was able to set the story straight about Sirius Black. PA 21, p. 396; 22, p. 423. This event occurred during Harry Potter's third year at Hogwarts. Newt Scamander received the Order of Merlin, Second Class, in 1979 for his services to the study of magical beasts. FB, p. vi. A wizarding family that performed a batch of Memory Charms during the Ilfracombe Incident of 1932 received the Order of Merlin, First Class. FB, p. xvi. Sirius Black's grandfather was awarded the Order of Merlin, First Class for "Services to the Ministry." OP 6, p. 116. Cornelius Fudge's title included the Order of Merlin First Class. OP 19, p. 415.

Order of Suspension. An order issued by the twelve governors of Hogwarts to remove Albus Dumbledore as headmaster for his failure to prevent the attacks on muggles. This event occurred during Harry Potter's second year at Hogwarts. Lucius Malfoy presented the order to Dumbledore in Rubeus Hagrid's hut. CS 14, pp. 262-63.

Order of the Phoenix. A secret society founded by Albus Dumbledore for the witches and wizards who fought against Lord Voldemort prior to his first attack on Harry Potter when Harry was an infant. OP 4, p. 67. The headquarters of the Order of the Phoenix was secretly located at Number Twelve, Grimmauld Place, London. The members of the Order of the Phoenix included: Alastor "Mad Eye" Moody, Remus Lupin, Nymphadora Tonks, Kingsley Shacklebolt, Elphia Doge, Dedalus Diggle, Emmeline Vance, Sturgis Podmore and Hestia Jones. OP 3, pp. 46-49, 58. Arthur, Bill, Charlie and Molly Weasley and Severus Snape were also members. OP 4, pp. 61, 69-70. Mundungus Fletcher was a member who understood crooks. OP 5, p. 81. Sirius Black and Minerva McGonagell were also members. OP 4, p. 78; 6, p. 118. Membership in the Order was limited to overage wizards. OP 5, p. 97. During year seven, the activity of the Order was discussed at a meeting between the Death Eaters and Voldemort in the Malfoy manor. DH 1, p. 3.

Ordinary Wizarding Levels. A degree of academic achievement, also known as O.W.L.s, earned after taking certain exams at Hogwarts. CS 4, p. 46. A student could not take the test until the student was 15 years old. GF 5, p. 55. After Harry Potter's first year at Hogwarts, Percy Weasley earned twelve O.W.L.s. Bill Weasley also received that number and was Head Boy at Hogwarts. CS 4, p. 46. Fred and George Weasley took the exams during Harry's third year at Hogwarts. PA 16, p. 314. They each received a handful of O.W.L.s. PA 22, p. 430. O.W.L.s were given to fifth-year students at Hogwarts. The examinations affected which jobs a wizard could later apply for and other matters. OP 12, p. 226. The grading scale, from top to bottom, was: O for "outstanding"; E for "exceeds expectations"; A for "acceptable"; P for "poor"; D for "dreadful"; T for "troll" (according to George Weasley). The grades from P and lower were considered failing grades. OP 15, pp. 310-11. By comparison, at Beauxbatons, students could not take O.W.L.s until after six years of study. Harry Potter, along with Hermione Granger and Ron Weasley received their grades during the summer prior to Harry's sixth year at Hogwarts. Both Ahrry and Ron achieved seven passing results each; Hermione received ten "O"s, all except for Defense Against the Dark Arts, in which she received an "E". Because Harry did not achieve an "O" in Potions, he could not be considered for the position of an auror. HP 5, pp. 101-04. Neville Longbottom received only "acceptable" for Transfiguration. HP 7, p. 138.

Orion. A constellation that was on the star chart of the Astronomy practical examination for the O.W.L. that Harry Potter took during his fifth year at Hogwarts. OP 31, p. 718.

Ornithomancy. A magical art. Dolores Umbridge kept asking questions of Sybil Trelawney about ornithomancy and heptomology. This event occurred during Harry Potter's fifth year at Hogwarts. OP 25, p. 552.

Ottery St. Catchpole. A village located near the Burrow, the residence of the Weasley family. CS 3, p. 31. DH 8, p. 137. More specifically, it was along the south coast of England and, according to *A History of Magic*, was one of several villages where Wizarding families lived alongside Confunded Muggles. DH 16, p. 319.

Ouagadogou. A village where Gilderoy Lockhart claimed to have witnessed something similar to the Transmogrifian Torture and where he provided amulets to the villagers to cure them of the curse. Gilderoy made this claim to Argus Filch and others who attempted to diagnose the paralysis of Mrs. Norris. This event occurred during Harry

Potter's second year at Hogwarts. CS 9, p. 142. (Ouadadogou is a city and the capital of Burkana Faso, a country in West Africa.)

Owl Office. The office from which wizards and witches sent owls for the delivery of mail. PA 22, p. 433. The owls were referred to as post owls. GF 3, p. 36. Prior to the commencement of year seven, Harry Potter still received his *Daily Prophet* by delivery owl. DH 2, p. 22.

Owl Order Service. A service offered by Weasleys' Wizard Wheezes to customers who needed their purchases to be mailed to them by Owl Post. HP 15, p. 306.

Owl-Order. The type of business that Fred and George Weasley continued to operate during year seven from the back room of Auntie Muriel's house. DH 25, p. 513. See also **Owl Order Service**.

O.W.L.s. See **Ordinary Wizarding Levels**. CS 4, p. 46. DH 33, p. 675.

Owl Treats. Food for post owls that Ron Weasley asked Harry Potter to feed to Pigwidgeon. This event occurred in the Burrow during the summer prior to Harry's fourth year at Hogwarts. GF 10, p. 155.

Owlery. The room in Hogwarts that housed the messenger owls. SS 8, p. 135. Harry Potter's owl, Hedwig, stayed in the Owlery. PA 8, p. 153. The Owlery was located at the top of the West Tower and was a circular stone room. It had windows with no glass in them. Hundreds of different types of owls rested in this room until they were dispatched for mail delivery. GF 15, p. 229.

Owlery Tower. Another name for the West Tower of Hogwarts, the top of which held the Owlery. OP 14, p. 289.

PACIFIC OCEAN – PYGMY PUFFS

Pacific Ocean. One of the natural habitats of the sea serpent. FB, p. 38.

Padfoot. A wizard who was responsible, along with three others, for the creation of the Marauder's Map. The other wizards were nicknamed Wormtail, Moony and Prongs. Fred and George Weasley gave the map to Harry Potter as a Christmas present during Harry's third year at Hogwarts. PA 10, pp. 191-194. Sirius Black was Padfoot. PA 18, p. 355. DH 10, p. 180.

Paisley. The location where a witch lived who sent a supportive letter to Harry Potter after his interview appeared in the March issue of *The Quibbler.* This event occurred during Harry's fifth year at Hogwarts. OP 26, p. 579. (Paisley is a city in the Strathclyde region in Southwestern Scotland and west of Glasgow.)

Pakistan. The Ministry of Magic in Pakistan regarded quidditch with some suspicion. QA 8, p. 46. (Pakistan is a country in South Asia between India and Afghanistan.)

Papua, New Guinea. The location where Flavius Belby vacationed in 1782 when he was attacked by a lethifold. Flavius survived the encounter by invoking the patronus charm. FB, pp. 26-27. (Papua, New Guinea is one of two countries located on a large island in the West Pacific Ocean.)

Paracelsus. A famous wizard who was featured on the collectors cards inside packages of Chocolate Frogs. Harry Potter obtained the Paracelsus card on the Hogwarts Express. This event occurred during the summer prior to Harry's first year at Hogwarts. SS 6, p. 102. There was a statue of Paracelsus along a corridor at Hogwarts near the Gryffindor tower. OP 14, p. 281.

Paris. A location where Gladrags Wizardwear had a store. The store was advertized on the flashing advertisement in the stadium at the

Quidditch World Cup. This event occurred during the summer prior to Harry Potter's fourth year at Hogwarts. GF 8, p. 96. (Paris is a city located along the Seine River and is the capital of France.)

Parkin, Walter. A wizarding butcher whose seven children formed the Wigtown Wanderers quidditch club in 1422. QA 7, p. 37.

Parkin's Pincer. A widely known quidditch move named after one of the original members of the Wigtown Wanderers. QA 10, p. 53.

Parkinson, Pansy. A student who was sorted by the Sorting Hat during Harry Potter's first year at Hogwarts. Pansy was a member of the Slytherin house. SS 7, p. 121; 9, p. 148. She and her gang of Slytherin girls taunted Harry Potter in Potions class about being selected as a school champion for the Triwizard Tournament. This event occurred during Harry's fourth year at Hogwarts. GF 18, p. 298. Pansy went to the Yule Ball that year with Draco Malfoy. GF 23, p. 413. During Harry's fifth year at Hogwarts, Pansy was a prefect, along with Draco Malfoy, for Slytherin. OP 10, p. 188. DH 31, p. 610.

Parselmouth. The name given to a witch or wizard who had the unusual ability to talk to snakes. CS 11, pp. 195-96. Parselmouths were considered to be Dark Wizards. CS 11, p. 199. During his trip to a zoo with the Dursley family, Harry Potter discovered that he could speak to snakes. However, Harry didn't know what the ability was called until an incident at a Dueling Club meeting during his second year at Hogwarts. Salazar Slytherin was a famous parselmouth. CS 11, p. 196. Parselmouths conversed with runespoors about their habits and translated the information back for non-parselmouths to understand. FB, p. 37.

Parseltongue. The language spoken by snakes and parselmouths. The ability to speak the language was deemed the mark of a Dark Wizard. Salazar Slytherin was famous for speaking paresletongue and was called "Serpent-tongue." Harry Potter spoke the language, but could only do so in front of a snake. CS 11, pp. 196-199. DH 17, p. 347. Ron Weasley imitated parseltongue that he heard Harry speak during year seven to gain access to the Chamber of Secrets. DH 31, p. 623.

Patil, Parvati. A student who, together with her twin sister Padma, was sorted by the Sorting Hat during Harry Potter's first year at Hogwarts. Parvati was a member of the Gryffindor house. SS 7, p. 221; 9, p. 147; GF 12, p. 174; 23, p. 12. Her worst fear was a blood-stained, bandaged mummy. This information was apparent after a Defense Against the Dark Arts class involving a bogart. This event occurred during Harry's third year at Hogwarts. PA 7, p. 137. Parvati was Harry's date to the Yule Ball the following year. GF 22, p. 401. DH 29, p. 578.

Patil, Padma. A student who, together with her twin sister Parvati, was sorted by the Sorting Hat during Harry Potter's first year at Hogwarts. SS 7, p. 121; GF 22, p. 402. Padma was a member of the Ravenclaw house. GF 12, p. 174. At the request of Harry Potter, Padma went to the Yule Ball with Ron Weasley during Harry's fourth year at Hogwarts. GF 22, p. 402; 23, p. 412. During the following school year, Padma was a prefect, along with Anthony Goldstein, for the Ravenclaw house. OP 10, p. 188. DH 29, p. 578.

Patonga Proudsticks. A quidditch team from Uganda. QA 8, p. 42.

Patronus. A kind of positive force and a projection of the things on which Dementors fed (i.e. hope, happiness, the desire to survive). Because a patronus could not feel despair, it could not be affected by a dementor. The patronus was an image selected by the conjurer from a happy memory. Remus Lupin instructed Harry Potter on the invocation of a patronus during Harry's third year at Hogwarts. PA 12, p. 237. During the following year, Harry conjured a patronus in the third task of the Triwizard Tournament. GF 31, p. 623. The Patronus Charm was the only effective means to fend off an attack from a lethifold. FB, p. 26. DH 7, p. 121. The following lists the witches and wizards, who were known to produce a patronus, and the type of patronus they conjured: Aberforth Dumbledore – goat; Albus Dumbledore – phoenix; Seamus Finnegan – fox; Hermione Granger – otter; Minerva McGonagell – cat; Ernie Macmillan – boar; Kinglsey Shacklebolt – lnyx; Harry Potter – stag; James Potter – stag; Lilly Potter – doe; Severus Snape – doe; Dolores Umbridge – cat; Arthur Weasley – weasel; Ron Weasley - terrier.

Patronus Charm. A highly advanced charm invoked with the magic words "*expecto patronum*," and used to conjure a Patronus and to turn away a Dementor. Remus Lupin taught Harry Potter this charm during Harry's third year at Hogwarts. PA 12, p. 237. During the following year, Harry used the charm in the third task of the Triwizard Tournament. GF 31, p. 623. A patronus in the shape of a silver lynx that was conjured by Kingsley Shacklebolt in year seven was capable of speaking. DH 8, p. 159. A patronus in the shape of a silver doe lead Harry to a frozen pool in the Forest of Dean that year. DH 19, p. 366. Albus Dumbeldore's patronus was a phoenix. DH 20, p. 390.

Patented Daydream Charms. A magic device sold in Weasley's Wizard Wheezes during the summer prior to Harry Potter's sixth year at Hogwarts. The device, invented by Fred and George Weasley, was advertised to provide a top-quality, highly realistic 30-minute daydream. It was not sold to wizards under 16 years of age. HP 6, p. 117.

Paws, Mr. A cat owned by Mrs. Figgs. Mrs. Figgs had three other cats who were named Tibbles, Snowy and Tufty. SS 2, p. 22.

Payne, Mr. One of the site managers at the camp site set up for patrons of the Quidditch World Cup. Amos and Cedric Diggory were directed by Basil to meet Mr. Payne for specific instructions about their camp site. Another site manager was Mr. Roberts. This event occurred during the summer prior to Harry's fourth year at Hogwarts. GF 7, p. 76.

Peakes, Jimmy. A student at Hogwarts who was a member of Gryffindor house and who Harry Potter chose to be a beater on the house quidditch team during Harry's sixth year at the school. That year, Jimmy was a third year student. HP 11, p. 225. DH 31, p. 611.

Pear Drop. A candy sold in the wizarding world. During his fourth year at Hogwarts, Harry Potter unsuccessfully tried to use the password "sherbet lemon" to open the secret passageway to Albus Dumbledore's office. He then tried several candy names on the door, including Pear Drop. Cockroach Cluster finally worked as the password. GF 29, p. 579.

Peasegood, Abraham. An eighteenth century wizard who invented quodpod in the United States. QA 8, p. 44.

Peasegood, Arnold. A wizard who worked for the Accidental Magic Reversal Squad as an obliviator. Arthur Weasley pointed out Arnold to Harry Potter and Hermione Granger at the camp on the grounds of the Quidditch World Cup. This event occurred during the summer prior to Harry's fourth year at Hogwarts. GF 7, p. 86.

Peeves the Poltergeist. A poltergeist who performed pranks on students at Hogwarts during the time that Harry Potter attended the school. SS 7, pp. 115, 129. The only person who could control Peeves was the Bloody Baron. SS 7, p. 129. DH 16, p. 324; 32, p. 644.

Pennifold, Daisy. A witch who had the idea of bewitching a quaffle so that if it were dropped it would fall slowly to earth. The modern quaffle was named the Pennifold Quaffle. QA 6, p. 21.

Pensieve. A magical, shallow, stone basin that Albus Dumbledore kept in a black cabinet in his office at Hogwarts. The basin had odd carvings around the edge. Inside the basin was a liquid or gas substance that emitted silvery light and had the appearance of clouds. GF 30, p. 583. The pensieve allowed a person to siphon excess thoughts into it and examine them at leisure later. It helped a person to spot patterns and links from previous events. GF 30, p. 597. Harry Potter discovered the pensieve in Dumbledore's office during his fourth year at Hogwarts. From looking into this magical device, Harry witnessed several important hearings before the Council of Magical Law that resulted in certain Death Eaters being sent to Azkaban. GF 30, pp.

583-96. Harry used the pensieve during year seven to witness a story about Severus Snape. DH 12, p. 228; 33, p. 662.

Pepper Imps. A candy sold at Honeydukes in Hogsmeade. This candy emitted smoke when eaten. Ron Weasley described the candy to Hermione Granger during Harry Potter's third year at Hogwarts. PA 5, p. 77.

Pepper, Octavius. A wizard who vanished according to an edition of the *Daily Prophet* published during Harry Potter's sixth year at Hogwarts. HP 21, p. 457.

Peppermint Toads. A candy that Ron Weasley ate and probably purchased from Honeydukes in Hogsmeade during Harry Potter's third year at Hogwarts. PA 11, p. 213.

Pepperup Potion. A potion used by Madam Pomfrey to help students and staff of Hogwarts who suffered from colds. After drinking Pepperup Potion, one's ears emitted smoke for a few hours. Madam Pomfrey administered the potion during Harry Potter's second year at Hogwarts. CS 8, p. 122. Madam Pomfrey gave some of the potion to Harry after he completed the second task of the Triwizard Tournament during his fourth year at the school. GF 26, pp. 504-05.

Perkins. An old warlock who was employed by the Misuse of Muggle Artifacts Office and worked with Arthur Weasley. Ron Weasley mentioned Perkins as he described the operations of the office to Harry Potter. This event occurred during the summer prior to Harry's second year at Hogwarts. CS 3, p. 31. Arthur Weasley borrowed two tents from Perkins, who no longer camped due to lumbago, so that the Weasleys, Harry and Hermione Granger would have shelter at the Quidditch World Cup. The tents reminded Harry of Mrs. Figgs' house. This event occurred during the summer prior to Harry's fourth year at Hogwarts. GF 7, p. 80. Perkins attended the wedding of Fleur Delacourt and Bill Weasley during year seven. DH 8, p. 139.

Perks, Sally-Anne. A student of Hogwarts who was sorted by the Sorting Hat during Harry Potter's first year at Hogwarts. Sally Anne's placement into a house was unspecified. SS 7, p. 121.

Permanent Sticking Charm. A charm that Mrs. Black was believed to have placed on the back of the life-size portrait of herself at Number Twelve, Grimmauld Place, London. This event occurred during the summer prior to Harry Potter's fifth year at Hogwarts. OP 5, p. 79. DH 10, p. 178.

Peru. According to Charlie Weasley, the national quidditch team from Peru was flattened by the team from Ireland in the semifinal games that led to the World Quidditch Cup. This event occurred during the summer prior to Harry Potter's fourth year at Hogwarts. GF 5, p. 63.

Peru was the natural habitat of the Peruvian vipertooth. FB, p. 13. The most skilled quidditch team in South America was from Peru. QA 8, p. 45. Fred and George Weasley imported Instant Darkness Powder from Peru during the summer prior to Harry's sixth year at Hogwarts. HP 6, p. 119. (Peru is a western country in South America.)

Peruvian Instant Darkness Powder. A magic powder that caused pitch blackness in an area where it was thrown into the air. Weasleys Wizarding Wheezes sold the powder and Draco Malfoy purchased some of it during Harry Potter's sixth year at Hogwarts. HP 29, p. 618. DH 7, p. 132.

Peruvian Vipertooth. One of ten pure-bred dragon types. While the smallest of all dragons, the Peruvian vipertooth was the fastest in the air. In the nineteenth century the International Confederation of Wizards was forced to exterminate some of these dragons because there were too many. FB, pp. 13-14.

Peskipiksi Pesternomi. The magic words used in a charm, unsuccessfully invoked by Gilderoy Lockhart, to subdue Cornish Pixies. Lockhart allowed the pixies to escape during a Defense Against the Dark Arts class that Harry Potter attended. This event occurred during Harry's second year at Hogwarts. SS 6, p. 102.

Pest Advisory Bureau. An office located in the Department for the Regulation and Control of Magical Creatures on level four of the Ministry of Magic. OP 7, p. 130. DH 12, p. 245.

Pest Sub-Division. A division in the Department for the Regulation and Control of Magical Creatures that was used to rid a house of bundimun when they became too large to remove with a simple magical cleaning fluid. The division also was used to remove chizpurfles. FB, pp. 6-7. A dozen albino bloodhounds were kept in the division to help locate nogtails. FB, p. 31.

Pet Menagerie. The shop on Diagon Alley where Hermione Granger purchased a large orange cat who she named Crookshanks. This event occurred during the summer prior to Harry Potter's third year at Hogwarts. PA 4, pp. 59-60.

Petrification Curse. The rigid state that persons suffered if they looked indirectly into the eyes of a basilisk. Harry Potter shared this information with Ron Weasley as they attempted to explain some of the events surrounding the reopening of the Chamber of Secrets. This event occurred during Harry's second year at Hogwarts. CS 16, p. 291. The cure for the curse was obtained from a mature mandrake. CS 18, p. 330. DH 36, p. 738.

Petrificus Totalus. The magic words used to invoke a charm in order to make a person's body stiff as a board and to prevent that person from moving or speaking. Hermione Granger used this charm on Neville Longbottom during Harry Potter's first year at Hogwarts. SS 16, p. 273. DH 9, p. 166.

Pettigrew, Peter. A friend of James Potter who was a student at Hogwarts at the same time as James. It was believed that Peter attempted to seek revenge on the death of James and Lilly Potter by going after Sirius Black, whom Pettigrew suspected of handing over the Potters to Lord Voldemort. According to eye witnesses, Sirius blew Pettigrew into smithereens and the largest piece left was one of Pettigrew's fingers. PA 10, pp. 207, 208. Pettigrew was also an unregistered animagus, in the form of a rat, and was known to his close friends as Wormtail. PA 17, p. 348; PA 18, p. 355; PA 19, pp. 363-366. Harry learned an important revelation about Pettigrew during his third year at Hogwarts. PA 17, p. 348. DH 5, p. 81. Pettigrew's fate was witnessed by Harry Potter and Ron Weasley during year seven. DH 23, pp. 470-71. Pettigrew's magic wand was made of chesnut and dragon heartstring. It was nine and one-quarter inches long. DH 24, p. 494.

Peverell. An old wizard family name. Mr. Gaunt wore a ring that featured the Peverell coat of arms on it. HP 10, p. 207. Hermione Granger suspected that the family had something to do with the Elder Wand. Three brothers in the family, Antioch, Cadmus and Ignotus, were believed to have been the Three Brothers who originally owned the Deathly Hallows. DH 21, pp. 412-13. The family was one of the first to become extinct because of no male heir and one of its descendants was Marvolo Gaunt. DH 22, pp. 427-28.

Peverell, Antioch. A wizard who may have been one of the Three Brothers that owned the Deathly Hallows. DH 21, p. 413.

Peverell, Cadmus. A wizard who may have been one of the Three Brothers that owned the Deathly Hallows. DH 21, p. 413.

Peverell, Ignotus. The name that appeared on a tombstone in Godric's Hollow. Ignotus may have been one of the Three Brothers that owned the Deathly Hallows. DH 21, p. 413. Harry Potter believed that he was a descendant of Ignotus. DH 22, p. 430.

Philosophy of the Mundane: Why the Muggles Prefer Not to Know. The title of a book written by Professor Mordicus Egg in 1963. The book was published by Dint and Mildewe. FB, p. xvii, fn. 8.

Philpott, Arkie. A wizard who was a customer at Gringotts Wizarding Bank and who had a Probity Probe stuck up a part of his body there due to increased security at the bank. HP 6, p. 108.

Phlegm. A nickname that Ginny Weasley gave to Fleur Delacourt during the summer prior to Harry Potter's sixth year at Hogwarts. HP 6, pp. 92-93.

Phoenix. A magical bird with red and gold plumage that periodically burst into flames and then was reborn from its own ashes. Its tears had healing powers and it made a faithful pet. Albus Dumbledore had a pet phoenix named Fawkes in his office at Hogwarts. Harry Potter met Fawkes during his second year at Hogwarts. CS 12, pp. 205-07. Fawkes assisted Harry to escape from the Chamber of Secrets. CS 17, pp. 318-25. During his duel with Lord Voldemort after the Triwizard Tournament, Harry heard the Phoenix's song and it assisted him in the struggle. GF 33, pp. 664-65. The Phoneix was native to Egypt, India and China. It was a very difficult beast to domesticate. FB, p. 32, fn. 32. The Moutohora Macaws, a quidditch team from New Zealand, had a phoenix mascot named Sparky. QA 8, p. 42. A tear of a Phoenix was the only known antidote for basilisk venom. DH 6, p. 104. Two phoenixes were on top of the cake at the Fleur Delacourt and Bill Wealsey wedding during year seven. DH 8, p. 151.

Piertotum Locomotor. The magic words used by Minerva McGonagell to invoke a charm that animated all of the statues and suits of armor in Hogwarts during year seven. DH 30, p. 602.

Pig. See **Pigwidgeon.**

Pig Snout. A password used to gain access to theGryffindor house during Harry Potter's first year at Hogwarts. SS 9, p. 156.

Pigwidgeon. The name given by Ginny Weasley to the Weasley's post owl, which was gray and small enough to fit into one's hand. Ron Weasley nicknamed the bird "Pig." GF 3, p. 35. Pigwidgeon delivered a message to Harry Potter to confirm that Arthur Weasley obtained the tickets for the Quidditch World Cup. This event occurred during the summer prior to Harry's fourth year at Hogwarts. GF 5, p. 57. Pidwidgeon continued to serve as the post owl for the Weasleys during year seven. DH 5, p. 83.

Pillock. A derogatory name that Rita Skeeter used to refer to the Gringotts Charm Breakers. Bill Weasley, as a charm breaker for Gringotts, was upset that Skeeter called them "long-haired pillocks." This event occurred during Harry Potter's fourth year at Hogwarts. GF 10, p. 152.

Pillsworth, Bernie. The ficitious name for a wizard in the Ministry of Magic that Ron Weasley invented during a ride in an elevator with Arthur Weasley during year seven. DH 13, p. 255.

Pince, Madam Irma. The librarian of Hogwarts during the time that Harry Potter attended the school. SS 12, p. 198. Madam Pince was thin, irritable and looked like an underfed vulture. CS 10, p. 163. During his fourth year at Hogwarts, Harry asked Madam Pince to help him locate a book that contained a spell to survive without oxygen. GF 26, p. 482; QA, pp. i, vii.

Pitch. The name for the field on which quidditch was played. QA 6, p. 17.

Pittiman, Radolphus. A famous wizard biographer who wrote about Uric the Oddball's episode with augureys. FB, p. 3, fn. 3.

Pixie. A magical beast found mostly in Cornwall. FB, p. 32.

Placement Charm. A charm used to apprehend a kelpie. The Placement Charm allowed the wizard casting it to throw a bridle over the head of the kelpie. FB, p. 23.

Plangentine. A plant that Bathilda Bagshot picked one winter in Godric's Hollow. DH 11, p. 218.

Platform Nine and Three-Quarters. The train platform at King's Cross where students boarded the Hogwarts Express to travel to Hogwarts. Muggles could not see or access the platform. SS 5, p. 87; 6, p. 93. Harry Potter was mysteriously prevented from reaching the platform on the way to his second year at Hogwarts. CS 5, p. 68. For the identity of the person who caused this event, see CS 10, 176. DH 33, p. 668.

PlayStation. In a letter to Sirius Black, Harry Potter described a PlayStation as a sort of computer thing you can play games on. According to Harry, Dudley Dursley threw his PlayStation out of a window in anger when told by his parents that they would no longer give him pocket money if he did not stop smuggling donuts into his room. Dudley was on a diet and used his PlayStation to play *Mega-Mutilation Part Three.* This event occurred during the summer prior to Harry's fourth year at Hogwarts. GF 2, p. 25.

Plimpy. A magical fish that inhabited deep lakes. FB, p. 32. See also, **Freshwater Plimpies**.

Plumpton, Roderick. A notable seeker for the Tutshill Tornados. Roderick held the record for the fastest capture of the snitch, which time was three and one-half seconds. This event occurred during a game in 1921 against the Caerphilly Catapults. QA 7, p. 37. The Plumpton Pass was named after Roderick. QA 10, p. 53.

Plumpton Pass. A quidditch move that was widely known. It was named after Roderick Plumpton. QA 10, p. 53.

Pluto. Sibyl Trelawney instructed Harry Potter's Divination class that Pluto was capable of disrupting everyday life in many ways. This event occurred during Harry Potter's fourth year at Hogwarts. GF 21, p. 371. (Pluto is the ninth planet from the sun in the solar system that includes Earth.)

Pocket Sneakoscope. A miniature, glass, spinning top that lighted up and spun when an untrustworthy person was near. Ron Weasley sent Harry Potter a sneakoscope from Egypt as a thirteenth birthday present. This event occurred during the summer prior to Harry's third year at Hogwarts. PA 1, p. 10. Harry observed a large sneakoscope in Mad-Eye Moody's office, as part of his collection of Dark Detectors, during Harry's fourth year at Hogwarts. GF 19, pp. 342-343. During year seven, Harry still had a sneakoscope in his trunk and Hermione Granger gave him a new one for his seventeenth birthday. DH 2, p. 14; 7, p.114.

Podmore, Sturgis. A wizard who was a member of the Order of the Phoenix and the advance guard that rescued Harry Potter from the Dursley home during the summer prior to Harry's fifth year at Hogwarts. OP 3, pp. 47-49. Sturgis lived at 2, Laburnum Gardens, Clapham and was convicted by the Wizengamot of attempting to break into a top-security area of the Ministry of Magic on August 31 prior to Harry's fifth year at Hogwarts. OP 14, p. 287.

Pogrebin. A magical beast native to Russia. The Pogrebin was often repulsed by Stupefying Charms and simple hexes. FB, pp. xix, 33.

Poisoning Department. A department at the St. Mungo's Hospital. DH 21, p. 413.

Pokeby, Gulliver. The author of *Why I Didn't Die When the Augurey Cried.* The book was published by Little Red Books in 1824. FB, p. 3, fn. 4.

Poland. The home country of the Grodzisk Goblins. The world's most innovative seeker, Josek Wronski, played for the Goblins. QA 8, p. 41. Ladislaw Zamojski was the top chaser of Poland's team. OP 19, p. 400. Rubeus Hagrid ran into a couple of mad trolls on the Polish border. OP 20, p. 426. (Poland is a country in East Central Europe on the Baltic Sea.)

Poliakoff. A student from the Durmstrang Institute who came to Hogwarts to be selected as his school's champion for the Triwizard Tournament. Poliakoff was rebuffed by Igor Karkaroff when he asked for some wine. These events occurred during Harry Potter's fourth year at Hogwarts. GF 16, p. 257.

Polkiss. A muggle family that lived near the Dursley home and had a child who played with Dudley Dursley. OP 1, p. 3.

Polkiss, Piers. A muggle friend of Dudley Dursley. Piers was a guest on a zoo trip that the Dursleys took on Dudley's eleventh birthday. Piers was also one of the members of Dudley's gang that liked to tease Harry Potter by playing "Harry Hunting." The other members, in addition to Dudley, were Dennis, Malcolm and Gordon. SS 2, p. 23; 3, p. 31.

Polyjuice Potion. A potion that allowed a witch or wizard to take the shape of another person temporarily. The recipe was contained in *Moste Potente Potions.* The book was located in the restricted section of the library at Hogwarts. CS 9, pp. 159, 160. The ingredients for the potion included: lacewing flies, leeches, fluxweed, knotgrass, powered horn of a bicorn, shredded skin of a boomslang and a bit of whoever the potionmaker wanted to turn into. CS 10, p. 165. The effect of the potion lasted for only an hour. Harry Potter, Ron Weasley and Hermione Granger made Polyjuice Potion during Harry's second year at Hogwarts. Harry took the form of Gregory Goyle and Ron took the form of Vincent Crabbe. CS 12, pp. 214-15. An important Death Eater used Polyjuice Potion during Harry Potter's fourth year. GF 35, p. 682. At the beginning of year seven, members of the Order of the Phoenix took some of the potion to look like Harry. DH 4, pp. 50-51. Polyjuice Potion works on humans only, not other creatures such as half-giants. DH 5, p. 71.

Pomfrey, Madam. A witch who was the nurse in the hospital of Hogwarts. SS 1, p. 11; 9, p. 156. The professors called her "Poppy." PA 5, p. 89. DH 31, p. 608.

Pontner, Roddy. A wizard with whom Ludo Bagman had a wager relating to the outcome of the Quidditch World Cup. This event occurred during the summer prior to Harry Potter's fourth year at Hogwarts. GF 7, p. 88.

Poppy. See **Pomfrey, Madam.**

Porlock. A magical beast found in Dorset, England and Southern Ireland that protected horses. Burdock Muldoon slipped on a pile of porlock dung during an important summit that he convened in the fourteenth century of the Wizards' Council. FB, pp. xi, 33. The subject of porlocks was often tested on O.W.L.s. OP 15, p. 323.

Porskoff, Petrova. A famous Russian quidditch player who was a chaser. The Porskoff Ploy was named after her. QA 10, p. 53.

Portable Swamp. A joke device that Fred and George Weasley invented during Harry Potter's fifth year at Hogwarts. They set the Portable Swamp off on the fifth floor of the east wing. Professor Flitwick thought it such a good bit of magic that he roped off a portion of it as a monument of sorts to the Weasley twins. OP 29, p. 674; 30, p. 676; 38, p. 848.

Porskoff Ploy. One of the quidditch plays recorded by the omnioculars Harry Potter looked through at the Quidditch World Cup during the summer prior to his fourth year at Hogwarts. This play was executed by Troy in order to fool a Bulgarian chaser into dropping the quaffle to Moran. Anther play was the Hawkshead Attacking Formation. GF 8, p. 106. The Porskoff Ploy was named after the Russian chaser Petrova Porskoff. QA 10, p. 53.

Portkey. An unobtrusive object, such that muggles would consider it a piece of litter, used to transport wizards from one spot to another at a prearranged time. Large groups of wizards could use a portkey at once. Two hundred portkeys were placed in Britain for transporting wizards to the Quidditch World Cup. This event occurred during the summer prior to Harry Potter's fourth year at Hogwarts. The closest portkey to the Burrow was an old boot lying on the ground at Stoatshead Hill. Members of the Weasley family, Harry and Hermione Granger used the boot as a portkey, along with Amos and Cedric Diggory. One simply needed to touch a portkey with a finger to be transported away. GF 6, pp. 70, 73. Other portkeys were an old newspaper, an empty drink can and a punctured football. GF 7, p. 75. The Weasleys and Harry used an old rubber tire to get back to Stoatshead Hill from the Quidditch World Cup. GF 10, p. 145. A portkey was secretly placed into the third task of the Triwizard Tournament. GF 32, p. 636. A quidditch referee's broomstick was turned into a portkey that transported the referee to the Sahara Desert. QA 6, p. 30. The magi word used to create a Portkey was "*portus*." OP 22, pp. 472, 474. During year seven, Pius Thicknesse made it an imprisonable offense to connect the Dursley residence to a portkey. DH 4, p. 46. A silver-backed hairbrush at the Tonks residence was a portkey to the Burrow during year seven for Harry and Rebeus Hagrid. DH 5, p. 67. Other portkeys that year were: a rusty oil can, an ancient sneaker and a bent coathanger. DH 5, pp. 68, 72.

Portkey Office. An office in the Department of Magical Transport located on level six of the Ministry of Magic. OP 7, p. 129.

Portsmouth. The location where Elias Grimstone resided. Elias made the first Oakshaft 79 in 1879. QA 9, p. 47. (Portsmouth is a seaport in South Hampshire, in Southern England on the English Channel.)

Portugal. The home country of the braga broomfleet. QA 8, p. 41. (Portugal is a country in Southwest Europe on the Iberian Peninsula, west of Spain.)

Portus. A magic word used in a charm invoked by Albus Dumbledore to make an old blackened kettle glow with an odd blue light and become a portkey. This event occurred during Harry Potter's fifth year at Hogwarts. OP 22, pp. 472, 474.

Post Owl. An owl used by a witch or wizard to deliver mail. GF 3, p. 37. There were many types of post owls. Harry Potter's post owl was a snowy owl named Hedwig. SS 5, p. 81. The Weasley family had the following owls: Errol, CS 3, p. 30; Hermes, CS 3, p. 30; and a tiny one named Pig. GF 3, p. 35. The post owl used by the Malfoy family was an eagle owl. SS 9, p. 144. Neville Longbottom's grandmother used a barn owl. SS 9, p. 145.

Potions. A subject taught at Hogwarts by Severus Snape. Severus summarized the subject as the subtle science and exact art of potion-making. SS 8, p.136. Potions was required only through the fifth year at Hogwarts. After that year, Severus took only the best students into the sixth year N.E.W.T. Potions class. OP 12, p. 232.

Potter. The wizard family to which Harry Potter belonged. Harry's parents were James and Lily. SS 1, p. 2.

Potter, Albus Severus. The middle child of Harry and Ginny Potter's three children. Albus attended Hogwarts for the first time 19 years after the conclusion of events during year seven. He was the only child of Harry's who had Lily's eyes. DH Epilogue, pp. 753, 758.

Potter, Harry James. The wizard son of James and Lily Potter. SS 1, p. 4. Harry had his father's looks and wild hair, and his mother's green eyes. SS 12, p. 208; PA 22, p. 427. Harry's parents were killed by Lord Voldemort on Halloween when Harry was a baby. SS 1, p. 12; 4, p. 55. Harry was renowned throughout the wizarding world for the lightning bolt scar on his forehead which he received from a failed curse that Lord Voldemort tried to place on him in order to kill him. SS 1, p. 15. The failed curse severely injured Lord Voldemort, forced him into hiding and thus made Harry a legend. SS 1, p. 13. Although Harry's Aunt Petunia and Uncle Dursley lied to him about his parents' death and his background, Rubeus Hagrid informed Harry of his past and that he was a wizard. SS 4, p. 50. Harry attended Hogwarts and was a member of the Gryffindor house. SS 7, p. 121. He became the seeker on that house's quidditch team during his first year at Hogwarts, a feat that had not occurred for one hundred years. SS 9, p. 151. Harry's birthday was July 31. SS 8, pp. 141-42. Harry's name appeared last on the list of borrowers found inside the cover of *Quidditch Through the Ages*. QA, p. i. Around the time of Harry's birth a prophecy was made by a seer regarding Harry's future. OP 37, p. 841. During his sixth year at Hogwarts, Harry was the captain of the Gryffindor quidditch team. HP 6, p. 106. That year, Harry kissed Ginny Weasley after Gryffindor won the Championship game against Ravenclaw, in which game Ginny was the seeker. With that kiss, Ginny and Harry began to date each other. HP 24, pp. 533-34. The protective charm that was placed on the Dursley residence to protect Harry expired on Harry's seventeenth birthday. The exact date on which Voldemort attacked Harry as an infant was October 31, 1981. DH 3, p. 33; 17, p. 332. During year seven, Harry agreed to be the godfather of Ted Lupin. DH 25, p. 514. Unknown to Voldemort, Harry had a piece of Voldemort's soul in himself. DH 33, p. 686. The final duel between Harry and Voldemort occurred at the end of year seven, when each of their fates was revealed. DH 36, pp. 743-44.

Potter, James. The father of Harry Potter. SS 1, p. 12. James attended Hogwarts and was head boy. SS 4, p. 55. James was also an excellent quidditch player. SS 9, p. 152. During his fifth year at Hogwarts,

James learned to turn himself into an animagus in the form of an antlered stag. He never registered that ability with the Ministry of Magic. PA 18, p. 354; 20, p. 385; 21, pp. 411-412; 22, p. 424. James' close friends nicknamed him Prongs. PA 18, p. 355. He was in the same class as Severus Snape and saved Snape's life during a prank. PA 18, p. 357. James and his wife, Lilly, were killed by Lord Voldemort on Halloween when Harry was a baby SS 4, pp. 54-55. James was a member of the Order of the Phoenix. OP 9, p. 174. Harry's middle name was James, like his father; it was printed on his Ordinary Wizarding Level results during the summer prior to his sixth year at Hogwarts. HP 5, p. 102. James was born on March 27, 1960. The tombstone of his grave, which he shared with Lilly Potter, was only two rows behind that of Kendra and Ariana Dumbledore's in Godric's Hollow. The inscription on the tombstone read: "The last enemy that shall be destroyed is death." DH 16, p. 328. James as a youth appeared in a story watched by Harry in the pensieve during year seven. DH 33, p. 671.

Potter, James. The oldest of Harry and Ginny Potter's three children. James was two years older than his sister, Lily. DH Epilogue, p. 753.

Potter, Lily (Evans). The mother of Harry Potter. SS 1, p. 12. Lily attended Hogwarts and was head girl. SS 12, p. 208. She and her husband, James, were killed by Lord Voldemort on Halloween when Harry was a baby. SS 4, pp. 54-55. Lilly was a member of the Order of the Phoenix. OP 9, p. 174. Her maiden name was Evans and she was a mudblood. OP 28, pp. 647, 648. She was one of the brightest students that Professor Horace Slughorn ever taught. HP 4, p. 70. Lily was especially skillful at making potions. HP 9, p. 191. DH 10, p. 181. Lily was born on January 30, 1960. The tombstone of her grave, which she shared with James Potter, was only two rows behind that of Kendra and Ariana Dumbledore's in Godric's Hollow. The inscription on the tombstone read: "The last enemy that shall be destroyed is death." DH 16, p. 328. Lily as a young girl was part of a story that Harry watched in the pensieve during year seven. DH 33, p . 663. Lily's patronus took the form of a silver doe. DH 36, p. 740.

Potter, Lily. The youngest of Harry and Ginny Potter's three children. She was two years younger than her brother, James. DH Epilogue, p. 753.

Potterwatch. A radio show broadcast to wizards during year seven. It was the only true news source to tell its listeners what was happening and was not controlled by Lord Voldemort. The secret password to access the program was "Albus" and Lee Jordan was the announcer for the program. DH 22, pp. 437-38. The password that followed "Albus" was "Made-Eye." DH 22, p. 444.

Potts, Nugent. A quidditch referee who was struck in the nose by a Shooting Arrow that had been fired by a member of the Appleby Arrows during a quidditch match in 1894. QA 7, p. 32.

Powers You Never Knew You Had and What To Do with Them Now You've Wised Up. The title of a book that Harry Potter consulted in order to find a way to breathe underwater in the second task of the Triwizard Tournament. This event occurred during Harry's fourth year at Hogwarts. GF 26, p. 488.

Practical Defensive Magic and Its Use Against the Dark Arts. A series of books that Harry Potter received as Christmas gifts from Sirius Black and Remus Lupin during Harry's fifth year at Hogwarts. OP 23, p. 501. During year seven, Harry tucked an obituary from the *Daily Prophet* into his copy of the first volume of this series. DH 2, p. 21.

Practical Potioneer, The. A periodical in the Wizarding World. Albus Dumbledore had some of his papers published in *The Practical Potioneer*. DH 2, p. 17.

Prang, Ernie. The driver of the Knight Bus. Harry Potter met Ernie after running away from the Dursley residence during the summer prior to his third year at Hogwarts. PA 3, p. 35.

Predicting the Unpredictable: Insulate Yourself Against Shocks. The title of a book relating to Divination that Harry Potter observed in Flourish and Blotts. This event occurred during the summer prior to Harry's third year at Hogwarts. PA 4, p. 53.

Prefect. A title of distinction that was conferred on certain accomplished students at Hogwarts. Students with the title received special privileges and had oversight responsibilities with respect to the other students. Percy Weasley became a prefect during Harry Potter's first year at Hogwarts. SS 6, p. 96. During Harry's fourth year at Hogwarts, Cedric Diggory was a prefect. GF 15, p. 236. The prefects had their own bathroom at Hogwarts. GF 23, p. 431. During Harry's fifth year at the school, Ron Weasley and Hermione Granger were the prefects for the Gryffindor house. Prefects were not chosen until a class had started its fifth year. OP 9, pp. 161-62, 166. Remus Lupin was a prefect when he attended Hogwarts. OP 9, p. 170. The other prefects selected from Harry's classmates were: Draco Malfoy and Pansy Parkinson, for the Slytherin house; Ernie MacMillan and Hannah Abbott, for the Hufflepuff house; and Anthony Goldstein and Padma Patil, for the Ravenclaw house. OP 10, pp.188-89. The captain of a house quidditch team at Hogwarts had the same "status" as a prefect. HP 6, p. 107. Tom Riddle was a prefect when the attended Hogwarts. HP 17, p. 370. DH 31, p. 608.

Prefects' Bathroom. A special bathroom restricted to the prefects of Hogwarts. The bathroom was located on the fifth floor, at the fourth door to the left of a statue of Boris the Bewildered. The door to the prefects' bathroom was opened by using the password "pine fresh." Cedric Diggory gave this information to Harry Potter after the conclusion of the Yule Ball. GF 23, p. 431. The bathroom had a rectangular swimming pool with approximately one hundred golden taps around it, each with a different colored jewel set into its handle. The taps emitted different types of water and bubblebath. There was also a diving board and a picture of a mermaid on the wall. GF 25, p. 459. Harry used this bathroom during his fourth year at Hogwarts to discover the secret of a golden egg he obtained during the second task of the Triwizard Tournament. Moaning Myrtle gave Harry assistance. GF 25, pp. 459-64.

Prefects Who Gained Power. The title of a book that Percy Weasley found in a tiny junk shop on Diagon Alley. This event occurred during the summer prior to Harry Potter's second year at Hogwarts. CS 4, p. 58.

Prentice, Mr. A muggle who was a neighbor of Mrs. Figg in Little Whinging. OP 2, p. 21.

Prewett. A family of wizards who, according to Rubeus Hagrid, were some of the best witches and wizards of the age, including the Bones and the McKinnons, that was killed by Lord Voldemort. SS 4, p. 56.

Prewett, Fabian. A wizard who was a member of the Order of the Phoenix and killed fighting for the Order. It took five Death Eaters to kill Fabian and his brother, Gordon. OP 9, p. 174. Antonin Dolohov was convicted of Fabian's murder. OP 25, p. 543.

Prewett, Gordon. A wizard who was a member of the Order of the Phoenix and killed fighting for the Order. It took five Death Eaters to kill Gordon and his brother, Fabian. OP 9, p. 174. Antonin Dolohov was convicted of Gordon's murder. OP 25, p. 543.

Pride of Portree. A quidditch team in the league that was from the Isle of Skye in Scotland. One of its most famous players was Catriona McCormack. Her daughter Meaghan also played for the team. QA 7, p. 36.

Prime Minister. Dudley Dursley was so uninterested in news that Vernon Dursley doubted whether Dudley even knew the identity of the Prime Minister. This event occurred during the summer prior to Harry Potter's fifth year at Hogwarts. OP 1, p. 2. The Prime Minister was visited by Cornelius Fudge prior to Harry's sixth year at Hogwarts. HP 1, p. 4.

Prince, Eileen. A student at Hogwarts who had been the Captain of the Hogwarts Gobstones Team years before Harry Potter attended the school. Hermione Granger suspected that Eileen could have been the half-blood prince. HP 25, p. 537. Eileen was the mother of Severus Snape. Her husband was Tobias Snape, a muggle. HP 30, p. 637.

Principal Exceptions to Gamps Law of Elemental Transfiguration. Food was the first of five exceptions to a magical law. The exception prohibited witches and wizards form producing food out of thin air. DH 15, p. 292.

Principles of Rematerialization, The. The title of an essay that Hermione Granger wrote during Harry Potter's sixth year at Hogwarts. HP 10, p. 195.

Pringle, Apollyon. The caretaker of Hogwarts around the time that Arthur and Molly Weasley were students at the school. According to Mrs. Weasley, Apollyon caught Arthur after the two students took a nighttime stroll and Arthur still had the marks from the punishment he received from Apollyon. GF 31, p. 616.

Prior Incantatem. The magic words used to invoke the Reverse Spell Effect. The effect occurred when two magic wands of the same core came into contact with each other. One of the wands forced the other to regurgitate the spells it had performed in reverse order so that the most recent spell was replayed first. GF 35, p. 697. The wands of Harry Potter and Lord Voldemort displayed this effect after the third event of the Triwizard Tournament. This event occurred during Harry's fourth year at Hogwarts. GF 34, pp. 663-68.

Prior Incantato. The magic words used in a charm to cast the last spell that a wand performed. The charm was extinguished by the word "*deletrius*." Amos Diggory invoked the charm to determine the last spell cast by Harry Potter's wand during the aftermath of the Quidditch World Cup that Harry attended. This event occurred during the summer prior to Harry's fourth year at Hogwarts. GF 9, pp. 135-36.

Priori Incantatem. A charm used to invoke the prior charms invoked from a wand. DH 24, p. 496. See **Prio Incantato**.

Pritchard, Graham. A student who was sorted by the Sorting Hat during Harry Potter's fourth year at Hogwarts. Graham was a member of the Slytherin house. GF 12, p. 180.

Privet Drive. The street on which the Dursley family lived. Their full address was 4 Privet Drive, Little Whinging, Surrey. They lived in a four bedroom house. SS 1, p. 1; 3 pp. 37. Letters sent to Harry Potter in the house before his first year at Hogwarts included the addresses: "The Cupboard Under the Stairs," SS 3, p. 34; and "The Smallest Bedroom." SS 3, p. 38. Mrs. Number Seven lived on Privet drive in Little Whinging. OP 1, p. 5. DH 2, p. 13.

Probity Probe. A magic device that was used by the goblins at Gringotts Wizarding Bank on Arkie Philpott, one of the bank's customers, as part of tighter security measures at the bank during the summer prior to Harry Potter's sixth year at Hogwarts. HP 6, p. 108. The device, capable of detecting spells of concealment and hidden magical objects, was used at Gringotts the following year as well. DH 26, p. 529.

Prod, Warlock D.J. A warlock from Didsbury who took the Kwikspell course and afterward was able to use a charm to turn his wife into a yak. This information was listed on a piece of parchment that advertised the Kwikspell course. Harry Potter read the advertisement in Argus Filch's office during Harry's second year at Hogwarts. CS 8, p. 127.

Prongs. A wizard who was responsible, along with three others, for the creation of the Marauder's Map. The other wizards were nicknamed Wormtail, Moony and Padfoot. Fred and George Weasley gave the map to Harry Potter as a Christmas present during Harry's third year at Hogwarts. PA 10, pp. 191-194. James Potter was Prongs. PA 18, p. 355.

Prophecy. During Harry Potter's fifth year at Hogwarts, Albus Dumbledore used a pensieve to retrieve a memory of Sibyll Trelawney in which she made an important prophecy about Harry. The prophecy was: "The one with the power to vanquish the Dark Lord approaches... Born to those who have thrice defied him, born as the seventh month dies... and the Dark Lord will make him as his equal, but he will have power the Dark Lord knows not...and either must die at the hand of the other for neither can live while the other survives...The one with the power to vanquish the Dark Lord will be born as the seventh month dies. OP, 37, p. 841.

Protean Charm. A charm that Hermione Granger placed on fake galleons in order for the coins to reveal the date and time of the next meeting of Dumbledore's Army. The ability to perform a Protean Charm was N.E.W.T. standard. This event occurred during Harry Potter's fifth year at Hogwarts. OP 18, p. 398.

Protego. A magic word that Harry Potter used , as part of a Shield Charm, to defend himself against a spell of Severus Snape's. This event occurred during one of Harry's special occlumency classes in his fifth year at Hogwarts. OP 26, p. 591. DH 9, p. 160. Hermione Granger invoked the Shield Charm in Gringotts Wizarding Bank during year seven. DH 26, p. 535.

Protego Horribilis. The magic words used by Professor Flitwick to invoke a protective charm around Hogwarts during year seven. DH 30, p. 600.

Protego Totalum. The magic words used by Hermione Granger to invoke one of several protective enchantments over her camping area during year seven. DH 14, p. 272.

Proudfoot. An auror who was stationed at Hogwarts to provide the school with extra security during Harry's sixth year at Hogwarts. Proudfoot was joined by Nymphadora Tonks, Savage and Dawlish. HP 8, p. 158.

Prudence. The sister of Madam Modesty Rabnott of Kent. Prudence resided in Aberdeen and was the recipient of an important letter written by Madam Modesty about the first quidditch match, conducted in 1269, that used a snidget. QA 4, p. 12.

Pucey, Adrian. A chaser on the Slytherin quidditch team during Harry Potter's first, second and fifth years at Hogwarts. SS 11, p. 186; CS 10, p. 168; OP 19, p. 409.

Puddlemere United. A quidditch team from Puddlemere. Albus Dumbledore wished good luck to Puddlemere United in his foreword to *Quidditch Through the Ages*. QA, p. viii. Puddlemere United was the oldest team in the league. Its anthem: "Beat Back Those Bludgers, Boys, and Chuck That Quaffle Here" was recorded by Celestina Warbeck as a fund raiser for St. Mungo's Hospital for Magical Maladies and Injuries. QA 7, p. 36. The team pattern included golden bulrushes. Harry Potter did not support Puddlemere United. DH 6, p. 88.

Puddlemere United Reserve Team. A quidditch team that Oliver Wood signed on to after graduating from Hogwarts. Oliver informed Harry Potter of this fact at the camp site near the Quidditch World Cup. This event occurred during the summer prior to Harry's fourth year at Hogwarts. GF 7, p. 84.

Puffapod. A plant that Harry Potter, Ron Weasley and Hermione Granger worked on in Herbology class during Harry's third year at Hogwarts. The plant had fat pink pods with shiny beans. Its beans burst into bloom if they were not handled carefully. PA 8, p. 147.

Puffer-fish. A fish, the eyes of which were used as an ingredient in a Potions class during Harry Potter's second year at Hogwarts. CS 11, p. 186.

Puffskein. A magical beast found worldwide. The puffskein was a popular wizarding pet. According to Ron Weasley, he had a puffskein for a pet, but Fred Weasley used it for bludger practice. FB, pp. vii, 34. A nest of dead puffskeins was under the sofa at Number Twelve, Grimmauld Place during the summer prior to Harry Potter's fifth year at Hogwarts. OP 6, p. 101. Miniature versions of them were sold, under the name Pygmy Puffs, in Weasleys Wizard Wheezes during the following year. HP 6, p. 121.

Puking Pastilles. One of the chews invented by Fred and George Weasley that collectively were referred to as Skiving Snackboxes. Fred and George developed the candies during the summer prior to Harry Potter's fifth year at Hogwarts. Two of the other chews were

Fainting Fancies and Nosebleed Nougat. OP 6, pp. 104-05. DH 12, p. 235.

Pumpkin Pasties. Pastries sold in the wizarding world. Harry Potter purchased some of these pastries on the Hogwarts Express as he traveled to his first year at Hogwarts. SS 6, p. 101.

Pure-blood. A name given to a person whose parents were both wizards. Being a pure-blood did not necessarily guarantee that a person was capable of performing magic; Neville Longbottom was one such example. CS 7, p. 116.

Purge and Dowse, Ltd. An old department store located in muggle London that served as a front for the entrance to St. Mungo's Hospital for Magical Maladies and Injuries. OP 22, p. 483.

Purkiss, Doris. A witch who lived at 18 Acanthia Way, Little Norton. According to a report in *the Quibbler*, Doris believed that Sirius Black was Stubby Boardman, lead singer of the popular singing group, the Hobgoblins. The report was published during the summer prior to Harry Potter's fifth year at Hogwarts. OP 10, pp. 191-92.

Put-Outer. A magical device shaped like a cigarette lighter that allowed one by clicking it to extinguish lights. The device was used by Albus Dumbledore to extinguish the streetlights along Privet Drive during the night that Harry Potter was rescued from Lord Voldemort's failed attempt to murder him. SS 1, p. 9. Alastor "Mad Eye" Moody borrowed Albus Dumbledore's Put-Outer the evening that the advance guard of the Order of the Phoenix rescued Harry Potter from the Dursley home. This event occurred during the summer prior to Harry's fifth year at Hogwarts. OP 3, p. 58.

Pye, Augustus. A trainee healer of the "Dangerous" Dai Llewellyn Ward at St. Mungo's Hospital for Magical Maladies and Injuries. OP 22, p. 487.

Pygmy Puffs. A magical beast sold in Weasleys Wizard Wheezes during the summer prior to Harry Potter's sixth year at Hogwarts. They were miniature puffskeins. HP 6, p. 120. Ginny.Weasley had a pygmy puff as a pet that school year. Its name was Arnold. HP 7, p. 132.

QUAFFLE - QUODPOT

Quaffle. A bright red ball, the size of a soccer ball, used to play quidditch. If a chaser passed the quaffle through one of the opponents' three hoops, the chaser's team scored ten points. SS 10, p. 167. The year 1269 was the earliest known date for the use of a quaffle in a game of quidditch. The event was recorded in a letter written by Madam Modesty Rabnott. QA 3, p. 8; 4, p. 12. A quaffle was seamless and twelve inches in diameter. QA 6, p. 21. Dragomir Gorgovitch, chaser of the Chudley Cannons, was the record holder for most Quaffles dropped in a season. DH 7, p. 112.

Quafflepocking. The name of one of the ten most common fouls committed in quidditch. QA 6, p. 30.

Quality Quidditch Supplies. A shop on Diagon Alley that sold quidditch supplies. During the summer prior to Harry Potter's second year at Hogwarts, Ron Weasley looked at a full set of Chudley Canon robes in the window of Quality Quidditch Supplies. CS 4, p. 58. Harry had his first glimpse of a Firebolt in the shop before the beginning of his third year at Hogwarts. PA 4, pp. 50-51.

Queerditch Marsh. The location where the game of quidditch was first played. QA 1, p. 6.

Quibbler, The. The title of a magazine in the wizarding world. OP 7, p. 133. Luna Lovegood's father was the editor of *The Quibbler*. OP 10, p. 193. During the summer prior to Harry Potter's sixth year at Hogwarts an edition of *The Quibbler* included a free pair of Spectrespecs. HP 7, p. 137. DH 15, p. 299.

Quiberon Quafflepunchers. A quidditch team from France that was a frequent league winner. QA 8, p. 40. (Quiberon is a peninsula of the northwest coast of France on the southern coast of Brittany.)

Quick-Quotes Quill. A magical quill pen that Rita Skeeter used in her interview of Harry Potter about the selection of Harry as a school champion for the Triwizard Tournament. The quill wrote on parchment without Rita holding it and sensed her thoughts. This event occurred during Harry's fourth year at Hogwarts. GF 18, pp. 304-05. DH 2, p. 24.

Quidditch. The major sport in the wizarding world. Quidditch was played in the air on brooms with four balls. SS 5, pp. 77, 79. Some of the points were scored by sending the balls through one of three golden hoops with poles that were positioned on each end of the playing field, known as a pitch. Each team had seven players. Three players were the chasers, who had the duty to pass between themselves a bright red ball, known as the quaffle. The quaffle was the size of a soccer ball. If a chaser passed the quaffle through one of the opponents' three hoops on the field, the chaser's team scored ten points. One of the players, known as the keeper, had the duty to keep the quaffle from going through the hoops. SS 10, pp. 166-68. Two of the players were called beaters. SS 9, p. 153. The beaters had the duty to use short baseball bats to prevent two other jet black balls, slightly smaller than the quaffle and known as bludgers, from striking the other players of their team off of their brooms. SS 10, p. 168. The most important member of the team was the seeker. SS 9, p. 151. The seeker was responsible for capturing the smallest ball, known as the golden snitch. The golden snitch was the size of a large walnut and bright gold with little fluttering silver wings. The team that captured the golden snitch received an additional 150 points, so that team usually won the game. The game did not end until the golden snitch was captured by one of the teams. SS 10, p. 169. The basic rules for playing quidditch were established by the Department of Magical Games and Sports in 1750. There were 700 types of fouls and all of them occurred during the first World Cup held in 1473. QA 6, pp. 27-30. The ten most common fouls were, according to their names, as follows: Blagging; Blatching; Blurting; Bumphing; Cobbing; Flacking; Haversacking; Quaffle-pocking; Snitchnip; Stooging; QA 6, pp. 27-30. The following moves were well-known in the game: Bludger Backbeat; Dopplebeater Defence; Double Eight Loop; Hawkshead Attacking Formation; Parkin's Pincer; Plumpton Pass; Porskoff Ploy; Reverse Pass; QA 10, pp. 52-53. The captain of a house quidditch team at Hogwarts had the same "status" as a Prefect. HP 6, p. 107. DH 2, p. 15.

Quidditch Committee. A committee in the International Confederation of Wizards that frowned upon the Japanese practice of ceremonially setting quidditch broomsticks on fire when Japanese teams were defeated. QA 8, p. 46.

Quidditch Cup. A silver cup awarded each year to the house team that won the final quidditch match of the Inter-House Quidditch Cup at Hogwarts. SS 9, p. 153. During Harry Potter's second year at Hogwarts, the championship game was called off due to safety concerns surrounding the reopened Chamber of Secrets. CS 14, p. 256; PA 8, p. 143. During Harry's fourth year at Hogwarts, the competition was cancelled due to the demands placed on the staff for the Triwizard Tournament. GF 12, pp. 183-84.

Quidditch Teams of Britain and Ireland. The title of a book that Hermione Granger gave to Harry Potter as a Christmas present during Harry's fourth year at Hogwarts. GF 23, p. 410. DH 6, p. 94.

Quidditch Through the Ages. The title of a book on the sport of quidditch found in the library at Hogwarts. Hermione Granger read broom flying tips from the book after her first flying lesson. This event occurred during Harry Potter's first year at the school. SS 9, p. 144; 11, p. 181. The book was written by Kennilworthy Whisp and published by Whizz Hard Books in 1952. QA, p. iii; FB, p. 39, fn 13.

Quidditch World Cup. The championship quidditch match played in the wizarding world. The four-hundred and twentieth time this event took place was during the summer prior to Harry Potter's fourth year at Hogwarts. GF 8, p. 102. According to Ron Weasley, Arthur Weasley usually got tickets for the event from the Ministry of Magic, specifically the Department of Magical Games and Sports. PA 22, p. 431; GF 3, p. 30. The event drew one hundred thousand wizards from all over the world to Britain and many members of the Ministry of Magic were on duty to watch for signs of unusual activity and to check identities. GF 1, p. 8: 6, p. 69. The game that took place two weeks prior to Harry's fourth year at Hogwarts was the first time in thirty years that Britain hosted the game. GF 3, pp. 30-31; 4, p. 39. The teams that played each other that year were Ireland and Bulgaria. GF 3, p. 35. The event was played in a special stadium. GF 8, pp. 95-96. The final score was later revealed. GF 8, p. 113. The first Quidditch World Cup was held in 1473 and the teams from Transylvania and Flanders were in the final match. It was the most violent match in history. The Quidditch World Cup was played every four years. QA 8, pp. 39-40. During year seven, Hermione Granger apparated with Harry and Ron to the site of the Quidditch World Cup that had been held in a forest several years earlier. DH 14, p. 271.

Quietus. A magic word used by Ludo Bagman to invoke a charm to ease his hoarse throat after the Quidditch World Cup was concluded. This event occurred during the summer prior to Harry Potter's fourth year at Hogwarts. GF 8, p. 116.

Quigley. A member of the Irish National Quidditch Team who played in the Quidditch World Cup that Harry Potter attended during the summer prior to his fourth year at Hogwarts. Quigley was a beater. The other members of the team were: Connolly, Ryan, Troy, Mullet, Moran and Lynch. GF 8, p. 105.

Quijudge. The name for the referee in a fourteenth century quidditch match. QA 6, p. 18.

Quintaped. A magical beast found only on the Isle of Drear, off the northernmost tip of Scotland. Quintapeds had actually been a clan of wizards, the MacBoons, and were transfigured into five-legged creatures. Quintapeds resisted capture by the Department for the Regulation and Control of Magical Creatures. FB, pp. xix, 34-36.

Quintessence: A Quest. The title of a book that Harry Potter read during Charms class during his sixth year at Hogwarts. HP 15, p. 304.

Quirke, Orla. A student who was sorted by the Sorting Hat during Harry Potter's fourth year at Hogwarts. Orla was a member of the Ravenclaw house. GF 12, p. 180.

Quirrell, Professor. A professor with a distinctive stutter and a turban on his head. Professor Quirrell taught Defense Against the Dark Arts at Hogwarts during the first year that Harry Potter attended the school. SS 5, p. 70. The mystery of the turban was later revealed. SS 17, p. 293.

Quod. A modified quaffle used to play quodpot in the United States. QA 8, pp. 44-45.

Quodpot. A broomstick game popular in the United States that competed in popularity with quidditch. Quodpot was invented by Abraham Peasegood, an eighteenth century wizard. QA 8, pp. 44-45.

R.A.B. – RYAN, BARRY

R.A.B. The initials of a witch or wizard who placed a handwritten note inside a locket retrieved by Harry Potter and Albus Dumbledore from a remote cave during Harry's sixth year at Hogwarts. The author of the note intended for it to be read by Lord Voldemort. HP 28, p. 609. Hermione Granger identified two reasonably well-known wizards as having those initials: Rosalind Antigone Bungs and Rupert 'Axebanger' Brookstanton. HP 30, p. 636. The identity of the person whose initials were R.A.B. was revealed during year seven as Regulus Arcturus Black. DH 10, p. 186.

Rabastan. A Death Eater for Lord Voldemort who was present in the Department of Mysteries when Harry Potter retrieved the prophecy relating to himself and Lord Voldemort. This event occurred during Harry's fifth year at Hogwarts. OP 35, p. 788.

Rabnott, Madam Modesty. A witch who lived in Kent and wrote an eyewitness account of the first quidditch game that used a snidget. This event occurred in 1269. QA 4, p. 12. A snidget reservation was named after Madam Rabnott in Somerset. QA 4, p. 14.

Rackharrow, Urquhart. A wizard who lived from 1612 through 1697 and invented the Entrail-Expelling Curse. A portrait of Urquhart hung in the "Dangerous" Dai Llewellyn ward at St. Mungo's Hospital for Magical Maladies and Injuries. OP 22, p. 487.

Radulf. A blacksmith who played on the same kwidditch team as Goodwin Kneed during the tenth century. Radulf played the position of catcher. QA 3, p. 9.

Ragnok. A leader of the goblins who was described by Bill Weasley as "anti-wizard" at the moment because the Ministry of Magic, through Ludovic Bagman, covered-up a situation that denied the goblins some gold they had been promised. OP 5, pp. 85-86.

Ragnok the First. A goblin who was, according to Griphook, the original owner of the goblin-made sword that later became known as the Gryffindor Sword. Griphook claimed that Godric Gryffindor stole the sword from Ragnok. Hermione Granger could not confirm or deny Griphook's account of the sword. DH 25, p. 506.

Railview Hotel, Room 17. The place in Cokeworth where Vernon Dursley moved his family and Harry Potter after dozens of letters were delivered for Harry at the Dursley residence. This event occurred during the summer prior to Harry's first year at Hogwarts. SS 3, p. 42.

Ramora. A magical fish found in the Indian Ocean. The ramora was highly valued by the International Confederation of Wizards, which established many laws to protect it. FB, p. 36.

Rapier. A code name that Fred Weasley preferred to use on *Potterwatch* during year seven. Fred abandoned Rodent in favor of Rapier. DH 22, p. 443.

Ravenclaw. One of the four dormitory houses at Hogwarts. SS 6, p. 106. It was named after Rowena Ravenclaw. CS 9, p. 150. Ravenclaw's mascot was an eagle. SS 3, p. 34. During Harry Potter's third year at Hogwarts, the Ravenclaw quidditch team was much better than the Hufflepuff team. PA 10, p. 189. The Ravenclaw team color was blue and during Harry's third year at Hogwarts the only female on the team was Cho Chang. PA 13, p. 259. During Harry's fourth year at the school, a blue banner bearing a bronze eagle for Ravenclaw decorated the Great Hall for the Triwizard Tournament. GF 15, p. 237. The Ravenclaw dormitory was located in a tower on the west side of the Hogwarts castle. OP 18, p. 396. The hourglass for Ravenclaw in the entrance hall at Hogwarts contained sapphires. OP 38, p. 853. The Ravenclaw tower was accessed by using a bronze knocker in the shape of an eagle and answering a question asked by the knocker. When Harry tired to enter, it asked him: "Which came first, the phoenix or the flame?" The answer was: "A circle has no beginning." In the common room was a white marble statue of Rowena Ravenclaw. The following phrase was etched on the plinth: "Wit beyond measure is man's greatest treasure." DH 29, pp. 587-88. Another question to gain access to the Ravenclaw common room was: "Where do Vanished objects go?" The answer was: "Into nonbeing, which is to say, everywhere." DH 30, pp. 590, 591.

Ravenclaw, Helena. The daughter of Rowena Ravenclaw and the ghost known as the Gray Lady at Hogwarts. The Bloody Baron had loved Helena and when she refused his advances he stabbed her to death and then committed suicide. DH 31, pp. 614-16

Ravenclaw, Rowena. One of the four great witches and wizards who established Hogwarts. CS 9, p. 150. According to the Sorting Hat at the sorting ceremony during Harry Potter's fourth year at Hogwarts, Rowena was considered to be the cleverest of the four witches. GF 12, p. 177. Xenophilius Lovegood had a stone bust of Rowena in his residence. DH 20, pp. 403-04. Rowena was the mother of Helena Ravenclaw. DH 31, p. 615.

Ravenclaw Tower. The name of the tower at Hogwarts where the Ravenclaw house was located. DH 30, p. 592.

Reasonable Restriction of Underage Sorcery. A law that Mrs. Figg mentioned to Harry Potter during the summer prior to Harry's fifth year at Hogwarts. OP 2, p. 21. See also **Decree for the Reasonable Restriction of Underage Wizardry** and **Decree for the Restriction of Underage Wizardry**.

Red Cap. Nasty, little goblin-like creatures that lurked whenever there was bloodshed. Red caps appeared in castle dungeons and potholes of deserted battlefields and waited to bludgeon persons who got lost in those places. Harry Potter studied Red Caps in the Defense Against the Dark Arts class during his third year at Hogwarts. PA 8, p. 141. The red cap was found mostly in Northern Europe. FB, p. 36.

Reducio. The magic word for a charm that reduced the size of an object or creature. Harry Potter used the charm during year seven to reduce the size of a spider he had just enlarged with the Engorgement Charm. DH 20, p. 392.

Reductor Curse. A curse that caused solid objects to be blasted out of the way. Harry Potter learned this curse for and used it in the third task of the Triwizard Tournament during his fourth year at Hogwarts. GF 31, pp. 608, 626. Parvati Patil learned the Reductor Curse during a meeting of Dumbledore's Army. This event occurred during Harry's fifth year at Hogwarts. OP 19, p. 397. The magic word to invoke the curse was "*reducto.*" HP 27, p. 594.

Re'em. A magical beast that had its natural habitat in the wilds of North America and the Far East. The blood of the Re'em, when drunk by a wizard, gave immense strength. FB, p. 36.

Refilling Charm. A charm used to refill an empty bottle. Harry Potter invoked the charm, silently for the first time, in Rubeus Hagrid's hut during his sixth year at Hogwarts. HP 22, p. 487.

Registry of Proscribed Charmable Objects. A document that Arthur Weasley relied on to establish an embargo on flying carpets. Barty Crouch warned Arthur that Ali Bashir was upset about the embargo at the Quidditch World Cup during the summer prior to Harry Potter's fourth year at Hogwarts. Arthur's response was that he had informed Ali one hundred times that flying carpets were defined as a muggle artifact under the Registry of Proscribed Charmable Objects. GF 7, p. 91.

Relashio. The magic word of a charm used by Harry Potter to propel a jet of boiling water from his wand. Harry used the charm to free himself from the clutches of a grindylow as part of the second task of the Triwizard Tournament. This event occurred during Harry's fourth year at Hogwarts. GF 26, p. 496. DH 13, p. 263.

Rematerialization, The Principles of. The title of an essay that Hermione Granger wrote during Harry Potter's sixth year at Hogwarts. HP 10, p. 195.

Remembrall. A glass ball about the size of a marble that appeared to be full of white smoke and told a wizard, by turning red, if there was something the wizard had forgotten to do. Neville Longbottom received a remembrall from his grandmother during Harry Potter's first year at Hogwarts. SS 9, p. 145.

Rennervate. The magic word for a charm that Harry Potter used to revive Albus Dumbledore in a cave during Harry's sixth year at Hogwarts. HP 26, p. 574.

Reparo. The magic word used by Hermione Granger to invoke a charm to repair a broken window in a compartment door on the Hogwarts Express. Ron Weasley had closed the door so hard that the glass in it shattered and needed to be repaired. This event occurred during the summer prior to Harry Potter's fourth year at Hogwarts. GF 11, p. 169. During year seven, Hagrid used the charm to try to mend the side car attached to Sirius Black's motorcycle. DH 4, p. 58. This was the last charm invoked at the end of year seven. DH 36, p. 749.

Repelling Spell. Wizards watching a game of quidditch in 1269 used repelling spells to force a snidget to remain on the field for sport. The event was recorded in a letter written by Madam Modesty Rabnott. QA 4, p. 12.

Repello Muggletum. The magic words used by Hermione Granger to invoke one of several protective enchantments over her camping area during year seven. DH 14, p. 272.

Resurrection Stone. A magic stone that, according to wizard legend, was able to bring back the dead. It was one of the Deathly Hallows and its origin was from The Tale of the Three Brothers. The tale appeared in *The Tales of Beedle the Bard.* Three brothers received gifts from Death: the Elder Wand, a wand more powerful than any other; the Resurrection Stone, a stone that could help bring back the dead; and the Cloak of Invisibility. DH 21, pp. 406-09. The location of the Resurrection Stone was made known to Harry during year seven. DH 34, p. 698.

Revealer. A device that Hermione Granger purchased on Diagon Alley to reveal hidden writing. Hermione unsuccessfully used the device on a diary discovered in Moaning Myrtle's toilet during Harry Potter's second year at Hogwarts. CS 13, p. 233.

Reverse Pass. A quidditch move that was widely known. QA 10, p. 53.

Reverse Spell Effect. The effect caused when two magic wands of the same core came into contact with each other. Also known as "*prior incantatem*," this effect meant that one of the wands forced the other to regurgitate the spells it had performed in reverse order so that the most recent spell replayed first. The wands of Harry Potter and Lord Voldemort experienced the effect after the Triwizard Tournament. This event occurred during Harry's fourth year at Hogwarts. GF 35, p. 697.

Revulsion Jinx. A jinx used by Hermione Granger to force a Death Eater to loosen his grip on her sleeve after she had apparated to Grimmauld Place. This event occurred during year seven. DH 14, p. 271.

Rictusempra. The magic word used to invoke the Tickling Charm. CS 11, p. 192. Harry Potter used the charm to defend himself against Draco Malfoy during the first meeting of the Dueling Club. This event occurred during Harry's second year at Hogwarts. CS 11, p. 192.

Riddikulus. The magic word used, when accompanied by laughter, to repel a bogart. Remus Lupin instructed his Defense Against the Dark Arts class about the charm during Harry Potter's third year at Hogwarts. PA 7, p. 134. During the following year, Harry used the charm in the third task of the Triwizard Tournament. GF 31, p. 623.

Riddle, Marvolo. The grandfather of Tom Marvolo Riddle. CS 13, p. 244. His real name was Marvolo Gaunt. HP 10, pp. 210-12.

Riddle, Tom. The muggle father of Tom Marvolo Riddle. CS 13, p. 244. Tom lived in a manor house in Little Hangleton and was murdered there with his wife and son about 50 years prior to Harry Potter's fourth year at Hogwarts. GF 1, p. 2. The identity of Tom's murderer was revealed later that school year. GF 33, p. 646. Tom and Merope Gaunt were the parents of Tom Marvolo Riddle. HP 10, pp. 210-12. DH 6, p. 103.

Riddle, Tom Marvolo. The author of a secret diary that was discarded in Moaning Myrtle's toilet and that was found by Harry Potter, Ron Weasley and Hermione Granger during Harry's second year at Hogwarts. CS 13, pp. 231, 240. Tom purchased the diary from a variety store on Vauxhall Road, London. CS 13, p. 231. Tom received an award for special services to the school 50 years before that event, which award was memorialized on a shield in the trophy room at Hogwarts . CS 13, p. 231. When not in attendance at the school, Tom lived in an orphanage. His father was a muggle and his mother a witch. His father was Tom and his grandfather was Marvolo. CS 13, p. 244. When he was a student at Hogwarts, Tom rearranged the letters in his name to form a new name. CS 17, p. 314. The villagers in Little Hangleton believed that Tom was murdered with his parents about 50 years prior to the start of Harry's fourth year at Hogwarts. GF 1, p. 2. Tom's mother died after giving birth to him. The identity of a family member who Tom murdered was revealed later that year. GF 33, p. 646. His mother's name was Merope Gaunt. HP 10, pp. 210-12. He was born in a London orphanage, operated by Mrs. Cole, on Christmas Eve. His mother died one hour after his birth. HP 13, p. 266. Albus Dumbledore informed Tom that he was a wizard while Tom lived in the orphanage. HP 13, p. 271. When he arrived at Hogwarts, Tom was sorted into the Syltherin house. HP 17, p. 360. He became a prefect. HP 17, p. 370. Tom was also head boy at Hogwarts. HP 20, p. 430. He worked at Borgin and Burkes, after he was turned down by Professor Dippet for a teaching position at Hogwarts. HP 20, p. 431. He murdered Hepzibah Smith and made her house-elf admit to poisoning her. HP 20, p. 438. DH 19, p. 374.

Riddle House. A manor house located in Little Hangleton. The house stood on a hill overlooking the village. During Harry Potter's lifetime the Riddle House was damp, derelict and unoccupied. It was considered creepy because of an incident that had occurred there 50 years prior in which three members of the Riddle family were found dead in the drawing room. GF 1, pp. 1-2. DH 22, p. 437.

Riddle-Harry. The form of Harry Potter that lifted out of the opened locket containing a horcrux during year seven. DH 19, p. 376.

Riddle-Hermione. The form of Hermione Granger that lifted out of the opened locket containing a horcrux during year seven. DH 19, p. 376.

Ripper. Marge Dursley's favorite bulldog. Ripper chased Harry Potter up a tree during Dudley Dursley's twelfth birthday party and kept Harry up in the tree past midnight. This event occurred during the summer prior to Harry's third year at Hogwarts. PA 2, p. 18.

Rise and Fall of the Dark Arts, The. The title of a book read by Hermione Granger and that included information about Harry Potter. Hermione read this book prior to Harry's first year at Hogwarts. SS 6, p. 106. Hermione also pointed out that the book contained information about the Dark Mark. This event occurred during the summer prior to Harry's fourth year at Hogwarts. GF 9, p. 141. DH 6, p. 93.

River. The code name of Lee Jordan on *Potterwatch* during year seven. DH 22, p. 438.

Robards, Gawain. A wizard who was head of the Auror Office after Rufus Scrimgeour became Minister of Magic. This event occurred during Harry Potter's sixth year at Hogwarts. HP 16, p. 345.

Roberts, Mr. One of the muggle site managers at the campsite set up for patrons of the Quidditch World Cup. The Weasleys, Harry Potter and Hermione Granger were directed by Basil to meet Mr. Roberts for specific instructions about their camp site. Another site manager was Mr. Payne. This event occurred during the summer prior to Harry's fourth year at Hogwarts. GF 7, p. 76.

Roberts, Mrs. The wife of Mr. Roberts and the mother of two children who was taunted as the subject of a cruel procession of hooded wizards after the end of the Quidditch World Cup. The entire Roberts family was elevated high off the ground and jeered at by a rough crowd. This event occurred during the summer prior to Harry Potter's fourth year at Hogwarts. GF 9, p. 120.

Robins, Demelza. A student at Hogwarts and a member of the Gryffindor house during year six. HP 11, p. 224.

Rock Cakes. Cakes that Rubeus Hagrid made and offered to Harry Potter, Ron Weasley and Hermione Granger during Harry's first year at Hogwarts. The cakes were shapeless lumps with raisins that almost broke one's teeth when eaten. SS 8, p. 140.

Rodent. The code name used by Fred Weasley on *Potterwatch* during year seven. DH 22, p. 442.

Romania. The place where Professor Quirrell reportedly met a vampire. Professor Quirrell's classroom smelled like garlic, which the students believed was placed there by the professor to ward off vampires. This event occurred during Harry Potter's first year at Hogwarts. SS 8, p. 134. Romania was the native habitat of the Romanian Longhorn. The world's most important dragon reservation was founded in Romania. FB, p. 14. DH 6, p. 109. (Romania is a country in Southeast Europe that borders the Black Sea.)

Romanian Longhorn. One of ten pure-bred dragons. FB, p. 14.

Romulus. The code name for Remus Lupin on *Potterwatch* during year seven. DH 22, p. 441.

Ronan. A centaur who lived in the Forbidden Forest. Ronan became transfixed by staring up at the stars. Harry Potter met Ronan during his first year at Hogwarts. SS 15, p. 252. DH 36, p. 734.

Rookwood, Augustus. A Death Eater who spied for Lord Voldemort as an employee of the Department of Mysteries. Igor Karkaroff attempted to gain his own release from Azkaban by giving Augustus' name to the Ministry of Magic. However, the ministry already had Augustus in custody. During his fourth year at Hogwarts, Harry Potter learned this information from the pensieve in Albus Dumbledore's office.

GF 30, p. 590. Augustus was actually convicted of leaking Ministry of Magic secrets to Lord Voldemort. OP 25, pp. 543-544. He was a Death Eater for Lord Voldemort and was present in the Department of Mysteries when Harry retrieved the prophecy relating to himself and Lord Voldemort. This event occurred during Harry's fifth year at Hogwarts. OP 35, p. 788. Rookwood fought against several students in the battle at Hogwarts during year seven. DH 32, p. 640. Augustus' fate was revealed at the end of year seven. DH 36, p. 735.

Room of Requirement. A special room in Hogwarts, also referred to as the Come and Go Room, that magically appeared when someone really needed it. Dobby the House Elf made Harry Potter aware of the room's existence and used it to hide Winky from time to time. The Room of Requirement was located on the seventh floor opposite the tapestry of Barnabas the Barmy being clubbed by trolls. Dumbledore's Army conducted its meetings in the room. OP 18, pp. 386-88. The room could be made unplottable. HP 21, p. 452. DH 20, p. 400. During year seven, it was used as a hideout for many students. DH 29, p. 577. Draco Malfoy referred to the room as the "Room of Hidden Things." DH 31, p. 629.

Room of Hidden Things. The name used by Draco Malfoy for the Room of Requirement at Hogwarts. DH 31, p. 629. See **Room of Requirement**.

Rosier, Evan. A Death Eater who was killed by an Auror the year before Lord Voldemort fell. GF 27, p. 531. During his fourth year at Hogwarts, Harry Potter learned about Evan's connection to Igor Karkaroff from the pensieve in Albus Dumbledore's office. GF 30, p. 589.

Rosmerta, Madam. A witch who was the landlady of the Three Broomsticks in Hogsmeade. Harry Potter ventured into the Three Broomsticks during his third and fourth years at Hogwarts. PA 10, p. 200; GF 19, p. 321. Madam Rosmerta was under the Imperius Curse during Harry's sixth year at Hogwarts. HP 27, p. 588.

Rotfang Conspiracy. According to Luna Lovegood, a group formed by aurors to bring down the Ministry of Magic from within using a combination of Dark Magic and gum disease. HP 15, p. 320.

Rowle, Thorfinn. A wizard and one of three Death Eaters who followed Harry Potter, Ron Weasley and Hermione Granger into a muggle cafe during year seven. DH 9, p. 166.

Royal. The code name of Kingsley Shacklebolt for *Potterwatch* during year seven. DH 22, p. 440.

Runcorn, Albert. A wizard who worked in the Ministry of Magic. During year seven, Harry Potter used Polyjuice Potion to turn into Albert. DH 12, pp. 242, 245.

Runespoor. A magical, three-headed serpent that originated in Burkins Faso. Runespoor eggs were very valuable for use in potions that stimulated mental agility. FB, pp. 36-38.

Russia. One of the natural habitats of the nogtail and the home of the pogrebin. FB, pp. 30-31, 33. (Russia is a former empire in Eastern Europe and North and Central Asia.)

Ryan, Barry. A member of the Irish National Quidditch Team who played in the Quidditch World Cup that Harry Potter attended during the summer prior to his fourth year at Hogwarts. Ryan was a keeper. Other members of the team were: Connolly, Troy, Mullet, Moran, Quigley and Lynch. GF 8, pp. 105, 108. At a quidditch practice, Ron Weasley hit the quaffle so hard that it traveled the distance of the pitch and scored. This move was similar to one made around that time by Barry Ryan, who was the Irish International Keeper. This event occurred during Harry Potter's fifth year at Hogwarts. OP 19, p. 400.

SAGE – SYKES, JOCUNDA

Sage. A plant material, along with mallowsweet, that Harry Potter burned in the first Divination class taught by Firenze. This event occurred during Harry's fifth year at Hogwarts. OP 27, p. 603.

Sahara Desert. The place where quidditch referees were known to appear months after a quidditch match that they called was over. Harry Potter learned this information from reading *Quidditch Through the Ages* during Harry's first year at Hogwarts. SS 11, p. 181. Quidditch referee broomsticks were occasionally made into portkeys that transported the referees to the Sahara Desert. QA 6, p. 30. (The Sahara Desert is located in North Africa and extends from the Atlantic Ocean to the Nile Valley.)

Salamander. A fire-dwelling lizard that consumed flames. FB, p. 38. Salamander blood was one of the ingredients in Strengthening Solution. OP 17, p. 363.

Salem Witches' Institute. An institute of witches based in the United States. Harry Potter observed a group of middle-aged American witches from the institute gossiping happily at the campground near the Quidditch World Cup. This event occurred during the summer prior to Harry's fourth year at Hogwarts. GF 7, p. 82.

Salvio Hexia. The magic words used by Hermione Granger to invoke one of several protective enchantments over her camping area during year seven. DH 14, p. 272.

Sanguini. A vampire and friend of Eldred Worple who attended the Christmas party given by Horace Slughorn at Hogwarts. This event occurred during Harry Potter's sixth year at Hogwarts. HP 15, p. 315.

Santa Claus. Gnomes placed in muggle gardens as ornaments did not look like real gnomes. Instead, they looked like fat little Santa Clauses with fishing rods. CS 3, p. 36. See also **Father Christmas**.

Saturn. Sibyl Trelawney incorrectly thought that Harry Potter was born in mid-winter under the planet Saturn. According to Sibyl, Saturn was in a position of power at the moment of Harry's birth. She made this statement to Harry in a Divination class during Harry's fourth year at Hogwarts. GF 13, pp. 200-01. (Saturn is the sixth planet from the sun in the solar system.)

Saucy Tricks for Tricky Sorts. The title of a book that Harry Potter consulted in order to find a way to breathe underwater in the second task of the Triwizard Tournament. This event occurred during Harry's fourth year at Hogwarts. GF 26, p. 486.

Savage. An auror who was stationed at Hogwarts to provide the school with extra security during Harry Potter's sixth year at Hogwarts. Savage was joined by Nymphadora Tonks, Proudfoot and Dawlish. HP 8, p. 158.

Saxon. The original language in which Gertie Keddle wrote about the earliest form of quidditch played at Queerditch Marsh in the eleventh century. QA 3, p. 7. (Saxon refers to the region of England settled by the Saxons, a Germanic people, during the fifth and sixth centuries.)

Scabbers. A gray rat originally owned by Percy Weasley and then given to his younger brother, Ron. SS 6, p. 100. Harry Potter met Scabbers on the Hogwarts Express on the way to his first year at Hogwarts. SS 6, p. 100. See **Wormtail**.

Scabior. A snatcher who assisted Fenrir Greyback capture Harry Potter, Ron Weasley and Hermione Granger during year seven. DH 23, p. 448.

Scamander, Newt (Newton Artemis Fido). The author of *Fantastic Beasts and Where to Find Them.* The book was required for first-year students during Harry Potter's first year at Hogwarts. SS 5, p. 67. Newt was born in 1897 and attended Hogwarts. He lived with his wife Porpentina and three kneazles in Dorset and worked for a while in the Dragon Research and Restraint Bureau. FB, p. vi.

Scamander, Porpentina. The wife of Newt Scamander. Porpentina and Newt lived with their three kneazles in Dorset. FB, p. vi.

Scandinavia. One of three locations that served as the natural habitat for the bowtruckle. The other two locations were the west of England and Southern Germany. FB, p. 5. (Scandinavia is the area consisting of Norway, Sweden and Denmark and, according to some sources, includes Finland, Iceland and the Faeroe Islands.)

Scarab Beetle. Powdered scarab beetles were one of the ingredients in Wit-Sharpening Potion. The other ingredients were armadillo bile and ginger root. Harry Potter worked on the potion during his fourth year at Hogwarts. GF 27, pp. 513-14, 518.

Scaprin's Revelation. A method of identifying the ingredient's of a potion. HP 18, p. 375.

Schmidt, Bruno. A six-year-old wizard who lived in Germany and committed the most recent attack on an erkling. Master Schmidt hit the creature over the head with his father's collapsible cauldron. FB, p. 15.

Scintillation Solution. An unidentified substance made by Madam Z. Nettles, a witch from Topsham. Madam Nettles was quoted as having taken the Kwikspell course and afterwards became the center of attention at parties for her Scintillation Solution recipe. Harry Potter read this information on a piece of parchment in Argus Filch's office during Harry's second year at Hogwarts. CS 8, p. 127.

Scops Owls. Little owls that were used in the wizarding world for local delivery of mail only. They were small enough to fit in the palm of a wizard's hand. Harry Potter and Ron Weasley observed scops owls in the Hogsmeade post office during Harry's third year at Hogwarts. PA 14, p. 278.

Scotland. According to Charlie Weasley, the national quidditch team from Scotland was slaughtered by the team from Luxembourg. This event occurred during the summer prior to Harry Potter's fourth year at Hogwarts. GF 5, p. 63. Scotland repeatedly violated Clause 73 of the International Code of Wizarding Secrecy by allowing muggles to view the world's largest kelpie in Loch Ness. FB, p. xvii. In 1949, merpeople off the coast of Scotland discovered a superb blue roan hippocampus. FB, p. 21. Wizards played creaothceann, the most dangerous of all broom games, in Scotland. QA 2, p. 5. The Banchory Bangers was a famous Scottish quidditch team. QA 5, pp. 16-17. DH 16, p. 315. (Scotland is a country in the northern part of Great Britain.)

Scourgify. The magic word for a charm that Nymphadora Tonks used to clean Hedwig's dirty cage and Ginny invoked to clean-up Stinksap. These events occurred during the summer prior to Harry Potter's fifth year at Hogwarts. OP 3, p. 53; 10, p. 188.

Scouring Charm. A charm that Hermione Granger attempted to teach Neville Longbottom in order to remove frog guts from under his fingernails. This event occurred during Harry Potter's fourth year at Hogwarts. GF 134, p. 209. The Scouring Charm was used to rid a house of bundimuns. FB, p. 6.

Screaming Yo-yo. A magic yo-yo included on Argus Filch's list of objects that were forbidden within Hogwarts. The list consisted of about 437 items and during Harry's fourth year the list was expanded to include not only Screaming Yo-yos, but Fanged Frisbees and Ever-Bashing Boomerangs as well. GF 12, p. 183.

Screechsnap. A plant that Harry Potter studied in Herbology class during his fifth year at Hogwarts. OP 25, p. 550.

Scrimgeour, Brutus. The author of *The Beaters' Bible*, a book on quidditch. Brutus was quoted as giving praise to *Quidditch Through the Ages*. QA, p. iv. Brutus' first rule for beaters was:"Take out the seeker." QA 6, p. 27.

Scrimgeour, Rufus. A wizard who Nymphadora Tonks did not trust because he asked her and Kingsley Shacklebolt funny questions. This event occurred during the summer prior to Harry Potter's fifth year at Hogwarts. OP 7, p. 122. The following year, Rufus succeeded Cornelius Fudge as the Minister of Magic. HP 1, p. 15. According to Luna Lovegood, Rufus was a vampire and the Ministry of Magic suppressed the release of that information from her father's paper. HP 15, p. 314. During year seven, Rufus remained the Minister of Magic. DH 1, p. 5; 7, p. 121. His fate was announced at the wedding reception between Fleur Delacourt and Bill Weasley. DH 8, p. 159.

Scrivenshaft's Quill Shop. A shop located on High Street in Hogsmeade. It displayed pheasant-feather quills in its window. Hermione paid fifteen sickles and two knuts for a quill at the shop. This event occurred during Harry Potter's fifth year at Hogwarts. OP 16, p. 348.

Scurvy Cur. A password used to gain access to the Gryffindor house of Hogwarts during Harry Potter's third year at Hogwarts. PA 12, p.230.

Scurvy-grass. One of the ingredients in the Confusing Draught and Befuddlement Draught. OP 18, p. 383.

Sea Serpent. A magical beast found in the Atlantic Ocean, Pacific Ocean and the Mediterranean Sea. FB, p. 38.

Secret-Keeper. The name given to a person who served to store a secret for someone else, brought about by a Fidelius Charm. The secret could not be wrenched out of that person unless he chose to tell it. When James and Lilly Potter learned that Lord Voldemort was after them, Dumbledore suggested the charm to them. PA 10, p. 205. Dumbledore was the secret-keeper for the location of the Order of the Phoenix. DH 6, p. 90. Bill Weasley was the secret-keeper for the hiding place of the Weasley family during year seven. DH 24, p. 482.

Secrets of the Darkest Art. The title of a book that, among other things, described how to build and destroy a horcrux. Hermione Granger retrieved the book from the Albus Dumbledore's office at the end of Harry Potter's sixth year at Hogwarts. DH 6, p. 102.

Secrecy Sensor. A magical device, considered a Dark Detector, that Mad-Eye Moody kept in his office at Hogwarts. The device looked like a golden television aerial and vibrated when it detected concealment or lies. Harry Potter observed the device in Mad-Eye's office during his fourth year at Hogwarts. GF 19, pp. 342-43. Argus Flich used secrecy sensors on the students of Hogwarts when they entered the school two years later. HP 11, p. 234.

Sectumsempra. The magic word used in a charm "for enemies" that the Half-Blood Price wrote in his copy of *Advanced Potion-Making*. Harry Potter discovered the charm during his sixth year at Hogwarts. HP 21, p. 447. Harry uttered the curse against Draco Malfoy in a boys' bathroom on the sixth floor of the school that year. The curse had the effect of slashing through skin like a sword. HP 24, p. 522. During year seven, Seveus Snape used the charm, which was one of his specialties. It removed one of George Weasley's ears that year and was regarded as Dark Magic. DH 5, p. 73.

Seeker. The most important member of a quidditch team. SS 9, p. 151. The seeker was responsible for capturing the golden snitch. SS 10, p. 169. The following persons were seekers on various teams: Cho Chang, Cedric Diggory, Terence Higgs, Viktor Krum, Gilderoy Lockhart, Aiden Lynch, Draco Malfoy and Harry Potter. The seeker was usually the lightest and fastest player on a quidditch team. QA 6, pp. 26-28. DH 7, p. 127.

Self-Correcting Ink. A magical device banned from the O.W.L. examination hall during Harry Potter's fifth year at Hogwarts. OP 31, p. 709.

Self-Defensive Spellwork. The title of a book found inside the Room of Requirement during Harry Potter's fifth year at Hogwarts. OP 18, p. 390.

Self-Fertilizing Shrub. The subject of an essay demanded by Professor Sprout during Harry Potter's fifth year at Hogwarts. OP 14, p. 289.

Self-Inking Quill. A special type of joke writing quill that was sold, in addition to the Spell-Checking and Smart-Answer varieties, at Weasleys' Wizard Wheezes during the summer prior to Harry Potter's sixth year at Hogwarts. HP 6, p. 117.

Self-Shuffling Playing Cards. Playing cards that shuffled themselves and were located in Ron Weasley's bedroom at the Burrow. Harry Potter stepped on a pile of these cards while visiting the Burrow during the summer prior to his second year at Hogwarts. CS 3, p. 40.

Selkies. Another name for the merpeople who lived in Scotland. See **Merpeople**. FB, pp. 28-29.

Selwyn. One of the Death Eaters who chased Harry Potter and Rubeus Hagrid as they fled the Dursley residence at the beginning of year seven. DH 4, p. 62. The Selwyn was a pure-blood family and Dolores Umbridge claimed to be related to the family. DH 13, p. 261. Selwyn was one of two Death Eaters, the other was Travers, who appeared at Xenophilius' house during year seven. DH 21, p. 421.

Serpensortia. The magic word used in a charm to form a snake from the end of a wand. CS 11, p. 194. Draco Malfoy used the charm against Harry Potter during the first meeting of the Dueling Club and Harry Potter responded by speaking to the snake in parseltongue. This event occurred during Harry's second year at Hogwarts. CS 11, p. 194.

Severing Charm. A charm that Ron Weasley used to trim the lacy cuffs off of the formal robe he wore to the Yule Ball. This event occurred during Harry Potter's fourth year at Hogwarts. GF 23, p. 411. A crup owner was legally required to invoke the Severing Charm in order to remove the tail of the crup when the magical beast was between six to eight weeks old. FB, p. 8. DH 17, p. 346.

Shacklebolt, Kingsley. A wizard who was a member of the Order of the Phoenix and the advance guard that rescued Harry Potter from the Dursley home during the summer prior to Harry's fifth year at Hogwarts. Kingsley was an auror. OP 3, p. 47-49, 52. As an auror he was placed in charge of the hunt for Sirius Black during that year. OP 5, p. 95. The following year, he served as an undercover bodyguard to the Prime Minister. The Prime Minister thought that Kingsley was just another efficient secretary. HP 1, p. 17. He continued to protect the Prime Minister at the beginning of year seven. DH 3, pp. 32, 34; 4, p. 46. At that time, Kingsley escorted Hermione Granger, who had taken Polyjuice Potion to look with Harry, on a thestral from the Dursley residence. DH 4, p. 53. He conjured a patronus in the form of a lynx that was able to speak. DH 8, p. 159. Kingsley used the code name "Royal" for *Potterwatch*. DH 22, p. 440. At the end of year seven, Kinglsey was appointed the temporary Minister of Magic. DH 36, p. 745.

Shell Cottage. The name of the residence of Bill and Fleur Weasley during year seven. DH 20, p. 397. It was located on the outskirts of Tinworth. DH 23, p. 468.

Shield Charm. A charm used to place a temporary invisible wall around someone that deflected minor curses. Harry Potter attempted to learn the charm for the third task of the Triwizard Tournament during his fourth year at Hogwarts. GF 31, p. 608. Harry taught the charm to members of Dumbledore's Army during his fifth year at Hogwarts. OP 25, p. 553. The charm was summoned with the magic word "*protego*." OP 25, p. 553; 26, pp. 591-592. DH 6, p. 94.

Shield Cloak. A magic device, along with Shield Gloves and Hats, invented by Fred and George Weasley during the summer prior to Harry Potter's sixth year at Hogwarts. The device provided the wearer of it against moderate hexes or jinxes. HP 6, p. 119.

Shield Glove. A magic device, along with Shield Cloaks and Hats, invented by Fred and George Weasley during the summer prior to Harry Potter's sixth year at Hogwarts. The device provided the wearer of it against moderate hexes or jinxes. HP 6, p. 119.

Shield Hat. A magic device invented by Fred and George Weasley and sold at Weasleys' Wizard Wheezes during the summer prior to Harry Potter's sixth year at Hogwarts. The device provided the wearer of it against moderate hexes or jinxes, which just bounced off. The Ministry of Magic purchased 500 of them. HP 6, p. 119.

Shooting Star. The make of a quidditch broom. During Harry Potter's second year at Hogwarts, Ron Weasley owned a Shooting Star that was old and often outstripped in speed by passing butterflies. CS 4, p. 46.

Shrake. A magical beast found in the Atlantic Ocean. FB, p. 38.

Shreaking Shack. A dwelling located in Hogsmeade and believed to be the most severely haunted building in Britain. PA 5, p. 77. The resident ghosts of Hogwarts avoided the Shrieking Shack. PA 14, p. 279. Harry Potter, Ron Weasley and Hermione Granger ventured into the Shreaking Shack during their third year at Hogwarts. PA 18, pp. 352-53. DH 15, p. 305; 32, p. 642.

Shrinking Door Key. An enchanted key that kept shrinking in size until it disappeared. The key was made by wizards to bait muggles into thinking that they had misplaced their keys. Arthur Weasley explained the use of the key to Fred and George Weasley during the summer prior to Harry Potter's second year at Hogwarts. CS 3, p. 38.

Shrinking Potions. The subject of a holiday work assignment that Severus Snape gave to Harry Potter during the summer prior to Harry's third year at Hogwarts. PA 1, p. 3.

Shrinking Solution. A bright, acid green solution that Severus Snape's Potions class made during Harry Potter's third year at Hogwarts. The ingredients for the solution included daisy roots, shrivelfigs (that were skinned), caterpillars, a rat spleen and a pinch of leech juice. PA 7, pp. 124-26.

Shrivelfigs. A substance used as an ingredient in shrinking solution. Harry Potter made the solution in a Potions class during his third year at Hogwarts. PA 7, p. 124.

Shunpike, Stan. The conductor of the Knight Bus. Harry Potter met Stan after running away from the Dursley residence during the summer prior to his third year at Hogwarts. PA 3, pp. 33-34. Stan tried to impress a villa during the aftermath of the Quidditch World Cup that Harry attended. This event occurred during the following summer. GF 9, p. 126. Stan lived in Clapham and during Harry's sixth year at Hogwarts, when he was 21 years old, was arrested on suspicion of Death Eater activity. HP 11, p. 221. During year seven, Stan was one of the Death Eaters that attacked Harry as he fled the Dursley residence. DH 4, p. 59.

Shuntbumps. A crude form of jousting played on broomsticks in Devon. In more recent times, shuntbumps was mainly played as a children's game QA 2, p. 6.

Sickle. A silver coin used for currency in the wizarding world. Seventeen sickles equaled a galleon and 29 knuts equaled a sickle. SS 5, p. 75. In Diagon Alley, an apothecary shop sold dragon liver for 17 sickles an ounce, which one customer thought was excessive. SS 5, p. 72. While on the Hogwarts Express as he traveled to his first year at Hogwarts, Harry Potter bought one of each candy for sale and paid for them with eleven sickles and seven knuts. SS 6, p. 101. Hermione Granger planned on charging two sickles to join S.P.E.W. during Harry's fourth year at Hogwarts. GF 14, p. 225. Fred and George Weasley paid six sickles for knarl quills. OP 9l, p. 171. The barman at Hog's Head charged Harry Potter six sickles for three bottles of butterbeer. OP 16, p. 337. It cost eleven sickles to ride the Knight Bus from Number Twelve, Grimmauld Place in London to Hogwarts. OP 24, p. 525.

Side-Along Apparition. Apparition when one wizard is joined by another wizard. HP 17, p. 356. DH 3, p. 37.

Silencing Charm. A charm applied to fwoopers in order to silence their dangerous song. The charm had limited usefulness and had to be reinforced each month. FB, p. 18. Harry Potter and Ron Weasley studied the Silencing Charm during their fifth year at Hogwarts. OP 18, p. 382.

Silver Arrow. A make of quidditch broom that Madam Hooch learned to ride on. The broom was not made during Harry Potter's lifetime. Madam Hooch said that the Firebolt reminded her of the Silver Arrow. PA 13, p. 254. The Silver Arrow was the true forerunner of the racing broom for quidditch. The Silver Arrow was made exclusively by Leonard Jewkes. QA 9, p. 49.

Sinistra, Professor. A witch and the professor of Astronomy at Hogwarts during the time that Harry Potter attended the school. CS 11, p. 204. Professor Sinistra assisted Professor Flitwick with carrying the rigid body of Justin Flinch-Fletchley to the hospital wing after the Chamber of Secrets was reopened during Harry Potter's second year at Hogwarts. CS 11, p. 204. Professor Sinistra danced with Mad-Eye Moody at the Yule Ball during Harry's fourth year at the school. GF 23, p. 420.

Sirens. Another name for the merpeople who lived in Greece. FB, pp. 28-29. See **Merpeople**.

Sites of Historical Sorcery. The title of a book that Hermione Granger read during Harry Potter's third year at Hogwarts. The book stated that

Hogsmeade was the location of the 1612 goblin rebellion and the site of the Shrieking Shack. PA 5, p. 77.

Skeeter, Rita. A reporter who worked for the *Daily Prophet.* Rita did not report favorably on the operations of the Ministry of Magic. She faulted the Ministry of Magic for having lax security at the Quidditch World Cup that Harry Potter attended. This event occurred during the summer prior to Harry Potter's fourth year at Hogwarts. GF 10, p. 147. During that school year, Rita covered the Triwizard Tournament. GF 18, p. 303. She also contributed to the *Witch Weekly.* GF 27, p. 511. Rita was an unregistered animagus and took the form of a fat beetle. GF 37, p. 727. She was quoted as giving "praise" to *Quidditch Through the Ages*. Her exact words were: "I've read worse." QA, p. iv. During Harry Potter's fifth year at Hogwarts, Rita was unemployed, but agreed to interview Harry for an article to be published in *The Quibbler.* OP 25, p. 564. During year seven, Rita authored the book *The Life and Lies of Albus Dumbledore*. DH 2, p. 22.

Skele-Gro. A healing agent that regrew bones. CS 10, p. 174. Madam Pomfrey applied Skele-Gro to Harry Potter's arm after Gilderoy Lockhart's failed attempt to heal it resulted in eliminating thirty-three bones in Harry's arm. This event occurred during Harry's second year at Hogwarts. CS 10, p. 174. Draco Malfoy commented that Rubeus Hagrid's large size was caused by swallowing a bottle of Skele-Gro when he was young. Draco made the comment during Harry's fourth year at Hogwarts. GF 24, p. 440. Fleur Weasley used Skele-Gro on Griphook's injuries during year seven. DH 24, pp. 480, 482.

Skiving Snackbox. An invention that Fred and George Weasley developed during the summer prior to Harry Potter's fifth year at Hogwarts, which invention included a range of sweets that made a student ill enough to miss classes. The sweets were double-ended, color-coded chews, three of which were called Fainting Fancies, Nosebleed Nougat and Puking Pastilles. Two of the ingredients were doxy venom and the black seed pods of the venomous tentacula. OP 6, pp. 104-05; 9, p. 171.

Skrewt. See **Blast-Ended Skrewt**.

Skower, Mrs. A witch who invented Mrs. Skower's All-Purpose Magical Mess Remover. Argus Filch unsuccessfully used this cleaner to erase a message that mysteriously appeared on the wall of Hogwarts. This event occurred during Harry Potter's second year at Hogwarts. CS 9, p. 146

Sleekeazy's Hair Potion. A potion that Hermione Granger used to style her bushy hair for the Yule Ball. This event occurred during Harry Potter's fourth year at Hogwarts. GF 24, p. 433.

Sleeping Draft. A potion that Charlie Weasley and several other wizards used to subdue four dragons that were brought to Hogwarts for the first event of the Triwizard Tournament. This event occurred during Harry Potter's fourth year at Hogwarts. GF 19, p. 327.

Sleeping Draught. A potion that Hermione Granger added to chocolate cakes. The cakes were intended for Vincent Crabbe and Gregory Goyle so that they would fall asleep and allow Harry Potter and Ron Weasley to safely assume their identities from a Polyjuice Potion. This event occurred during Harry's second year at Hogwarts. CS 12, p. 215.

Slinkhard, Wilbert. The author of *Defensive Magical Theory*. This book was required reading during Harry Potter's fifth year at Hogwarts. OP 9, p. 160.

Sloper, Jack. A student at Hogwarts who was a member of the Gryffindor house and became a beater for the house team, along with Andrew Kirke, when Fred and George Weasley were banned from the team by Dolores Umbridge. This event occurred during Harry Potter's fifth year at Hogwarts. OP 21, p. 453.

Sloth Grip Roll. A quidditch move that was widely known. QA 10, p. 53. During Harry Potter's fifth year at Hogwarts, Angelina Johnson wanted the team to work on the Sloth-Grip Roll. OP 17, p. 351.

Slow-Acting Venoms. A topic discussed in Gilderoy Lockhart's book *Gadding with Ghouls*. CS 10, p. 162. Hermione Granger used this topic as a means to obtain Lockhart's signed approval for access to the restricted section of the library at Hogwarts. This event occurred during Harry Potter's second year at the school. CS 10, p. 162.

Slug Club. The name given by Horace Slughorn to the group of students he taught and admired. HP 7, p. 147.

Slughorn, Horace. A wizard who lived temporarily in a muggle house in Budleigh Babberton. Horace was an old friend and colleague of Albus Dumbledore's. HP 4, pp. 64-66. He was a professor at Hogwarts when Lily Evans, before marrying James Potter, attended the school. At that time, Horace was the head of the Slytherin House and one of the students in that house was Regulus Black. HP 4, p. 70. Arthur and Molly Weasley were also some of Horace's students. He started teaching at Hogwarts the same time as Albus Dumbledore. HP 5, p. 84. During Harry Potter's fifth year at Hogwarts, Horace was the Potions teacher, which allowed Severus Snape to teach Defense Against the Dark Arts. HP 8, p. 166. His favorite candy was crystalized pineapple. HP 23, p. 495. At the end of Harry's sixth year at Hogwarts, Professor McGonagall appointed Horace as the Head of Slytherin. HP 29, p. 625. DH 6, p. 102; 30, p. 598.

Slytherin. One of the four dormitory houses at Hogwarts. SS 5, p. 77. It was named after Salazar Slytherin. CS 9, p. 150. Lord Voldemort was a member of the house when he attended Hogwarts. SS 6, pp. 106-07. Severus Snape was the head of the house at the time Harry Potter attended the school. SS 8, p. 135. The house colors were green and silver and its mascot was a serpent. SS 17, p. 304. During Harry's fourth year at Hogwarts, a green banner bearing a silver serpent for Slytherin decorated the Great Hall for the Triwizard Tournament. GF 15, p. 237. Slytherin turned out more Dark witches and wizards than any of the other three houses together. CS 5, p. 77. The Slytherin quidditch team had no female members on it. CS 7, p. 110. The entrance to the house was found behind a bare, damp stone wall in the dungeon area of the school. CS 12, p. 220. A password to enter the house during Harry Potter's second year at Hogwarts was "pure-blood." CS 12, p. 221. The hourglass for Slytherin in the entrance hall at Hogwarts contained emeralds. OP 28, p. 626. During the years when Lily (Evans) Potter attended Hogwarts, Horace Slughorn was the head of Slytherin. HP 4, p. 70. At the end of Harry's sixth year at Hogwarts, Professor McGonagall appointed Horace as the head of the house. HP 29, p. 625. The light in the house was green because the house was under the lake. DH 23, p. 450.

Slytherin, Salazar. One of the four great witches and wizards who established Hogwarts. Salazar believed that Hogwarts should not accept students who were born to muggle parents even if the students showed signs of magic. CS 9, p. 150. Salazar had a serious disagreement with Godric Gryffindor over this subject, which caused Salazar to leave the school. CS 9, p. 150. Salazar was a famous parselmouth and was nicknamed "Serpent-tongue." CS 11, p. 199. According to remarks made by the Sorting Hat in the sorting ceremony during Harry Potter's fourth year at Hogwarts, Salazar was power-hungry and loved students who showed great ambition. GF 12, p. 177. DH 36, p. 732.

Smart-Answer Quill. A special type of joke writing quill that was sold, in addition to the Self-Inking and Spell-Checking varieties, at Weasleys' Wizard Wheezes during the summer prior to Harry Potter's sixth year at Hogwarts. HP 6, p. 117.

Smeek, Enid. A witch or wizard who lived outside Godric's Hollow and who was quoted in *The Life and Lies of Albus Dumbldore* by Rita Skeeter regarding the reaction of Aberforth Dumbledore to the death of his mother. DH 18, p. 354.

Smelting stick. A special stick used by Vernon Dursley to discipline Dudley Dursley and Harry Potter. SS 3, p. 33.

Smeltings. The private muggle school that was attended by Vernon Dursley and later Dudley Dursley. SS 3, p. 32.

Smethley, Veronica. A witch who was a fan of Gilderoy Lockhart. Harry Potter wrote a reply to Veronica on behalf of Lockhart as part of Harry's detention for being in the flying car that injured the Whomping Willow. This event occurred during Harry's second year at Hogwarts. CS 7, p. 120.

Smethwyck, Elliot. A wizard who invented the Cushioning Charm in 1820. The charm was used to make broomsticks more comfortable to ride. QA 9, p. 47.

Smethwyck, Hippocrates. A wizard who was Healer-in-Charge of the "Dangerous" Dai Llewellyn ward at St. Mungo's Hospital for Magical Maladies and Injuries. OP 22, p. 487.

Smith, Hepzibah. A witch who had a house-elf named Hokey. Hepzibah was a distant relative of Helga Hufflepuff. She possessed a cup that had belonged to Helga and purchased a locket from Borgin and Burkes that Slytherin had owned. She died two days after a visit from Tom Riddle and her house-elf, Hokey, was convicted of poisoning her. HP 20, pp. 433, 436. During year seven, the cup was found in the Lestrange vault at Gringotts Wizarding Bank. DH 26, p. 538.

Smith, Zacharias. A student at Hogwarts who was a member of the Hufflepuff house and a member of its quidditch team. Zacharias appeared at Hog's Head, along with several other students, to discuss formation of a club to study Defense Against the Dark Arts. OP 16, p. 338, 340. He was hexed by Ginny Weasley on the Hogwarts Express as it made its way to Hogwarts for Harry Potter's sixth year there. HP 7, p. 147. During that school year, Zacharias was the quidditch commentator. HP 14, p. 296. When on the team he was a chaser. HP 19, p. 409. DH 5, p. 71; 31, p. 613.

Snackbox. See **Skiving Snackbox**.

Snape, Severus. The professor of the Potions class at Hogwarts durin the time that Harry Potter attended the school. SS 7, p. 126. Severus always wanted to teach the Dark Arts class but never got the chance. SS 7, p. 126. He was the head of the Slytherin house during the time that Harry attended the school. SS 8, p. 135. Harry was Severus' least favorite student. CS 5, p. 77. Severus had a mark on his left forearm that he tried to kept secret. GF 25, p. 472. He attended Hogwarts as a student at the same time that Sirius Black did. According to Sirius, Severus came to the school knowing more curses than the seventh-year students. Severus was always fascinated with the Dark Arts and half of the gang he associated himself with at school turned out to be Death Eaters. GF 27, p. 531. Severus was a member of the Order of the Phoenix. OP 4, p. 69. During Harry's fifth year at Hogwarts,

Severus had taught there for 14 years. OP 17, p. 363. He was a Death Eater before the Dark Lord's disappearance. HP 2, p. 27. During Harry's sixth year at Hogwarts, Severus declared that he was the Half-Blood Prince. HP 28, p. 604. Severus' parents were Tobias Snape, a muggle, and Eileen Prince, a witch. HP 30, p. 637. During year seven, Severus attended a meeting of the Death Eaters and Voldemort at the Malfoy manor house. DH 1, p. 1. On September 1 of that year, Severus was appointed Headmaster of Hogwarts. DH 12, p. 226. During that year, he revealed that he had the ability to fly like a bat. DH 30, p. 599. Severus' fate was witnessed by Harry Potter in the Shreaking Shack. DH 32, pp. 656-58. Harry watched a story about Severus' life in the Pensieve during year seven. Severus' childhood home was in Spinner's End. DH 33, pp. 663, 665. As a youth, James Potter called Severus the derogatory nickname "Snivellus." DH 33, p. 672. When Severus attended Hogwarts as a student in the Slytherin house, he befriended Avery and Mulciber. DH 33, p. 673. Severus' Patronus took the form of a silver doe. DH 33, p. 687.

Snape, Tobias. The muggle father of Severus Snape. His wife was Eileen Prince. HP 30, p. 637.

Snargaluff. A magical plant that was studied in Harry Potter's Herbology class during his sixth year at Hogwarts. The plant was described in *Flesh-Eating Trees of the World.* HP 14, p. 279. DH 20, p. 398. Professor Sprout intended to use snargaluff pods as a defense against Death Eaters during year seven. DH 30, p. 600.

Snatchers. A group of witches or wizards that acted like a gang to earn gold by rounding up muggle-borns and blood-traitors and turning them over to the Ministry of Magic. DH 19, pp. 381-382. Scabio was a snatcher who assisted Fenrir Greyback during year seven. DH 23, p. 449.

Sneakoscope. See **Pocket Sneakoscope**. DH 2, p. 14.

Sneezewort. One of the ingredients in the Confusing Draught and Befuddlement Draught. OP 18, p. 383.

Snidget, Golden. An extremely rare, protected species of magical bird. The snidget's golden feathers and eyes were so prized that it almost became extinct. FB, p. 39. The bird was hunted from the 1100's. The golden snitch replaced the golden snidget in the game. QA 4, p. 10. The Wizards' Council in the mid-1300's prohibited the use of snidgets in the game. QA 4, p. 14.

Snitch, Golden. The smallest ball used in the game of quidditch. The golden snitch was the size of a large walnut and was bright gold with little fluttering silver wings. The team that captured the golden snitch received an additional 150 points, so that team usually won. The game was not over until the golden snitch was captured. SS 10, p.

169. The golden snitch was invented by Bowman Wright of Godric's Hollow. QA 3, p. 10; 4, p. 14. DH 7, p. 119. A snitch was not touched by bare skin prior to its release during a match. It had "flesh memory," meaning that it carried an enchantment by which it could identify the first human being to lay hands on it, in case of a disputed capture during a quidditch match. DH 7, p. 127.

Snitchnip. The name of one of the ten most common fouls committed in quidditch. QA 6, p. 30.

Snow White and the Seven Dwarfs. A story that was read by muggles. DH 7, p. 135.

Snowy. A cat who was owned by Mrs. Figgs. Mrs. Figgs had three other cats named Tibbles, Mr. Paws and Tufty. SS 2, p. 22.

Snuffles. The secret name that Sirius Black asked Harry Potter, Ron Weasley and Hermione Granger to call him while he was in hiding. This event occurred during Harry's fourth year at Hogwarts. GF 27, p. 534.

Society for the Promotion of Elfish Welfare. A club that Hermione Granger founded during Harry Potter's fourth year at Hogwarts. Hermione established the club to fight against the enslavement of elves. She made badges that bore the club's acronym: S.P.E.W. The club's manifesto heading was: "Stop the outrageous abuse of our fellow magical creatures and campaign for a change in their legal status." Hermione explained that the club's short-term objectives were to secure fair wages and working conditions for elves. Its long-term aims were to change the law about non-wand use and to get an elf into the Department for the Regulation and Control of Magical Creatures because they were shockingly under represented. Hermione planned on charging two sickles to become a member. GF 14, pp. 224-25.

Society for the Protection of Ugly Goblins. Harry Potter teased Hermione Granger about starting a club for the protection of goblins, S.P.U.G., in addition to the one she established for house elves, S.P.E.W. Hermione sarcastically added that goblins did not need protection because they could deal with wizards. This discussion occurred in the Three Broomsticks during Harry's fourth year at Hogwarts. GF 24, p. 449.

Somerset. The location of the Madam Modesty Rabnott Snidget Reservation. QA 4, p. 14. Somerset also sustained a "hurricane" caused by giants and Death Eaters during the summer prior to Harry Potter's sixth year at Hogwarts. HP 1, p. 13. (Somersetshire is a county in Southwest England.)

Sonorus. The magic word spoken by Ludo Bagman to invoke a charm at the Quidditch World Cup. The charm activated the public address system so that Ludo could announce and comment on the game. GF

8, p. 102. He also used the spell during the second and third tasks of the Triwizard Tournament. These events occurred during Harry Potter's fourth year a Hogwarts. GF 26, p. 493; 31, p. 620.

Sonnets of a Sorcerer. The title of a dangerous book that, according to Ron Weasley, caused anyone who read it to speak in limericks for the rest of their lives. Ron used this book as an example to warn Harry Potter about tampering with the diary of T.M. Riddle. This event occurred during Harry's second year at Hogwarts. CS 13, p. 231.

Sorcerer's Stone. A legendary substance produced from the ancient study of alchemy and that had some unusual powers. The Sorcerer's Stone was able to transform any metal into gold and produce the Elixir of Life, which made the person who consumed it immortal. Harry Potter learned about the Sorcerer's Stone during his first year at Hogwarts. SS 13, p. 220. DH 21, p. 416.

Sorting Hat. A magic hat that, during the Sorting Ceremony, sorted first-year students into the four dormitory houses at Hogwarts. This event was the first order of business each school year and occurred in the Great Hall. The ceremony began with the hat singing a special song and then each student took turns wearing it. The hat then decided in which house to place the students and announced its decision to the entire school body. SS 7, pp. 117-119. Godric Gryffindor created the Sorting Hat. This historical fact was introduced in the song sung by the Sorting Hat during Harry Potter's fourth year at Hogwarts. The song was different each year. GF 12, pp. 176-78. At the beginning of Harry Potter's fifth year at Hogwarts, the Sorting Hat added a warning to the song it sang. The warning was unusual because the Sorting Hat generally only described the quality looked for by each of the four houses and its own role in sorting them. OP 11, p. 207. DH 7, p. 129. Voldemort used the Sorting Hat as he reverted back to his "original plan" at the end of year seven. DH 36, p. 732.

South America. In South America, quidditch competed with the game of quodpot. QA 8, p. 45.

Spattergroit. A highly contagious illness caused by fungus. Arthur, Fred and George Weasley conjured a charm to make it appear that the ghoul in the attic of the Burrow looked like Ron Weasley with spattergroit. DH 6, p. 99.

Sparky. A phoenix that served as the mascot of the Moutohora Macaws, a quidditch team from New Zealand. QA 8, p. 42.

Special Advisor to the Wizengamot. The title given to Elphias Doge during year seven. DH 2, p. 24.

Special Award for Services to the School. An award given at Hogwarts that was displayed in the trophy room at Hogwarts. CS 7, p. 121. The award was one of the awards that Ron Weasley had to polish and clean as part of his detention for driving the flying car into the Whomping Willow. This event occurred during Harry Potter's second year at Hogwarts. CS 7, p. 121.

Specialis Revelio. The magic words used to invoke a charm that detected anything odd about an object. Hermione Granger placed the charm on Harry Potter's copy of *Advanced Potion-Making* during his sixth year at Hogwarts. HP 9, p. 193.

Spectrespecs. A magical device that was included free inside an edition of *The Quibbler* read by Luna Lovegood on the Hogwarts Express. HP 7, p. 137.

Spell-Checking Quill. A special type of joke writing quill that was sold, in addition to the Self-Inking and Smart-Answer varieties, at Weasleys' Wizard Wheezes during the summer prior to Harry Potter's sixth year at Hogwarts. HP 6, p. 117.

Spellman's Syllabary. The title of a book that Hermione Granger used for homework during Harry Potter's fifth year at Hogwarts. OP 26, p. 575. She also continued to carry it around the following year. HP 24, p. 517. DH 6, p. 94.

Spellotape. A product that Ron Weasley attempted to use in order to put his wand back together after it had been destroyed from the car accident on the Whomping Willow. This event occurred during Harry Potter's second year at Hogwarts. CS 6, p. 95. Ginny Weasley used spellotape to mend her copy of *One Thousand Magical Herbs and Fungi* during the summer prior to Harry's fourth year at Hogwarts. GF 10, p. 151. DH 13, p. 251.

S.P.E.W. See **Society for the Promotion of Elfish Welfare**.

Sphinx. A creature that had a body of a large lion and a head of a woman. It had great-clawed paws and a long yellowish tail that ended in a brown tuft. Harry Potter encountered a sphinx in the third task of the Triwizard Tournament during his fourth year at Hogwarts. The sphinx offered him a riddle. The creature was also featured in the *Monster Book of Monsters*. GF 31, pp. 628-630. Sphinxes were often employed by wizards to guard treasure. FB, pp. 20, 39.

Spinner's End. A deserted street on which was a house that Narcissa Malfoy and her sister, Bellatrix Black, visited during the summer prior to Harry Potter's sixth year at Hogwarts. The house was occupied by Severus Snape and Wormtail, who Severus regarded as his servant. HP 2, p. 21. Spinner's End was the childhood home of Severus. DH 33, p. 665.

Spinnet, Alicia. A chaser on the Gryffindor quidditch team during Harry Potter's first, second and third years at Hogwarts. SS 11, p. 186; CS 7, p.107; PA 8, p. 144. The other two chasers on the team were Katie

Bell and Angelina Johnson. Alicia was one year ahead of Harry Potter at Hogwarts. OP 26, p. 575. DH 30, p. 603.

Spirit Division. An office within the Department for the Regulation and Control of Magical Creatures of the Ministry of Magic. FB, p. xii, fn. 2. DH 12, p. 245.

Splinch. The act of leaving part of oneself behind after attempting to apparate. According to Arthur Weasley, a couple of people were fined by the Department of Magical Transportation for apparating without a license and splinching themselves. They had to be sorted out by the Accidental Magic Reversal Squad. This event occurred during the summer prior to Harry Potter's fourth year at Hogwarts. GF 6, pp. 66-67. Two years later Susan Bones splinched her left leg during Apparition Lessons at Hogwarts. HP 18, p. 385. DH 14, p. 269. One of the ways to cure splinching was to use Essence of Dittany. DH 14, p. 269.

Spore, Phyllida. The author of *One Thousand Magical Herbs and Fungi*. The book was required for first-year students during Harry Potter's first year at Hogwarts. SS 5, p. 66.

Sprout, Pomona. A witch who taught the Herbology class at Hogwarts during the time that Harry Potter attended the school. Professor Sprout taught the class in greenhouses located behind the school. SS 8, p. 133. She was the Head of the Hufflepuff house. GF 18, p. 293. Professor Sprout's preferred brand of fertilizer was dragon dung. OP 13, p. 263. Her first name was Pomona. HP 22, p. 479. DH 30, p. 598.

Spudmore. See **Ellerby and Spudmore**.

S.P.U.G. See **Society for the Protection of Ugly Goblins.**

Squib. A person who was born into a wizarding family but had no magic powers. CS 9, p. 145. Argus Filch claimed that Harry Potter knew he was a squib because he suspected Harry of reading his Kwikspell correspondence. This event occurred during Harry's second year at Hogwarts. CS 9, pp. 142-143. Mrs. Figg informed Harry Potter that she was a squib. This event occurred during the summer prior to Harry's fifth year at Hogwarts. OP 2, p. 20. During year seven, Auntie Muriel claimed that Albus Dumbledore's sister, Ariana, was a squib and had not attended Hogwarts, as it was the custom in those days to send squibs to muggle schools and communities. DH 8, pp. 154-55. Magical abilities were revealed in a child by the time the child was seven years old. DH 11, p. 218.

Squid. A giant squid that lived in the lake on the Hogwarts grounds. SS 16, p. 263.

St. Brutus' Secure Center for Incurably Criminal Boys. A muggle school that Vernon Dursley told Marge Dursley that Harry Potter attended.

Vernon lied to Marge so that she would not learn that Harry attended a school for wizards. This event occurred during the summer prior to Harry's third year at Hogwarts. PA 2, p. 19. The Dursleys told the lie to other people as well. GF 2, p. 19.

St. Mungo's Hospital for Magical Maladies and Injuries. A hospital that Lucius Malfoy gave a very generous contribution to, according to Cornelius Fudge. Fudge disclosed the fact to Arthur Weasley in the top box at the Quidditch World Cup. GF 8, p. 101. This event occurred during the summer prior to Harry Potter's fourth year at Hogwarts. According to an article in the *Daily Prophet*, the hospital denied comment on whether Barty Crouch was confined there with a critical illness. GF 27, p. 522. This event also occurred during Harry's fourth year at the school. Frank Longbottom and his wife, who became insane as a result of a Cruciatus Curse, were admitted to the hospital. GF 30, p. 603. Celestina Warbeck recorded the anthem of the Puddlemere United club as a fund raiser for St. Mungo's. QA 7, p. 36. Arthur Weasley was a patient at St. Mungo's during Harry Potter's fifth year at Hogwarts. St. Mungo's was located in muggle London in an old department store, Purge and Dowse, Ltd., that bore a sign stating "closed for refurbishment." OP 22, pp. 473, 483. A Junior Minister named Herbert Chorley was scheduled to be transferred to this hospital during the summer prior to Harry's sixth year at Hogwarts. HP 1, p. 10. During that school year Katie Bell suffered a curse and was removed to St. Mungo's. HP 13, p. 258. DH 8, p. 156. One of the departments within the hospital was the Posioning Department. DH 21, p. 413.

Stalk, Blenheim. The author of *Muggles Who Notice* which was published in 1972. Stalk claimed that some residents of Ilfracombe escaped the batch of Memory Charms summoned to make muggles forget about a Welsh green dragon that swooped down on sunbathing muggles there in 1932. FB, p. xvi, fn. 7.

Standard Book of Spells, Grade 1. The title of a book required for first-year students during Harry Potter's first year at Hogwarts. SS 5, p. 66.

Standard Book of Spells, Grade 2. The title of a book required for second-year students during Harry Potter's second year at Hogwarts. CS 4, p. 43.

Standard Book of Spells, Grade Three. The title of a book that Harry Potter purchased in Flourish and Blotts for his third year at Hogwarts. PA 4, p. 54.

Standard Book of Spells, Grade 4. The title of a book written by Miranda Goshawk and that Molly Weasley purchased for Harry Potter, Ron Weasley and Hermione Granger on Diagon Alley during the summer prior to Harry's fourth year at Hogwarts. GF 10, pp. 152, 155.

Standard Book of Spells, Grade 5, The. The title of a book written by Miranda Goshawk that was required reading for Harry Potter during his fifth year at Hogwarts. OP 9, 160.

Standard Book of Spells, Grade Six, The. The title of a book used at Hogwarts. HP 9, pp. 178-79

Statute of Secrecy. A law, section 13 of which was enacted by the International Confederation of Wizards, to forbid underage wizards from performing magic under certain circumstances. The statute was breached in 1749, which event was of such historical importance that it appeared as a question on the History of Magic O.W.L. that Harry Potter took during his fifth year at Hogwarts. OP 8, p. 140; 31, p. 725. Mrs. Figg mentioned the law to Harry during the summer prior to his fifth year at Hogwarts. OP 2, p. 21. DH 18, p. 357. See also **International Confederation of Warlocks' Statute of Secrecy.**

Starfish and Stick. A quidditch move that was widely known. QA 10, p. 53.

Stealth and Tracking. A course of instruction for Auror training. OP 3, p. 52.

Stealth Sensoring Spell. A spell that Dolores Umbridge placed around the doorway to her office at Hogwarts during Harry Potter's fifth year at the school. OP 32, p. 741.

Stebbins. A student of Hogwarts who was a member of the Hufflepuff house. At the Yule Ball, Severus Snape took ten points away from the Hufflepuff house because he caught Stebbins in the rosebushes with Miss Fawcett. This event occurred during Harry Potter's fourth year at Hogwarts. GF 23, p. 426. Stebbins was a student at Hogwarts during the time when James Potter attended the school. OP 28, p. 642.

Stichstock. An ancient German game that dated from at least 1105 and was an early version of quidditch. Stichstock was shown on a famous painting from that year titled "Gunther the Violent Is the Winner." QA 2, p. 4.

Stimpson, Patricia. A student at Hogwarts in Fred and George Weasley's class who kept fainting during their fifth year O.W.L.s. OP 12, p. 226.

Stingers. A name that referred to the fans of the Wimbourne Wasps. QA 7, p. 38.

Stinging Hex. A hex that Harry Potter placed on Severus Snape during Harry's first Occlumency lesson. This event occurred during Harry's fifth year at Hogwarts. OP 24, p. 534.

Stinging Jinx. A jinx that Hermione Granger placed on Harry Potter during year seven in order for Harry not to look recognizable. DH 23, p. 458.

Stink Pellets. Prank devices sold at Zonko's Joke Shop in Hogsmeade. Ron Weasley intended to purchase some Stink Pellets at Zonko's during Harry Potter's third year at Hogwarts. PA 8, p. 145.

Stinksap. The liquid ejected from the plant Mimbulus mimbletonia. The liquid smelled like rancid manure, but was not poisonous. OP 10, p. 187.

Stoatshead Hill. A large black mass that rose beyond the village of Ottery St. Catchpole. The hill was the location of a portkey in the shape of a boot, which portkey was the closest one to the Burrow. Some of the members of the Weasley family, along with Harry Potter and Hermione Granger used the portkey to get to the Quidditch World Cup. This event occurred during the summer prior to Harry's fourth year at Hogwarts. GF 6, p. 70.

Stonewall High. A local public school attended by muggles, including Dudley Dursley and Harry Potter before Harry began his education at Hogwarts. SS 3, p. 32.

Stonewall Stormers. A quidditch team from Canada. QA 8, p. 43.

Stooging Penalty. A penalty established by rule of the Department of Magical Games and Sports on June 21, 1884. The rule prohibited more than one chaser in the scoring area of the quidditch field at one time. This rule was published in the *Daily Prophet.* A crowd of wizards who were angry over the newly-announced stooging penalty for quidditch matches, threatened to stooge the Minister of Magic. QA 6, pp. 26, 30.

Streeler. A magical snail native to several African countries, but later raised in Europe, Asia and the Americas. FB, pp. xvii, 40. Its venom was used in a few substances that killed horklumps. FB, p. 40.

Strengthening Solution. A potion that Harry Potter brewed during a fifth year Potions class. Two of the ingredients were salamander blood and powdered griffin claw. OP 15, p. 309; 17, p. 363.

Stretching Jinx. A spell that could be used to make a person grow. Molly Weasley mentioned the jinx, in reference to Harry Potter's and Ron Weasley's height, during the summer prior to Harry's sixth year at Hogwarts. HP 5, p. 83.

Strout, Miriam. A healer at St. Mungo's Hospital for Magical Maladies and Injuries. Miriam was in-charge at the time that Broderick Bode was strangled by Devil's Snare. This event occurred during Harry Potter's fifth year at Hogwarts. OP 25, p. 546.

Stubbs, Billy. A child who was an orphan at the same London orphanage where Tom Riddle lived during his childhood. The orphanage was operated by Mrs. Cole. Other orphans there were Eric Whalley, Amy Benson and Dennis Bishop. HP 13, pp. 264, 268.

Study of Recent Developments in Wizardry. The title of a book located in the library at Hogwarts. Harry Potter, Ron Weasley and Hermione Granger consulted the book regarding the identity of Nicolas Flamel, only to discover that he was not discussed in it. This event occurred during Harry's first year at Hogwarts. SS 12, p. 197.

Stump, Grogan. A wizard who was the newly-appointed Minister for Magic in 1811. Grogan decreed that any creature with sufficient intelligence to understand the laws of the magical community and assume part of the responsibility in shaping those laws was a "being." FB, p. xii. Grogan established the following three divisions in the Department for the Regulation and Control of Magical Creatures: Beast Division, Being Division and the Spirit Division. FB, p. xii, fn. 2.

Stunners. Blinding flashes of light used by wizards from the Ministry of Magic in order to subdue the person or persons who conjured the Dark Mark during the aftermath of the Quidditch World Cup that Harry Potter attended. The charm was invoked by speaking the magic word "*stupefy*." This event occurred during the summer prior to Harry's fourth year at Hogwarts. GF 9, p. 129.

Stunning Charm. A charm invoked with the magic word "*stupefy*." The wizards who subdued the dragons used for the first event of the Triwizard Tournament also used the charm. This event occurred during Harry Potter's fourth year at Hogwarts. GF 19, p. 326. During year seven, Harry used Stunning Charms against Death Eaters as he fled the Dursley residence. DH 4, p. 57.

Stupefy. The magic word used to invoke the Stunning Charm. The charm was invoked by 20 wizards in order to subdue the person or persons who conjured the Dark Mark during the aftermath of the Quidditch World Cup that Harry Potter attended. The magic word summoned stunners and sent blinding flashes of light. The light made Harry's hair ripple as though a wind was passing through it. This event occurred during the summer prior to Harry's fourth year at Hogwarts. GF 9, p. 129. The wizards that subdued the dragons for the first event of the Triwizard Tournament also used the charm. GF 19, p. 326. Harry relied on the charm to defend himself against a blast-ended skrewt in the third task of the tournament. GF 31, pp. 625; 631. These events occurred during Harry's fourth year at Hogwarts. During year seven, Harry used the charm against a Death Eater while Harry fled the Dursley residence. DH 4, p. 56.

Stupefying Charm. A charm that Flavius Belby unsuccessfully invoked against a lethifold in 1782. FB, p. 26. The Stupefying Charm was effective in repelling the pogrebin. FB, p. 33.

Substantive Charm. A charm that Seamus Finnigan and Dean Thomas studied while preparing for the O.W.L.s they were going to take during Harry Potter's fifth year at Hogwarts. OP 31, p. 710.

Sugar Quill. Candy sold in the wizarding world. During his fourth year at Hogwarts, Harry Potter unsuccessfully tried to use the password "sherbet lemon" to open the secret passageway to Albus Dumbledore's office. He then tried several candy names on the door, including Sugar Quill. Cockroach Cluster finally worked as the password. GF 29, p. 579.

Sumbawanga Sunrays. A quidditch team from Tanzania. The team was known for its formation looping. QA 8, p. 43.

Summerby. A student at Hogwarts who was a member of the Hufflepuff house and a seeker for that house's quidditch team. OP 26, p. 575.

Summers, Mr. A student who attended Hogwarts. Mr. Summers was a member of the Hufflepuff house and was sixteen years old during Harry Potter's fourth year at Hogwarts. During that school year, Mr. Summers attempted to use an Aging Potion in order to qualify for the Triwizard Tournament and failed. Other students who tried the same trick and also failed were Fred and George Weasley and Miss Fawcett of the Ravenclaw house. GF 16, p. 260.

Summoning Charm. A charm used by Molly Weasley to produce joke toffees hidden by Fred and George Weasley. GF 6, p. 68. Hermione Granger read about the charm from *The Standard Book of Spells, Grade 4* and attempted to learn it on the Hogwarts Express prior to Harry Potter's fourth year at Hogwarts. GF 11, p. 167.

Sunday Prophet. The name of the Sunday edition of the *Daily Prophet.* Harry Potter read the *Sunday Prophet* at the end of his fifth year at Hogwarts. OP 38, p. 846.

Supersensory Charm. A charm mentioned by Ron Weasley that would have helped him to park a muggle car. DH Epilogue, p. 755.

Supreme Mugwump. A title conferred by the International Confederation of Wizards on Albus Dumbledore. SS 4, p. 51. The title, perhaps associated with or another name for the chairmanship of the confederation, was removed from Albus during the summer prior to Harry Potter's fifth year at Hogwarts. OP 15, p. 308.

Surrey. The county in which the Dursley family lived. Their full address was Number Four Privet Drive, Little Winging, Surrey. SS 3, p. 34. The news reported that a helicopter also crashed in Surrey during the summer prior to Harry Potter's fifth year at Hogwarts. OP 1, p. 4. (Surrey is a county in Southeast England, bordering South London.)

Sweden. Beginning in the tenth century, Sweden celebrated an annual broom race where fliers raced from Kopparberg to Arjelog. The course went through a dragon reservation. QA 2, p. 4. Luna Lovegood insisted that the crumple-horned snorkack lived in Sweden. OP 38, p. 848. (Sweden is a kingdom in Northern Europe and the eastern part of the Scandinavian Peninsula.)

Swedish Short-Snout. A type of dragon that was used in the first task of the Triwizard Tournament hosted at Hogwarts. The dragon was blue-gray and smaller than the other dragons used in the task. Charlie Weasley was part of the team that controlled the dragons. This event occurred during Harry Potter's fourth year at Hogwarts. GF 19, pp. 326-327. Cedric Diggory fought a Swedish short-snout in the tournament and went first in order of the champions who competed. GF 19, p. 350. The Swedish short-snout was one of ten pure-bred dragon types. The skin of the Swedish short-snout was prized for the manufacture of protective gloves and shields. FB, p. 14.

Sweetwater All-Stars. A quidditch team from Texas. QA 8, p. 45.

Swelling Solution. A potion made in part from puffer-fish that the Potions class worked on during Harry Potter's second year at Hogwarts. CS 11, p. 186. Swelling solution had the effect of swelling parts of the body it came into contact with (i.e. Draco Malfoy's nose swelled like a balloon, Gregory Goyle's eyes grew as large as dinner plates). The potion was counteracted by a deflating draft. CS 11, p. 187.

Swiftstick. A make of quidditch broom manufactured in 1962 by Ellerby and Spudmore, a company from the Black Forest. The Swiftstick's predeceasor was the Tinderblast. QA 9, p. 50.

Switch, Emeric. The author of *A Beginners' Guide to Transfiguration.* This book was required for first-year students during Harry Potter's first year at Hogwarts. SS 5, p. 66.

Switching Spells. Hermione Granger mentioned that she knew information about switching spells and received points for Gryffindor house from Minerva McGonagell for that knowledge. This event occurred during Harry Potter's first year at Hogwarts. SS 9, p. 155. During Harry's fourth year at Hogwarts, Hermione reasoned that a switching spell probably would not help Harry to subdue a dragon in the first task of the Triwizard Tournament. GF 19, p. 338.

Swivenhodge. A broomstick game played in Herefordshire. QA 2, p. 6.

Sword of Godric Gryffindor. A magical sword that Albus Dumbledore believed was the only weapon that could kill the Heir of Slytherin. During year seven, Severus Snape moved a fake copy of the Gryffindor sword to Gringotts for protection after several students attempted to steal it. DH 7, p. 129; 15, pp. 290, 298. See **Gryffindor, Godric.**

Sykes, Jocunda. The first witch to cross the Atlantic Ocean on a broomstick. Jocunda performed the feat in 1935. QA 9, p. 48.

TABOO – TWYCROSS, WILKIE

Taboo. A jinx placed on the name of Lord Voldemort so that whenever anyone said his name it had the effect of breaking protective enchantments around that person and made that person trackable by the Ministry of Magic. DH 19, p. 389.

Tadfoal. The name given to an unhatched hippocampus that could be seen through its large, semi-transparent egg. FB, p. 21.

Tail-Twig Clippers. An item included in the Broomstick Servicing Kit given by Hermione Granger to Harry Potter as a thirteenth birthday present. The kit also included Fleetwood's High-Finish Handle Polish, a tiny brass compass and a copy of *Handbook of Do-It-Yourself Broomcare.* This event occurred during the summer prior to Harry's third year at Hogwarts. PA 1, p. 12.

Tale of the Three Brothers, The. An old wizarding tale that served as the basis for the Deathly Hallows. The tale appeared in *The Tales of Beedle the Bard.* Three brothers received gifts from Death: the Elder Wand, a wand more powerful than any other; the Resurrection Stone, a stone that could help bring back the dead; and a Cloak of Invisibility. DH 21, pp. 406-09.

Tales of Beedle the Bard, The. The title of a book, written by Beedle the Bard, that Hermione Granger obtained during year seven. The title was set forth in runes. The book included such stories as: 'The Fountain of Fair Fortune'; 'The Wizard and the Hopping Pot'; and 'Babbitty Rabbitty and her Cackling Stump.' DH 7, pp. 126, 135.

Tanzania. The home country of the Sumbawanga Sunrays, a quidditch team. QA 8, p. 43. (Tanzania is a country in East Africa.)

Tarantallegra. The magic word used in a charm to force someone to dance uncontrollably in a quickstep. Draco Malfoy used the charm against Harry Potter during the first meeting of the Dueling Club. This event occurred during Harry's second year at Hogwarts. The charm was counteracted by speaking the magic words "*finite incantatem.*" CS 11, p. 192.

Tarapoto Tree-Skimmers. The most famous quidditch team from Peru. QA 8, p. 46. (Tarapoto is a city in North Peru.)

Tchamba Charmers. A quidditch team from Togo, Africa. The Charmers were masters in the use of the Reverse Pass. QA 8, p. 43. (Tchamba is a city located in the central region of Togo, Africa.)

Tebo. A magical warthog found in the Congo and Zaire. The Tebo's hide was valued for making protective shields and clothing. FB, pp. xvii, 40.

Tenebrus. The first thestral, a male, that was born in the Forbidden Forest. Tenebrus was Rubeus Hagrid's favorite from among all the thestrals he raised there. OP 21, p. 447.

Tentacula. A plant with magical properties. Professor Sprout intended to use Tenatacula as a defense against Death Eaters during year seven. DH 30, p. 600.

Tergeo. The magic word used in a charm that siphoned off dried blood from a body. HP 8, p. 162. Ron Weasley used the charm to clean a dirty handkerchief of grease during year seven. Harry Potter also used the charm to clean dust off of photographs in Bathilda Bagshot's residence that same year. DH 6, p. 94; 17, p. 336.

Texas. The location that served as the home of the Sweetwater All-Stars. QA 8, p. 44. (Texas is a southern state in the United States of America.)

Theories of Transubstantial Transfiguration. The title of a book that Albus Dumbledore borrowed from the Hogwarts library. When Dumbledore doodled in the book, a curse caused the book to beat him on the head. QA, p. viii.

Thestral. A rare breed of Winged Horse that had the ability to become invisible. Many wizards considered a thestral to be unlucky. FB, p. 42. Rubeus Hagrid trained thestrals at Hogwarts not to touch owls and raised the only domestic breed of thestrals in Britain. Thestrals pulled the carriages of students from Hogsmeade Station to Hogwarts Castle. Only a person who had seen death could see the creatures. The name of the first thestral Hagrid raised in the Forbidden Forest was Tenebrus. OP 10, p. 196; 17, p. 358; 20, p. 439; 21, pp. 444-46. Thestrals were able to fly through the air and carry a passenger on their backs. OP 33, p. 762. Thestrals were used by the Order of the Phoenix to escort Harry Potter from the Dursley residence during year seven. DH 4, p. 47; 36, p. 733.

Thickey, Janus. A wizard who faked his abduction by a Lethifold in 1973. Janus was later found five miles away from his home with the landlady of the Green Dragon. FB, p. 27, fn. 9. A ward at St.

Mungo's Hospital for Magical Maladies and Injuries was named after Janus. It housed long-term patients with permanent spell damage. OP 23, p. 511.

Thicknesse, Pius. A wizard who was Head of the Department of Magical Law Enforcement within the Ministry of Magic during year seven. Yaxley placed an Imperius Charm on him that year. DH 1, p. 5. Pius became the Minister of Magic that year, replacing Rufus Scrimgeour. DH 11, p. 208. Pius' fate was revealed at the end of year seven. DH 36, p. 735.

Thief's Curse. A curse placed on copies of *Fantastic Beasts and Where to Find Them,* which copies were released to the muggle world. FB, p. viii; QA, p. viii.

Thief's Downfall. A magical waterfall in the caverns of Gringotts Wizarding Bank that washed away all enchantments and magical concealment of anyone who passed underneath it. DH 26, p. 534.

Thomas, Dean. An ethnically black student who was sorted by the Sorting Hat during Harry Potter's first year at Hogwarts. Dean was a member of the Gryffindor house. SS 7, p. 122. His greatest fear was a bloody eyeball that could walk. That fact was made obvious after a Defense Against the Dark Arts class in which the students experimented with a bogart. This event occurred during Harry's third year at Hogwarts. PA 7, p. 138. Dean's parents were muggles. OP 11, p. 219. At the end of Harry Potter's fifth year at Hogwarts, Ginny Weasley expressed interest in dating Dean. OP 38, p. 866. Dean replaced Katie Bell as chaser on the house quidditch team the following school year. HP 14, p. 284. DH 15, p. 295. He was held as a captive in the cellar at the Malfoy mansion during year seven. DH 23, p. 465.

Thousand Magical Herbs and Fungi, A. The title of a book that Ron Weasley read during Harry Potter's sixth year at Hogwarts. HP 25, p. 539.

Three Broomsticks. A shop located in Hogsmeade that sold foaming mugs of butterbeer. PA 8, p. 158. The Three Broomsticks was owned and operated by Madam Rosmerta. Harry Potter ventured into the pub during his third and fourth years at Hogwarts. PA 10, p. 200; GF 19, p. 319. It was one of only two pubs in Hogsmeade; the Hog's Head was the other. HP 12, p. 245. DH 28, p. 554.

Thundelarra Thunderers. A quidditch team from Australia. The Thunderers dominated the Australian quidditch scene, along with the Woollongong Warriors, for over a century. QA 8, p. 42.

Tibbles, Mr. A cat owned by Mrs. Figgs. Mrs. Figgs' other three cats were named Snowy, Mr. Paws and Tufty. SS 2, p. 22. Mrs. Figg stationed Mr. Tibbles under a car near Privet Drive to stand guard. This event occurred during the summer prior to Harry Potter's fifth year at Hogwarts. OP 2, p. 20.

Tibet. A country that repeatedly violated Clause 73 of the International Code of Wizarding Secrecy by allowing muggles to view the yeti. The Confederation of Wizards responded by permanently placing an International Task Force in the mountains. FB, p. xvii. Kingsley Shacklebolt, as the auror in charge of the hunt for Sirius Black, fed the Ministry of Magic false information that Sirius Black was in Tibet. This event occurred during Harry Potter's fifth year at Hogwarts. OP 5, p. 95. (Tibet is an administrative division of China and is north of the Himalayas.)

Tickling Charm. A charm invoked with the magic word "*rictusempra*" that was used to tickle someone. CS 11, p. 192. Harry Potter used the charm to defend himself against Draco Malfoy during the first meeting of the Dueling Club. This event occurred during Harry's second year at Hogwarts. CS 11, p. 192.

Time Room. A special room in the Department of Mysteries in which time-turners were stored. OP 35, p. 795.

Time-Turner. A magical hourglass that allowed the user of it to turn back time. Hermione Granger obtained a time-turner from Minerva McGonagell during Harry Potter's third year at Hogwarts. PA 21, pp. 394-95. Time-turners were stored in the Time Room of the Department of Mysteries. OP 35, p. 794. During the attack on Harry Potter at the Ministry, all of the Ministry's time-turners were destroyed. HP 11, p. 231.

Timms, Agatha. A witch who Ludo Bagman had a wager with over the outcome of the Quidditch World Cup. According to Bagman, Agatha put up half the shares in her eel farm that the match would last a week. This event occurred during the summer prior to Harry Potter's fourth year at Hogwarts. GF 7, p. 88.

Tinderblast. A make of quidditch broom manufactured in 1940 by Ellerby and Spudmore, a company from the Black Forest. The Tinderblast was followed by the Swiftstick in 1952. QA 9, p. 50.

Tinworth. A village in Cornwall that, according to *A History of Magic*, was one of several villages where Wizarding families lived alongside confunded Muggles. DH 16, p. 319. Tinworth was the location of Shell Cottage, the newlywed home of Bill and Fleur Weasley during year seven. DH 23, p. 468.

Tofty, Professor. A wizard and professor who administered the practical examination of the O.W.L.s. to Harry Potter during Harry's fifth year at Hogwarts. Professor Tofty was a friend of Tiberius Ogden. OP 31, pp. 713, 714.

Togo. The home country of the Tchamba Charmers. QA 8, p. 43. (Togo is a country in Western Africa.)

Tom. The owner and innkeeper of the Leaky Cauldron. Harry Potter met Tom prior to his first year at Hogwarts. SS p. 5, p. 69. DH 26, p. 524.

Tongue-Tying Curse. A curse that Mad-Eye Moody set up in Number Twelve Grimmauld Place to affect Severus Snape if he ventured on the property during year seven. DH 9, p. 170.

Tonks, Andromeda. The wife of Ted Tonks and mother of Nymphadora. Andromeda's two sisters were Bellatrix Black and Narcissa Black, the later of whom married Lucius Malfoy. OP 6, p. 113. She looked very similar to Bellatrix and was called 'Dromeda by her husband. She was a pure-blood. DH 5, pp. 65-66; 15, p. 295.

Tonks, Nymphadora. A witch who was a member of the Order of the Phoenix. Nymphadora preferred to be called by her surname only and was one of the advance guard sent to rescue Harry Potter from the Dursley home during the summer prior to Harry's fifth year at Hogwarts. Tonks' father was a muggle. OP 3, pp. 47-50. She was a metamorphmagus by birth and an auror. OP 3, p. 52. Her mother, Andromeda, was Sirius Black's favorite cousin. OP 6, p. 113. She was stationed at Hogwarts to provide the school with extra security during Harry's sixth year at the school. HP 8, p. 158. She fell in love with Remus Lupin. HP 29, p. 624. Tonks and Remus were married immediately prior to the commencement of year seven. DH 1, p. 10; 4, p. 45. At the beginning of that year, Tonks escorted Ron Weasley, who had taken Polyjuice Potion to look with Harry, on a broomstick from the Dursley residence. DH 4, p. 53. Her father called her Dora. DH 5, p. 64. She became pregnant with Remus' child that same year. DH 11, p. 212. She and Remus had a boy and they named him Ted, after his maternal grandfather. DH 25, p. 514. Tonks' fate was explained at DH 33, p. 661.

Tonks, Ted. The husband of Andromeda and father of Nymphadora Tonks. Ted was muggle-born. OP 6, p. 113. Ted's home was scheduled to be the safe location for Harry to venture to once he vacated the Dursley residence at the beginning of year seven. He was not a pure-blood. DH 4, p. 48; 5, p. 64; 15, p. 295. Ted's fate was announced during a broadcast of *Potterwatch*. DH 22, p. 439.

Ton-Tongue Toffee. Joke candy invented by Fred and George Weasley. When eaten the candy caused a person's tongue to swell to over a foot in length. Dudley Dursley consumed the candy and felt its effects when the Weasleys came to pick up Harry Potter for the Quidditch World Cup. This event occurred during the summer prior to Harry's fourth year at Hogwarts. GF 5, p. 50.

Toothflossing Stringmints. Candy sold at Honeydukes in Hogsmeade. Ron Weasley wanted to purchase some of the candy as a Christmas present for his parents. This event occurred during Harry Potter's third year at Hogwarts. PA 10, p. 190.

Top Box. The uppermost box of seats at the Quidditch World Cup. The box was occupied by such officials as Ludo Bagman and Barty Crouch. Crouch complained that the Bulgarians demanded another twelve seats be added to the Top Box. GF 7, pp. 90-92. The Weasleys, Harry Potter and Hermione Granger sat in the Top Box. Cornelius Fudge sat in the Top Box and Winky reserved seats there for Mr. and Mrs. Lucius Malfoy and Draco Malfoy. Mr. Oblansk also sat in the Top Box. This event occurred the summer prior to Harry Potter's fourth year at Hogwarts. GF 8, pp. 96, 100-01.

Topsham. The residence of a witch, Madam Z. Nettles, who took the Kwikspell course and afterwards became the center of attention at parties for her Scintillation Solution recipe. Harry Potter discovered that information on a piece of parchment in Argus Filch's office during Harry's second year at Hogwarts. CS 8, p. 127. (Topsham was originally a port town in the Exe Estuary of Devon County, a southern county in England. It is currently part of the city of Exeter in Devon County.)

Tornados. See **Tutshill Tornados**.

Tottenham Court Road. A road in London where Harry Potter, Ron Weasley and Hermione Granger escaped to after the wedding of Fleur Delacourt and Bill Weasley ended abruptly during year seven. DH 9, p. 161. (Tottenham Court Road is a road in Central London.)

Towler, Kenneth. A student at Hogwarts in Fred and George Weasley's class who kept suffering from boils during their fifth year O.W.L.s. OP 12, p. 226.

Toyohashi Tengu. The most successful Japanese quidditch team to play the game during the last century. QA 8, p. 46. (Toyohashi is a city located in Aichi Prefecture in Japan.)

Trace. A charm that detected magical activity around a witch or wizard who was under seventeen years of age. The Trace was one way that the Ministry of Magic found out about underage magic. DH 4, p. 47.

Transfiguration. The ability of a wizard to turn an object into another object. SS 7, p. 125. The skill was taught in a class by Minerva McGonagell at Hogwarts during the time that Harry Potter attended the school. Minerva considered the subject to be some of the most complex and dangerous magic to be learned at Hogwarts. SS 8, pp. 133-34. The final exam for third-year students, including Harry, was to turn a teapot into a tortoise. PA 16, p. 317. Prior to becoming headmaster at Hogwarts, Albus Dumbledore taught the class. CS 17,

p. 313. During Harry's fourth year at Hogwarts, Mad-Eye Moody was reprimanded by Minerva for transfiguring Draco Malfoy into a ferret as a punishment. GF 13, p. 206. DH 10, p. 182.

Transfiguration Today. A periodical published in the wizarding world. When Harry Potter was temporarily housed in the Leaky Cauldron, he observed wizards debating the latest article in *Transfiguration Today.* This event occurred during the summer prior to Harry's third year at Hogwarts. PA 4, p. 49. Albus Dumbledore had some of his papers published in *Transfiguration Today.* DH 2, p. 17; 18, p. 354.

Transforming Spells. Spells used in transfiguration. Minerva McGonagell asked Harry Potter's Transfiguration class to describe the ways in which transforming spells had to be adapted to perform cross-species switches. This event occurred during Harry's fourth year at Hogwarts. GF 22, p. 385.

Transmogrifian Torture. A curse that Gilderoy Lockhart suspected had been invoked against Mrs. Norris, killing her and making her stiff as a statue. This event occurred during Harry Potter's second year at Hogwarts. CS 9, pp. 141-42.

Transylvania. The national quidditch team from Transylvania beat the team from England three hundred ninety to ten. According to Charlie Weasley, it was a shocking performance. This event occurred during the summer prior to Harry Potter's fourth year at Hogwarts. GF 5, p. 63. Percy Weasley was proud to announce to Ludo Bagman that he was going to meet with the Transylvanians to discuss their signing of the International Ban on Dueling in the new year. This discussion occurred during Harry's fourth year at Hogwarts. GF 23, p. 425. A quidditch team from Transylvania was in the final match of the first Quidditch World Cup held in 1473. QA 9, pp. 39-40. The other team was from Flanders. Dragomir Despard, the alias that Ron Weasley used in year seven, was supposedly from Transylvania. DH 26, p. 528. (Transylvania is a region and former province in Central Romania.)

Transylvanian Tackle. A quidditch move that was widely known. It was first seen at the World Cup in 1473. QA 10, p. 54.

Travels with Trolls. The title of a book written by Gilderoy Lockhart. The book was required for second-year students during Harry Potter's second year at Hogwarts. CS 4, p. 43. DH 6, p. 96.

Travers. A Death Eater who helped Lord Voldemort kill the McKinnons. Igor Karkaroff attempted to gain his own release from Azkaban by giving Travers' name to the Ministry of Magic. However, the Ministry already had Travers in custody. During his fourth year at Hogwarts, Harry Potter learned this information from the pensieve in Albus Dumbledore's office. GF 30, p. 590. Travers was one of the Death

Eaters that chased Harry after he left the protection of the Dursley residence during year seven. DH 5, p. 73. Travers was also one of two Death Eaters, the other was Selwyn, who appeared at Xenophilius' house during year seven. DH 21, p. 421.

Treacle fudge. Rubeus Hagrid offered treacle fudge to Ron Weasley during Harry Potter's second year at Hogwarts. CS 7, p. 115.

Trelawney, Cassandra. A celebrated seer who was the great-great-grandmother of Sibyll Trelawney. OP 15, p. 314.

Trelawney, Sibyll. The witch who taught Divination class at Hogwarts during the time that Harry Potter attended the school. Sibyll's classroom was located at the top of the North Tower and was accessed by climbing up a silvery ladder and through a trapdoor. PA 6, p. 101. Harry took Sibyll's class during his third year at Hogwarts. During the fall term of Harry's fifth year at Hogwarts, Sibyll had taught Divination almost sixteen years. Albus Dumbledore appointed her to the position. She was the great-great-granddaughter of the celebrated Seer Cassandra Trelawney. OP 15, p. 314. She made an important prophecy about Harry that Albus Dumbledore shared with Harry during Harry's fifth year at Hogwarts. OP 37, p. 841. For the text of the prophecy, see **Prophecy**. Sibyll rarely attended the start-of-term feast, although she did during Harry's sixth year at Hogwarts. HP 8, p. 164. She shared teaching the Divination classes with Firenze during the following school year. HP 9, p. 174. Sibyll had the power of cartomancy. HP 25, p. 544. DH 32, p. 646.

Trevor. The name of Neville Longbottom's toad. Trevor accompanied Neville to Hogwarts during the first year that Harry Potter attended the school. SS 6, p. 112.

Trimble, Quentin. The author of *The Dark Forces: A Guide to Self-Protection.* The book was required for first-year students during Harry Potter's first year at Hogwarts . SS 5, p. 67.

Trip Jinx. A jinx that Draco Malfoy placed on Harry Potter to trip him as Harry ran away from a D.A. meeting. This event occurred during Harry's fifth year at Hogwarts. OP 27, p. 609.

Triwizard Cup. The official award given to the winner of the Triwizard Tournament. In addition, the winner received one thousand galleons as a personal prize. This event occurred during Harry Potter's fourth year at Hogwarts. GF 12, p. 188.

Triwizard Tournament. A competition between the three wizarding schools: Beauxbatons Academy of Magic, Durmstrang Institute and Hogwarts that started seven hundred years prior to Harry Potter's lifetime. The competition was originally intended to be a friendly contest in which a champion from each of the schools competed in three magical tasks. The event occurred every five years and the schools took turns hosting it. The event was originally designed to be a means of establishing ties between young witches and wizards of different nationalities. It was later discontinued because the death toll from it rose too high. The Department of International Magical Cooperation and the Department of Magical Games and Sports permitted the event to resume during Harry Potter's fourth year at Hogwarts, with Hogwarts as the hosting school. The other schools arrived with their short-listed contenders on October 30 of that year and the three champions were selected on Halloween. The winner of the contest won the Triwizard Cup and one thousand galleons as a personal prize. The parties who organized the event established the rule that only students who were at least seventeen17 years old were eligible to enter the competition. GF 12, pp. 186-88; 15, p. 235. The panel of judges who decided the tournament consisted of the following five wizards: the heads of the three competing schools, Ludo Bagman and Bartemius Crouch. GF 15, p. 238; 16, p. p. 239. The Goblet of Fire selected four school champions to compete. They were: Viktor Krum, Fleur Delacour, Cedric Diggory and Harry Potter. GF 16, pp. 269-71. The identity of the person who placed Harry's name in the Goblet of Fire was revealed later that school year. GF 35, p. 675. The tasks were designed to test the magical prowess of the champions in the following three fields: their daring, their powers of deduction and their ability to cope with danger. GF 16, p. 255. The first of the three tasks took place on November 24 and was a test of daring. The champions were required to collect a golden egg from a nesting dragon. GF 17, p. 281; 19, pp. 349, 350-61. The second task took place on February 24. GF 19, p. 361. The champions were required to swim under the lake for an hour and retrieve something important to them that was being held by merpeople in the lake. GF 25, p. 463; 26, p. 491. The third task took place on June 24. GF 26, p. 507. It involved navigating through a hedge maze containing dangerous creatures. The hedge was grown on top of the quidditch field and was twenty feet high. GF 27, pp. 550-51; 31, pp. 620-35. DH 2, p. 27.

Troll. A dangerous creature that was about twelve feet tall, with dull granite gray skin, a lumpy body like a boulder and a bald head like a coconut. A troll had short legs and horny feet and carried a huge wooden club. Harry Potter encountered a troll during his first year at Hogwarts. SS 10, pp. 172, 174. According to Percy Weasley, Troll was one of 200 languages that Barty Crouch could speak. GF 7, p. 88. Trolls originated in Scandinavia and spread to Britain and Ireland and other areas of Northern Europe. FB, p. 40. Trolls sometimes rode graphorns, which were found in mountainous European regions.

However, it was more common to see a troll covered in graphorn scars because graphorns did not like to be ridden. FB, p. 20. DH 19, p. 382.

Trophy Room. A room in Hogwarts that was always unlocked and contained trophies and awards honoring past students and achievements of the school. Draco Malfoy challenged Harry Potter to a midnight duel in the room during Harry's first year at Hogwarts. SS 9, p. 153. Ron Weasley served a detention in the Trophy Room, under the direction of Argus Filch, as a punishment for flying his father's car into the Whomping Willow. This event occurred during Harry's second year at Hogwarts. CS 7, p. 118. The room contained, among other things, the Medal for Magical Merit and a list of head boys. CS 13, p. 234.

Troy. A member of the Irish National Quidditch Team who played in the Quidditch World Cup that Harry Potter attended during the summer prior to his fourth year at Hogwarts. Troy was a chaser. The other members of the team were: Connolly, Ryan, Mullet, Moran, Quigley and Lynch. GF 8, pp. 105-06.

True Seer. A witch or wizard who was an expert in divination. According to Minerva McGonagell, true seers were very rare. She explained this fact to her Transfiguration class during Harry Potter's third year at Hogwarts. PA 6, p. 109.

Truth Potion. Three drops of a truth potion's liquid, named Veritaserum, was enough to make a person spill his innermost secrets. Severus Snape threatened to use truth potion on Harry Potter after Harry denied breaking into Severus' office for boomslang skin and gillyweed. This event occurred during Harry's fourth year at Hogwarts. GF 27, p. 517.

Tufty. A cat owned by Mrs. Figgs. Mrs. Figgs' other three cats were named Tobbles, Snowy, and Mr. Paws. SS 2, p. 22.

Turkey. An English quidditch team with Ludovic Bagman as beater played the quidditch team from Turkey one week before Ludovic was brought up on charges before the Council of Magical Law. Ludovic's splendid performance in the game affected the outcome of his trial the following week. Harry Potter learned this information from the pensieve in Albus Dumbledore's office during Harry's fourth year at Hogwarts. GF 30, p. 593. (Turkey is a country located in West Asia and Southeast Europe.)

Turpin, Lisa. A student who was sorted by the Sorting Hat during Harry Potter's first year at Hogwarts. Lisa was a member of the Ravenclaw house. SS 7, p. 122.

Tutshill. See **Tutshill Tornados**.

Tutshill Tornados. A quidditch team in the league that was founded in 1520. Its most notable player in the last century was Roderick

Plumpton, who served as the team's seeker and captain. Roderick held the record for fastest capture of the snitch (three and a half seconds) during a match against the Caerphilly Catapults in 1921. QA 7, p. 37. According to a report in *The Quibbler*, the Tornados took control in the quidditch league through various forms of corruption. OP 10, pp. 190, 193. This report was published during the summer prior to Harry Potter's fifth year at Hogwarts. Cho Chang wore a sky-blue badge emblazoned with a double gold T and supported the team. OP 12, p. 230.

Twelve Fail-Safe Ways to Charm Witches. The title of a book that described everything one needed to know about girls. Ron Weasley gave the book to Harry Potter as a seventeenth birthday present during year seven. DH 7, p. 113.

Twigger 90. A make of quidditch broom manufactured by Flyte and Barker in 1990. Flyte and Barker intended for the Twigger 90 to replace the Nimbus, but it never acheived that status. The Twigger 90 had such features as the Warning Whistle and Self-Straightening Brush. QA 9, p. 51.

Twilfitt and Tatting's. A robe shop located in Diagon Alley. HP 6, p. 114.

Twitchy Ears. A hex that caused a person's ears to twitch. Harry Potter experimented with the hex after a Defense Against the Dark Arts class in which the students were supposed to practice hex-deflection. GF 27, p. 547.

Twycross, Wilkie. A wizard from the Ministry of Magic who taught a twelve-week class on apparition at Hogwarts. HP 18, p. 382. The students used a variety of nicknames for Wilkie, the most polite of which were Dogbreath and Dunghead. HP 18, p. 389.

UGANDA - URQUHART

Uganda. The national quidditch team from Uganda beat the team from Wales. This event occurred during the summer prior to Harry Potter's fourth year at Hogwarts. GF 5, p. 63. The Patonga Proudsticks, a quidditch team, was from Uganda. QA 8, p. 42. (Uganda is an independent state in East Africa.)

Ugga. A wizard who played on Goodwin Kneen's Kwidditch team during the tenth century. Ugga was probably a beater. QA 3, p. 9.

Ukranian Ironbelly. One of ten pure-bred dragon types and the largest. An Ukranian ironbelly carried off a sailing boat from the Black Sea in 1799. FB, p. 14.

Umbridge, Dolores Jane. A witch who served as the Undersecretary to the Minister of Magic. Dolores was an interrogator during Harry's Potter's disciplinary hearing held at the Wizengamot and served as the Defense Against the Dark Arts professor at Hogwarts during Harry's fifth year at the school. Dolores drafted anti-werewolf legislation that made it almost impossible for Remus Lupin to find employment. OP 8, p. 139; 11, p. 211, 14, p. 302. Also during Harry's fifth school year, Cornelius Fudge appointed Dolores as High Inquisitor and later Headmaster. OP 15, p. 306; 28, p. 624. During year seven her office at the Ministry was located on Level One. DH 12, pp. 229-30. That same year her titles were: Senior Undersecretary to the Minister and Head of the Muggle-born Registration Commission. Her Patronus was a cat. DH 13, pp. 250, 259.

Umfraville, Quintius. The author of *The Noble Sport of Warlocks* which was published in 1620. The book included the diagram of a seventeenth century quidditch pitch. QA 6, p. 18.

Umgubular Slashkilter. A magical device that Luna Lovegood claimed was possessed by Cornelius Fudge. Luna made the claim during Harry Potter's fifth year at Hogwarts. OP 18, p. 395.

Unbreakable Charm. A charm that Hermione Granger invoked on a glass jar that contained a large beetle. The beetle was actually Rita Skeeter in her animagus form. This event occurred during Harry Potter's fourth year at Hogwarts. GF 37, p. 728.

Unbreakable Vow. A binding promise made by a wizard to another. It required a third wizard to use his wand and invoke the magic for the vow. The third person was known as the Bonder. Severus Snape uttered an Unbreakable Vow to Narcissa Malfoy, the substance of which was to protect Draco Malfoy during Harry Potter's sixth year at Hogwarts and to carry out the duty if Draco failed to complete it. HP 2, p. 35.

Uncle Bilius. See **Weasley, (Uncle) Bilius**.

Undesirable. A derogatory name used by Pius Thicknesse, Minister of Magic, to refer to a "blood traitor" in the Ministry of Magic with whom Arthur Weasley was associating himself. This event occurred during year seven. DH 13, p. 247.

Undesirable Number One. The title given to Harry Potter on a poster in Dolores Umbridge's office during year seven. DH 13, p. 252.

Undetectable Potions. The subject of an essay that Harry Potter worked on for his Potions class. This event occurred during Harry's third year at Hogwarts. PA 12, p. 244.

Unfogging the Future. The title of a thick, black-bound book written by Cassandra Vablatsky. Harry Potter purchased the book for his third-year Divination class at Hogwarts. PA 4, p. 53. According to the manager of Flourish and Blotts where Harry purchased the book, it was a very good guide to all basic fortune telling methods, i.e. palmistry, crystal balls and bird entrails. The portion of the book on reading tea leaves stated that: a crooked cross meant trials and suffering; a sun meant great happiness; an acorn meant a windfall of unexpected gold; a falcon meant a deadly enemy; a club meant an attack; a skull meant danger in one's path and the grim meant death. PA 6, pp. 106-07. Harry and Ron Weasley used the book for Divination class during their fourth year at Hogwarts. GF 14, p. 221.

Unforgiveable Curses. The name for the three most terrible curses that a wizard could invoke. They were: the Cruciatus Curse, the Imperius Curse and the Killing (or "*Avada Kedarva*") Curse. Each of the curses was illegal to perform and if a wizard invoked one of them on a human being, he could be punished with a life sentence in Azkaban. Mad-Eye Moody introduced Harry Potter and his classmates to these curses during Harry's fourth year at Hogwarts. GF 14, p. 217.

Unicorn. A powerful, magical creature killed in the Forbidden Forest. SS 15, p. 250-51. The horn and tail of a unicorn was used in potions. Its silvery blood had magical properties and any person who drank the blood of a unicorn could be kept alive even if mortally injured. However, that person then lead a half-life, a cursed life. Harry Potter learned this information during his first year at Hogwarts. SS 15, p. 258. A unicorn foal was pure gold, unlike a mature unicorn. GF 26, p. 484. During Harry's fourth year at Hogwarts, Professor Grubbly-Plank showed the students in the Care of Magical Creatures class a unicorn. This event occurred after Rita Skeeter placed an article in the *Daily Prophet* that was critical of Albus Dumbledore and mentioned Rubeus Hagrid. GF 24, p. 437. Unicorns were found in the forests of Northern Europe. The unicorn's horn, blood and hair had highly magical properties. FB, p. 41. The subject of unicorns was often tested on O.W.L.s. OP 15, p. 323. A single strand of unicorn hair was worth ten galleons during Harry's sixth year at Hogwarts. HP 22, p. 487. DH 7, p. 120.

United States of America. The American game of quodpot competed for attention with quidditch in the United States. QA 8, p. 44. See **America** and **American Witches.**

Universal Brooms Ltd. A company that manufactured quidditch brooms. Universal first made the Shooting Star in 1955 and went out of business in 1978. QA 9, p. 50.

U-No-Poo. A magic device described as "the constipation sensation that's gripping the nation" on a poster outside of Weasley's Wizard Wheezes during the summer prior to Harry Potter's sixth year at Hogwarts. HP 6, p. 116.

Unplottable. A word used to describe a building that was so enchanted, its existence could not be plotted on a map. According to Hermione Granger, Durmstrang Institute was probably made unplottable to keep foreign wizards from finding it. Her remarks were made while riding the Hogwarts Express on the way to Harry Potter's fourth year at Hogwarts. GF 11, p. 166. The Ministry of Magic in Burkina Faso designated certain forests unplottable in order for the runespoor to be left alone. FB, p. 37. Sirius Black's father made Number Twelve, Grimmauld Place unplottable. OP 6, p. 115. A wizard could make the Room of Requirement at Hogwarts unplottable. HP 21, p. 452.

Unspeakables. The title given to wizards who worked for the Department of Mysteries within the Ministry of Magic. Their activities were top secret. Two of these wizards were Bode and Croaker. Arthur Weasley pointed out Bode and Croaker to Harry Potter and Hermione Granger in the camp at the Quidditch World Cup. This event occurred during the summer prior to Harry's fourth year at Hogwarts. GF 7, p. 86. DH 12, p. 230.

Untransfigure. The ability of witches or wizards who transfigured themselves into another form to change back. OP 29, p. 662.

Upper Flagley. A village in Yorkshire that, according to *A History of Magic*, was one of several villages where Wizarding families lived alongside confunded Muggles. DH 16, p. 319.

Uranus. In a Divination class during Harry Potter's fourth year at Hogwarts, Sibyl Trelawney pointed out to Lavender Brown that an unaspected planet on her parchment was Uranus. Lavender was working on an assignment about the planets that were visible on her date of birth. Ron Weasley said he would like to see Lavender's Uranus too. This joke did not escape Sibyl, who gave the class a lot of homework that day. GF 13, p. 201. (Uranus is the seventh planet from the sun in the solar system.)

Urg the Unclean. A goblin rebel who Ron Weasley complained he had to know for the History of Magic final exam he took the day of the third task in the Triwizard Tournament. Another goblin rebel's name was Bodrod the Bearded. This event occurred during Harry Potter's fourth year at Hogwarts. GF 31, p. 618.

Uric the Oddball. A famous wizard who was studied in the History of Magic class at Hogwarts during the time that Harry Potter attended the school. The students frequently confused Uric the Oddball with Emeric the Evil. SS 8, p. 133. Uric reportedly slept in a room with fifty pet augureys. FB, p. 3, fn. 3. He also tired to convince the Wizards' Council that the fwooper song was healthy. Uric appeared before the council wearing nothing but a toupee that was actually a dead badger. FB, p. 18, fn. 8.

Urquhart. A student at Hogwarts who, during Harry Potter's sixth year at the school, was the new captain of the Slytherin quidditch team. HP 14, p. 295.

VABLATSKY, CASSANDRA - VULCHANOV

Vablatsky, Cassandra. The author of *Unfogging the Future.* The book was required for students in Harry Potter's Divination class during his third year at Hogwarts. PA 4, p. 53.

Vaisey. A student at Howarts who was a member of the Slytherin House and its quidditch team. Vaisey was a chaser on the team during Harry Potter's sixth year at Hogwarts. HP 14, p. 294.

Vampire. One of the creatures, along with a hag, that Professor Quirrell reportedly encountered in the Black Forest. Rubeus Hagrid reported this information to Harry Potter when they observed Professor Quirrell on Diagon Alley. This event occurred during the summer prior to Harry's first year at Hogwarts. SS 5, p. 71. Gilderoy Lockhart claimed to have inflicted such injury on a vampire, that the creature was unable to eat anything but lettuce. Lockhart made the claim during a Defense Against the Dark Arts class that Harry attended during his second year at Hogwarts. CS 10, p. 161. According to Luna Lovegood, Rufus Scrimgeour was a vampire and the Ministry of Magic suppressed the release of that information from her father's paper. HP 15, p. 314.

Vance, Emmeline. A witch who was a member of the Order of the Phoenix and the advance guard that rescued Harry Potter from the Dursley home during the summer prior to Harry's fifth year at Hogwarts. OP 3, pp. 47-49. Emmeline was murdered, in addition to Amelia Bones, during the summer prior to Harry Potter's sixth year at Hogwarts. HP 1, pp. 4, 14.

Vane, Romilda. A student of Hogwarts who, on the Hogwarts Express, invited Harry Potter to join her. This event occurred during the summer prior to Harry's sixth year at Hogwarts. HP 7, p. 138.

Romilda was a member of the Gryffidnor house and tried out for the house quidditch team. HP 11, p. 224.

Vanishing Cabinet. A cabinet on the first floor of Hogwarts that Fred and George Weasley forced Montague into and expected him to be gone for weeks. This event occurred during Harry Potter's fifth year at Hogwarts. OP 28, p. 627. The following school year, Harry found the cabinet inside the Room of Requirement. There was a companion cabinet at Borgin and Burkes. HP 24, p. 526; 27, p. 587. DH 31, p. 627.

Vanishing Spell. A spell that made an object disappear. Harry Potter wished that he knew how to cast the spell during his second year at Hogwarts. CS 6, p. 98. A vanishing spell was easier to perform than a conjuring spell. Vanishing spells were on the O.W.L.s and among the most difficult magic tested. OP 13, p. 257.

Vauxhall Road. A road in London on which a variety store was located. The store's name and address appeared on the back of a secret diary owned by T. M. Riddle. Harry Potter, Ron Weasley and Hermione Granger learned this information during their second year at Hogwarts. CS 13, p. 231. (Vauxhall is an inner city area of South London, in the London borough of Lambeth.)

Vector, Professor. A witch who was the Arithmancy professor at Hogwarts during Harry Potter's third year at the school. PA 12, p. 244. Hermione Granger took Professor Vector's class the following year and bragged to Ron Weasley that Professor Vector had not given her any homework after the first class. GF 13, p. 202.

Veela. The name given to a witch who had exceptional beauty and whose beauty was so entrancing to men that they lost their concentration and focused entirely on the veela. A veela had skin that shown like moonlight and white-gold hair that appeared to fan out behind it without any wind. When a veela danced, men went completely and blissfully blank. The Bulgarian quidditch team mascot was the veela. Harry Potter first became entranced by the veela during the Quidditch World Cup that he attended during the summer prior to his fourth year at Hogwarts. When outraged, a veela turned its face into a sharp, cruel-beaked bird head and scaly wings burst from its shoulders. GF 8, pp. 103-11. DH 7, p. 116.

Venom antidotes. The subject of an essay Severus Snape gave to his fifth year students after their abysmal attempt at homework on the subject of moonstones. This event occurred during Harry Potter's fifth year at Hogwarts. OP 15, p. 309.

Venemous Tentacula. A spiky, dark red plant that had long feelers to ensnare people. Harry Potter experimented with the plant in a Herbology class during his second year at Hogwarts. CS 6, p. 93.

Fred and George Weasley used the shriveled black pods from venemous tentacula for their Skiving Snackboxes. The pods were a Class C Non-Tradeable Substance. They paid Mundungus Fletcher ten galleons for the pods. OP 9, p. 171. DH 32, p. 645.

Venus. Harry Potter and Ron Weasley used the planet Venus to fabricate answers for a Divination class homework assignment involving predictions of the future. Harry wrote that on the upcoming Tuesday he anticipated getting stabbed in the back by a friend because of the alignment of Venus. This event occurred during Harry's fourth year at Hogwarts. GF 14, p. 222. Venus was one of the planets on the star chart of the Astronomy practical examination of the O.W.L. that Harry took during his fifth year at the school. OP 31, p. 719. (Venus is the second planet from the sun in the solar system that includes Earth.)

Veritaserum. A truth potion that was very strong. Three drops of the clear potion was enough to make a person spill his innermost secrets. Severus Snape threatened using the potion on Harry Potter after he denied breaking into Severus' office for boomslang skin and gillyweed. GF 27, p. 517. Albus Dumbledore used the potion on a Death Eater after the conclusion of the Triwizard Tournament. GF 35, p. 682. These events occurred during Harry's fourth year at Hogwarts. Veritaserum took a full moon cycle to mature. OP 32, p. 744. Rita Skeeter also used the potion on Bathilda Bagshot to gather material for her book *The Life and Lies of Albus Dumbledore.* DH 18, p. 355.

Violet. A wizened witch who appeared in a painting in a room that was connected to the Great Hall of Hogwarts. GF 17, p. 273. Violet overheard the discussion regarding the Goblet of Fire's selection of four school champions instead of three and ran up to the painting of the Fat Lady to inform her of the news. GF 17, p. 284. Violet also celebrated Christmas with the Fat Lady in her painting. These events occurred during Harry Potter's fourth year at Hogwarts. GF 23, pp. 411, 432.

Viridian, Vindictus. The author of *Curses and Countercurses (Bewitch Your Friends and Befuddle Your Enemies with the Latest Revenges: Hair Loss, Jelly-Legs, Tongue-Tying and Much, Much More).* The book was sold in Flourish and Blotts and perused by Harry Potter before his first year at Hogwarts. SS 5, p. 80.

Voldemort, Lord. A powerful and evil wizard, commonly referred to as "You-Know-Who" by wizards who feared the sound of his true name. SS 1, p. 11. Lord Voldemort was also known as "He-Who-Must-Not-Be-Named." SS 5, p. 85. Lord Voldemort killed Harry Potter's parents on Halloween and his attempt to kill Harry, who was an infant at the time, failed. SS 1, p. 12, 4, p. 55. The failed attempt severely wounded Lord Voldemort and forced him into hiding in order to regain his strength and to regroup his supporters. His name was originally Tom Marvolo Riddle. CS 17, p. 313. Lord Voldemort confronted Harry after the Triwizard Tournament. GF 32, pp. 640-43. He was born in a London Orphanage, operated by Mrs. Cole, on Christmas Eve. His mother died one hour after his birth. HP 13, p. 266. During year seven, Voldemort discussed the activity of the Order of the Phoenix at a meeting with the Death Eaters in the Malfoy manor house; at the meeting he avowed to kill Harry himself. DH 1, pp. 3, 7. Voldemort's original magic wand was made of yew and phoenix feather. It was thirteen and one-half inches long. DH 24, p. 496. The final duel between Voldemort and Harry occurred at the end of year seven, when each of their fates was revealed. DH 36, pp. 743-44. See also **Tom Riddle**.

Volkov. A member of the Bulgarian National Quidditch Team who played at the Quidditch World Cup that Harry Potter attended during the summer prior to Harry's fourth year at Hogwarts. Volkov was a beater. The other members of the team were: Dimitrov, Ivanova, Zograf, Levski, Vulchanov and Viktor Krum. GF 8, pp. 104, 107.

Voyages with Vampires. The title of a book, written by Gilderoy Lockhart that was required for second-year students during Harry's second year at Hogwarts. CS 4, p. 43.

Vratsa Vultures. A quidditch team that was the European champion until defeated by the Appleby Arrows in 1932. QA 7, p. 32. The Vultures' home country was Bulgaria. QA 8, p. 40.

Vulchanov. A member of the Bulgarian National Quidditch Team who played at the Quidditch World Cup that Harry Potter attended during the summer prior to Harry's fourth year at Hogwarts. Vulchanov was a beater. The other members of the team were: Dimitrov, Ivanova, Zograf, Levski, Volkov and Viktor Krum. GF 8, pp. 104, 107.

WADDIWASI – WRONSKI, JOSEF

Waddiwasi. The magic word for a spell that Remus Lupin used on Peeves the Poltergeist during Lupin's first Defense Against the Dark Arts class. The spell had the effect of shooting a wad of chewing gum out of a keyhole and into Peeves' left nostril. This event occurred during Harry Potter's third year at Hogwarts. PA 7, p. 131.

Waffling, Adalbert. The author of *Magical Theory*. The book was required for first-year students during Harry Potter's first year at Hogwarts. SS 5, p. 66. Albus Dumbledore and Adalbert, who was a magical theoretician, shared regular correspondence. DH 2, p. 17.

Wagga Wagga Werewolf. A creature that Gilderoy Lockhart claimed to have defeated. CS 10, p. 162. Lockhart asked his Defense Against the Dark Arts class to write a poem about the event during Harry Potter's second year at Hogwarts. CS 10, p. 162.

Wailing Widow, The. A ghost from Kent who came to Nearly Headless Nick's five hundredth deathday party. This event occurred during Harry Potter's second year at Hogwarts. CS 8, p. 135.

Wakanda. A witch with whom Arthur Weasley had an interrupted conversation at the Ministry of Magic during year seven. DH 13, p. 254.

Wales. Stan Shunpike asked the driver of the Knight Bus whether the bus was flying over Wales. This event occurred during the summer prior to Harry Potter's third year at Hogwarts. PA 3, p. 36. According to Charlie Weasley, the national quidditch team from Wales was defeated by the team from Uganda. This event occurred during the summer prior to Harry's fourth year at Hogwarts. GF 5, p. 63. The Caerphilly Catapults, a quidditch team, was from Wales. QA 7, p. 33. DH 15, 0. 292. See also **Common Welsh Green Dragon**. (Wales is a division in Southwest Great Britain.)

Wand of Destiny, The. An extra-powerful wand that, according to historical accounts, was owned by a Dark wizard. DH 21, p. 415.

Wand-carrier. The generic name used by a goblin to refer to a witch or wizard. They were called wand-carriers because wizards refused to share their knowledge of wandlore with goblins, even though goblins could perform magic without the devices. Wands would have allowed goblins to extend their powers. DH 24, p. 488.

Wanderings with Werewolves. The title of a book, written by Gilderoy Lockhart, that was required for second-year students during Harry Potter's second year at Hogwarts. CS 4, p. 43.

Wandlore. A complex and mysterious branch of magic involving magic wands, as described by Mr. Ollivander during year seven. DH 24, pp. 293-94.

Warbeck, Celestina. A singing sorceress featured on the radio program "The Witching Hour." The program played on the radio in the Weasley residence when Harry Potter visited the family for the first time. This event occurred during the summer prior to Harry's second year at Hogwarts. CS 3, p. 34. Celestina recorded the anthem of the Puddlemere United club titled "Beat Back Those Bludgers, Boys, and Chuck That Quaffle Here." The recording was a fund raiser for St. Mungo's Hospital for Magical Maladies and Injuries. QA 7, p. 36. Celestina was a featured singer on a Christmas Eve radio broadcast at the Weasley home during Harry's sixth year at Hogwarts. She sang "A Cauldron Full of Hot, Strong Love" and "You Charmed the Heart Right Out of Me." HP 16, pp. 330-31. According to Ron Weasley, Fleur Delacourt hated Celestine Warbeck. DH 20, p. 397.

Warlocks' Convention of 1709. A law that prohibited dragon breeding. Ron Weasley stated to Rubeus Hagrid that everyone knew that law. This event occurred during Harry Potter's first year at Hogwarts. SS 14, p. 230.

Warrington, C. A student of Hogwarts who was a member of the Slytherin house. Warrington played the position of chaser on Slytherin's quidditch team during Harry Potter's third year at Hogwarts. PA 15, p. 306. The following year, Warrington was one of the first students to place his name in the Goblet of Fire for the selection of champions for the Triwizard Tournament. GF 16, p. 261. Warrington's name appeared on the list of borrowers found inside the cover of *Quidditch Through the Ages*. QA, p. i. Harry's opinion of Warrington's skills as a Slytherin quidditch team chaser, during Harry's fifth year at Hogwarts, was that his aim was pathetic. OP 19, p. 401.

Wartcap. A wizarding powder that Sirius Black accidentally applied to his hand, that caused it to be covered in an unpleasant crusty covering like a tough brown glove. OP 6, p. 116. DH 10, p. 189.

Watch wizard. A wizard who had the power to arrest witches and wizards on behalf of the Ministry of Magic. Eric Munch was a watch wizard who arrested Sturgis Podmore on August 31. This event occurred during the summer prior to Harry Potter's fifth year at Hogwarts. OP 14, p. 287.

Wattlebird. A password used to gain access to the Gryffindor house of Hogwarts during Harry Potter's second year at Hogwarts. CS 5, p.84.

Weasley. A family of red-headed, poor wizards who were friends of Harry Potter. SS 6, p. 92. The children in the family were in order of youngest to oldest: Ginny, Ron, twins named Fred and George, Percy, Bill and Charlie. Charlie had already graduated from Hogwarts by the time that Harry began his first year at the school. SS 6, pp. 92, 93, 99.

Weasley, Arthur. The father of the Weasley family. Arthur worked for the Misuse of Muggle Artifacts Office within the Ministry of Magic. CS 3, pp. 24, 30, 38; 4, p. 47. Harry Potter referred to Arthur as a fully qualified wizard. GF 2, p. 22. Arthur was obsessed with anything having to do with muggles. He admitted to the Dursley family that he collected electricity plugs and had a very large collection of batteries. This admission occurred during the summer prior to Harry's fourth year at Hogwarts. GF 4, p. 46. Arthur was a member of the Order of the Phoenix. He was also a second cousin once removed of Sirius Black. OP 4, p. 72; 6, p. 113. During the summer prior to Harry's sixth year at Hogwarts, Arthur was promoted to head of the new Office for the Detection and Confiscation of Counterfeit Defensive Spells and Protective Objects. HP 5, p. 84. Arthur's dearest ambition was to understand how airplanes fly. The private pet name his wife used for him was "Mollywobbles." HP 5, p. 86. DH 3, p. 32; 4, p. 45. At the beginning of year seven, Arthur escorted Fred Weasley, who had taken Polyjuice Potion to look like Harry, on a broomstick from the Dursley residence. DH 4, p. 52. Arthur conjured a partonus in the form of a bright silver weasel. DH 7, p. 121.

Weasley, Bilius. An uncle of Ron Weasley who died within twenty-four hours of seeing a grim. Ron Weasley shared that information with Hermione Granger to impress upon her the danger of observing a grim, which Harry Potter claimed to have seen. This event occurred during Harry Potter's third year at Hogwarts. PA 6, p. 110. Uncle Bilius had been very funny at weddings and was never married. DH 8, pp. 142-43.

Weasley, (William) Bill Arthur. One of the eldest children in the Weasley family who was head boy while at Hogwarts. After graduating from Hogwarts, Bill was employed in Africa for the Gringotts Wizarding Bank. SS 6, pp. 99, 107. Specifically, he worked as a curse breaker in Egypt. PA 1, p. 8. Bill's duties also involved delivering treasure to the bank. GF 5, p. 62. Harry Potter met Bill for the first time during the summer prior to Harry's fourth year at Hogwarts and in a word described him as "cool." GF 5, p. 52. Bill wore his long, red hair in a pony-tail. Bill was a member of the Order of the Phoenix. He applied for a desk job from Gringotts Bank so that he could live with his parents and help the Order during Harry's fifth year at Hogwarts. OP 4, p. 70. During the summer prior to Harry's sixth year at Hogwarts, Fleur announced that she was going to marry Bill the following summer. HP 6, p. 92. Bill was attacked by Fenrir Greyback at the end of that school year. HP 29, p. 612. DH 4, p. 45. At the beginning of year seven, Bill escorted Fleur Delacourt, who had taken Polyjuice Potion to look like Harry, on a thestral from the Dursley residence. DH 4, p. 52. Bill's full name was revealed at his wedding to Fleur Delacourt during year seven. DH 8, p. 145.

Weasley, Charlie. One of the eldest children in the Weasley family who was captain of the Gryffindor quidditch team while at Hogwarts. After graduating from the school, Charlie studied and worked with dragons in Romania. SS 6, pp. 99, 107. Harry Potter met Charlie for the first time during the summer prior to Harry's fourth year at Hogwarts. GF 5, p. 52. Charlie was a member of the Order of the Phoenix while he lived in Romania. OP 4, p. 70. During year seven, Charlie still worked in Romania. DH 6, p. 109; 7, p. 118; 36, p. 734.

Weasley, Fred. One of the seven children in the Weasley family who was a twin, the other being George, and who attended Hogwarts. Fred was a member of the Gryffindor house and was one of the beaters on the quidditch team for that house. SS6, p. 99; 9, p. 153. He was sixteen years old during Harry Potter's fourth year at Hogwarts. GF 2, p. 22. His birthday was in April. GF 12, p. 189. Fred's name appeared on the list of borrowers found inside the cover of *Quidditch Through the Ages*. QA, p. i. Fred was legally an adult during the summer prior to Harry's fifth year at Hogwarts. OP 5, p. 91. DH 4, p. 45. At the beginning of year seven, Fred, who had taken Polyjuice Potion to look like Harry, left the Dursley residence on a broomstick with his father. DH 4, p. 52. Fred used the code name "Rodent" or "Rapier" on *Potterwatch* that year. DH 22, p. 442. Fred's fate was witnessed by Percy Weasley at Hogwarts during year seven. DH 31, p. 637.

Weasley, George. One of the seven children in the Weasley family who was a twin, the other being Fred, and who attended Hogwarts. George was a member of the Gryffindor house and was one of the beaters on the quidditch team for that house. SS 6, p. 99; 9, p. 153. He was sixteen years old during Harry Potter's fourth year at Hogwarts. GF 2, p. 22. His birthday was in April. GF 12, p. 189. George Weasley was legally an adult during the summer prior to Harry's fifth year at Hogwarts. OP 5, p. 91. DH 4, p. 45. At the beginning of year seven, George, who had taken Polyjuice Potion to look like Harry, left the Dursley residence on a broomstick with Remus Lupin. DH 4, p. 52. During that same year, one of George's ears was "cursed" off and could not be replaced. DH 5, p. 71.

Weasley, Ginny. One of the seven children who was the only girl and the youngest child in the Weasley family. SS 6, p. 92. Ginny was one year behind Harry Potter at Hogwarts and was a member of the Gryffindor house. CS 5, p. 82. Ginny was Neville Longbottom's date to the Yule Ball. GF 22, p. 401. This event occurred during Harry's fourth year at Hogwarts. Ginny dated Michael Corner during Harry's fifth year at the school. She and Michael had met each other at the Yule Ball the previous year. OP 16, pp. 347-48. Ginny became seeker for the Gryffindor quidditch team after Harry was banned from the game by Dolores Umbridge. At the end of the year she stopped dating Michael Corner and chose Dean Thomas instead. These events occurred during Harry's fifth year at Hogwarts OP 21, p. 453; 38, p. 866. The following school year, she took a pygmy puff, named Arnold, to Hogwarts at a pet. HP 7, p. 132. Later that year, Harry kissed her after Gryffindor won the Championship game against Ravenclaw, in which game Ginny was seeker. With that kiss, Ginny and Harry began to date each other. HP 24, pp. 533-34. DH 4, p. 52; 5, p. 67. Ginny had a poster of the Weird Sisters and a picture of Gwenog Jones on her bedroom walls during year seven. DH 7, p. 115.

Weasley, Hugo. The son of Ron and Hermione Weasley. Hugo had an older sister, Rose. DH Epilogue, p. 755.

Weasley, Molly. The mother of the Weasley family. SS 6, p. 92; CS 4, p. 55. Every year Molly made and sent her children sweaters for Christmas presents. She also made one for Harry Potter during Harry's first year at Hogwarts. Ron Weasley complained that his Weasley sweater was always maroon. SS 12, pp. 200-01. Molly was a member of the Order of the Phoenix. OP 4, p. 61. DH 4, p. 48; 5, p. 67. She had a brother named Fabian. She gave Fabian's watch to Harry as a seventeenth birthday present during year seven. DH 7, p. 114.

Weasley, (Auntie) Muriel. A great aunt of Ron Weasley who, according to the jeers of Ginny Weasley, was the person who gave Ron the best kiss he ever received. HP 14, p. 287. Muriel was actually the Great

Aunt of the Weasleys and she owned a goblin-made tiara. HP 29, p. 623. She was Molly Weasley's aunt, referred to as "Auntie Muriel." DH 4, p. 48. During year seven, Muriel claimed to be one hundred seven years old. She had a brother, Lancelot, who was a Healer at St. Mungo's hospital. DH 8, pp. 141, 156.

Weasley, Percy Ignasius. One of the seven children in the Weasley family. Percy was a prefect of Hogwarts at the time Harry Potter began to attend the school. SS 6, p. 99. Percy became head boy at the beginning of Harry 's third year at Hogwarts. PA 1, p. 10. During the following year, Percy worked for Barty Crouch at the Ministry of Magic. GF 5, p. 57. At the Yule Ball held at Hogwarts that year, Percy bragged that he had been promoted to Personal Assistant to Crouch. GF 23, p. 415. Percy was promoted to Junior Assistant to the Minister of Magic during the summer prior to Harry Potter's fifth year at Hogwarts and also moved to London. OP 4, pp. 71-72. Percy was the court scribe of the Wizengamot during Harry's disciplinary hearing held that summer. OP 8, p. 139. DH 8, p. 138; 13, p. 255; 30, p. 605.

Weasley, Ronald Bilius. One of the seven children in the Weasley family who was one of Harry Potter's classmates and best friends at Hogwarts. SS 6, p. 93; CS 1, p. 7. Ron was a member of the Gryffindor house. SS 7, p. 122. His favorite quidditch team was the Chudley Cannons. CS 12, p. 212. His greatest fear was spiders which fear became obvious in a Defense Against the Dark Arts class involving a bogart. This event occurred during Harry's third year at Hogwarts. PA 7, p. 136. Ron was a prefect for the Gryffindor house during Harry's fifth year at Hogwarts. He was the fourth Weasley child to receive that honor. OP 9, pp. 161-162, 169. Ron also tried out for and made the position of keeper of the Gryffindor quidditch team that year. He beat out Vicky Frobisher and Geoffrey Hooper. OP 13, p. 275. The following year he beat out Cormac McLaggen for the position of keeper. HP 11, p. 226. After Gryffindor's quidditch match against Syltherin, Ron was observed kissing Lavender Brown. HP 14, p. 300. Lavender's pet name for Ron was "Won-Won." HP 17, p. 351. Ron's birthday was in March. HP 17, p. 354. DH 4, p. 45. At the beginning of year seven, Ron, who had taken Polyjuice Potion to look like Harry, was escorted by Nymphadora Tonks on a broomstick from the Dursley residence. DH 4, p. 53. Ron's middle name, Bilius, was not revealed until year seven. DH 7, p. 125. Ron's patronus took the form of a silver terrier. DH 32, p. 649.

Weasley, Rose. The daughter of Ron and Hermione Weasley. Rose's younger brother was Hugo. DH Epilogue, p. 755.

Weasley, Victoire. The daughter, presumably, of Bill and Fleur Weasley. She attended Hogwarts nineteen years after the concluding events of year seven. Victoire was observed kissing Teddy Lupin. DH Epilogue, p. 756.

Weasleys' Wildfire Whiz-Bangs. Magical Fireworks that Fred and George Weasley invented during Harry Potter's fifth year at Hogwarts. They included Basic Blaze box for five galleons, and Deflagration Deluxe, for twenty galleons. OP 28, p. 634.

Weasleys' Wizard Wheezes. The name given by Fred and George Weasley to a collection of joke devices including fake wands and trick candies that they invented and hoped to sell. Harry Potter was first introduced to the collection during the summer prior to his fourth year at Hogwarts. GF 5, pp. 54-55. Fred and George gave an enormous box of the devices to Harry as a seventeenth birthday present during year seven. DH 7, p. 114.

Weasleys' Wizarding Wheezes. The name of the joke and gag shop that Fred and George Weasley vowed to open at Number Ninety-three, Diagon Alley. This event occurred during Harry Potter's fifth year at Hogwarts. OP 29, p. 675. The shop was also referred to as Weasleys' Wizard Wheezes. HP 6, p. 128.

Weighing of the Wands Ceremony. A ceremony held as part of the Triwizard Tournament hosted by Hogwarts. Mr. Ollivander was the official for the ceremony and he inspected and weighed each wand that the school champions intended to use in the first task of the tournament. Fleur Delacour's wand was made of rosewood and contained a strand of hair from the head of a veela. Cedric Diggory's wand was made of ash and contained a single hair from the tail of a fine male unicorn. Viktor Krum's wand was a Gregorovitch creation and contained a hornbeam and dragon heartstring. Harry Potter's wand was made of holly and contained one feather from the tail of a phoenix. GF 18, pp. 307-10.

Weird Sisters. A musical group rumored to be the entertainment for the Yule Ball. This event occurred as part of the Triwizard Tournament held during Harry Potter's fourth year at Hogwarts. GF 22, p. 391. The Weird Sisters' instruments included a set of drums, several guitars, a lute, cello and some bagpipes. GF 23, p. 419. Kirley McCormack was the lead guitarist for The Weird Sisters. QA 7, p. 36. Nymphadora Tonks owned a t-shirt that displayed the name of The Weird Sisters. OP 38, p. 867. During year seven, Ginny Weasley had a poster of the band on her bedroom wall. DH 7, p. 115.

Weird Wizarding Dilemmas and Their Solutions. The title of a book that Hermione Granger consulted in order to help Harry Potter find a way to breathe underwater in the second task of the Triwizard

Tournament. One of the charms in the book made a person's nose hair grow into ringlets. This event occurred during Harry's fourth year at Hogwarts. GF 26, p. 487.

Wellington Boots. Boots placed outside the front door of the Burrow. Crookshanks chased gnomes into the boots during the summer prior to Harry Potter's fourth year at Hogwarts. GF 5, p. 60. DH 6, p. 106.

Wellington. The location in New Zealand where the New Zealand Ministry of Magic was located. QA 8, p. 41. (Wellington is a seaport in and the capital of New Zealand.)

Wendelin the Weird. A witch who lived during the fourteenth century and who enjoyed being burned so much that she allowed herself to be caught forty-seven times in various disguises. Harry Potter learned that information while working on a homework assignment prior to his third year at Hogwarts. PA 1, p. 2.

Werewolf. An animal that Gilderoy Lockhart claimed in one of his books to have been cornered in a telephone booth. CS 6, p. 94. Gilderoy also had Harry Potter act like a werewolf during a Defense Against the Dark Arts class to demonstrate how Lockhart had turned the creature back into a man using a complex Homorphus Charm. CS 10, p. 161. When Remus Lupin became ill and could not teach his Defense Against the Dark Arts class, Severus Snape substituted and began to teach the class about werewolves. PA 9, p. 171. Students at Hogwarts did not study the werewolf until their third year. PA 9, p. 171. These events occurred during Harry's third year at Hogwarts. Werewolves originated in Northern Europe but were found worldwide. FB, pp. 41-42. Most werewolves were loyal to Lord Voldemort because they thought their life would be better under his control of the wizarding world. Fenrir Greyback was the most savage werewolf of his time. He attacked Remus Lupin when Remus was a child and made Remus into a werewolf. HP 16, pp. 334-35. According to Madam Pomfrey there was no cure for a werewolf bite. If a werewolf attacked a person at a time other than full moon, the victim did not become a full werewolf but stood the chance of having some werewolf characteristics. HP 29, p. 613. Werewolves did not normally breed. DH 11, p. 213.

Werewolf Capture Unit. A special unit in the Beast Division. FB, p. xiii.

Werewolf Code of Conduct. A code of conduct that was approved in 1637. SS 16, p. 263. The code was included on the final exam in the History of Magic class during Harry Potter's first year at Hogwarts. SS 16, p. 263.

Werewolf Registry of 1947. A registry to keep track of werewolves that was created by Newt Scamander. The register was maintained by the Beast Division. FB, pp. vi, xiii.

Werewolf Support Services, Office of. An office in the Being Division. FB, p. xiii.

West Country. That portion of England in which an unforseeable freak hurricane occurred the summer prior to Harry Potter's sixth year at Hogwarts. The precise location of the hurricane, caused by giants and Death Eaters, was Somerset. HP 1, pp. 2, 13. One of the villages in the West Country was Godric's Hollow. DH 16, p. 319.

West Ham. A location that had a famous soccer team. Dean Thomas had a poster of the West Ham team hanging in his Gryffindor tower bedroom. This event occurred during Harry Potter's first year at Hogwarts. SS 9, p. 144. During Harry's fourth year at Hogwarts, Ron Weasley noticed that the soccer players were stationary in the poster. GF 12, p. 191. During Harry's fifth year at Hogwarts, Dean Thomas had a pair of pajamas in the West Ham colors. OP 11, p. 216.

West Tower. The name for one of the towers of Hogwarts. PA 21, p. 393. The Owlery was located at the top of the West Tower. GF 15, p. 229.

Whalley, Eric. A child who was an orphan at the same London orphanage where Tom Riddle lived during his childhood. The orphanage was operated by Mrs. Cole. Other orphans there were Billy Stubbs, Amy Benson and Dennis Bishop. HP 13, pp. 264, 268.

Where There's a Wand There's a Way. The title of a book that Harry Potter consulted in order to find a way to breathe underwater in the second task of the Triwizard Tournament. This event occurred during Harry's fourth year at Hogwarts. GF 26, p. 488.

Which Broomstick. The title of a book that Harry Potter borrowed from Oliver Wood for the Christmas vacation during Harry's third year at Hogwarts. PA 10, p. 190. The editor of *Which Broomstick* was quoted as giving praise to *Quidditch Through the Ages*. QA, p. iv. During the summer prior to Harry's fifth year at the school, *Which Broomstick* reported that the Comet Two Sixty was capable of accelerating from zero to sixty in ten seconds with a decent tailwind. OP 9, p. 170.

Whisp, Kennilworthy. The author of *Quidditch Through the Ages*. QA, p. iii; FB, p. 39, fn. 13. Whisp was a renowned quidditch expert and author of several other books on the subject: *Beating the Bludgers - A Study of Defensive Strategies in Quidditch*; *He Flew Like a Madman*; and *Wonder of Wigtown Wanderers, The*. Whisp lived in Nottinghamshire and was a devoted fan of the Wigtown Wanderers. His hobbies included backgammon, vegetarian cookery and collecting vintage broomsticks. QA, p. v.

Whitby, Kevin. The last student who was sorted by the Sorting Hat during Harry Potter's fourth year at Hogwarts. Kevin was a member of the Hufflepuff house. GF 12, p. 180.

Whizz Hard Books. A publisher of books in the wizarding world with an address of 129B Diagon Alley, London. Whizz Hard Books published *Quidditch Through the Ages*. QA, p. iii; FB, p. 39, fn. 13. The company also published *Hairy Snout, Human Heart* by an anonymous author in 1975. FB, p. 41, fn. 16.

Whizzing Worms. A joke device sold in Zonko's Joke Shop in Hogsmeade. Harry Potter and Ron Weasley purchased Whizzing Worms during Harry's third year at Hogwarts. PA 8, p. 153.

Whomping Willow. A magic willow tree on the grounds of Hogwarts that attacked people with its branches when approached. Ron Weasley crashed Arthur Weasley's Ford Anglia into the tree at the beginning of Harry Potter's second year at Hogwarts. CS 5, pp. 73, 79. The reason why the Whomping Willow was planted was revealed to Harry the following school year. PA 18, p. 353. DH 32, p. 650.

Why I Didn't Die When the Augurey Cried. The title of a book written by Gulliver Pokeby. The book was published by Little Red Books in 1824. FB, p. 3, fn. 4.

Widdershins, Willy. A wizard who was arrested by the Ministry of Magic for jinxing muggle toilets so that they regurgitated their contents. Willy was later acquitted of the charge, but then was caught selling biting doorknobs to muggles. He was present at the Hogs' Head when Harry Potter and other students met to discuss formation of Dumbledore's Army. These events occurred during Harry's fifth year at Hogwarts. OP 22, p. 489; 27, p. 613.

Wigtown. The location that had a quidditch team known as the Wigtown Wanderers. Kennilworthy Whisp wrote a book about Wigtown's team titled *The Wonder of Wigtown*. QA, p. v. (Wigtown is an historic county in Southwest Scotland.)

Wigtown Wanderers. A quidditch team from Wigtown. Kennilworthy Whisp wrote a book about the Wigtown Wanderers titled *The Wonder of Wigtown*. QA, p. v. The club was formed in 1422 by the seven children of Walter Parkin, who was a wizarding butcher. QA 7, p. 37. The Parkin's Pincer, a quidditch move, was named after one of its original players. QA 10, p. 53.

Wigworthy, Wilhelm. The author of *Home Life and Social Habits of British Muggles*. The book was published by Little Red Books in 1987. FB, p. 7, fn. 6.

Wilkins, Wendell and Monica. During year seven, Hermione Granger modified her parents memories so that they believed their names were Wendell and Monica Wilkins. They moved to Australia not realizing that they even had a daughter. DH 6, p. 96.

Wilkes. A wizard who was a Death Eater. Wilkes was killed by an auror during the year prior to the fall of Lord Voldemort. Sirius Black explained this event to Harry Potter during Harry's fourth year at Hogwarts. GF 27, p. 531.

Williamson. A wizard who was present in the Atrium of the Ministry of Magic during the fight between Albus Dumbledore and Lord Voldemort. Williamson witnessed Lord Voldemort grab Bellatrix Lestrange and then disapparate. Williamson was an auror for the Minstry of Magic. This event occurred during Harry Potter's fifth year at Hogwarts. OP 36, p. 817.

Wiltshire. The location where the Malfoy family lived in a mansion. OP 15, p. 307. (Wiltshire is a county in Southern England, having Salisbury as its county seat.)

Wimbledon. A location where a regurgitating public toilet was reported to the Ministry of Magic. This event occurred during the summer prior to Harry Potter's fifth year at Hogwarts. OP 7, p. 133. (Wimbledon was a former borough, now part of Merton, in Southeast England, near London.)

Wimbourne Wasps. A quidditch team on which Ludo Bagman played as a beater prior to becoming head of the Department of Magical Games and Sports. GF 7, p. 78. The Wimbourne Wasps won the quidditch league three times in a row while Ludo was the team's beater. GF 9, p. 127. Ludo was a beater for the team. QA, p. iv. The Wimbourne Wasps had a fierce rivalry with the Appleby Arrows. QA 7, p. 32.

Wimple, Gilbert. An employee of the Committee on Experimental Charms. Arthur Weasley pointed out Gilbert to Harry Potter and Hermione Granger at the camp on the grounds of the Quidditch World Cup. This event occurred during the summer prior to Harry's fourth year at Hogwarts. GF 7, p. 86.

Wingardium Leviosa. The magic words used in a charm to make objects fly. Harry Potter experimented with the charm in a Charms class during his first year at Hogwarts. SS 10, pp. 170-171. During year seven, Harry used the charm to try to mend the sidecar attached to Sirius Black's motorcycle. DH 4, p. 58.

Winged Horse. A magical beast found worldwide. The most common breeds of Winged Horse were as follows: Abraxan; Aethonan; Granian; and Thestral. The owner of a Winged Horse was required to keep a Disillusionment Charm on the beast. FB, p. 42.

Winged keys. Magical keys with wings that flew together like a flock of birds. The keys were located in a room with a locked door somewhere beneath the trapdoor on the third floor of Hogwarts. SS 16, p. 280. A big, old-fashioned, silver key unlocked the door. Harry Potter encountered the keys during his first year at Hogwarts. SS 16, p. 280.

Winky. A female house-elf who knew Dobby. Harry Potter met Winky in the Top Box at the Quidditch World Cup during the summer prior to his fourth year at Hogwarts. GF 8, pp. 97-98. Winky's master was Barty Crouch. GF 9, p. 132. Her mother and grandmother had both worked for the Crouches. GF 21, p. 381. After Barty dismissed Winky, she was given a job by Albus Dumbledore and worked in Hogwart's kitchen without pay because she was ashamed to be free. According to Winky, Ludo Bagman was a bad wizard. GF 21, pp. 376, 379, 382.

Wisteria Walk. The street on which Mrs. Figg lived near the Dursley family in Little Whinging. Wisteria Walk ran parallel to Magnolia Crescent and was connected to it by a narrow alleyway. OP 1, pp. 2, 13.

Wistful, Wilfred the. There was a statue of Wilfred the Wistful at Hogwarts. OP 14, p. 281.

Witch Weekly. A magazine sold in the wizarding world. Gilderoy Lockhart claimed that *Witch Weekly* had bestowed the "Most Charming Smile Award" on him five times. CS 6, p. 91. Pansy Parkinson had a copy of *Witch Weekly* in March of Harry Potter's fourth year at Hogwarts. That issue contained a story written by Rita Skeeter who reported that Harry's secret heartache was Hermione Granger. GF 27, pp. 511-12. There were old copies of *Witch Weekly* in the waiting room at St. Mungo's Hospital for Magical Maladies and Injuries. OP 22, p. 484.

***Witch Weekly's* Most-Charming-Smile Award.** An award given by *Witch Weekly* to Gilderoy Lockhart. CS 6, p. 91. Gilderoy claimed to have been awarded it five times. He bragged about the award to his Defense Against the Dark Arts class. This event occurred during Harry Potter's second year at Hogwarts. CS 6, p. 99.

Witching Hour, The. A radio program featuring the singing sorceress, Celestina Warbeck, that played on the radio in the Burrow. Harry Potter heard the program when he visited the Burrow for the first time prior to his second year at Hogwarts. CS 3, p. 34.

Wit-Sharpening Potion. A potion that Harry Potter's class was assigned to work on in a Potions class. Some of the ingredients for the potion were powdered scarab beetles, ginger root and armadillo bile. This event occurred during Harry's fourth year at Hogwarts. GF 27, pp. 513-14, 518.

Wizard Chess. A board game similar to muggle chess, except that the figures were alive. Ron Weasley was accomplished at the game and taught it to Harry Potter over the Christmas holidays. This event occurred during Harry's first year at Hogwarts. SS 12, p. 199.

Wizard Crackers. Fantastic party favors that exploded like cannons when pulled apart and engulfed the person opening them with a cloud of blue smoke. Inside the crackers were such items as a rear admiral's hat and several live, white mice. Wizard crackers were part of the Christmas dinner celebration during Harry Potter's first year at Hogwarts. SS 12, p. 203. See also **Cribbage's Wizarding Crackers**.

Wizard High Court. See **Wizengamot**.

Wizarding Examinations Authority. The organization responsible for conducting O.W.L.s. Griselda Marchbanks was the head of the organization during Harry Potter's fifth year at Hogwarts. OP 31, p. 707.

Wizarding Wireless Network (WWN). A radio network that wizards and witches listened to in the wizarding world. Harry Potter was unfamiliar with the radio network because he didn't have access to it at the Dursley residence. The network was mentioned in connection with the rumor that Albus Dumbledore had booked the Weird Sisters for the Yule Ball. This event occurred during Harry Potter's fourth year at Hogwarts. GF 22, p. 391. DH 22, p. 439.

Wizards' Council. The predecessor entity to the Ministry of Magic. FB, pp. x-xi. In 1269, Barberus Bragge was chief of the council. QA 4, pp. 11-12. During the fourteenth century the Wizards' Council was headed by Burdock Muldoon and then Madame Elfrida Clagg. FB, pp. x-xi; QA 4, p. 14.

Wizengamot. The name for the Wizard High Court in the Ministry of Magic. Albus Dumbledore was demoted from Chief Warlock on the Wizengamot during the summer prior to Harry Potter's fifth year at Hogwarts. OP 5, p. 95. The hearing room of the Wizengamot was the location where the Lestranges were sentenced to life imprisonment in Azkaban. Harry was required to attend a disciplinary hearing of the Wizengamot on August 12 during the summer prior to his fifth year at Hogwarts. OP 8, pp. 137-38. Griselda Marchbanks and Tiberius Ogden resigned from the Wizengamot in protest over the outcome in Harry's case. OP 15, p. 308. DH 2, p. 20. While Albus Dumbledore was a student at Hogwarts, he received the distinction as the British Youth Representative to the Wizengamot. DH 18, p. 353.

Wizengamot Administation Services. An office, incorporated in the Department of Magical Law Enforcement, that was located on level two of the Ministry of Magic. OP 7, p. 130. DH 12, p. 245.

Wizengamot Charter of Rights. The charter of the Wizengamot included a provision giving an accused the right to present witnesses. OP 8, pp. 142-43.

Wolfsbane. Another name for the plant known as aconite or monkshood used in potions. Severus Snape quizzed Harry Potter about the name of the plant during Harry's first Potions class at Hogwarts. SS 8, p. 137-138. See **Aconite**.

Wolfsbane Potion. A potion used to prevent a human being who was a werewolf from turning back into a werewolf. PA 18, p. 353. The potion was invented by Damocles Belby. HP 7, p. 144.

Wonder of Wigtown, The. The title of a book relating to quidditch that was written by Kennilworthy Whisp. QA, p. v.

WonderWitch. A manufacturer of love potions. Weasleys Wizarding Wheezes carried WonderWitch potions during the summer prior to Harry Potter's sixth year at Hogwarts. HP 6, p. 120.

Won-Won. The pet name that Lavender Brown used for Ronald Weasley during Harry Potter's sixth year at Hogwarts. HP 17, p. 351.

Wood, Oliver. The captain and keeper of the Gryffindor house quidditch team during Harry Potter's first year at Hogwarts. That year Wood was a fifth-year student. SS 9, pp. 150-51. He was also the captain during Harry Potter's second and third years at Hogwarts. CS 7, p. 105; PA 8, p. 143. Oliver was seventeen years old and in his final year during Harry Potter's third year at Hogwarts. PA 8, p. 143. The Gryffindor team had lost the quidditch cup every year until that point. PA 8, p. 143. Harry saw Oliver at the Quidditch World Cup and Oliver was pleased to announce that he was signed on to the Puddlemere United Reserve Team. This event occurred during the summer prior to Harry's fourth year at Hogwarts. GF 7, p. 84. Oliver's name was the first to appear on the list of borrowers found inside the cover of *Quidditch Through the Ages*. QA, p. i. DH 30, p. 603.

Woodcroft, Hengist of. See **Hengist of Woodcroft**.

Woollongong Shimmy. A quidditch move that was widely known. It was perfected by the Woollongong Warriors. QA 10, p. 55.

Woollongong Warriors. A quidditch team from Australia. The Warriors dominated the Australia quidditch scene, along with the Thundelarra Thunderers, for over a century. QA 8, p. 42.

Worcestershire. The location where Brother Benedict, a Franciscan monk, lived during the Middle Ages and encountered a talking "ferret" in his Herbe Garden. FB, p. xiv. (Worcestershire is a former county in West Central England and is now part of Hereford and Worcester.)

World Cup. The championship game for quidditch. The new Firebolt was claimed to be the favorite broomstick for the event during Harry Potter's third year at Hogwarts. PA 4, p. 51. The first World Cup was held in 1473. During that particular event all of the seven hundred types of fouls in quidditch were committed. QA 6, p. 28.

Wormtail. A wizard who was responsible, along with three others, for the creation of the Marauder's Map. The other wizards were nicknamed Moony, Padfoot and Prongs. Fred and George Weasley gave the map to Harry Potter as a Christmas present during Harry's third year at Hogwarts. PA 10, pp. 191-94. The identity of the wizards who created the map was revealed later that school year. PA 18, p. 355. During year seven, Wormtail was present at a meeting between Voldemort and Death Eaters that occurred in the Malfoy manor house. DH 1, p. 7.

Wormwood. A substance that when mixed with powered asphodel root made a sleeping potion so powerful that it was known as the Draught of Living Death. Severus Snape quizzed Harry Potter about the substance in Harry's first Potions class. This event occurred during Harry's first year at Hogwarts. SS 8, pp. 137-38.

Worme, Augustus. An employee of Obscurus Books who convinced Newt Scamander to write a book about magical beasts. FB, p. ix.

Worple, Eldred. The author of *Blood Brothers: My Life Amongst the Vampires.* Eldred attended a Christmas party given by Horace Slughorn, who claimed that Eldred was an old student of his, at Hogwarts. Eldred was accompanied to the party by his friend Sanguini. This event occurred during Harry Potter's sixth year at Hogwarts. HP 15, p. 315.

Wrackspurt. An invisible magical beast that, according to Luna Lovegood, floated through your ears and made your mind go fuzzy. HP 7, p. 140. DH 8, p. 149. Xenophilius Lovegood believed that wearing the siphons of a wrackspurt removed all distractions from the immediate area of the wearer. DH 20, p. 404.

Wright, Bowman. A wizard from Godric's Hollow who was a metal-charmer and inventor of the golden snitch. QA 4, p. 14. DH 16, p. 319.

Wronski Defensive Feint. A quidditch play that was a dangerous seeker diversion and flashed in purple in Harry Potter's Omniocular at the Quidditch World Cup that Harry attended during the summer prior to his fourth year at Hogwarts. Viktor Krum executed the play against Aiden Lynch and injured Aiden. GF 8, p. 109.

Wronski Feint.†

A quidditch move that was widely known. The Wronski Feint was named after Josef Wronski. QA 10, p. 55.

Wronski, Josef. The most innovative seeker in history. Josef played quidditch for the Grodzisk Goblins, a team from Poland. QA 8, p. 41.

YAXLEY – ZONKO'S JOKE SHOP

Yaxley. A Death Eater who failed to search for the Dark Lord after he disappeared. Other Death Eaters who failed to do so were: Avery, the Carrows, Greyback and Lucius Malfoy. HP 2, p. 26. During year seven, Yaxley attended a meeting of the Death Eaters and Voldemort at the Malfoy manor house. DH 1, p. 1. He worked at the Ministry of Magic. DH 12, p. 243. Yaxley's fate was revealed at the end of year seven. DH 36, p. 735.

Year with the Yeti. The title of a book written by Gilderoy Lockhart. The book was required for second-year students during Harry Potter's second year at Hogwarts. CS 4, p. 43.

Yeti. A creature who had a head cold that Harry Potter was forced to act like during a Defense Against the Dark Arts class taught by Gilderoy Lockhart. This event occurred during Harry's second year at Hogwarts. CS 10, p. 161. The yeti was also known as Bigfoot and the Abominable Snowman. FB, p. 42.

Yorkshire. A muggle town that reported a downpour of shooting stars on the day Lord Voldemort disappeared. Two other towns that made similar reports were Dundee and Kent. SS 1, p. 6. Two hooded figures in Hog's Head spoke with Yorkshire accents. This event occurred during Harry Potter's fifth year at Hogwarts. OP 16, p. 336. One of the villages in Yorkshire was Upper Flagley. DH 16, p. 319. (Yorkshire is a former county in North England, now part of several counties.)

Youdle, Cyprian. A quidditch referee from Norfolk who died during a friendly quidditch match in 1357. It was believed that Youdle was murdered by a spectator-invoked curse. QA 6, p. 30.

You-Know-Whats. The casual name given to horcruxes by Ronald Weasley during year seven. DH 6, p. 86.

You-Know-Who. A euphemism for Lord Voldemort. SS 1, pp. 5, 11. Another name was "He-Who-Must-Not-Be-Named." The names were used because many witches and wizards were afraid to speak Lord Voldemort's name. SS 5, p. 85. DH 6, p. 91. See **Voldemort, Lord**.

Yule Ball. A formal dance that was a traditional part of the Triwizard Tournament. The Yule Ball occurred on Christmas day during Harry Potter's fourth year at Hogwarts. Only fourth-year and older students were permitted to attend, but they were able to invite a younger student. The Yule Ball was also part of the tradition that school champions had to bring dance partners and open the ball with a dance. GF 22, pp. 386-87. DH 33, p. 679.

Yvonne. A friend of the Dursley family who was unable to watch Harry Potter on Dudley Dursley's eleventh birthday because she was on vacation in Majorca. This event occurred during the summer prior to Harry's first year at Hogwarts. SS 2, pp. 22-23.

Zaire. One of the natural habitats of the Tebo. FB, p. 40. (Zaire is the former name of the Democratic Republic of the Congo.)

Zabini, Blaise. A student who was sorted by the Sorting Hat during Harry Potter's first year at Hogwarts. Blaise was a member of the Slytherin house. SS 7, p. 122. Blaise was one of the privileged students to be invited into Compartment C of the Hogwarts Express to meet Professor Horace Slughorn on the way to Harry Potter's sixth year at Hogwarts. HP 7, p. 143. His mother was married seven times; each of her husbands had died mysteriously and left her mounds of gold. HP 7, p. 145.

Zamojski, Ladislaw. The top chaser of Poland's quidditch team. OP 19, p. 400.

Zeller, Rose. The last student sorted by the Sorting hat at the beginning of Harry Potter's fifth year at Hogwarts. Rose was sorted into the Hufflepuff house. OP 11, p. 208.

Zograf. A member of the Bulgarian National Quidditch Team who was introduced at the Quidditch World Cup that Harry Potter attended during the summer prior to his fourth year at Hogwarts. Zograf was a keeper. The other members of the team were: Dimitrov, Ivanova, Levski, Vulchanov, Volkov and Viktor Krum. GF 8, pp. 104, 109.

Zonko's Joke Shop. A shop that was located in Hogsmeade and that sold such items as Stink Pellets, Belch Powder, Whizzing Worms, Dungbombs, Hiccup Sweets, Frog Spawn Soup and Nose-Biting Teacups. Harry Potter and Ron Weasley ventured into this shop during Harry's third year at Hogwarts. PA 8, pp. 145, 151, 153; PA 14, p. 278. At the Yule Ball the following year, Ludo Bagman promised to get Fred and George Weasley in contact with a couple of his contacts at Zonko's Joke Shop. GF 23, p. 424. During Harry's sixth year at Hogwarts, Zonko's Joke Shop was boarded up and closed. HP 12, p. 243.

APPENDIX – QUICK REFERENCE LISTS

Beasts and Creatures.

There were many unusual animals in the wizarding world that Harry Potter met in his adventures and learned about in his classes at Hogwarts. The following is a list of the assorted magical beasts and creatures found in the wizarding world:

Abominable Snowman. FB, p. 42.
Abraxan. FB, p. 42.
Acromantula. FB, pp. xviii, 1, fn. 1.
Aethonan. FB, p. 42.
Antipodean Opaleye. FB, p. 11.
Aquavirius maggot. OP 34, p. 772.
Ashwinder. FB, p. 2.
Augurey (Irish Phoenix). FB, pp. vii, 2-3.
Bandon Banshee. CS 6, p. 99.
Basilisk. CS 13, p. 247; DH 6, p. 104.
Bicorn. CS 10, p. 165.
Bigfoot. FB, p. 42.
Billiwig. FB, pp. xviii; DH 25, p. 513.
Blast-Ended Skrewt. GF 13, pp. 196-197.
Blibbering Humdinger. OP 13, p. 262.
Blood-Sucking Bugbear. CS 11, p. 201.
Bogart. GF 31, p. 623.
Boomslang. CS 10, p. 165.
Bowtruckle. FB, pp. xvii, 5; DH 28, p. 560.
Bundimun. FB, pp. 5-6.
Centaur. SS 15, pp. 252-253.
Chameleon Ghoul. CS 11, p. 184.
Chimera. FB, p. 6.

Chinese Fireball Dragon. GF 19, pp. 326-327.
Chizpurfle. FB, pp. xviii, 6.
Clabbert. FB, p. 8.
Clauricorn. FB, p. 25.
Cockatrice. GF 15, p. 238.
Common Welsh Green Dragon. SS 14, p. 231.
Cornish Pixie. CS 6, p. 101.
Crumple-Horned Snorkack.OP 13, p. 262; DH 8, p. 149.
Crup. FB, p. 25.
Demiguise. FB, pp. xvii, 9.
Diricawl. FB, pp. xi, 9.
Double-Ended Newt. PA 4, p. 58.
Doxy. FB, p. 10; DH 28, p. 560.
Dragon. SS 6, p. 99; DH 7, p. 120.
Dugbog. FB, p. 15.
Dwarf. CS 13, p. 236.
Erkling. FB, p. 15.
Erumpent. FB, p. 16; DH 20, p. 401.
Fairy. FB, pp. 16-17.
Fire-Crab. GF 24, p. 438.
Flobberworm. PA 6, p. 121.
Freshwater Plimpies. DH 20, p. 402.
Fwooper. FB, p. xi.
Ghoul. CS 3, p. 29; DH 6, p. 98.
Giant. GF 23, p. 430.
Glumbumble. FB, p. 19.
Gnome. CS 3, p. 29.
Goblin. SS 5, p. 63.
Granian. FB, p. 42.
Graphorn. FB, p. 20.
Griffin. FB, p. 20.
Grim. PA 6, p. 107.
Grindylow. PA 8, p. 153.
Gulping Plimpies. HP 20, p. 425.
Hag. SS 5, p. 71.
Half-Giant. GF 23, p. 428.
Hebridean Black Dragon. SS 14, p. 231.
Hinkypuff. PA 15, p. 186.
Hippocampus. FB, pp. 20-21.
Horklump. FB, p. 40.
House-Elf. CS 2, p. 12.
Hungarian Horntail Dragon. GF 19, pp. 326-327.
Imp. FB, p. 22.

Jarvey. FB, pp. xii, 22.
Jobberknoll. FB, pp. 22-23.
Kappa. PA 8, p. 141.
Kelpie. CS 7, p. 114.
Knarl. FB, p. 24.
Kneazle. FB, pp. vi, 24.
Leeches. CS 10, p. 165.
Lethifold. FB, pp. 25.
Lobalug. FB, p. 27.
Loch Ness. FB, pp. xvii, 24.
Mackled Malaclaw. FB, p. 28.
Manticore. PA 11, p. 222.
Merpeople. GF 25, p. 464.
Moke. FB, p. 29; DH 7, p. 120.
Mooncalf. FB, pp. xviii, 29-30.
Murtlap. FB, p. 30.
Nargle. OP 21, p. 452; DH 22, p. 425.
Niffler. GF 27, pp. 542-543.
Nogtail. FB, pp. 30-31.
Norwegian Ridgeback Dragon. SS 14, p. 236.
Nundu. FB, p. 31.
Occamy. FB, p. 31.
Peruvian Vipertooth. FB, pp. 13-14.
Phoenix. CS 12, pp. 205-207.
Pixie. FB, p. 32.
Plimpy. FB, p. 32.
Pogrebin. FB, pp. xix, 33.
Porlock. FB, pp. xi, 33.
Puffskein. FB, pp. vii, 34.
Quintaped. FB, pp. xix, 34-36.
Ramora. FB, p. 36.
Red Cap. PA 8, p. 141; FB, p. 36.
Re'em. FB, p. 36.
Romanian Longhorn. FB, p. 14.
Runespoor. FB, pp. 36-38.
Salamander. FB, p. 38.
Shrake. FB, p. 38.
Snidget, Golden. FB, p. 39; QA 4, p. 10.
Sphinx. GF 31, pp. 628-630.
Squid, Giant. SS 16, p. 263.
Streeler. FB, p. 40.
Swedish Short-Snout Dragon. GF 19, pp. 326-327.
Tebo. FB, p. xvii, 40.

Thestral. FB, p. 42; OP 10, p. 196; DH 4, p. 47.
Troll. SS 10, pp. 172, 174.
Ukranian Ironbelly. FB, p. 14.
Unicorn. SS 15, pp. 250-251; DH 7, p. 120.
Vampire. SS 5, p. 71.
Wagga Wagga Werewolf. CS 10, p. 162.
Werewolf. CS 6, p. 94.
Winged Horse. FB, p. 42.
Wrackspurt. HP 7, p. 140; DH 8, p. 149.
Yeti. CS 10, p. 161.

Books and Publications (by title).

Witches and wizards learned about their world of magic through various printed materials, including books, newspapers and other periodicals. The following is a list of books and other publications in the wizarding world:

Achievements in Charming. OP 31, p. 709.
Advanced Potion-Making. HP 9, p. 183.
Advanced Rune Translation. HP 7, p. 129.
Alas, I've Transfigured My Feet. QA 8, p. 39.
Ancient Runes Made Easy. CS 14, p. 254.
Anthology of Eighteenth-Century Charms, An. GF 26, p. 488.
Appraisal of Magical Education in Europe, An. GF 9, p. 123; DH 6, p. 100.
Armando Dippet: Master or Moron? DH 13, p. 252.
Beating the Bludgers–A Study of Defensive Strategies in Quidditch. QA, p. v.
Beginners' Guide to Transfiguration, A. SS 5, p. 66.
Blood Brothers: My Life Amongst the Vampires. HP 15, p. 315.
Break with a Banshee. CS 4, p. 43; DH 6, p. 100.
Broken Balls: When Fortunes Turn Foul. PA 4, p. 53.
Challenges in Charming. DH 2, p. 17.
Charm to Cure Reluctant Reversers, A. PA 2, p. 27.
Charm Your Own Cheese. CS 3, p. 34.
Common Apparition Mistakes and How to Avoid Them. HP 22, p. 469.
Common Magical Ailments and Afflictions. GF 2, p. 21.
Compendium of Common Curses and Their Counter-Actions. OP 18, p. 390.
Confronting the Faceless. HP 9, p. 177.
Daily Mail. GF 3, p. 26.
Daily Prophet. SS 5, p. 64; DH 1, p. 12.
Dark Arts Outsmarted, The. OP 18, p. 390.
Dark Forces: A Guide to Self-Protection, The. SS 5, p. 66.

Death Omens: What to Do When You Know the Worst is Coming. PA 4, p. 54.

Defensive Magical Theory. OP 17, p. 267; DH 6, p. 100.

Dragon Breeding for Pleasure and Profit. SS 14, p. 233.

Dragon Species of Great Britain and Ireland: From Egg to Inferno, A Dragon Keeper's Guide. SS 14, p. 230.

Dreadful Denizens of the Deep. GF 26, p. 488.

Enchantment in Baking. CS 3, p. 34.

Encyclopedia of Toadstools. CS 4, p. 63.

Evening Prophet. CS 5, p. 79.

Fantastic Beasts and Where to Find Them. SS 5, p. 66; DH 20, p. 401.

Flying with the Cannons. CS 12, p. 212.

Fowl or Foul? A Study of Hippogriff Brutality. PA 15, p. 300.

Gilderoy Lockhart's Guide to Household Pets. CS 3, p. 35.

Great Wizards of the Twentieth Century. SS 12, p. 197.

Great Wizarding Events of the Twentieth Century. SS 6, p. 106.

Guide to Advanced Transfiguration, A. GF 19, p. 340.

Guide to Medieval Sorcery. GF 26, p. 488.

Guidelines for the Treatment of Non-Wizard Part-Humans. GF 10, p. 147.

Hairy Snout, Human Heart. FB, p. 41.

Handbook of Do-It-Yourself Broomcare. PA 1, p. 12.

Handbook of Hippogriff Psychology, The. PA 15, p. 300.

He Flew Like a Madman. QA, p. v.

Healer's Helpmate, The. HP 5, p. 100.

History of Magic, A. SS 5, p. 66; DH 16, p. 318.

Hogwarts, A History. SS 7, p. 117; DH 6, p. 96.

Holidays with Hags. CS 4, p. 43.

Home Life and Social Habits of British Muggles. PA 13, p. 264.

Important Modern Magical Discoveries. SS 12, p. 197.

Intermediate Transfiguration. PA 4, p. 54.

Invisibility Book of Invisibility. PA 4, p. 53.

Jinxes for the Jinxed. OP 18, p. 390.

Madcap Magic for Wacky Warlocks. GF 26, p. 488.

Magical Drafts and Potions. SS 5, p. 66.

Magical Hieroglyphs and Logograms. OP 26, p. 574.

Magical Me. CS 4, p. p. 58.

Magical Theory. SS 5, p. 66.

Magical Water Plants of the Mediterranean. GF 14, p. 220.

Magick Moste Evile. HP 18, p. 381.

Men Who Love Dragons Too Much. GF 19, p. 338.

Modern Magical History. SS 6, p. 106.

Monster Bok of Monsters, The. PA 1, p. 13; DH 6, p. 95.

Most Potente Potions. CS 9, p. 160.

Mudbloods and the Dangers They Pose to a Peaceful Pure-Blood Society. DH 13, p. 249.

Nature's Nobility: A Wizarding Genealogy. OP 6, p. 116***;*** DH 10, p. 190.

New Theory of Numerology. OP 23, p. 503.

Noble Sport of Warlocks, The. QA 6, p. 18.

Notable Magical Names of Our Times. SS 12, p. 197.

Numerology and Gramatica. PA 16, p. 315; DH 6, p. 93.

Olde and Forgotten Bewitchments and Charms. GF 26, p. 486.

One Minute Feasts--It's Magic. CS 3, p. 34.

One Thousand Magical Herbs and Fungi. SS 5, p. 66.

Philosophy of the Mundane: Why The Muggles Prefer Not to Know. FB, p. xvii, fn. 8.

Powers You Never Knew You Had and What To Do with Them Now You've Wised Up. GF 26, p. 488.

Practical Defensive Magic and Its Use Against the Dark Arts. OP 23, p. 501.

Predicting the Unpredictable: Insulate Yourself Against Shocks. PA 4, p. 53.

Prefects Who Gained Powers. CS 4, p. 58.

Practical Potioneer, The. DH 2, p. 17.

Quidditch Teams of Britain And Ireland. GF 23, p. 410; DH 6, p. 94.

Quidditch Through the Ages. SS 9, p. 144.

Quintessence: A Quest. HP 15, p. 304.

Rise and Fall of the Dark Arts, The. SS 6, p. 106; DH 6, p. 93.

Saucy Tricks for Tricky Sorts. GF 26, p. 486.

Secrets of the Darkest Art. DH 6, p. 102.

Self-Defensive Spellwork. OP 18, p. 390.

Sites of Historical Sorcery. PA 5, p. 77.

Sonnets of a Sorcerer. CS 13, p. 231.

Spellman's Syllabary. OP 26, p. 575; DH 6, p. 94.

Standard Book of Spells, Grade 1. SS 5, p. 66.

Standard Book of Spells, Grade 2. CS 4, p. 93.

Standard Book of Spells, Grade Three. PA 4, p. 54.

Standard Book of Spells, Grade 4. GF 10, pp. 152, 155.

Standard Book of Spells, Grade 5, The. P 9, 160.

Standard Book of Spells, Grade Six, The. HP 9, pp. 178-79

Study of Recent Developments in Wizardry. SS 12, p. 197.

Tales of Beedle the Bard, The. DH 7, p. 126.

Theories of Transubstantial Transfiguration. QA, p. viii.

Thousand Magical Herbs and Fungi, A. HP 25, p. 539.

Transfiguration Today. PA 4, p. 49; DH 2, p. 17.

Travels with Trolls. CS 4, p. 43; DH 6, p. 96.
Twelve Fail-Safe Ways to Charm Witches. DH 7, p. 113.
Unfogging the Future. PA 4, p. 53.
Voyages with Vampires. CS 4, p. 43.
Wandering with Werewolves. CS 4, p. 43.
Weird Wizarding Dilemnas and Their Solutions. GF 26, p. 487.
Where There's a Wand There's a Way. GF 26, p. 488.
Why I Didn't Die When the Augurey Cried. FB, p. 3, fn. 4.
Witch Weekly. CS 6, p. 91.

Charms.

One of the skills learned by students at Hogwarts was the conjuring of charms or spells. Charms were cast on muggles, animals, inanimate objects, magical forces and other witches and wizards. The following is a list of charms that were used in the wizarding world:

Accio. GF 6, p. 68; DH 4, p. 61.
Aguamenti Charm. HP 11, p. 218; DH 11, p. 222.
Alohomora. SS 9, p. 160; DH 10, p. 187.
Anapneo. HP 7, p. 144.
Anti-Cheating Charm. OP 31, p. 708.
Aparecium. CS 13, p. 233.
Atmospheric Charm. DH 12, p. 244.
Avada Kedavra. GF 14, p. 215.
Avis. GF 18, pp. 309-10.
Banishing Charm. GF 26, p. 479.
Bubble-Head Charm. GF 26, p. 506.
Caterwauling Charm. DH 28, p. 558.
Cave Inimicum. DH 14, p. 272.
Cheering Charm. PA 15, p. 294.
Colloportus. OP 35, p. 788.
Color-Changing Charm. OP 31, p. 713.
Confringo. DH 4, p. 59.
Confundus Charm. PA 21, p. 386; GF 16, p. 279; DH 1, p. 4.
Cushioning Charm. QA 9, p. 47; DH 26, p. 534.
Defodio. DH 26, p. 542.
Deprimo. DH 21, p. 422.
Descendo. DH 6, p. 97.
Disarming Charm. CS 11, p. 190.
Disillusionment Charm. FB, p. 42; DH 4, p. 45.
Drought Charm. GF 26, p. 486.
Duro. DH 32, p. 643.
Engorgement Charm. CS 7, p. 118; DH 20, p. 392.
Enlargement Charm. OP 26, p. 584.

Erecto. DH 14, p. 273.
Expelliarmus. CS 11, p. 190; DH 4, p. 59.
Expulso. DH 9, p. 165.
Extension Charm. DH 9, p., 162.
Fidelius Charm. PA 10, p. 205; DH 6, p. 90.
Finite. OP 36, p. 808; DH 31, p. 629.
Finite Incantatem. DH 12, p. 244.
Flame Freezing Charm. PA 1, p. 2.
Flying Charm. OP 14, p. 290.
Geminio. DH 13, p. 263.
Glisseo. DH 32, p. 643.
Gripping Charm. QA 6, p. 20.
Growth Charm. OP 31, p. 713.
Hair-Thickening Charm. OP 19, p. 400.
Homenum revelio. DH 9, pp. 171-72.
Homorphus Charm. CS 10, p. 162.
Horton-Keitch Breaking Charm. QA 9, pp. 49-50.
Hover Charm. CS 2, p. 21; DH 17, p. 346.
Impedimenta. HP 26, p. 575.
Imperturbable Charm. OP 4, p. 69.
Impervius Charm. OP 18, p. 379; DH 12, p. 244.
Inanimatus Conjurus. OP 14, p. 289.
Incarcerous. HP 26, p. 575.
Invisibility Spell. OP 24, p. 540.
Intruder Charm. HP 4, p. 67.
Levicorpus. HP 12, p. 239; DH 26, p. 539.
Levitation Charm. OP 31, p. 713.
Liberacorpus. HP 12, p. 239; DH 26, p. 540.
Memory Charm. CS 16, p. 303; DH 9, p. 167.
Meteolojinx, Recanto. DH 13, p. 255.
Muffliato. HP 12, p. 238; DH 7, p. 132.
Muggle Repelling Charm. GF 8, p. 95.
Nox. PA 17, p. 338; DH 32, p. 652.
Obliteration Charm. OP 20, p. 440.
Obscuro. DH 15, p. 301.
Oppugno. HP 14, p. 302.
Patronus Charm. PA 12, p. 237; DH 7, p. 121.
Permanent Sticking Charm. OP 5, p. 79; DH 10, p. 178.
Petrificus Totalus. SS 16, p. 273; DH 9, p. 166.
Piertotum Locomotor. DH 30, p. 602.
Placement Charm. FB, p. 23.
Portus. OP 22, p. 472.
Prior Incantato. GF 9, pp. 135-136.

Priori Incantatem. DH 24, p. 496.
Protean Charm. OP 19, p. 398.
Protego. DH 26, p. 535.
Protego Horribilis. DH 30, p. 600.
Protego Totalum. DH 14, p. 272.
Quietus. GF 8, p. 116.
Reducio. DH 20, p. 392.
Refilling Charm. HP 22, p. 487.
Relashio. GF 26, p. 496; DH 13, p. 263.
Rennervate. HP 26, p. 574.
Repelling Spells. QA 4, p. 12.
Repello Muggletum. DH 14, p. 272.
Salvio Hexia. DH 14, p. 272.
Scouring Charm. GF 14, p. 209; FB, p. 6.
Sectumsempra. HP 21, p. 447; DH 5, p. 73.
Severing Charm. GF 23, p. 411; DH 17, p. 346.
Shield Charm. GF 31, p. 608; OP 25, p. 553; DH 26, p. 535.
Silencing Charm. FB, p. 18.
Stealth Sensoring Spell. OP 32, p. 741.
Stunning Charm. GF 19, p. 326; DH 4, p. 57.
Stupefying Charm. FB, p. 26; DH 4, p. 56.
Substantive Charm. OP 31, p. 710.
Summoning Charm. GF 6, p. 68; GF 11, p. 167.
Supersensory Charm. DH Epilogue, p. 755.
Tergeo. HP 8, p. 162; DH 6, p. 94.
Tickling Charm. CS 11, p. 192.
Trace Charm. DH 4, pp. 46-47.
Unbreakable Charm. GF 37, p. 728.
Waddiwasi. PA 7, p. 131.

Countries and Exotic Locations.

The wizarding world known to Harry Potter was located in Great Britain, but witches and wizards roamed throughout the world. The following is a list of the various countries (excluding Great Britain which has its own list below) and exotic locations that are mentioned in the Harry Potter series:

Africa. GF 10, p. 150.
Albania. CS 18, p. 328; DH 15, p. 288.
America (United States of). GF 7, p. 82.
Andorra. GF 27, p. 556.
Argentina. QA 8, p. 45.
Arjeplog. QA 2, p. 4.
Armenia. CS 16, p. 297.
Asia. QA 8, p. 46.

Atlantic Ocean. QA 9, p. 48.
Australia. GF 5, p. 62; DH 6, p. 96.
Azkaban. CS 12, p. 224.
Bangladesh. QA 8, p. 46.
Black Forest. SS 5, p. 71.
Black Sea. FB, p. 15.
Borneo. FB, pp. xviii.
Brazil. GF 7, p. 84.
Bulgaria. GF 3, p. 35.
Burkins Faso. FB, pp. 36-38.
Cairo. DH 18, p. 353.
Canada. QA 8, p. 43.
Canary Islands. HP 4, p. 68.
China. FB, pp. 11-12, 32.
Congo. FB, p. 40.
Cork. QA 8, p. 38.
Dijon. OP 20, p. 426.
Egypt. CS 12, p. 211.
Ethiopia. QA 8, p. 43.
Far East. FB, p. 9.
Fiji. FB, p. 17.
Flanders. QA 9, pp. 39-40.
France. QA 8, p. 40; DH 5, p. 82.
Germany. FB, p. 5; QA 1, p. 2.
Greece. FB, 3.
Greenland. OP 5, p. 80.
India. FB, p. 31; QA 8, p. 46.
Indian Ocean. FB, p. 36.
Iran. QA 8, p. 46.
Ireland. GF 3, p. 35.
Japan. FB, p. 23; QA 8, p. 46.
Kopparberg. QA 2, p. 4.
Lake Windermere. DH 2, p. 24.
Liechtenstein. OP 31, p. 725.
Lithuania. QA 8, p. 46.
Luxembourg. GF 5, p. 63; QA 8, p. 41.
Majorca. SS 2, pp. 22-23.
Massachusetts. QA 8, p. 45.
Mauritius. FB, p. 9.
Mediterranean Sea. FB, p. 21.
Minsk. OP 20, p. 426.
Mongolia. PA 9, p. 172.
Mykonos. QA 7, p. 33.

New Guinea. FB, pp. 26-27.
New Zealand. FB, p. 11.
North Sea. FB, p. 27; HP 1, p. 8.
Northern Ireland. QA 7, p. 32.
Norway. GF 5, p. 64.
Ouagadogou. CS 9, p. 142.
Pacific Ocean. FB, p. 38.
Pakistan. QA 8, p. 46.
Papua, New Guinea. FB, pp. 26-27.
Paris. GF 8, p. 96.
Peru. GF 5, p. 63.
Poland. QA 8, p. 41.
Portugal. QA 8, p. 41.
Quiberon. QA 8, p. 40.
Romania. SS 8, p. 134.
Russia. FB, pp. 30-31, 33.
Sahara Desert. SS 11, p. 181.
Salem. GF 7, p. 82.
Scandinavia. FB, p. 5.
South America. QA 8, p. 45.
Sweden. QA 2, p. 4.
Tarapoto. QA 8, p. 46.
Togo. QA 8, p. 43.
Transylvania. GF 5, p. 63; DH 26, p. 528.
Turkey. GF 30, p. 93.
Tanzania. QA 8, p. 43.
Texas. QA 8, p. 44.
Tibet. FB, p. xvii.
Uganda. GF 5, p. 63.
Wellington. QA 8, p. 41.
Zaire. FB, p. 40.

Currency.

Witches and wizards purchased everything from food and candy to ingredients for potions and magical paraphernalia in the wizarding world with a form of currency that was different than those used in the muggle world. The following coins were used as currency in the wizarding world:

Knut (Bronze)29 Knuts = 1 Sickle.
Sickle (Silver)17 Sickles = 1 Galleon.
Galleon (Gold). SS 5, pp. 62, 75.

Curses.

Curses were sometimes invoked by witches and wizards to inflict harm on or to direct the actions of another person. Some curses were prohibited under wizarding law because of the severity of the injuries they caused. The following is a list of the curses that were used in the wizarding world:

Babbling Curse. CS 10, p. 161.
Body-Bind Curse. SS 16, p. 273; DH 8, p. 138.
Confundus Curse. PA 21, p. 386.
Conjunctivitus Curse. GF 23, p. 406.
Cruciatus Curse. GF 14, p. 214.
Curse of the Bogies. SS 9, p. 157.
Entrail-Expelling Curse. OP 22, p. 487.
Fiendfyre. DH 31, p. 635.
Flagrante Curse. DH 26, p. 537.
Gemino Curse. DH 26, p. 537.
Impediment Curse.GF 31, pp. 626, 631.
Impediment Jinx. OP 19, p. 397; DH 4, p. 58.
Imperius Curse. GF 14, p. 217; DH 1, p. 5.
Killing Curse. GF 14, p. 217; DH 4, p. 57.
Langlock Hex. HP 19, p. 420.
Petrification Curse. CS 16, p. 291.
Reducto. HP 27, p. 594.
Reductor Curse. GF 31, pp. 608, 626; OP 19, p. 397.
Revulsion Jinx. DH 14, p. 271.
Stinging Hex. OP 24, p. 534.
Stinging Jinx. DH 23, p. 458.
Stretching Jinx. HP 5, p. 83.
Thief's Curse. FB, p. viii; QA, p. viii.
Tongue-Tying Curse. DH 9, p. 170.
Trip Jinx. OP 27, p. 609.
Unforgivable Curses. GF 14, p. 217.

Food and Candy.

Witches and Wizards eat some unusual foods and beverages. They also enjoyed a variety of sweets, both as dessert and as candy treats at any time. The following is a list of the various kinds of foods, beverages and candies that Harry Potter was familiar with in the wizarding world:

Acid Pops. PA 10, p. 200.
Babbling Beverage. OP 32, p. 746.
Bath Buns. PA 14, p. 273.
Bertie Botts' Every Flavor Beans. SS 6, p. 101; DH 21, p. 406.
Butterbeer. PA 8, p. 158; DH 8, p. 146.
Canary Creams. GF 21, p. 366.

Cauldron Cakes. SS 6, p. 101.
Chipolatas. PA 11, p. 230.
Chocoballs. PA 5, p. 77.
Chocolate Frogs. SS 6, pp. 101-102; DH 2, p. 24.
Cockroach Clusters. PA 10, p. 197.
Drooble's Best Blowing Gum. SS 6, p. 101.
Every Flavor Beans. DH 21, p. 406.
Fainting Fancies. OP 6, p. 104.
Firewhisky. OP 31, p. 708; DH 5, p. 79.
Fizzing Whizbees. PA 10, p. 197.
Fudge Flies. PA 13, p. 265.
Ginger Newt. OP 12, p. 248.
Ice Mice. PA 10, p. 197.
Jelly Slugs. PA 10, p. 196.
Lemon Drops. SS 1, p. 10.
Licorice Wands. SS 6, p. 101.
Mars Bars. SS 6, p. 101.
Nosebleed Nougat. OP 6, p. 104.
Ogden's Old Firewhisky. CS 6, p. 100.
Owl Treats. GF 10, p. 155.
Pear Drop. GF 29, p. 579.
Pepper Imps. PA 5, p. 77.
Peppermint Toads. PA 11, p. 213.
Puking Pastilles. OP 6, p. 104; DH 12, p. 235.
Pumpkin Pastries. SS 6, p. 101.
Rock Cakes. SS 8, p. 140.
Skiving Snackboxes. OP 6, p. 104.
Sugar Quill. GF 29, p. 579.
Toothflossing Stringmints. PA 10, p. 190.
Treacle Fudge. CS 7, p. 115.

Great Britain Locations.

All of the action in the first four books of the Harry Potter series occurs in Great Britain. Many of the places actually exist. The following is a list of the places in Great Britain that appear in the entire series (fictitious places are presented in italics):

Aberdeen. PA 3, p. 41.
Abergavenny. PA 3, p. 36.
Anglesea. PA 3, p. 41.
Argyllshire. PA 9, p. 165.
Axminster. GF 7, p. 91.
Arbroath. QA 1, p. 2.
Barnsley. OP 1, p. 4.

Barnton. QA 6, p. 19.
Bath. CS 13, p. 231.
Bethnal Green. OP 7, p. 133.
Birmingham. OP 24, p. 525.
Blackpool. SS 7, p. 125.
Bodmin Moor. QA 6, p. 23.
Bottom Bridge. DH 20, p. 404.
Bristol. SS 1, p. 15.
Budleigh Babberton. HP 4, p. 59.
Clapham. OP 14, p. 287.
Cokeworth. SS 3, p. 42.
Cornwall. FB, p. 32; DH 16, p. 319.
Devon. SS 13, p. 220.
Didsbury. CS 8, p. 127.
Dorset. FB, pp. vi, 33.
Downing Street. DH 5, p. 77.
Drear, Isle of. FB, pp. 34-36.
Dundee. SS 1, p. 6.
Elephant and Castle. OP 7, p. 133; HP 5, p. 87.
Forest of Dean. DH 19, p. 364.
Gaddley. DH 22, p. 439.
Godric's Hollow. SS 1, p. 12.
Great Hangleton. GF 1, p. 3.
Herefordshire. QA 2, p. 6.
Hogsmeade. PA 1, p. 14; DH 15, p. 305.
Ilfracombe. FB, pp. xvi, 12.
Isle of Skye. QA 7, p. 36.
Isle of Wright. SS 3, p. 34.
Kent. SS 1, p. 6.
King's Cross. SS 5, p. 87; DH 35, p. 712.
Lancashire. QA 8, p. 38.
Little Hangleton. GF 1, p. 1; DH 35, p. 721.
Little Norton. OP 10, p. 191.
Little Whinging. SS 3, p. 34.
London. SS 3, p. 32; DH 27, p. 544.
Montrose. QA 1, p. 2.
Mould-on-the-Wold. DH 11, p. 217.
Norfolk. CS 5, p. 79.
Nottingham. OP 5, p. 85.
Nottinghamshire. QA, p. v.
Ottery, St. Catchpole. CS 3, p. 31; DH 16, p. 319.
Paisley. OP 26, p. 579.
Portsmouth. QA 9, p. 47.

Queerditch Marsh. QA 1, p. 6.
Scotland. GF 5, p. 63; DH 16, p. 315.
Somerset. QA 4, p. 14; HP 1, p.13.
Spinner's End. HP 2, p. 21; DH 33, p. 665.
Stoatshead Hill. GF 6, p. 70.
Surrey. SS 3, p. 34; OP 1, p. 4.
***Tinworth,* Cornwall.** DH 16, pp. 318-319.
Topsham. CS 8, p. 127.
Tottenham Court Road. DH 9, p. 161.
Tutshill. QA 7, p. 37.
***Upper Flagley,* Yorkshire.** DH 16, p. 319.
Vauxhall (Road). CS 13, p. 231.
Wales. PA 3, p. 36; DH 15, p. 292.
West Country. HP 1, p. 2; DH 16, p. 319.
West Ham. SS 8, p. 144.
Wigtown. QA, p. v.
Wiltshire. OP 15, p. 307.
Wimbledon. OP 7, p. 133.
Worcestershire. FB, p. xiv.
Yorkshire. SS 1, p. 6; DH 16, p. 319.

Hogwarts School of Witchcraft and Wizardry - House Rosters.

There were four houses at Hogwarts where the students studied, socialized and slept. The following is a list of the students in each of the four houses at Hogwarts who attended the school at the same time as Harry Potter and before. There are a few students whose membership in a house was not identified; those students are listed at the end.

Gryffindor

Abercrombie, Euan. OP 11, pp. 207-208.
Bell, Katie. SS 11, p. 186.
Brown, Lavender. SS 7, p. 119.
Coote, Ritchie. HP 11, p. 225.
Creevy, Colin. CS 6, p. 96.
Creevy, Dennis. GF 12, p. 174.
Finnegan, Seamus. SS 7, p. 120.
Frobisher, Vicky. OP 13, p. 276.
Granger, Hermione. SS 6, pp. 105-106.
Hooper, Geoffrey. OP 13, p. 276.
Johnson, Angelina. SS 1, p. 185.
Jordan, Lee. SS 6, p. 94.
Kirke, Andrew. OP 21, p. 453.
Longbottom, Neville. SS 7, p. 120.
McDonald, Natalie. GF 12, p. 180.

McLaggen, Cormac. HP 7, p. 143.
Patil, Parvati. SS 7, p. 121.
Peakes, Jimmy. HP 11, p. 225.
Potter, Harry. SS 7, p. 121.
Robins, Demelza. HP 11, p. 224.
Sloper, Jack. OP 21, p. 453.
Spinnet, Alicia. SS 11, p. 186.
Thomas, Dean. SS 7, p. 122.
Weasley, Fred. SS 6, p. 99.
Weasley, George. SS 6, p. 99.
Weasley, Ginny. CS 5, p. 82.
Weasley, Percy. SS 6, p. 99.
Weasley, Ron. SS 6, p. 93.
Wood, Oliver. SS 9, pp. 150-151.

Hufflepuff:

Abbot, Hannah. GF 13, 195.
Bones, Susan. SS 7, p. 119.
Branstone, Eleanor. GF 12, p. 178.
Cadwallader. HP 19, p. 414.
Cauldwell, Owen. GF 12, p. 179.
Diggory, Cedric. PA 9, p. 168.
Finch-Fletchley, Justin. SS 7, p. 120.
Lovegood, Luna. OP 10, pp. 185-186.
MacMillan, Ernie. CS 11, pp. 198-200.
Madley, Laura. GF 12, p. 178.
Smith, Zacharias. OP 16, pp. 338, 340.
Stebbins, Mr. GF 23, p. 426.
Summerby. OP 26, p. 575.
Summers, Mr. GF 16, p. 260.
Whitby, Kevin. GF 12, p. 180.
Zeller, Rose. OP 11, p. 208.

Ravenclaw:

Ackerly, Stewart. GF 12, p. 178.
Belby, Marcus. HP 7, p. 143.
Boot, Terry. SS 7, p. 119.
Brocklehurst, Mandy. SS 7, p. 119.
Carmichael, Eddie. OP 31, p. 708.
Chambers. OP 31, p. 704.
Chang, Cho. PA 13, p. 254.
Clearwater, Penelope. CS 12, p. 219.
Corner, Michael. OP 16, p. 338.
Davies, Roger. PA 13, p. 259.
Fawcett, Miss. CS 11, p. 192.

Goldstein, Anthony. OP 10, p. 189.
Patil, Padma. SS 7, p. 121.
Quirke, Orla. GF 12, p. 180.
Turpin, Lisa. SS 7, p. 122.
Bradley. OP 30, p. 684.
Slytherin:
Avery. DH 33, p. 673.
Baddick, Malcolm. GF 12, p. 178.
Bletchley, Miles. OP 19, p. 400.
Bole. PA 15, p. 308.
Bulstrode, Millicent. SS 7, p. 119.
Crabbe, Vincent. SS 6, p. 108.
Derrick. PA 15, p. 308.
Flint, Marcus. SS 10, p. 185.
Goyle, Gregory. SS 6, p. 108.
Harper. HP 14, p. 296.
Higgs, Terence. SS 11, p. 187.
Malfoy, Draco. SS 5, p. 77.
Montague. PA 15, pp. 306-307.
Mulciber. DH 33, p. 673.
Parkinson, Pansy. SS 7, p. 121.
Pritchard, Graham. GF 12, p. 180.
Pusey, Adrian. SS 11, p. 186.
Riddle, Tom. HP 17, p. 360.
Snape, Severus. DH 33, p. 673.
Urquhart. HP 14, p. 295.
Vaisey. HP 14, p. 294.
Zabini, Blaise. SS 7, p. 122.
Other Students:
Aubrey, Bretram. HP 24, p. 532.
Bobbin, Melinda. HP 11, p. 233.
Bundy, K. QA, p. i.
Capper, S. QA, p. i.
Dawlish. OP 27, p. 620.
Derek. PA 11, p. 230.
Dingle, Harold. OP 31, p. 708.
Dobbs, Emma. GF 12, p. 179.
Doge, Elphia. DH 2, p. 16.
Dorney, J. QA, p. i.
Dumbledore, Albus. DH 2, p. 16.
Dunstan, B. QA, p. i.
Edgecombe, Marietta. OP 27, p. 612.
(Evans) Potter , Lilly. OP 28, p. 547.

Goldstein, Anthony. OP 10, p. 188.
Greengrass, Daphne. OP 31, p. 713.
Macdonald, Mary. DH 33, p. 673.
MacDougal, Morag. SS 7, p. 120.
Nott, Theodore. SS 7, p. 121; OP 26, p. 583.
Prince, Eileen. HP 25, p. 537.
Stebbins. OP 28, p. 642.
Stimpson, Patricia. OP 12, p. 226.
Towler, Kenneth. OP 12, p. 226.
Vane, Romilda. HP 7, p. 138.

Hogwarts School of Witchcraft and Wizardry - Professors and Staff. There were many professors who taught the magical arts and classes at Hogwarts. An assorted team of staff persons was also necessary to operate the school. The following is a list of the witches and wizards who were professors or staff at Hogwarts prior to and during the time that Harry Potter attended Hogwarts:

Binns, Professor. History of Magic. SS 8, p. p. 133; DH 21, p. 415.
Black, Phineas Nigellus. Head Master. HP 13, p. 259.
Bloody Baron. Slytherin House Ghost. SS 7, p. 124.
Burbage, Charity. Muggle Studies. DH 1, p. 11.
Cadogan, Sir. Painting Ghost. PA 6, pp. 99-101.
Carrow, Alecto. Muggle Studies. DH 12, p. 226.
Carrow, Amycus. Defense against the Dark Arts. DH 12, p. 226.
Delaney-Podmore, Sir Patrick (a.k.a. Nearly Headless Nick). Gryffindor House Ghost. CS 8, p. 124.
Derwent, Dilys. Headmaster. OP 22, pp. 468-469, 485.
Dippet, Armando. Headmaster. CS 13, pp. 241.
Dobby. Liberated house-elf; Kitchen Staff person. GF 21, p. 375.
Dumbledore, Albus. Headmaster; Fmr. Transfiguration Professor. SS 1, p. 8; CS 17, p. 313.
Everard. Headmaster. OP 22, pp. 468-469.
Fat Friar. Hufflepuff House Ghost. SS 7, p. 115
Fat Lady. Painting Ghost. SS 7, p. 129.
Filch, Argus. Caretaker and custodian. SS 7, p. 127.
Firenze. Divination. OP 26, p. 598.
Flitwick, Professor (Filius). Charms. SS 8, p. 133.
Grubbly-Plank, Professor. Care of Magical Creatures. GF 4, p. 435.
Gryffindor, Godric. Cofounder of Hogwarts. CS 9, p. 150.
Hagrid, Rubeus. Keeper of Keys and Grounds; Care of Magical Creatures Prof. SS 4, p. 48; PA 5, p. 93.
Hooch, Madam. Broomstick lessons; Quidditch Match Referee. SS 7, p. 127; SS 9, p. 146.

Hufflepuff, Helga. Cofounder of Hogwarts. CS 9, p. 150.

Kettleburn, Professor. Care of Magical Creatures. PA 5, p. 93.

Lockhart, Gilderoy. Defense Against the Dark Arts. CS 4, p. 60.

Longbottom, Neville. Herbology. DH Epilogue, p. 757.

Lupin, Remus J. Defense Against the Dark Arts. PA 5, p. 74.

Malfoy, Lucius. Governor of Hogwarts. CS 12, p. 221.

McGonagell, Minerva. Deputy Headmistress; Transfiguration.SS 4, p. 51.

Merrythought, Galatea. Defense Against the Dark Arts. HP 17, p. 368; 20, p. 432.

Moody, Alastor "Mad-Eye." Defense Against the Dark Arts. GF 12, pp. 184-186.

Myrtle, Moaning. Ghost of First Floor Girls' Bathroom. CS 8, p. 132.

Nigellus, Phineas (Black). Headmaster. OP 6, p. 113.

Norris, Mrs. Pet cat of Argus Filch. SS 8, p 132.

Ogg. Gamekeeper. GF 31, p. 617.

Peeves the Poltergeist. Resident poltergeist at Hogwarts. SS 7, p. 115, 129.

Pince, Madam. Librarian. SS 12, p. 198.

Pomfrey, Madam. Nurse. SS 1, p. 11.

Pringle, Apollyon. Caretaker. GF 31, p. 616.

Quirrell, Professor. Defense Against the Dark Arts. SS 5, p. 70.

Ravenclaw, Rowena. Cofounder of Hogwarts. CS 9, p. 150.

Sinistra, Professor. Astronomy. CS 11, p. 204.

Slughorn, Horace. Potions. HP 4, pp. 64-66.

Slytherin, Salazar. Cofounder of Hogwarts. CS 9, p. 150.

Snape, Severus. Potions; Defense Against the Dark Arts; Headmaster (year seven). SS7, p.126; HP 8, p. 166; DH 12, p. 226.

Sorting Hat. Sorted Students into Houses. SS 7, pp. 117-119.

Sprout, Pomona. Herbology. SS 8, p. 133; HP 22, p. 479.

Trelawney, Sibyll. Divination. PA 6, p. 101.

Tufty, Professor. O.W.L. Practical Examiner. OP 31, p. 713.

Twycross, Wilkie. Ministry Apparitions . HP 18, p. 382.

Umbridge, Dolores. Defense Against the Dark Arts; Head. OP 11, pp. 211, 624.

Vector, Professor. Arithmancy. PA 12, p. 244.

Violet. Painting ghost. GF 17, p. 273.

Winky. Liberated house-elf; Kitchen staff. GF 21, p. 376.

Hogwarts School of Witchcraft and Wizardry - Subjects of Instruction.

The students at Hogwarts had many subjects to learn before they completed their formal wizarding education. Some subjects were required, while others were elected by each student. The following is a list of the subjects offered to students at Hogwarts or that were other magical arts known in the wizarding world:

Ancient Runes. CS 14, 252.
Arithmancy. CS 14, p. 252.
Astronomy. CS 1, p. 204.
Care of Magical Creatures. CS 8, p. 130.
Charms. SS 8, p. 133.
Crystal Gazing. PA 15, p. 297.
Defense Against the Dark Arts. SS 8, p. 134.
Divination. CS 14, p. 252.
Flying Lessons. CS 9, p. 146.
Heptomology. OP 25, p. 552.
Herbology. CS 6, pp. 91-93
History of Magic. SS 8, p. 133.
Legilimency. OP 24, p. 531.
Magizoology. FB, p. vi.
Muggle Studies. CS 14, p. 252.
Occlumency. OP 24, p. 530.
Ornithomancy. OP 25, p. 552.
Potions. SS 8, p. 133.
Transfiguration. SS 7, p. 125.

Joke and Gag Devices.

Fred and George Weasley frequently pulled practical jokes and gags on their family members and friends. Some of the gags they purchased from shops and others they invented themselves. The following jokes and gag items were mentioned in the Harry Potter series:

Belch Powder. PA 8, p. 153.
Blood Blisterpod. OP 14, p. 293.
Bulbadox Powder. OP 12, p. 226.
Canary Creams. GF 21, p. 366.
Decoy Detonators. HP 6, p. 119; DH 12, p. 236.
Dr. Filibuster's Fabulous Wet-Start No Heat Fireworks. CS 4, p. 58.
Dungbomb. PA 10, p. 191; DH 2, p. 26.
Edible Dark Marks. HP 6, p. 118.
Fever Fudge. OP 18, pp. 378-379.
Filibuster's Fabulous No-Heat, Wet Start Fireworks. GF 11, p. 162.
Frog Spawn Soup. PA 14, p. 278.

Headless Hats. OP 24, p. 540.
Hiccup Sweets. PA 14, p. 278.
Instant Darkness Powder. HP 6, p. 119.
Nosebleed Nougat. OP 6, pp. 104-105; DH 12, p. 236.
Nose-Biting Teacup. PA 14, p. 278.
Patented Daydream Charms. HP 6, p. 117.
Portable Swamp. OP 29, p. 675.
Pygmy Puffs. HP 6, p. 121.
Self-Inking Quill. HP 6, p. 117.
Shrinking Door Key. CS 3, p. 38.
Smart-Answer Quill. HP 6, p. 117.
Spell-Checking Quill. HP 6, p. 117.
Stink Pellets. PA 8, p. 145.
Ton-Tongue Toffee. GF 5, p. 50.
U-No-Poo. HP 6, p. 116.
Weasleys' Wizard Wheezes. GF 5, pp. 54-55; DH 7, p. 114.
Whizzing Worms. PA 8, p. 153.

Laws.

Wizards and witches established their own set of laws and regulations. The following is a list of some of the laws that regulated the actions of witches and wizards in the wizarding world:

Ban on Experimental Breeding. FB, p. vi.
Code of Wand Use. GF 9, p. 132.
Decree for Justifiable Confiscation. DH 7, p. 123.
Decree for the Reasonable Restriction of Underage Wizardry. CS 2, p. 21.
Decree for the Restriction of Underage Wizardry. CS 5, p. 81.
Gamp's Law of Elemental Transfiguration. DH 15, p. 292.
Guidelines for the Treatment of Non-Wizard Part-Humans. GF 10, p. 147.
International Ban on Dueling. GF 23, p. 425.
International Code of Wizarding Secrecy. GF 26, p. 482.
International Confederation of Warlocks' Statute of Secrecy. CS 2, p. 21.
International Statute of Secrecy. DH 2, p. 20.
International Statute of Wizarding Secrecy. QA 1, p. 2.
Law Fifteen B. OP 33, p. 754.
Magical Law (as a profession). DH 7, p. 123.
Muggle Protection Act. CS 4, p. 51.
Principal Exceptions to Gamp's Law of Elemental Transfig. DH 15, p. 292.
Reasonable Restriction of Underage Sorcery. OP 2, p. 21.

Registry of Proscribed Charmable\Objects. GF 7, p. 91.
Statute of Secrecy. OP 2, p. 21; DH 18, p. 357.
Warlocks' Convention of 1709. SS 14, p. 230.
Werewolf Code of Conduct. SS 16, p. 263.
Werewolf Registry of 1947. FB, pp. vi, xii.

Magical Devices and Objects.

In addition to magic wands, witches and wizards used many other devices to perform magic and experience life in the wizarding world. The following is a list of magical devices and objects that appear in the Harry Potter series:

Age Line. GF 16, pp.256, 259.
Auto-Answer Quills. OP 31, pp. 708-709.
Baruffio's Brain Elixir. OP 31, p. 708.
Bezoar. SS 8, pp. 137-138.
Cloak of Invisibility, The. DH 21, p. 409.
Dark Detector. GF 19, pp. 342-343.
Deathly Hallows. DH 20, p. 404.
Deathstick, The. DH 21, p. 415.
Deluminator. DH 7, p. 125.
Detachable Cribbing Cuffs. OP 31, p. 709.
Dr. Ubbly's Oblivious Unction. OP 38, p. 847.
Elder Wand, The. DH 21, p. 409.
Erised, Mirror of. SS 12, p. 207.
Ever-Bashing Boomerang. GF 12, p. 183.
Everlasting Ink. DH 17, p. 333.
Exploding Snap. CS 12, pp. 210-211.
Fanged Frisbee. GF 12, p. 183.
Floo Powder. CS 4, p. 47.
Foe-Glass. GF 19, p. 343.
Goblet of Fire. GF 16, pp. 255-256.
Gubraithian fire. OP 20, p. 428.
Hand of Glory. CS 4, pp. 52-53.
Howler. CS 6, p. 87.
Invisibility Booster. CS 5, p. 67.
Invisibility Cloak. SS 12, p. 201; DH 2, p. 15.
Invisibility Marquee. OP 17, p. 372.
Leprechaun Gold. GF 27, p. 544.
Lunascope. PA 4, p. 50.
Marauder's Map. PA 10, pp. 191-194.
Metamorph-Medal. HP 5, p. 87.
Mokeskin. DH 7, p. 120.
Mrs. Skower's All-Purpose Magical Mess Remover. CS 9, p. 146.
Omniocculars. GF 7, p. 93.

Pensieve. GF 30, p. 583.
Peruvian Instant Darkness Powder. HP 29, p. 618; DH 7, p. 132.
Pocket Sneakoscope. PA 1, p. 10.
Portkey. GF 6, pp. 70, 73.
Probity Probe. HP 6, p. 108; DH 26, p. 529.
Put-Outer. SS 1, p. 9.
Quick Quotes Quill. GF 18, pp. 304-305.
Remembrall. SS 9, p. 145.
Resurrection Stone, The. DH 21, p. 409.
Revealer. CS 13, p. 233.
Screaming Yo-Yo. GF 12, p. 183.
Secrecy Sensor. GF 19, pp. 342-43.
Self-Correcting Ink. OP 31, p. 709.
Self-Shuffling Playing Cards. CS 3, p. 40.
Shield Cloak. HP 6, p. 119.
Shield Glove. HP 6, p. 119.
Shield Hat. HP 6, p. 119.
Shrinking Door Key. CS 3, p. 38.
Skele-Gro. CS 10, p. 174; DH 24, p. 480.
Sleekeazy's Hair Potion. GF 24, p. 433.
Slide-Along-Apparition. HP 3, p. 42.
Sorcerer's Stone. SS 13, p. 220; DH 21, p. 416.
Sorting Hat. SS 7, pp. 117-119.
Spectrespecs. HP 7, p. 137.
Spellotape. CS 6, p. 95.
Stunner. GF 9, p. 129.
Thief's Downfall. DH 26, p. 534.
Time-Turner. PA 21, pp. 394-395.
Umgubular Slashkilter. OP 18, p. 395.
Vanishing Cabinet. OP 28, p. 627; DH 31, p. 627.
Wand of Destiny, The. DH 21, p. 415.
Wartcap. OP 6, p. 116; DH 10, p. 189.
Weasleys' Wildfire Whiz-Bangs. Basic Blaze. Deflagration Deluxe. OP 28, p. 634.
Winged Key. SS 16, p. 280.
Wizard Chess. SS 12, p. 199.
WonderWitch products. HP 6, p. 120.

Ministry of Magic.

There was a large government in the wizarding world that consisted of numerous departments, committees, offices and squads. It was known as the Ministry of Magic and it imposed order on the many creatures that inhabited the wizarding world. The following is a list of the various departments and offices that comprised the Ministry of Magic:

Accidental Magic Reversal Department. PA 3, p. 44.

Accidental Magic Reversal Squad. GF 6, p. 67.

Auror Headquarters. OP 7, p. 130.

Auror Office. DH 1, p. 4.

Beast Division. FB, p. xii, fn 2.

Being Division. FB, p. xii, fn 2.

Centaur Liaison Office. FB, p. xiii, fn 3.

Committee for the Disposal of Dangerous Creatures. PA 11, p. 218.

Committee on Experimental Charms. CS 3, p. 38.

Department of International Magical Cooperation. GF 3, p. 36.

Department of Magical Catastrophes. PA 10, p. 208.

Department of Magical Games and Sports. GF 3, p. 30.

Department of Magical Law Enforcement. QA 6, p. 26.

Department of Mysteries. GF 7, p. 86.

Department for the Regulation and Control of Magical Creatures. GF 6, p. 71.

Dragon Research and Restraint Bureau. FB, p. vi.

Experintmental Charms. DH 13, p. 253.

Ghoul Task Force. FB, pp.18-19.

Goblin Liaison Office. GF 7, p. 86.

Improper Use of Magic Office. CS 2, p. 21.

Magical Law Enforcement Patrol. OP 7, p. 133.

Magical Law Enforcement Squad. PA 10, p. 208.

Magical Maintenance. OP 7, p. 131.

Misuse of Muggle Artifacts Office. CS 3, p. 30.

Muggle Liason Office. HP 1, p. 9.

Muggle-born Registration Commission. DH 11, p.209.

Office for House-Elf Relocation. FB, p. vi.

Office for the Detection and Confiscation of Counterfeit Defensive Spells and Protective Objects. HP 5, p. 84.

Office of Misinformation. FB, p. xx.

Pest Sub-Division. FB, p. 31.

Werewolf Capture Unit. FB, p. xiii.

Werewolf Support Services, Office of. FB, p. xiii.

Wizengamot (Wizard High Court). OP 5, p. 95.

Plants.

The wizarding world had an abundance of unusual plant life. Some of the imaginary plants were very alive indeed. Many real plants found in the muggle world were used as ingredients in potions by wizards and witches. The following is a list of both types of plants:

Abyssinian Shrivelfig. CS 15, p. 268.
Aconite. SS 8, pp. 137-138.
Alihotsy. FB, p. 19.
Asphodel. SS 8, p. 137-138.
Bouncing Bulb. GF 18, p. 293.
Bubotubor. GF 13, pp. 194-195.
Chinese Chomping Cabbage. OP 16, p. 332.
Devil's Snare. SS 16, pp. 277-278; DH 30, p. 600.
Dirigible Plums. DH 20, p. 398.
Fanged Geranium. OP 31, p. 714.
Flitterbloom. OP 25, p. 547.
Flutterby Bush. GF 19, p. 345; DH 6, p. 106.
Fluxweed. GF 26, p. 491.
Gillyweed. GF 26, p. 491.
Ginger. GF 27, pp. 513-514, 518.
Gurdyroot. HP 20, p. 425.
Hellebore. OP 12, p. 234.
Knotgrass. CS 10, p. 165.
Leaping Toadstool. CS 14, p. 251.
Lovage. OP 18, p. 383.
Mallowsweet. OP 27, p. 603.
Mandrake. CS 6, p. 93.
Mimbulus mimbletonia. OP 10, p. 186.
Mistletoe. DH 20, p. 398.
Monkshood. SS 8, pp. 137-138.
Plangentine. DH 11, p. 218.
Puffapod. PA 8, p. 147.
Sage. OP 27, p. 603.
Scurvy-grass. OP 17, p. 383.
Screechsnap. OP 25, p. 550.
Shrivelfig. PA 7, p. 124.
Shrub, Self-Fertilizing. OP 14, p. 289.
Snargaluff Pods. HP 14, p. 279; DH 30, p. 600.
Whomping Willow. CS 5, pp. 73, 79.
Sneezewort. OP 18, p. 383.
Tentacula. DH 30, p. 600.
Venomous Tentacula. OP 9, p. 171.

Wolfsbane. SS 8, pp. 137-138.
Wormwood. SS 8, pp. 137-138.

Potions.

Potions were concoctions of assorted ingredients that when combined produced liquids or gases with magical properties. Harry Potter learned about the science of potion-making from Severus Snape at Hogwarts. During Harry's sixth year, the subject was taught by Horace Slughorn. The following is a list of the potions that were used in the wizarding world:

Amortentia. HP 9, P. 185.
Befuddlement Draught. OP 18, p. 383.
Blood-Replenishing Potion. OP 22, p. 488.
Calming Draught. OP 27, p. 606.
Confusing Concoction. PA 16, p. 318.
Confusing Draught. OP 18, p. 383.
Deflating Draft. CS 11, p. 187.
Draught of Living Death. SS 8, pp. 137-138.
Draught of Peace. OP 12, p.232.
Elixir of Life. SS 13, pp. 219-220.
Essence of Dittany. DH 14, pp. 269-70.
Euphoria. HP 22, p. 475.
Everlasting Elixirs. HP 15, p. 305.
Felix Felicis. HP 9, p. 187.
Hiccuping Solution. HP 22, p. 475.
Invigoration Draught. OP 29, p. 660.
Love Potion. GF 6, p. 73.
Mandrake Restorative Draught. CS 18, p. 330.
Memory Potions. FB, p. 23.
Polyjuice Potion. CS 9, p. 159.
Scintillation Solution. CS 8, p. 127.
Shrinking Potions. PA 1, p. 3.
Shrinking Solutions. PA 7, pp.124-126.
Sleekeazy's Hair Potion. GF 24, p. 433.
Sleeping Draft. GF 19, p. 327.
Sleeping Draught. CS 12, p. 215.
Strengthening Solution. OP 15, p. 309.
Swelling Solution. CS 11, p. 187.
Truth Potion. GF 27, p. 517.
Truth Serums. FB, p. 23.
Undetectable Potion. PA 12, p. 244.
Veritaserum. GF 27, p. 517; DH 18, p. 355.
Wit-Sharpening Potion. GF 27, pp. 513-514, 518.
Wolfsbane Potion. PA 18, p. 353.

Quidditch Broomsticks.

A quidditch player's success depended in part upon the player's speed on the quidditch field. Having the right broomstick on which to ride made a noticeable difference in one's speed and agility for the game. Just as there are different makes and models of vehicles to drive in the muggle world, so there were different manufacturers that produced and marketed quidditch broomsticks for sale in the wizarding world. The following is a list of the various makes and models of broomsticks that were used to play quidditch and the persons or teams who rode them:

Blue Bottle. Advertised as a family broom. GF 8, p. 96.

Cleansweep One. QA 9, p. 49.

Cleansweep Two. QA 9, p. 50.

Cleansweep Three. QA 9, p. 50.

Cleansweep Eleven. OP 9, p. 170; 13, p. 271.

Cleansweep Five. Fred and George Weasley.CS 7, p. 111.

Cleansweep Six. OP 10, p. 193.

Cleansweep Seven. Ravenclaw House Team. PA 12, p. 251.

Cleansweep Eleven. Ron Weasley. OP 13, p. 271.

Comet 140. QA 9, p. 49.

Comet 180. QA 9, p. 50.

Comet 260. Draco Malfoy. SS 10, p. 165. Cho Chang. PA 13, p. 254.

Comet 290. OP 9, p;. 170.

Firebolt. Irish International Side. PA 4, p. 51. Harry Potter (Third Year). PA 11, p. 223; DH 4, p. 43.

Moontrimmer. QA 9, p. 48.

Nimbus 1000. QA 9, pp. 50-51.

Nimbus 1001. QA 9, pp. 50-51.

Nimbus 1500. QA 9, pp. 50-51.

Nimbus 1700. QA 9, pp. 50-51

Nimbus Two Thousand. Harry Potter (First and Second Years). SS 5, p. 72.

Nimbus Two Thousand and One. Slytherin House Team. CS 7, p. 111.

Oakshaft 79. QA 9, p. 47.

Shooting Star. Ron Weasley. CS 4, p. 46.

Silver Arrow. Madam Hooch. PA 13, p. 254.

Swiftstick. QA 9, p. 50.

Tinderblast. QA 9, p. 50.

Twigger 90. QA 9, p. 51.

Quidditch Teams and Rosters of Players.

Many witches and wizards were obsessed with following the sport of quidditch. Quidditch matches were played at Hogwarts and by many professional teams throughout the wizarding world. The following is a list of the quidditch teams and their players that are referenced in the Harry Potter series:

Appleby Arrow. QA 5, p. 17

Ballycastle Bats. GF 22, p. 393.

Banchory Bangers. QA 5, pp. 16-17.

Bigonville Bombers. QA 8, p. 41.

Bludger Backbeat. QA 10, p. 52.

Bragga Broomfleet. QA 8, p. 41.

Bulgarian National Quidditch Team. Dimitrov (chaser). GF 8, p. 104, pp. 107-108.

Ivanova (chaser). GF 8, p. 104, pp. 107-108.

Krum, Viktor (seeker). GF 8, p. 104, pp. 107-108; DH 8, p. 143.

Levski (chaser). GF 8, p. 104, pp. 107-108.

Volkov (beater). GF 8, p. 104, pp. 107-108.

Vulchanov (beater). GF 8, p. 104, pp. 107-108.

Zograf (keeper). GF 8, p. 104, pp. 107-108.

Caerphilly Catapults. QA 7, p. 33.

Chudley Cannons. Jenkins, Joey (beater). GF 22, p. 393.

Gorgovitch, Dragomir. DH 7, p. 112.

Falmouth Falcons. QA 7, p. 34.

Fitchburg Finches. QA 8, p. 45.

Gimbi Giant-Slayers. QA 8, p. 43.

Gorodok Gargoyles. QA 8, p. 46.

Grodzisk Goblins. QA 8, p. 41.

Gryffindor House Team. Bell, Katie (chaser). SS 11, p. 186.

Coote, Ritchie (beater). HP 11, p. 225.

Johnson, Angelina (chaser; capt.). SS 11, p. 185; OP 12, p. 224.

Kirke, Andrew (beater) OP 21, p. 453.

McLaggen, Cormac (keeper substitute). HP 19, p. 412.

Peakes, Jimmy (beater) HP 11, p. 225.

Potter, Harry (seeker; capt). SS 9, p. 151; HP 11, p. 224.

Robins, Demelza (chaser) HP 11, p. 224.

Sloper, Jack (beater). OP 21, p. 453.

Spinnet, Alicia (chaser). SS 11, p. 186.

Thomas, Dean (chaser substitute). HP 14, p. 284.

Weasley, Fred (beater). SS 9, p. 153.

Weasley, George (beater). SS 9, p. 153.

Weasley, Ginny (seeker; chaser). OP 21, p. 453; HP 11, p. 224.

Weasley, Ron (keeper). OP 13, p. 275; HP 11, p. 226.

Montague (chaser; capt.). PA 15, pp. 306-307; OP 19, p. 405.
Pusey, Adrian (chaser). SS 11, p. 186.
Urquhart (captain). HP 14, p. 295.
Vaisey (chaser). HP 14, p. 294.
Warrington (chaser). OP 19, p. 401.
Stonewall Stormers. QA 8, p. 43.
Sumbawanga Sunrays. QA 8, p. 43.
Sweetwater All-Stars. QA 8, p. 45.
Tchamba Charmers. QA 8, p. 43.
Thundelarra Thunderers. QA 8, p. 42.
Repelling Spells. QA 4, p. 12.
Toyohashi Tengu. QA 8, p. 46.
Tutshill Tornados. QA 7, p. 37.
Vratsa Vultures. QA 8, p. 40.
Wigtown Wanderers. QA, p. v; 7, p. 37; 10, p. 53.
Wimbourne Wasps. Bagman, Ludo (beater). GF 7, p. 78.
Woollongong Warriors. QA 8, p. 42.

Quidditch Terminology.

Just as with other sports, the wizarding world developed its own terminology for quidditch. The following is a list of the terms used in quidditch:

All-Africa Cup. QA 8, p. 43.
Beater. SS 9, p. 153.
Blagging. QA 6, p. 29.
Blatching. QA 6, p. 29.
Blooder. QA 3, p. 9.
Bludger. SS 10, p. 168.
Blurting. QA 6, p. 29.
Bumphing. QA 6, p. 29.
Catcher. QA 3, p. 9.
Chaser. SS 10, p. 167; DH7, p. 112.
Chaser Hawkshead Attacking Formation. QA 7, p. 35.
Cobbing. QA 6, p. 29.
Cuaditch. QA 4, p. 12.
Dangerous Dai Commemorative Medal. QA 7, p. 33.
Dopplebeater Defence. QA 10, p. 52.
Double Eight Loop. QA 10, p. 52.
European Cup. QA 7, p. 38.
Flacking. QA 6, p. 30.
Flesh Memory. DH 7, p. 127.
Haversacking. QA 6, p. 30.
Hawkshead Attacking Formation. GF 8, p. 106.

Hunter. QA 4, p. 13.
Keeper. SS 10, p. 168.
Latin World Cup. QA 8, p. 45.
League. QA 7, p. 32.
League Cup. QA 7, pp. 32.
Parkin's Pincer. QA 10, p. 53.
Pitch. QA 6, p. 17.
Plumpton Pass. QA 10, p. 53.
Porskoff Ploy. QA 10, p. 53; GF 8, p. 106.
Quaffle. SS 10, p. 167.
Quafflepocking. QA 6, p. 30.
Quidditch. SS 5, pp. 77, 79.
Quidditch Cup. SS 9, p. 153.
Quidditch World Cup. GF 8, p. 102; DH 14, p. 271.
Quidjudge. QA 6, p. 18.
Quod. QA 8, pp. 44-45.
Quodpot. QA 8, pp. 44-45.
Reverse Pass. QA 10, p. 53.
Seeker. SS 9, p. 151; DH 7, p. 127.
Sloth Grip Roll. QA 10, p. 53.
Snitch, Golden. SS 10, p. 169; DH 7, p. 119.
Snitchnip. QA 6, p. 30.
Starfish and Stick. QA 10, p. 53.
Stichstock. QA 2, p. 4.
Stooging Penalty. QA 6, pp. 26, 30.
Swivenhodge. QA 2, p. 6.
Transylvanian Tackle. QA 10, p. 54.
Woollongong Shimmy. QA 10, p. 55.
Wronski Defensive Feint. GF 8, p. 109.

Shops and Stores.

Witches and wizards purchased goods from various shops and stores throughout the wizarding world. The following is a list of the business establishments that existed at several locations:

Diagon Alley:
Apothecary. PA 4, p. 52.
Eeylops Owl Emporium. SS 5, p. 72.
Florean Fortescue's Ice Cream Parlor. PA 4, p. 50.
Flourish and Blotts. SS 5, p. 80; DH 8, p. 153.
Gambol and Japes Wizarding Joke Shop. CS 4, p. 58.
Gringotts Wizarding Bank. SS 5, pp. 63-64; DH 15, p. 290.
Leaky Cauldron. SS 5, p. 68; DH 9, p. 163.
Madam Malkin's Robes for All Occasions. SS 5, p. 76; DH 23, p. 459.

Magical Menagerie. PA 4, p. 58.
Ollivander's. SS 5, p. 81.
Pet Menagerie. PA 4, pp. 59-60.
Quality Quidditch Supplies. CS 4, p. 58.
Twilfitt and Tatting's. HP 6, p. 114.
Weasleys' Wizarding Wheezes. OP 29, p. 675.
Hogsmeade:
Gladrags Wizardwear. GF 8, p. 96.
Hog's Head. SS 16, p. 265.
Honeydukes. PA 5, p. 77.
Madam Puddifoot's Tea Shop. OP 25, p. 559.
Scrivenshaft's Quill Shop. OP 16, p. 348.
The Three Broomsticks. PA 8, p. 158.
Zonko's Joke Shop. PA 8, p. 145.
Knockturn Alley:
Borgin and Burkes. CS 4, p. 50; DH 15, p. 288.
Little Hangleton:
The Hanged Man. GF 1, p. 2.
Others:
Building Society. DH 9, p. 165.
Green Dragon. FB, p. 27, fn. 9.
Millamant's Magic Marquees. DH 6, p. 109.

ABOUT THE COMPILER OF THIS DICTIONARY

Duane M. Searle lives in Boiling Springs, Pennsylvania with his wife and three children. He has thoroughly enjoyed reading and rereading and discussing again and again the Harry Potter books with his family and desperately needed this resource book to keep up with the vast material in the series. Mr. Searle is not affiliated with J.K. Rowling, Bloomsbury Publishing, Scholastic Press, Warner Bros. or any of their assigns, authorized agents or representatives.

Made in the USA
Lexington, KY
04 December 2013